THE OTHER HALF OF THE GRAVE

JEANIENE FROST

The Other Half of the Grave
Copyright © 2022 by Jeaniene Frost
Ebook ISBN: 9781641971928
KDP Print ISBN: 9798433280809
IS Print ISBN: 9781641971980

NYLA Publishing

121 W 27th St., Suite 1201, New York, NY 10001

http://www.nyliterary.com

THE OTHER HALF OF THE GRAVE

1

Author's Note:

Readers have long asked me if I'd ever write Bones's side of the story, and I said no because I didn't "hear" Bones in my head the same way that I heard Cat. Well, a couple years ago, Bones finally started talking to me, and wow, did he have a lot to say. I thought I knew everything about him, and Bones proved me wrong. Writing this also showed Cat in a brand-new light for me, as well as Ian, Spade, and others. Reliving their story through Bones's perspective made me laugh, cry, and fall in love with him and Cat all over again. I hope you enjoy it as much as I did!

When you read, you'll notice that I updated the technology to today's time because I didn't want to confuse readers by *not* mentioning things that are commonplace now. I also didn't want to pull readers out of the story by keeping the now-defunct technology of the early 2000s. Example: Bones had a beeper as a receiver for Cat's panic alert back in the original version (Gen Z, you'll have to look up what a "beeper" is.) I laughed out loud when

I re-read that part, and it's not supposed to be a funny scene. So, I thought upgrading the technology was a better choice. I also gave Cat a cell phone in this version. Her not having one back when HALFWAY TO THE GRAVE was first published was unusual, but not unheard of. Today, however, the average middle schooler has a cell phone, so a college student like Cat would definitely have one, too.

Finally, since this is told through Bones's point of view, there are slight changes in context and dialog. Anyone who's been in a relationship knows that couples can have two versions of the same incident, and both will swear that their version is correct. Such is the case with how Bones remembers things versus how Cat did. Hey, I'm not going to tell Bones that he's wrong. This is his story, and he's sticking to it.

—*Jeaniene Frost*

∾

*T*onight, Bones hunted.

Devon was his prey. According to Bones's sources, Devon ran the books for an undead cabal that operated from Mexico all the way to this poor imitation of a high-end nightclub in Columbus, Ohio. Devon was supposed to be here tonight, hence Bones sitting in the frayed, fake-velvet booths of the club's VIP area. The music was atrocious, and so loud that the humans had to shout in order to hear each other. With a vampire's heightened senses, the annoying beat felt as if it were being pumped directly into Bones's skull.

He was, as the cliché went, getting too old for this. At least when it came to frequenting human nightclubs. When it came to hunting, Bones's two-centuries-plus was to his advantage. The same held true for his other pursuits.

One example of those pursuits flashed a smile at him as she came nearer. She was attractive enough, if he ignored the heavy chemical scent of perfume she'd doused herself with. But he couldn't ignore the way her eyes were dilated from something other than feminine interest.

"Hi," she purred, leaning over his table to better display her décolleté. "What do you say to buying me a drink, sexy?"

Shagging might be his favorite pastime, but Bones never touched a woman under the influence of drugs. She was also now blocking his view of the club's entrance. If Devon slipped in, Bones wouldn't know it. Normally, he'd let her down gently, but lives were on the line.

"I'd say lay off whatever drugs made your pupils larger than olives," he replied with a rudeness meant to send her away.

She huffed and straightened, clearing his line of sight to the door. "Bastard," she snapped before stalking off.

Bones hefted his glass in salute. "Right you are."

Two more women and a man made similar advances over the next hour. He sent them away as well. He'd just rebuffed his latest admirer when a glimpse of almost luminescent skin caught his eye.

Vampire, was Bones's first thought as he studied the woman entering the club. Her hair was a crimson splash that hid her face as she waited while the bouncer checked her identification. Must be a young-looking vampire, for the bouncer to double-check her license. After a moment, she was allowed to pass.

Bones only caught glimpses of her as she threaded her way through the crowd. She wore oversized denim trousers with construction-style pockets, long black gloves, and a nondescript white top with elbow-length sleeves. If not for its scooped neck-line, he wouldn't have caught sight of her distinctive skin, especially since her long red tresses shielded most of her face.

Push your hair back, Bones thought. *Show me your face...*

Wait, who cared what the vampire looked like, if she was even a vampire at all? He had his doubts now. Yes, her skin held that faint tinge of incandescence that usually meant "vampire," but she moved like a human, and she also had too much flush in her skin for a vampire's stationary pulse.

Must be a human with unusually lovely skin, nothing more. Bones finished his whisky and left cash for his bill. A tour of the club was now in order. Devon could've slipped in when he was distracted by the redhead. That wouldn't do.

An hour later, Bones was back in the booths with their elevated view of the entrance. Devon hadn't shown up yet, and it was approaching midnight. If this were a vampire club, the evening would just be starting, but this was a human establishment so it would only be open another two hours.

Perhaps his intelligence on Devon had been wrong. Vampires *had* been known to lie to stop the pain when a silver knife was shoved into their sternum—

Ash blond hair caught Bones's eye as a man walked into the club. He moved with distinct, purposeful grace, and his skin held the same faint tinge of luminescence as Bones's own.

Devon. Finally.

The redhead he'd admired earlier suddenly came toward Bones with an unsteady gait. Before Bones could send her away, she dropped into the seat across the table from him.

"Hello handsome," she said, her faint slur turning a poor impression of a seductive voice into a terrible one.

"Not now," he replied shortly.

She blinked as if she'd never been rejected before. With her beauty, she probably hadn't. Dark red brows arched over storm-cloud gray eyes while very little makeup graced her high cheek-bones, elegant nose, and luscious, full lips. No perfume masked her scent, either, allowing him to catch a subtle mix of sweet cream, vanilla, and...cherries.

"Excuse me?" she said.

4

He could no longer see Devon now. Lovely or no, he wouldn't let her cost him years of hunting.

"I'm busy, so off you go."

She touched his hand. Her warmth erased any doubt as to her humanity, as did the heartbeat he could now hear from her nearness. She stammered out something he ignored until she finished it with "Want to fuck?"

As soon as she said it, a horrified look crossed her features. Her hand also paused midway to her mouth as if she'd been about to physically attempt stuffing the words back.

His lips curled. Not afraid to say what she wanted even if it embarrassed her, was she? Under other circumstances, he'd make her forget that embarrassment in the nearest, darkest corner, but now wasn't the time.

"Bad timing, luv. Be a good bird and fly away. I'll find you later."

At that, she got up and walked away, shaking her head. Bones didn't spare her another look. His gaze was all for the blond vampire moving through the crowd with the arrogance of an apex predator surrounded by prey.

Bones flew up to the ceiling. His all-black attire plus the darkness around the booths meant that no one noticed. Once there, he went behind the network of lights. Anyone who looked up would only see the constant flash of strobes or the roving beams of spotlights. Not the dark figure behind them.

His perch gave him a clear view of Devon. The other vampire paused by several women during his slow sweep of the club, leaning in to catch their scent, brush their skin, or run his fingers through their hair. Devon made it seem subtle, almost accidental, but shoppers in a grocery store tested their produce in much the same way.

Devon was picking out his next meal.

Bones's jaw tightened when he saw Devon catch a glimpse of the redhead. He'd hoped she'd leave the club after his refusal, but she'd done a circle of the place as if looking for him, and then sat at the bar. When Devon saw her, he stopped talking to the petite blond he'd been conversing with and stared.

Distractingly lovely, isn't she? Bones thought, feeling an odd twinge of anger. Yes, vampires were territorial over their possessions or their people, but the redhead was neither to him. Still, that twinge grew when Devon left the blonde and went straight over to her.

He couldn't hear what Devon said over the pulsating music. He could only watch as Devon leaned behind the redhead and spoke. She turned around, annoyance clear on her features.

Good. Send him on his way!

A bright smile wreathed her face, turning up the dial on her already irresistible beauty. Whatever she said had Devon sitting next to her and signaling the bartender for a drink.

Anger surged again. Bones told himself it was fueled by sympathy, not more irrational jealousy.

Bad choice, pet. He intends to eat you in an entirely different way than I did.

Her choices soon worsened. Within half an hour, the redhead was following Devon out the door. Bones slid across the ceiling to a corner, and then jumped down and left the club. Once outside, he flew high to avoid being spotted and kept his aura tamped down so that Devon couldn't detect it.

The redhead could barely walk as she followed Devon to his car. Clearly, she'd had too much to drink. Devon didn't care. He smirked as he helped her into the passenger seat, and then climbed into the driver's side and pulled away.

Bones stayed high as he followed the Volkswagen. No surprise, Devon drove to a deserted, wooded area. Bones dropped lower, tensing when the car stopped. Almost immediately, the passenger door opened, and the redhead stumbled out.

Bones was low enough to hear Devon laugh when she staggered away, screaming. Drunk as she was, she only made it a few meters before she tripped and fell. Not that she would have been able to escape Devon even if she'd been sober. No human could outrun a vampire.

Bones dropped even lower as Devon walked over to the girl. His back was to Bones, but from the new green glow bathing the redhead's features, he'd released the inhuman light in his gaze. Seeing it, she whimpered and crawled backward faster.

Don't fret, luv, Bones thought grimly. *I'm coming. Just need to catch him unawares so you don't get hurt in the process.*

"Don't hurt me!" she cried out when Devon knelt next to her and grabbed her by the back of the neck.

"It will only hurt for a moment," Devon hissed.

Bones braced against the nearest tree trunk, about to springboard off it to maximize his speed to knock Devon away—

The redhead's hand whipped out, ramming something into Devon's chest. Before Bones could react, she gave it a vicious twist, and Devon collapsed on top of her. She kept twisting until Devon shriveled into a vampire's true state of death.

Bones was too stunned to do anything other than stare.

What the bloody hell was this?

"You were right," she said in a tone that no longer bore a hint of a drunken slur. "It only hurt for a moment."

Bones's disbelief gave way to anger. All the answers he'd sought for the past several years, gone. All because of a lovely, murdering redhead who'd fooled both him and Devon, though only one of them had lived to regret it.

She shoved Devon's body aside. No hysterics, no remorse, and she'd shown no hesitation before stabbing Devon, either. If she had, Bones could have stopped her. But no, she'd been swift and merciless. This wasn't her first kill, especially with how brisk and businesslike she was as she opened the trunk and hefted Devon's body into it.

Little chit must be a professional. He'd be sure to use that to his advantage when he met her again. He'd been her first intended victim, after all.

I promised to find you. I'll keep that promise.

She whistled as she closed the trunk and got back into Devon's car. Bones flew high and followed her. He had no idea who she was, but he was going to find out.

2
-----

*T*he redhead drove back to the club, where she parked Devon's car next to an old Ford truck at the far side of the club's parking lot. She got out and quickly transferred Devon's body from the trunk to the truck bed and covered him with black plastic sheeting. Then, she left Devon's car and drove off in her truck. Smart. Now, Devon's car wouldn't be traced back to her murder scene, and anyone looking for Devon would assume he'd left his vehicle at the club himself after catching a ride.

She drove for about an hour, until she reached a cherry orchard in a small, rural town. Once there, she chopped Devon's head off and buried him on the far edge of the orchard. Then, she went inside the lone house on the property and slept so soundly Bones could hear her snores from his nearby tree perch.

He didn't sleep. He spent the rest of the early morning hours looking up everything he could find on the mysterious redhead. Thanks to the orchard's name painted on a faded sign in front of the property, it was easy.

Catherine Kathleen Crawfield appeared to be a normal college girl whose only oddity was her utter lack of social media presence. The only online images Bones could find of her were yearbook pictures and an old family photo on the Crawfield Cherry Orchard's official website. The orchard was owned by Catherine's grandparents, who were as boring a couple as Bones had ever researched. Nothing interesting popped up regarding Catherine's mum, either, and her father was unknown. On paper, the Crawfields were no more than a family of cherry farmers going back five generations.

Yet Catherine was a vampire killer. If he hadn't seen it himself, let alone smelled evidence of other kills buried in the family orchard, he wouldn't believe it, but there it was. How did Devon fit in? Catherine had only focused on him after Bones had rebuffed her. Had Bones been Catherine's intended target all along? Or had Devon? Bones's brown hair was currently dyed blond, and Devon was a blond, so Catherine could have confused one of them for the other.

Or had Catherine been after both of them? The head of the cabal Bones was investigating could have found out that Bones was after Devon. Perhaps he'd decided to get rid of the pair of them as a precaution? If so, a human woman seemed a poor choice of assassins, though Devon would doubtless disagree.

Well, if the lady wanted to kill him, he'd let her try.

Catherine went to the same club the next night. As soon as she entered, she did what Bones realized was a sweep of the premises. When she didn't find what she was looking for, she sat at the bar. Bones was behind her before she could order a drink.

"I'm ready to fuck now."

A line offensive enough to send all except a person with ulterior motives running. *Last chance to show you're a lamb instead of a wolf, Catherine.*

"What?" she gasped out, spinning around. Then, the outrage in her expression died as she recognized him. Oddly, she flushed as if embarrassed by remembering what she'd said. Then her chin lifted and determination filled her gaze.

"Yes, well…drink first?"

"Don't bother," he said, waving away the bartender she'd started to hail. "Let's go."

"Now?" She looked startled.

"Yeah, now."

When she hesitated, he said, "Changed your mind?" and turned as if to leave.

She grabbed her purse and practically lunged toward him. *Not a lamb at all, then.*

"No, no. Lead the way," she said.

As if he'd turn his back on her even once tonight. His arm swept out. "Ladies first."

She glanced over her shoulder at him so much, he was surprised she didn't trip on her way from the club to the parking lot. Once they were outside, she opened her mouth as if to speak, but Bones beat her to it.

"Well? Get your ride, and let's be off."

"My ride?" she all but stammered. "I don't have a ride. Where's your car?"

"I drove a bike here," he lied. "Fancy a ride on it?"

"A motorcycle?" she said with such obvious consternation, he stifled a laugh. Was she imaging how difficult it would be to transport his body on one of those? "Um, we should take my vehicle instead. It's over there."

She began to walk toward the old Ford, staggering after a few steps as if remembering that she was supposed to act drunk.

"Thought you didn't have a ride?" Bones called out.

She turned around, her expression saying "Oh shit" louder than words. Sweet bleedin' hell, she was terrible at this.

"I forgot it was here, is all," she said in a too-bright tone. Then, she started to slur her words again. "Think I drank too much. You want to drive?"

"No thanks," he said at once.

Anger flashed across her features before she covered it with a smile. "Really, I think you should drive. I'd hate to wrap us around a tree."

And be distracted while she launched a new attempt to murder him? "If you want to beg off until another night..." he said, turning away again.

"No!" she replied with such obvious desperation, he almost laughed. She must have realized she'd revealed too much because at once she tried to backtrack.

"I mean, you're so good-looking and"—her brow furrowed as she quickly tried to think up more flattery—"I *really* want to get it on."

This time, he couldn't stifle his laughter. She blanched, and he almost pitied her, except for how she'd twist silver into his heart the first chance she got.

His tongue traced the inside of his lip as he stared at her until she flinched. But he only said, "Right, then, let's be off." Relief filled her face until he added, "You're driving."

With that, Bones climbed into the passenger seat of her pickup truck. *Your move.*

She shifted on her feet for a few moments. Then, decision made, she got into the truck.

Bones didn't take his eyes off her as she drove. She must have felt it, but she didn't look at him. Instead, her breathing hitched, her heart rate sped up, and her scent wavered between fear and resolve. Didn't she know vampires could scent emotions? She should have worn perfume. The harsh chemical odor would've helped mask her true feelings.

Ten minutes into the silent standoff, she said "What's your name?" in a sharp, tense tone.

Trying to verify your target? "Does it matter?"

She finally looked his way. Uncertainty filled her features before determination tightened her jaw.

"I just wanted to know. Mine's Cat," she said as she left the freeway for a gravel road.

"Cat, hmm?" he mocked. "From where I sit, you look more like a Kitten."

She shot him an irritated glance. "It's Cat. Cat Raven."

"Whatever you say, Kitten Tweety," Bones drawled.

She slammed on the brakes. "You got a problem, mister?"

I don't, but you do. Temper, temper. "No problem, pet. Have we stopped here for good? Is this where you want to shag?"

She flushed again before looking away. Perhaps this part wasn't an act. His would-be murderess was a prude? Priceless.

"Um, no," she said. "Further up. It's prettier there."

And well off the main road so no one could stumble across them. Prude or no, she was still doing her level best to kill him. Pity he'd have to disappoint her.

"I just bet it is, luv," Bones said with a chuckle.

After a few minutes, she stopped at the edge of a lake. Bones didn't move. He only watched with more amusement as she fidgeted and kept glancing at the pocket on her right thigh. Even though her trousers were oversized, Bones could still see the outline of her weapon. She couldn't pull it out without being obvious, and without the element of surprise, he could snatch it from her before she could raise it to stab him.

She had to know that. How would she attempt to distract him? She couldn't play the helpless victim if she wasn't being attacked, and Bones wasn't moving a muscle. Frustration nearly boiled off her as the minutes ticked by.

Bones hid his smile. She had no idea what to do now, did she?

"Don't you want to go outside and...shag?" she said at last.

Bones didn't attempt to conceal his grin. "Oh, no. Right here. Love to do it in a truck."

He could hear her teeth grind as she said "Well..." while doubtless searching for an excuse to leave his sight long enough to pull her weapon. "There's not much room in here," she settled on, and began to open her door.

"Plenty of room, Kitten," Bones replied. "I'll stay here."

"*Don't* call me Kitten," she said, anger sharpening both her tone and her scent.

Lucifer's bouncing balls, she had to be the worst faux-seductress ever! Devon should be spinning in his grave over letting her slay him.

"Take off your clothes," Bones said while raking her with a gaze. "Let's see what you've got."

Now the red in her cheeks was from rage. "Excuse me?"

"You weren't going to shag me with your clothes on, were you, Kitten?" he taunted her. "Guess all you'll need is your knickers off, then. Come on. Don't take all bloody night."

She shot him a look of pure hatred before her expression turned crafty. "You first."

She thought modesty would be *his* downfall? Bones grinned.

"Shy bird, are you? Didn't peg you for it, what with walking up to me and practically begging for a shag. How about this? We'll take our clothes off at the same time."

Her expression mottled with more fury, but either she gave up on her attempt to kill him, or she continued with the seductress charade. She chose the charade and began to unbutton her trousers. When Bones undid his and pulled up his shirt, her fingers actually shook.

Once again, he almost pitied her. Then he saw her hand slip to the weapon in her pocket. As soon as she touched it, her trembling eased. She wanted him dead so much that the prospect calmed her.

She'd made her move. *My turn.*

"Look here, luv, see what I have for you," Bones said, pulling his cock out.

Her cheeks flamed and she looked away. It was all the distraction he needed.

His fist shot out and connected with her head. She slumped into his arms, her right hand still curled around the weapon she'd tried so hard to murder him with.

Bones pulled it out. A wooden stake? That wouldn't kill any vampire...wait. It was heavier than it should be.

Bones broke off a piece of the wood...and smiled.

"Well," he said to his unconscious companion. "Aren't you full of surprises, Kitten?"

3

*H*ours later, she regained consciousness and immediately threw up. The unshaded lamp between them meant she didn't see his wince. Concussions were nasty things. Good thing he'd chained her in a standing position instead of flat on her back. Otherwise, her vomit might have gone back down her throat.

Bones waited until she stopped heaving before he came into the bright circle of light. "I thawt I thaw a putty tat." A sarcastic Tweety Bird impression was the least she deserved after trying to kill him. "I *did*, I *did* thee a putty tat!"

Anger flashed across her features. Good. The concussion wasn't addling her wits, then. Time to get answers. "Now, luv, let's get down to business. Who do you work for?"

She had the nerve to look surprised. Then, disappointingly, she lied. "I don't work for anyone."

"Bollocks," he said, and came nearer.

Her heart rate increased as she glanced down at herself. He'd stripped her of her weapons and outer garments while she was unconscious, leaving her only in her bra and knickers. Sadly, her clothing had revealed nothing except an extra silver weapon shaped like a cross, of all things, and her mobile only had texts and phone calls to and from her mother.

But someone had taught her how to kill vampires. Someone had sent her after him and Devon. If it was who Bones thought it was, she was protecting the same mass murderer he'd chased across two different countries.

He couldn't allow that, but he'd ask her nicely one more time. "Who do you work for?"

"No one," she lied again.

The hard way, then. He slapped her, hiding his distaste for it behind a deep scowl.

She glared at him and snapped, "Go to hell!"

Why wouldn't she tell him who her boss was? Was she in love with the sod? Or was she so greedy that she didn't care how many people suffered, as long as she received whatever reward she'd been promised?

If she were a man, Bones would ask again with his knife, but he couldn't bring himself to torture a woman, even one that had tried to kill him. Still, she was a murderer at best and a conspirator in a cartel that had murdered hundreds at worst. He gave her a firmer slap.

"Once again, who do you work for?"

She spat out the blood he'd drawn onto his feet. "No one, ass munch!"

Laughter burst from him. He hadn't been called such a creatively vile name in decades. It merited giving her another chance to talk without more unpleasantness. Still, she couldn't think he'd gone soft. That's why he let her see his fangs before he leaned in very close.

"I know you're lying," he said, brushing those fangs near her neck. Her whole body went rigid and her pulse tripled in speed. "Because last night, I went looking for a bloke," Bones whispered against her skin. "When I spotted him, I saw the same lovely red-haired girl who'd been rubbing on me leaving with him. I followed, thinking I'd sneak up on him while he was occupied. Instead, I watched you plug a stake into his heart, and what a stake!"

He held up her impressive weapon between them. Her eyes widened when she saw it.

"Wood on the outside, silver on the inside," Bones said, tapping the stake. "Poof, down goes Devon, yet it didn't stop there. You transported him to your truck, drove home, chopped his head off, and buried him in pieces, all while whistling a merry tune. How in the bloody hell could you do that, hmm?"

With every word, her expression became more stricken. His tone hardened.

"You don't work for anyone? Then why, when I take a deep whiff here," he inhaled near her neck, "do I smell something other than human? Faint, but unmistakable. *Vampire.*"

She flinched at the word. Bones pounced. She needed to know there was no point lying to him anymore.

"You've got a boss, you do. Feeds you some of his blood, right? Makes you stronger and faster, but still only human. Us poor vamps never see it coming. All we see is"—he pressed on the vibrating pulse in her neck—"food. Now, for the last time before I forget my manners, tell me *who* your boss is."

Anger and hatred soured her scent, but her gaze burned into his with a defiant sort of despair. "I don't have a boss." *Idiot*, her tone added. "You want to know why I smell like a human and a vampire? *Because that's what I am.* Years ago, my mother went on a date with what she thought was a nice guy. He turned out to be a vampire, and he raped her. Five months later there was me, premature but fully developed, with a whole slew of funky abilities."

Ah, Bones thought. *She's unhinged.*

Poor lass. Someone should tell her that while modern fiction might have half-breeds aplenty, in reality, the only one that Bones knew of had died nearly six hundred years ago.

"When she finally told me about my father," Cat went on. "I promised her I'd kill every vampire I found to ensure no one else suffers the way she did. She's been afraid to leave our home ever since! I hunt for her," her voice rose to a scream, "and the only thing I regret about dying now is that I didn't take more of you bloodsuckers with me!"

With that, she closed her eyes and braced.

Bones's brows rose. Did she think he was about to rip her throat out? As if he'd murder someone barking mad...or was there more to it than that?

Her voice had held the distinct ring of truth. Could a vampire have compelled her to believe such an impossible story? A simple "kill these blokes" order would've been easier, but some vampires tended toward the dramatic.

After a few moments, her eyelids peeked open. "Well?" she demanded. "Kill me already, you pathetic suck-neck!"

Bones stifled a laugh. "Ass-munch. Suck-neck. You kiss your mum with that mouth?"

She puffed up in outrage. "Don't you talk about my mother, murderer! Your kind isn't fit to speak of her!"

"I've seen you do murder," Bones reminded her, then couldn't resist adding, "And if what you're telling me is true, you're the same kind I am."

She shook her head so hard, her hair flew. "I am nothing like your kind! You're all monsters, preying on innocent people and caring nothing about the lives you wreck. The vampires I killed all attacked me. It was just their bad luck that I was ready for them. I might have some of this cursed blood in my veins, but at least I was using it to—"

"Oh, stick a sock in it already." Bigoted little bird, wasn't she? "You always ramble on so? No wonder your dates went right for your throat. Can't say as I blame them."

Her jaw dropped, and he almost laughed at the look on her face. The Queen couldn't be more offended if someone had farted on her crumpets. Still, the brief silence was welcome as he continued to weigh whether she was mental or under vampiric compulsion. Now, he gave either possibility fifty-fifty odds.

"I hate to interrupt your sympathy sessions over the other dead vampires," she said in a scathing tone. "But are you going to be killing me soon or what?"

Mental without a doubt, he thought until he put his mouth near the pounding pulse in her throat. Then, her scent changed his mind. Few humans knew that courage and cowardice smelled the same: like fear. The only difference between the courageous and cowards was whether or not they overcame that fear.

Even with the creature she despised most at her throat, Cat didn't grovel or try to offer someone else's life in exchange for her own. She only stiffened as his fangs grazed her skin.

Bravery like that deserved another chance before he drank the answers he needed out of her. He leaned back. She sagged in relief, but he pretended not to notice.

"In a hurry to die, are you?" he asked in a casual way. If she didn't believe her life was in danger, she'd have no incentive to tell him the truth. "Not before you answer a few more questions."

Her mouth turned down. "What makes you think I will?"

He had to fight not to smile. She couldn't know how much he admired her courage. Little chit would only use it against him.

"Believe me, you'll like it much more if you do," he said in a suitably menacing tone.

She gulped but said, "What do you want to know? *Maybe* I'll tell you."

This time, he couldn't stop his smile. It was also getting harder to ignore how her plain cotton knickers hugged her shapely hips, or how her bra had slipped during her struggle.

Before, he hadn't given her near nakedness a thought beyond ensuring that she had no more weapons. Now that she likely wasn't a willing participant in the cartel he was hunting, her charms were becoming distracting. He fancied many things about women, but courage outweighed them all, and she had courage to spare.

"Brave little Kitten, I'll give you that," he said, tracing his tongue along the inside of his lip. "Right, then. Suppose I believe you're the offspring of a human and a vampire. Almost unheard of, but we'll get back to that. Then let's say I believe you troll clubs hunting us evil deads to avenge your mum. How did you know what to use to kill us?"

Someone had to tell her. If she revealed who, he'd know the vampire who'd compelled her into believing such nonsense.

"It's not an open secret," Bones went on. "Most humans think good ol' wood will do it. But not you. You're telling me you've never dealt with vampires before, except to kill them?" *Impossible,* his tone stressed.

"You got anything to drink around here?" was her surprising response. "Nothing with clots in it, I mean, or that can be classified as O-negative or B-positive. Hmm?"

Once again, he had to bite back his laughter. He'd been asked —or begged—for many things during an interrogation, but never before had someone dared to request a booze break.

Courage to spare, indeed.

"Thirsty, luv? What a coincidence. So am I."

The implied threat made her blanch. Bones pulled out a flask and held it to her mouth. As soon as it brushed her lips, she bit the rim, tilted her head back, and emptied all of his good whisky down her throat. She even sighed with regret when she released her bite and the flask dropped back into his hand.

Bones held the bottle upside down. No, not a drop remained. She was a brash, brave, foul-mouthed, murdering *drunk,* and God help him, he hadn't found anyone this enticing in centuries.

"If I'd have known you were such a lush, I'd have given you the cheap stuff." Then, lest she sense the effect she had on him, he added, "Going to go out with a bang, are you?"

Instead of quailing, she managed to shrug. "What's the matter?

Did I ruin my flavor for you? I'm sure I'll be turning over in my grave worrying that you didn't like how I tasted. I hope you choke on my blood, you jerk."

Laughter spilled out of him. If he were in her position, he'd give his interrogator nothing but scathing sarcasm, too.

"Good form, Kitten! But enough stalling. How did you know what to use if no vampire told you?"

She looked away. "I didn't. Oh, I'd read a hundred books or more about our...your kind after hearing about my father. Some said crosses, sunlight, wood, or silver. It was pure luck, really." Her tone darkened. "One night, a vampire approached me at a club and then took me for a drive. Of course, he couldn't have been nicer, right up until he tried to eat me alive. I made up my mind that I was going to kill him or die trying, and the big silver cross dagger was all I had on me. It worked, though it took a bit of doing. So presto, I knew about silver."

Bones listened, expressionless, but inside, he tipped his hat. *Well done, you.*

"Later, I found out that wood didn't work at all. Got a nice scar on the thigh to prove it. The vamp laughed when he saw my stake, too, so clearly, he wasn't afraid of wood. Then, when I was making caramel apples it occurred to me to hide the silver in something a vampire would think was harmless." She gave him a baleful look. "Though most of you are so busy eyeing my neck, you don't even see me pull out my pointy friend."

He'd started shaking his head at the caramel apples part. By the time she finished, he was almost agog. "You're telling me caramel apples and books taught you how to kill vampires?"

At her nod, he started to pace. Could she...could she be telling the truth? No vampire in his right mind would make up such a ridiculous story simply to compel a human to kill.

"Then it's a damn good thing most of the recent generations disklike reading, or we'd all be in serious trouble," he finished with a sharp laugh. "But how did you know he was a vampire when you saw him?" What were the facts amidst the fiction that another vampire *must* have implemented in her mind? "Did you not find out until he tried to have an artery party?"

She flinched at how close he'd come. Bones backed up, but only a step. She was too brave to be allowed to feel truly comfortable. That could cause her to think lying was an option.

"I don't know how I knew. I just did. For starters, your kind looks different. Your skin looks...ethereal, almost. You move differently, more purposeful. And when I'm near you, I feel it in the air, like static electricity."

He'd been surprised at her perceptiveness about a vampire's skin and movements. Most humans didn't notice such things. But when she said she could *feel* vampires, he was shocked. Only vampires could feel another vampire's aura.

"Happy now?" she suddenly demanded, her voice cracking a bit. "Heard what you wanted?"

"Almost. How many vampires have you killed? Don't lie to me, or I'll know it."

She paused as if silently counting. Then, "Sixteen, including your friend from last night."

"Sixteen?" *How?* She'd failed utterly at being a seductress, and her only other act was being a marginally-believable drunk. "Sixteen vampires you took out yourself with nothing but a stake and your cleavage? Makes me ashamed of my kind, it does."

Her chin lifted. "I would have killed *more* if I hadn't been too young to get into bars, since they're vampire trolling grounds, not to mention all the times I had to take off when my grandfather got sick."

A mechanical "ping" came from the other side of the cave, indicating a new text. Bones left to read it. He'd uploaded Cat's SIM card from her mobile and sent it to his hacker friend, Ted. If there was deleted information on there from Cat's vampire boss, Ted would find it.

Nothing, Ted's text read, dashing Bones's hopes. *Most boring phone I've ever cracked. U owe me.*

Bones's jaw tightened. Yes, he did, but it left him no closer to answers. Only Catherine had those.

Chains clanged and he heard her grunt. Bones came back to her section of the cave to see her bent forward, straining as she tried to wrest her chains from the wall. He switched the light off to disorient her and chuckled as she cursed him.

"Oh, sorry about that," he mocked. "Those chains won't budge. They're not going anywhere, and neither are you. Good of you to try, though. Hate to think your spirit's broken already."

"I hate you," she said, out of breath from her efforts.

More truth, but not enough. Still, he had another path. A vampire compulsion could be broken by a stronger vampire, and Bones was strong. All it would take was drinking her blood.

"Time's up, luv," he said softly.

Her heart hammered when he smoothed her hair back from her neck. His lips thinned. He hated terrifying her, but drinking her blood was the only way to break the hold the other vampire had on her. Who knew what else Cat had been forced to do?

She thought he was about to kill her, but in reality, he was freeing her. If he thought she'd believe him, he'd tell her that. But in case he was wrong about her being under vampiric compulsion and this had been her best acting job yet…

"Last chance, Kitten. Who do you work for? Tell me the truth, and I'll let you live."

"I told you the truth," she gasped out, her pulse vibrating against his lips.

He rested his fangs over it. "I don't believe you," he murmured, glancing up to give her one more chance to confess—

Holy Mother of Christ, her *eyes.*

4

"*B*loody hell, look at your eyes," Bones breathed out, staggering back.

She said nothing. Just stared at him with eyes that, impossibly, were now the same glowing emerald green as his own.

Bones lunged forward and gripped her head. "Look at your bloody eyes!" he thundered, stunned into repetition.

Her expression was half terror, half annoyance. "Don't need to look at them, I've seen them. They change from gray to green when I'm upset. Happy now? Going to enjoy your meal more?"

He let her go before shock made him forget to check his strength and he accidentally hurt her. Then he began to pace.

"Bugger, you're telling the truth." No vampire was compelling her or controlling her. Somehow, she *was* the offspring of a human and a vampire. "You have to be," he went on, as if some part of him still needed convincing. "You have a pulse, but only vampires have eyes that glow green. This is unbelievable!"

"Glad you're excited," she said in a suddenly weary voice.

He stopped pacing to stare at her. Her hair tangled around her shoulders and her gaze lost some of its glowing intensity now that his fangs were nowhere near her throat. Did she have fangs, too?

No, he only saw flat teeth when she nibbled on her bottom lip, and if she was upset enough for her eyes to transform, her canines would have, too, if they could.

Vampire eyes, human teeth. It shouldn't be possible. *She* shouldn't be possible, yet here she was. Half human and half vampire…and pathological in her hatred of the latter.

That hatred would get her killed. She had no idea what was happening in Ohio now, but if she kept throwing herself in vampires' paths, she'd find out. The mass grave he'd uncovered two weeks ago flashed in his mind. If she kept on this path, she'd be one of those skeletons, tossed away like rubbish after the most hellish of existences…

Rage suffused him, followed by a stronger swell of determination. It didn't matter that she'd tried to kill him. Didn't matter that she wasn't one of his people. Also didn't matter that his near-pathological need to protect her made no bloody sense. He wouldn't let her become one of the lost.

She wanted to kill vampires? He could work with that.

"This is perfect," he said as if he'd been looking his entire life for a half breed. "In fact, it could come in right handy."

"What could come in handy?" she asked in an irate tone. "Either kill me, or let me go already. I'm tired."

He turned the light back on. She blinked under its brightness before scowling at him. He grinned. Oh yes, she'd stake him right and proper if she could. Now, to give her a compelling reason not to.

"How would you like to put your money where your mouth is?"

"What?" she asked with open suspicion.

"I can kill you, or let you live." His tone was bland, as if either option meant nothing to him. "But living comes with conditions. Your choice, your pick. Can't let you go without conditions; you just try to stake me."

"Aren't you the smart one?" she muttered.

He stifled his laugh. "You see, we're in the same boat. You hunt vampires. *I* hunt vampires. Both of us have our reasons, and we both have our problems. Other vampires can sense me whenever I'm close, so that makes it difficult for me to stake them without them expecting the try and running. You, on the other hand, put them at ease with that juicy jugular of yours, but you aren't strong enough to bring down the really big fish."

She stiffened in offense.

Bones continued as if he hadn't noticed. "Oh, you may have beaten some green ones, probably no older than twenty years undead, tops. Barely out of their nappies, as it were. But a Master vampire, like me?" He let scorn drip from his tone. "You couldn't bring me down with both weapons blazing. I'd be picking you out of my teeth in minutes. Therefore, I propose a deal. You continue doing what you love most—killing vampires—but you only hunt the ones *I'm* looking for. No exceptions," he stressed when she opened her mouth. "You're the bait. I'm the hook."

She stared at him as if he'd taken leave of his senses. Perhaps he had. Recruiting the half dead to kill the undead *was* a bit unorthodox, but he needed to keep her safe, and she needed to kill vampires. At least for now.

I hunt for her, she'd said of her mother. *To ensure no one else suffers the way she did...*

Except every time she risked her life hunting vampires, Cat was punishing herself for merely existing. That sort of self-destructive imperative couldn't easily be remedied. He knew that from experience. He hadn't become a bounty hunter of people even his kind was afraid of by accident. Once, like Cat, he'd thought it was all he deserved, too.

With time, Cat would realize there was more to life. Until then, he'd keep her safe, and trained to handle the monsters she thought she needed to kill. Until then...

Bones tapped his foot. "Don't have all night. The longer you wait, the hungrier I get. Might change my mind in a few minutes."

27

"I'll do it," she said quickly. Then she added, "But I have a condition of my own."

He chuckled. "You're hardly in a position to demand conditions."

Her chin jutted out. "Just challenging you to put *your* money where your mouth is. You said I wouldn't last against you even with both my weapons. I disagree. Unchain me, give me my stuff, and let's go. Winner takes all."

Damn good thing he wasn't in profile, or she'd notice that he'd just turned rock hard.

"And what you do you want if you win?" he asked while sending his blood to a less distracting place in his body.

"Your death."

First seething courage, now brutal honesty. She was just *trying* to switch him on, wasn't she?

"If I can beat you, I don't need you," she continued. "And as you put it, if I just let you walk, you'd come after me. But if you win"— a shrug—"I play by your rules."

Every bit of him felt like it was waking up. He'd think it was more lust, except it didn't stop there. No, it grew until it penetrated parts of him he hadn't realized existed.

He'd heard poets talk about things like this. They gave it fanciful names like "love at first sight" or "destiny." He'd always dismissed such claims as nonsense. Now, he wasn't so certain.

"You know, pet," he said to cover those new, startling emotions. "With you chained there, I could have a nice long drink out of your neck and go about my business as usual. You're pushing your luck quite a bit saying this to me."

"You don't seem the type that likes a boring drink out of a chained-up jugular," she countered.

Right you are.

"You seem like the type who likes danger. Why else would a vampire hunt vampires? Well? Are you in, or am I out?"

She held her breath after throwing down the gauntlet. He

came nearer, his gaze raking her while those inexplicable sensations kept growing until they felt as if they'd breach his skin and boil over onto the ground between them. Her breathing hitched and her heartbeat sped up, but her gaze remained hard, desperate...and fixed on him with deadly intent.

He almost laughed. Here he was, feeling as if Cupid's arrow had pierced his heart, and the source of his affection wanted nothing more than to see him dead. But first, she'd demanded a demonstration of his abilities.

Very well. As she'd soon learn, he was always happy to fulfill a lady's request.

Bones unlocked her manacles. "Let's see what you've got," he said, and meant it this time.

5

"Give me my clothes back," were her first words once she was free.

"You *are* trying to kill me, right?" Bones asked, chuckling. "Those trousers will cost you fluidity."

And wearing them will ensure I'm not distracted by your lovely form, he didn't add, though she should have known that, and she also should've used it to her advantage.

"Fluidity or not, I refuse to fight you in my underwear," she said between gritted teeth.

Worst. Murderess. Ever.

But if these were her terms… "Very well. Wait here."

Bones left her alone, not fretting about her running away. What this cave lacked in conveniences, it made up for in security. It's why he'd chosen to stay here instead of more comfortable surroundings. No one would think to look for him in a cavernous hole in the ground.

Unlike Hollywood's common portrayal of vampires in ramshackle castles or dark crypts, most of his kind wouldn't be caught dead in such hovels when there were modern—and luxurious—conveniences available. Vampires hadn't survived millenniums without detection because they'd failed to evolve. No, most vampires were very versatile, and they enjoyed their comforts as much as any human.

Bones did, too, especially since he'd had more than his share of poverty as a lad. But growing up destitute had taught him never to value anything more than he could afford to lose. He might not like staying in a cave, but he didn't value his comfort more than his advantage over his enemies. He'd return to his normal, posh lifestyle once this was over.

The echoing factor in the cave also gave Bones an acoustical image of everything Cat did. From the sounds, she didn't stray far from where he'd left her. Smart. The light bulb only illuminated a small section of that area, and there were several steep drops and crevasses beyond her sight. More natural security, all for the price of temporarily sleeping rough.

He went to the flatter, large section he used as his living quarters to fetch her things. When he returned, he tossed them at her. "Here."

She caught them with reflexes far faster than an average human. What other vampire traits did she have?

She gave him a pointed look before she pulled on her trousers. "You could pretend to be polite and turn your back."

He snorted. "With you armed? Shall I put a big red X over my heart for you as well, Kitten?"

"Don't call me that," she snapped.

Oh, it was her name forever now. "Whatever you say, luv."

That earned him another death glare. He only grinned, still basking in the unfamiliar yet wondrous sensations she brought out in him. Yes, she was fantasizing about ripping both of her weapons through his heart while he was feeling things he'd only heard of before, but who said romance was perfect?

"Are we doing this here?" she asked in an abrupt tone when she finished dressing.

Where she could barely see and the uneven terrain could fell her with one wrong step? She had so much to learn.

"Start walking straight ahead. Soon, you'll see lights."

She gave him several wary glances when she passed him, but then she moved with surer steps once she was several paces ahead. He followed, brows raised when she went well beyond the lamp's glow without a pause in her stride.

Can see in the dark, he added to her list of preternatural attributes.

She stopped when she reached the large antechamber he'd recently renovated. It now had lights strung up in several spots plus a desk and a chair. He'd intended to add other items now that he knew his stay here would be extended, but his delay in getting those meant they had plenty of room for their duel.

He cracked his knuckles and rolled his head around his shoulders; a prefight ritual dating back to his humanity. Then he steeled himself against his repugnance at the thought of hurting her. She'd demanded this duel. He'd give her the respect she was due by honoring that demand.

"All right, Kitten. Because I'm a gentleman, I'll let you have the first try. Come on. Let's do this."

She charged at him with impressive speed for a human, but too slow to be effective against him. She also seemed to have no strategy beyond pointing her weapons in his direction and lunging. He didn't bother criticizing her. He just whirled and let her sail past him.

"Going jogging, pet?"

She glared at him before attacking again from his right. He blocked her overhead stab, but—good on her!—she simultaneously scored a slash in his abdomen with her other weapon. Before she could dig it deeper, he gave her a light kick in the midsection.

She sprawled onto the cave floor.

"I liked this shirt," he muttered, examining the new rip. "Now you've gone and ripped it."

And for what? His heart wasn't in his stomach, as she very well knew.

She stayed doubled over for a few seconds, breathing raggedly. *Insufficient abdominal muscles,* he added to his list. How would her reflexes hold up, now that she'd been winded?

He moved at half speed, raising his arm to telegraph his intentions. Her eyes widened, and she ducked, but too slow, and she didn't let go of her midsection to block his strike. He gave her a glancing blow to the side of her head in reprimand.

Next time, stop clutching your belly and block me!

She staggered and almost fell. Then she attacked him with impressive enthusiasm. For several minutes, he let her, dialing down his strength, speed, and skill until he fought with no more force than an average young vampire.

Under these conditions, could she win?

No, he realized after several minutes. She kept getting up, though, proving her will was as formidable as her rage. But her reflexes, strength, and speed were still too human.

When he'd learned what he needed to know, he flung her off. She landed on the floor with a thud, groaning. Then, she opened bloodshot eyes. They were glowing green, her gaze a mixture of rage, pain, and desperation.

He'd seen that same desperation earlier. Why did she feel it now? Did she think he'd go back on his word not to kill her? Or was there something else behind that look—

Silver flashed in her hand. In the next instant, agony flared, and he looked down to see the hilt of her cross dagger embedded only a few centimeters above his heart. That's what he got for allowing his concern for her to distract him!

He snatched it out, snarling "Bloody hell, woman, that hurts!"

Though excellent throwing skills, he silently added.

She got back on her feet, but from her slow, careful movements, it took a great deal of effort.

"Had enough?" he asked, inhaling to see if her scent indicated worse injuries than he could see.

That desperate look leapt back into her gaze. "Not yet."

She couldn't win. She had to know that, but she refused to concede. If he was any other vampire, her need to continue this fight would be the last thing she ever did. The thought of that made him feel...bloody hell, more than he could handle right now.

He steeled himself against it, and against his near-overwhelming urge to call off this duel and heal her. If he didn't collect on her agreement to let him train her, her need to kill vampires combined with her human weaknesses would get her killed, and if she had even an inkling of knowledge about what he felt for her, she'd use it to slaughter him.

But if she thought she needed him to accomplish her goals... he could use her vampire-slaying compulsion to save her.

Bones resumed their fight, now showing her with crisp, ruthless efficiency that she was outmatched in every way. When she fell to the ground and didn't get back up, he knelt next to her.

"Enough now?"

One swollen eye slit open to glare at him. Her lips moved, but no sound came out. Still, Bones could make out what she mouthed at him.

Fuck you.

Then she passed out.

Admiration and those deeper, mystifying emotions swelled in him as he bit his wrist and held the bloody gash to her mouth. Even unconscious, she swallowed, at first weakly, and then stronger as his blood healed her bruises, cuts, and fractures.

She didn't stir as he picked her up and carried her to the bedroom he'd made from a cozy alcove in the cave. He set her on the bed, and then sealed them both in by blocking the entranceway with a heavy stone slab. Now he could sleep without fretting about anything—or anyone—disturbing them.

Dawn was upon them, and his brave, ferocious Kitten wasn't the only one who could use some rest.

6

----

*B*ones let the first several tugs go despite their revealing more of his body to the cave's chilly air. But when she yanked the last of his blankets off him, he ceased being a gentleman.

"If you're going to take *all* the covers, you can sleep on the floor!"

Cat's eyes opened, then widened when she saw him next to her in bed. Horror suffused her features, and she jumped up with such alarm, she banged her head on the room's low ceiling.

"Owww," she moaned while her gaze darted around, looking for a way to escape. When she realized the small room was sealed, she backed into the corner. Then she glanced down at herself, relief suffusing her expression when she saw that she was still fully clothed.

He suppressed a scoff. She thought he'd assault her while she was unconscious? She had so much to learn.

"Why am I not in a hospital?" she asked with more alarm than relief.

Bones sat up, moving slowly so he didn't startle her. "I healed you."

She blanched, fingers flying to her throat. As if she could wake up as a vampire and not realize it at once.

"How?" she demanded. "How did you do that?"

He leaned back. "Blood, of course."

She paled even more, if possible. Then her voice elevated to a shriek. "Tell me what you did to me!"

He hid his urge to comfort her behind an eye roll.

She tracked his every movement, her body coiled to fight while her heart rate tripled. To show he had no interest in harming her, he fluffed his pillow and pulled it nearer.

"Gave you a few drops of my blood," he said in a neutral tone. "Figured you wouldn't need much, what with you being a half-breed. You probably heal fast naturally, but then you were banged up a bit. Your own fault, of course, having suggested that stupid match," he added just to rile her.

He could stand her anger, but her fear hit him places he had no defense against yet. They were too new.

"Now, if you don't mind, it's daylight and I'm knackered. Didn't even get a meal out of all this," he said as further ammunition for her ire.

She barely seemed to hear that last part. "Vampire blood heals?" she asked in a shocked tone.

He closed his eyes. "You didn't know? Blimey, but you're ignorant about your own kind."

"Your kind is not my kind," she said at once.

Neither was humanity. Eventually, she'd have to reckon with that. But he only replied, "Whatever you say, Kitten."

She was quiet for a moment. He resisted the urge to open his eyes because if he did, he might stare at her sleep-tousled crimson hair. Or her eyes, dark as an approaching storm. Or the elegant curve of her throat, the soft swell of her breasts, and the round arse she'd unwittingly snuggled against him earlier...

"Would too much blood turn me?"

The question interrupted his thoughts. Good thing, too, or he might have tented the sheets over his hips.

"How much is too much?" she went on.

He opened one eye. It was all he dared, considering where his previous thoughts had taken him.

"Look, school's out now," he replied in a gruff tone. "I'm going to sleep. You're going to shut up. Later, when I'm awake, we'll go over all these niceties and more. Until then, let a fellow get some rest."

She drew herself up with a huff. "Show me the way out, and you can sleep all you want."

He snorted. "Sure. Shall I fetch your weapons for you as well, and close my eyes while you plug holes into my heart?"

She glanced away.

He stifled another snort. She'd been thinking that exact thing. Time to give her something else to think about.

"Not likely," he said, tone hardening. "You're in until I let you out. Don't bother trying to escape, you'd never make it. Now, I suggest you let me get some rest, because if you keep me awake much longer, I'm going to want breakfast."

To punctuate his point, he shut his eyes, yet heard her suck in an appalled breath.

"I'm not sleeping with you."

Not yet, Kitten, but if I have my way, you will soon.

He yanked the blanket off and threw it in her general direction. A peek through his lashes revealed that she let it hit her in the face.

Bloody hell, the woman needed to learn how to *duck*.

"Sleep on the floor, then. You're a cover hog, anyhow."

For the next half hour, he listened to her move around as if searching for a softer spot. She wouldn't find one. The cave floor was hard limestone, not mud. Would she swallow her pride—and hatred—enough to share the king-sized mattress with him?

She didn't. Eventually, she settled down in one spot and her breathing became regular and deep. Then snores filled the room.

Bones's lips twitched. Somehow, despite avoiding this feeling for nearly two hundred and fifty years, he was now head-over-heels for a prissy, murdering half-breed who hated the sight of him and *snored*. If this wasn't repayment for his many sins, he didn't know what was.

Wait until he told Charles. His best mate would hurt himself from laughing too hard.

But before he told anyone, he had to show her there was far more to vampires than what she believed. Yes, it meant upending his life, but the feelings she elicited left him no choice. No wonder songwriters droned on and on about such things. Shockingly, Bones wanted to tell everyone, too, including the snoring redhead who'd go right for her stakes if she had any inkling of what he felt for her.

No, he'd tell her none of it. Instead, he'd be a stern taskmaster while he trained her to survive against odds that would kill her with her current, under-developed abilities. The rest would have to wait until she looked at him and saw a man instead of a monster...and looked at herself and saw a woman instead of a sin to atone for.

In the meantime, he'd be reacquainting himself with something he was very unfamiliar with—celibacy.

He gave his right hand a wry glance. *You and I are about to become a lot closer, mate.*

With how long it would probably take for his Kitten to warm up to him, he might well become the first vampire to ever develop calluses.

～

Six hours later, Bones stood over her. She didn't stir. *No sense of being watched,* he added to his list of things she'd need to improve upon. Then he bent and shook her shoulder.

"Rise and shine, we have work to do."

She rolled over with a groan, then gave him an accusing look as her joints creaked when she sat up.

He only grinned. "Serves you right for trying to kill me. Last bloke who did that ended up with much more than a stiff neck. You're right lucky you're useful, or you'd be nothing more than a flush in my cheeks by now."

"Yeah, that's me," she muttered. "Lucky."

Bones wagged a finger at her. "Don't be glum. You're about to get a first-class education in nosferatu. Believe me, not many humans get to learn this stuff. Then again, you're not really human."

She flinched. "Stop saying that. I'm more human than I am...thing."

She seemed oblivious to the fact that every time she insulted vampires, she also reviled herself. "Yes, well, we'll find out just how much shortly," was all he said. "Move away from the wall."

She seemed glad for an excuse to get as far away from him as the small room allowed. He'd expected that, but he was surprised that it still stung. Then he chided himself for a fool. Was she supposed to forget everything she'd seen and been taught simply because he hadn't murdered her in her sleep? She was right not to trust him until he gave her a reason.

Time to start giving her one.

Bones hefted the stone boulder up and moved it aside. "Come along," he said.

She didn't move.

"Don't dawdle."

She came out of the room, and then glanced around at the antechamber they'd fought in with an embarrassed sort of dismay.

"I don't suppose...is there a bathroom in here?"

39

Bones stopped mid-step. Right. He should have anticipated she'd have that need—

"*One* of us still has functioning kidneys," she added, with a look of distaste in his direction.

Another "dead monster" crack, was it? Very well, he'd treat her with the same rudeness. "Think this is a bloomin' hotel? What, next you'll be wanting a bidet?"

She flushed, and then ground out, "Unless you like it messy, I suggest you show me an alternative, and fast."

He sighed as if exasperated. "Follow me. Don't trip or twist anything, damned if I'll carry you. Let's see what we can come up with. Sodding woman," he added. If she was angry, she would no longer be embarrassed about her normal bodily functions.

She muttered under her breath as she followed him. He didn't catch all of it, but the words "stake" and "heart" were clear. He hid his smile. Not embarrassed at all now, was she?

"There," he said after leading her to the underground river that cut through the cave. "That water runs downstream. You can climb on those rocks and do your business."

She ran over, her lips edging up in a smile that was too triumphant to only be anticipated bladder relief.

"By the way, if you're thinking you'll just jump off and swim out of here, it's a bad idea," he called out. "That water's about forty degrees and snakes over two miles before it exits these caves. Not a nice way to be, hypothermic and lost in the dark. You'd also have broken our agreement, so when I found you, I would be really, really displeased."

Her shoulders stiffened, but she had the grace not to deny any of it. Progress.

"See you in a bit," he said, walking far enough away to give her the illusion of privacy.

"I suppose toilet paper's out of the question?" she called out a few moments later.

He snorted in amusement. "I'll put it on my shopping list, Kitten."

"Stop calling me that. My name is Cat."

Not to me, he thought, hearing her come closer. When he could feel her warmth in the air and smell the creamy, vanilla-and-cherries scent that clung to her, he closed his eyes. She hit his senses with the impact of a sledgehammer, making his need to touch her almost painful.

He forced that back, surprised by how difficult it was. He'd never lacked self-control before. Granted, his looks ensured that women seldom rebuffed his attentions, so he supposed he *was* out of practice when it came to this form of discipline.

"What's your name, by the way?" she asked, a thread of hesitation running through her tone. "You never told me."

She hadn't truly wanted to know before. He'd been nothing more than a target to be eliminated to her.

"If we're going to be working together, at least I should know what to call you," she went on, as if rationalizing to herself why she'd asked him this. "Unless you simply prefer answering to profanity, of course," she finished in a clear attempt to further distance herself from the question.

Too late, he thought, a grin playing about his lips as he turned around. *I caught you treating me—however briefly—like a person instead of a monster.*

"My name is Bones."

7

"First things first," Bones said, settling himself onto a boulder as if it were a chair. "If you're going to be truly good at killing vampires, you need to know more about them."

After a moment, Cat sat on the boulder opposite him. He'd picked this spot because it was toward the entrance of the cave, where light filtered in through cracks in the rocky ceiling. She might be able to see well in the dark, but he didn't have to keep her limited to darkness.

"Sunlight doesn't do anything but give us a sunburn if we expose our skin to it for too long," he began with.

Interest flicked on her face, as if he'd answered a question she'd long wondered about.

"But we won't explode into flames in the sun like we do in the movies," he continued. "However, we do like to sleep in the day because we are most powerful at night. During the day we are slower, weaker, and less alert, especially at dawn."

Brand new vampires couldn't even stay conscious for the first few weeks at dawn, but he left that part out. No need to whet her appetite for a kill that would never happen.

"By dawn, you'll find most vampires tucked into whatever they call a bed, which, as you could tell from last night, doesn't mean a coffin," he went on. "Oh, some of the old-fashioned ones only sleep in coffins, but most of us sleep in whatever's comfortable. In fact, some vamps will have coffins staged in their lair so some Van Helsing wannabe will go there first while the vampire sneaks up on them. Done that trick a time or two myself. So, if you think throwing up the blinds and letting the sun stream in will do the trick, forget it."

Her expression was rapt. If she still had her mobile, he expected she would've started taking electronic notes. Inwardly, Bones smiled. She might be listening in anticipation of turning herself into a better killer, but she was still learning more about the other half of her nature than she had before. Nothing chipped at blind bigotry more effectively than knowledge.

"Crosses. Unless they're rigged up like yours, they'll only make us laugh before we eat you. Wood, as you are aware, can give us splinters, but it won't stop us from ripping your throat out. Holy water...well." Bones gave a dismissive grunt. "I've had more damage done by someone throwing dirt in my face. The whole religious thing is bunk when it comes to hurting our kind, got it?" *No god worshipped has a problem with us*, he didn't add, but hoped she realized from the subtext. "Your only advantage is that when a vampire sees that special stake of yours, they won't be put off by it."

"Aren't you afraid I'll use this information against you?" she asked.

Bones leaned forward. At once, she leaned back. The single gesture reinforced how much she despised all things vampire, including him. Before he could change that, she was right; he couldn't have her using this information to plot his demise.

Time for the stick.

"You and I are going to have to trust one another to accomplish our objectives, so I'll make this very, very simple: If you so much as look cross-eyes at me and I even *wonder* if you're thinking about betraying me, I'll kill you. Now, that might not scare you, being the big brave girl that you are, but remember this: I followed you home the other night. Got anyone you care about in that barn of a house?"

He let the sentence dangle.

She gulped, paling a shade whiter than death. He could practically hear her mind filling in terrible threats he'd never be evil enough to utter. In this, her revulsion of vampires would be to his benefit.

Stick, accomplished. Now, the carrot.

"Besides," he said in a more cheerful tone. "I can give you what you want."

Her expression couldn't be more doubtful. "What could you possibly know about what I want?"

"You want what every abandoned child wants. You want to find your father."

Her heart skipped a beat before accelerating into a loud staccato.

"But you don't want a happy reunion," Bones went on, his tone deepening. "You want to kill him."

Her gaze fixed on him as if he'd used his power to mesmerize her. "You can help me find my father? *How?*"

Bones shrugged as if he didn't know firsthand the kind of hatred a person could harbor against someone who'd hurt and abandoned their mother. "For starters, I know a great many undead types, so without me, you're looking for a needle in a fangstack. Even if I don't personally know him, I already know more about him than you do."

"What? How?" she sputtered.

"His age, for example." When her confusion didn't abate, he sighed. She knew *nothing* about the species she'd committed her young life to killing. "You're what, twenty-one?"

"Twenty-two," she corrected in a whisper. "Last month."

"Indeed? Then you have the wrong age as well as the wrong address on that fake license of yours."

Her chin lifted. "How do you know it's a fake?"

He snorted. "Didn't we just cover this? I know your real address, and it's not the one on that license."

Though it was clever of her to have false identification on her when she hunted. If Bones hadn't followed her home, he would have been chasing down information on the wrong person.

"Come to think of it, you are a liar, possessor of false identification, and a murderer," he said, enjoying the little huff she made when she was indignant.

"Your point?"

"Not to mention a tease," he went on. "Foulmouthed as well. Yep, you and I will get along famously."

She gave him a withering look. "*Bollocks.*"

Bones grinned. "Imitation is the sincerest form of flattery. But back to the subject. You said your mum carried you for what? Five months?"

At once, her expression changed, going back to the haunted one that no one her age should wear. "Yes, why?"

He leaned forward. This time, she didn't lean back.

"When you're changed into a vampire, it takes a few days for some of the human functions to stop completely. Oh, the heartbeat stops right off and the breathing does as well, but tears still look normal for the first day or so before you cry only pink due to the blood-to-water ratio in our bodies. You might even piss once or twice to get it out of your system. But the main point is, you father still had swimmers in his sacks."

"Excuse me?" she said in her prissiest tone.

"You know, luv. *Sperm.* Your father still had living sperm in his juice. Now, that could only be possible if he'd been newly changed. Within a week at most, I'd wager. Right off, then, you can pinpoint almost exactly how old he is, in vampire years. Add

45

that to any recent deaths around that time and place matching his description, and bingo! There's your da."

Shock suffused her features as she processed this. Bones waited, saying nothing. When she finally looked back at him, that shock had been replaced by flintlike determination.

She'd worn the same look all those times she'd gotten back up after he knocked her down during their fight. Nothing would stop her from seeing their arrangement through now. But, of course, she was still suspicious.

"Why do you want to help me find my father? In fact, why do you kill other vampires at all? They're your own kind."

Yours too, Bones didn't say, but it was true despite her denial. "I'll help you find your father because you hate him more than me, so it'll keep you motivated to do what I say."

She gave a nod she didn't even seem to be aware of.

"As for why I hunt vampires…you don't need to bother about that now." She wouldn't believe him even if he told her. "Suffice it to say that some people just need killing, and that goes for vampires as well as humans."

She didn't argue, which meant she must've met some evil sods with heartbeats, too. God knew the world had no shortage.

"Back to the subject," he said. "Guns don't work on us, either, with only two exceptions. One, if the bloke is lucky enough to shoot our necks in two. Decapitation *does* work; not many things can live without a head, and a head is the only part on a vampire that won't grow back if you cut it off. Two, if the gun has silver bullets and enough are fired into the heart to destroy it. That's not as easy as it sounds," he warned. "No vampire will stand still and pose for you. Likely, he'll rip you apart before any real damage is done. But those silver bullets hurt, so you can use them to slow a vamp down and then stake him, though you'd better be quick with that silver because you'll have a very brassed-off vampire on your hands."

She nodded, giving him that laser-like attention again. Staring into her dark gray eyes was like starting into the heart of a storm. Even dirty and blood-streaked, she was ridiculously beautiful, and so earnest it broke his heart.

She shouldn't be concerned with the best way to murder anyone, especially vampires. But somehow, she was convinced that she didn't deserve more to life than this.

I'll change that, he swore. But for now, he'd hold up his end of their bargain.

"Strangulation, drowning, none of that does anything. Vampires only breathe about once an hour for preference, and we can go indefinitely without oxygen. Our version of hyperventilating is to breathe once every few minutes. That's one way to tell a vamp is tiring; he'll start to breathe a bit to perk up. Electrocution, poisonous gas, ingestible poisons, drugs…none of those work."

"Sure we can't test some of those on you?" she muttered.

He wagged his finger in mock rebuke. "None of that, now. You and I are partners, remember? If you start to forget that, maybe you'd remember the things I mentioned would work really well on you."

"It was a joke," she said with no conviction.

Such a terrible liar. "The bottom line is that we are very hard to put down. How *you* managed to plant sixteen of us in the ground is beyond me, but then the world never lacks for fools."

She huffed. "I would have had you in pieces if you hadn't made me drive and then sucker-punched me when I wasn't looking."

He laughed. She stared at him before quickly looking away as if something she'd seen had rattled her.

"Kitten, why do you think I made you drive?" he said, still chuckling. "I had you pegged five seconds after speaking with you. You were a novice, green to the gills, and once off your routine, helpless as a babe. Of course, I 'sucker-punched' you. There is only one way to fight, and that's dirty. Clean, gentlemanly fighting will get you nowhere but dead, and fast. Take every cheap shot, every low blow, *absolutely* kick someone when they're down, and then maybe you'll be the one who walks away." He'd learned that at great cost during his youth. The memory made his laughter fade. "Remember, this isn't a boxing match. You can't win by scoring the most points."

"I get it," she said in grim tone.

She probably did. She'd killed over a dozen vampires, and any one of them would have murdered her for the attempt, had they been lucky enough to survive it. She'd known that. Must be why she carried false identification so her family wouldn't be harmed in retaliation, if one of her targets rifled through her things after murdering her. Many people could be brave in the heat of battle, but for years, she'd prepared for her own death with the kind of ice-cold courage that few had.

Yet another thing to admire, but she had to think this was a business arrangement he cared little about.

"Now we're off topic," he said. "We've covered our weaknesses. Onto our strengths, and we have many. We can scent you long before we see you, and we can hear your heartbeat from nearly a mile away. In addition to that, a vampire can suck a pint of your blood and seconds later, you won't even remember seeing one. Our fangs secrete a substance that, when combined with the power in our gaze, makes humans easy to hypnotize. So, for example, you wouldn't know that a vampire just sucked a meal out of your neck. Instead, all you'd remember is that you met a bloke, had a chat, and now you're sleepy."

And Master vampires like him didn't even need the narcotic-like property in their venom in order to control humans' minds. The power in their gaze alone was enough.

"That's how most of us feed," he stressed in case she didn't connect the dots herself. "If every vampire killed to eat, we'd have been outed from our closet centuries ago—"

"You can control my mind?" she interrupted, horrified.

Doubtful, but no need to wonder when he could be sure. His eyes flared green as he let his power out.

"Come to me."

Any regular human would be on their feet and moving toward him. She recoiled and hissed, "No fucking way."

He grinned and let his eyes return to their normal dark brown shade. "Appears not. Good on you. Can't have you getting all weak-minded and forgetting your goals, can we? Must be your bloodline. It doesn't work on other vampires, either." She bristled and he clarified, "Or other humans who imbibe of vampire blood. Some humans are immune to it, but only a small percentage. Have to have extraordinary mind control or natural resistance not to let us meddle about in your heads. Video games have solved that as far as most of humanity goes. That, and telly."

"Telly?" she repeated in confusion.

Americans. "Television. Don't you speak English?"

"You sure don't," she mumbled.

Please. He'd spent so little time in England recently, he probably sounded more like a Yank than a Brit.

"Daylight's burning, and we still have a lot to cover. We've gone through the senses and the mind control, but don't forget our strength. Or our teeth. Master vampires are strong enough to break you in half and carry the pieces with a finger. We can throw your car at you if we want to, and we'll rip you apart with our teeth. The question is, how many of our strengths do you have in you?"

Her head lowered, and she hunched as if about to reveal damning secrets. "Darkness doesn't affect me. I can see as well at night as in the day. I'm faster than any human I know," she added, now giving him a glance through her lashes. "I can hear things from far away, maybe not as far as you can. But sometimes in my room at night, I could hear my grandparent's downstairs whispering to each other about me—"

She paused at his raised brow. He schooled his expression to show nothing, but anger burned. Her whole bloody family had ostracized her when she couldn't help how she'd been born?

"I don't think I can control anyone's mind," she went on. "I mean, I've never tried it, but I think if I could, people would have treated me differently...anyway," she continued in a brisker tone. "I know I'm stronger than the average person. When I was fourteen, I beat up three boys, and they were all bigger than me." Bitterness crept into her tone. "That was when I couldn't hide anymore from the fact that something was very wrong with me. You've seen my eyes."

She said it as if they were the most hideous of deformities. He couldn't disagree more. Her glowing green eyes were a miracle, as was she.

"I have to control them when I'm upset so other people don't see them glow. My teeth are normal, I guess. They've never poked out funny, anyhow."

Her voice trailed off and she kept glancing at him as if expecting him to rain insults upon her. She spoke of her dazzling uniqueness with more shame than he'd heard genocidal murderers speak of mass atrocities.

"Let me get this straight," he said in a carefully controlled tone. "You said at fourteen you truly realized your uniqueness. You didn't know what you were before then? What did your mum tell you about your father when you were growing up?"

Pain filled her gaze. "She never mentioned my father. If I'd ask, as I did when I was little, she'd change the subject or get angry. But the other children let me know. They called me a bastard from the time they could speak."

She closed her eyes. Briefly, Bones did too.

Oh, how well I know that pain, Kitten...

"Like I said, when I hit puberty I started to feel even more different," she said, opening her eyes. "It got harder to hide my weirdness like my mom told me to. I liked the night most." For a moment, her tone softened. "I'd wander for hours in the orchard. Sometimes, I wouldn't even sleep until dawn..."

Of all the things she'd spoken of, this was the only memory that didn't seem strafed with pain. He almost smiled at the image of a young Cat playing in the orchard all night. Then her tone hardened and tightness filled her features.

"But it wasn't until those boys cornered me that I knew how bad it was."

"What did they do?" he asked softly.

She closed her eyes again. "They were pushing me, calling me names, the usual stuff. That didn't set me off; it happened almost every day."

It was a damn good thing she couldn't see his expression or she'd leap back in fear. *All I need are names,* he thought coldly. *Never too late for bullies to pay for their crimes.*

"But then one of them called my mother a slut, and I lost it. I threw a rock at him and busted his teeth out. The others jumped me, and I beat them."

She opened her eyes. His expression was schooled back into blankness. If she saw his pride in her, she'd be suspicious.

"They never told anyone what happened."

Bet they didn't, the sniveling little shits.

"Finally, on my sixteenth birthday, my mother decided I was old enough to know the truth about my father. I didn't want to believe her, but deep down, I knew it was true. That was the first night I saw my eyes glow. She held a mirror up to my face after stabbing me in the leg-"

She did *what?* His horror must've pierced his controlled mask because at once, she began to defend her mum.

"She wasn't being mean. She needed me really upset so I could see what my eyes did. About six months after that, I killed my first vampire."

Her words excused her mum's actions, but her eyes filled with tears that she tried to blink away. Those tears kept Bones from pointing out that even after she'd tried to kill him, he—a "cursed" vampire!—hadn't been cruel enough to stab her, and he'd thought she might be working for a murdering slaver.

No wonder her gaze held such desperation. Her own mum had broken her, and she'd done it when Cat had been at her most vulnerable.

Yet Cat hadn't stayed broken. Somehow, she'd picked up the pieces and molded herself into an avenger of the very woman who'd shattered her. Now, with every vampire she slew, Cat was trying to murder the parts of herself her mum had caused her to despise...and also to buy back her mother's love.

She shouldn't have had to be that strong. No one should.

Suddenly, she stood. "Speaking of my mother, I have to call her. She'll be worried sick. I've come home late before, but I've never been out this long. She'll think one of you bloodsuckers finally killed me."

That smashed through his control. "Your mum knows you've been hunting vampires? And she allows you do to do this?"

Blimey, she didn't have to hunt for monsters. She *lived* with one!

"I thought you were joking when you said your mum knew you were putting a dent in our population. If you were my child, I'd have you nailed inside your room at night to keep you from doing this."

Her face went red from rage, but once again, her eyes stopped him. She hadn't looked this hurt when she thought he was going to kill her. Deep down, she must know how wrong her mum's actions were. She just couldn't bring herself to admit it.

"Don't speak about her that way! She knows I'm doing the right thing! Why wouldn't she support that?"

Because she should love you more than she hates the species of the sod who raped her.

He didn't say it. The only reason she'd agreed to partner with him was so she could learn to be a better vampire killer. If he pointed out that no amount of superior slaying skills would make her mum love her if she didn't love her already, he'd never see her again.

So, he forced himself to shrug. "Whatever you say."

Then he stood in front of her.

She blinked, startled by his speed. If she knew all his abilities, she might faint, so for now, he'd only show her what was necessary.

"You've got good aim when you throw things. Found that out when you chucked your cross at me. Just think, a few centimeters lower, and you'd be planting daisies over my head by now. We'll work to improve your speed and accuracy. You'll be safer if you can kill from a distance. You're too vulnerable up close."

To emphasize that, he grasped her upper arms. She tried to pull away and couldn't.

His brow arched. *Exactly.*

"Your strength leaves much to be desired. You're stronger than a human man, but as weak as the weakest vampire. Also, your flexibility is shit, and you don't use your legs at all when you fight. They're valuable weapons and should be treated as such. As for your speed...that might be hopeless. But," his tone brightened, "we'll give it a go. The way I figure it, we have five weeks of hard training, and one week to work on your looks before we can get you out in the field."

"My looks?" she repeated, her cheeks filling up with a lovely, angry shade of red. "What's wrong with them?"

Bones gave her his most patronizing smile. "Oh, nothing *horrible*, but still, something that needs fixing."

His needling had her forgetting all about the pain of her mum's rejection. Indeed, if her face got any redder, it would soon match her hair. "How dare you—"

"After all, we're going after some big fish," he interrupted her. "Baggy jeans and plain tee-shirts won't cut it. You wouldn't know sexy if it bit you in the arse."

Green flashed in her eyes. "By God, I am going to—"

"Quit blathering," he cut her off again, now fighting to hold in his laughter. It wasn't all lies. She was stunning, but she didn't present herself that way. Maybe she didn't even realize it. By the time he was through, she would, as would everyone who set eyes on her.

Besides, it *would* help with hunting vampires. A beautiful woman in a tight, tiny dress would be irresistible to them...and Bones couldn't wait to see her in one himself.

"Didn't you want to call your mum?" he tempted her. "Come with me. My mobile's in the back."

Once again, he heard her mutter threats under her breath, this time involving silver-studded barb wire and his nether regions. But once again, she also followed him.

8

*I*t took two weeks for her to stop smelling of fear. Granted, she wore rage and resentment as if they were designer perfumes, but he could hardly blame her. He trained her with the same ruthlessness that the poverty-ridden streets of London had trained him, but instead of the chronic hunger he'd endured, he strapped boulders to her back while she climbed up the steep terrain in the cave. Instead of running from the law after he'd stolen food to survive, he ran her through the woods until she vomited. And instead of the endless times he was beaten and robbed by older lads, she got hand-to-hand combat with him.

Each day, he wondered if she would quit. Part of him hoped she would. That hope increased the first week, when she threw off the boulders he'd strapped onto her and said, "Enough!"

"That so?" Bones replied mildly. "If you no longer want to hunt vampires, then by all means, quit."

"I'm not quitting *that*," she snapped. "I'm quitting *this*. I hunted vampires just fine before your back-breaking techniques. If I'd known what you intended with that stupid bargain, I would have gladly chosen death!"

She would be choosing death, if she kept hunting vampires

without his training. She might have survived on sheer luck plus the element of surprise before, but those were unreliable. Skill wasn't, and he'd make damn sure she had it even if she didn't think she needed it.

That's why he smiled wide enough to show his fangs. "You'd rather die? Come here and prove it."

She stared at him.

He stared back, knowing her prejudice made her believe he'd really drain the life from her without a second thought.

After a long moment, she began strapping the boulders back onto the harness he'd fashioned for her, and then resumed her trek up the cave's steep incline.

He'd never been so proud of her...or so irritated by her low opinion of him.

By the second week, she'd made remarkable gains, so much that she stopped losing consciousness during their bouts. She looked rightfully pleased with herself over that, until she realized she would now be awake when he gave her his blood to heal her.

"I won't do it," she said in her most obstinate tone.

"Two of your ribs are broken, your arm's dislocated, and your eyes are so black, you could double as a raccoon," Bones countered, thrusting his bitten finger toward her. "Going to return home to your family that way?"

Her jaw clenched. "I'll tell them I was in a car crash."

"You'd also be breaking our bargain because you wouldn't be able to continue your training for weeks," he said, now wagging his blood-smeared finger at her. "That's not an option, so quit complaining, open your mouth, and swallow."

"Don't you sound like every other guy?" she muttered, but finally popped his bloody finger into her mouth.

With anyone else, he would have found the quip amusing. With her, jealousy hit him so hard that he was briefly robbed of rational thought. Her mouth was so warm, so inviting...and how many other blokes had thought the same under much more erotic circumstances?

"Disgusting," she garbled as she swallowed his blood. "How can you things live off that?"

Things. His patience stretched to the breaking point.

"Necessity is the mother of all appetites," he said in a curt tone.

"All this blood better not turn me into a vampire," she muttered, and almost spat his finger out. Then she looked at the moistened digit, at him, and blushed as if thinking of something other than his finger sliding between her lips.

Lust strafed the unexpected jealousy that still gripped him. Never before had she looked at him that way. Finally, she saw him as a *man*, and judging from that blush, a man she was having naughty thoughts about.

It took all his control to wipe his finger as if nothing had occurred. She wasn't ready to act on the thought. From her expression, it was already gone, but it *had* been there.

"Trust me, luv, this won't turn you into a vampire," he said. "Since you keep fretting about it, however, I'll tell you how it works. First, I'd have to drain you to the very point of death. Then, I'd open a vein, and let you drink from me until you were stuffed full of my blood. Only *that* would trigger the change. These measly drops aren't doing more than healing your injuries. They're probably not even enhancing your strength, so stop fretting every time you have to lick a few bits off my pieces."

Her face turned scarlet, and not from any lustful twinges this time. She simply couldn't handle even unintended innuendo.

"That's another thing you have to stop," he said, addressing it head-on. "You can't turn red as a sunset while pretending to be a confident, *horny* woman. No bloke's going to believe that act if he says 'cock' and you faint. Your virginity's going to get you killed."

"I'm not a virgin," she countered.

Insane jealousy slammed him, until he couldn't think past the need to kill any man who'd touched her. Right then, he was every inch the monster she'd repeatedly accused him of being.

"...change the subject," she was saying. "We're not friends. I don't want to discuss this with you."

Entirely reasonable. Her sexual history was her business, not his. But when he opened his mouth, none of those logical statements came out. Only his maddened jealousy did, inflamed by his feelings for her and the seething territoriality that all vampires had.

"Well, well, well. Kitten's catted around, has she?"

Shut it, fool! the sane part of him urged. *Shut it now!*

But he didn't. "Chap must be quite a lad. Is he waiting for you to finish your training? Or did you tire of him? Didn't peg you for the promiscuous type, but then you did offer me a taste when we first met. I wonder—did you plan on staking me before or *after* you got your itch scratched? What about the other vampires? Did they die with smiles on their faces—"

She slapped him.

He'd never deserved it more. He only caught her wrist when she tried it again because her violence fed the beast that he was now using all his strength to contain.

She whipped her free hand at his cheek. He caught that, too. Then, her expression tore through his insanity. If anyone else had caused her that level of hurt, he'd rip them to pieces.

"Don't talk to me that way, scum." Her voice shook. "I've heard enough of it. Just because my mother had me out of wedlock, our stupid neighbors thought she was a slut, and me, too, by default. Not that it's your business, but I've only been with one guy, and he dropped me right afterward, so no, I didn't duplicate the sexual escapades of my peers. Now, I mean it, we are never talking about this again!"

Rage and humiliation had her panting, and her pulse lashed him with its rapid beat. He barely even registered the "scum" insult. He was too gutted for causing her such pain.

"Kitten, I apologize."

It wasn't nearly enough, but how could he explain the reason behind his sudden, unhinged attack? Besides, his lack of control was his problem, not hers. So, he went with the logic that had failed him before.

"I had no right to say that to you. No one does. But just because your ignorant neighbors took their bigotry out on you and your mum, or some pimply teenager pulled a one-nighter—"

"Stop it," she interrupted, tears brightening her eyes. "Just stop. I can do the job, I can fake sexy, horny, whatever. But we are not discussing this."

As if he cared about the bloody job! "Look, luv—"

"Bite me," she spat, and stalked off.

Bones stayed where he was until the last echoes from her footsteps dissipated. Stalactites on the antechamber's ceiling caught the additional lights he'd set up for her, scattering them over the ground like discarded stars. He'd also gotten a couch for her to sit on, a table so she had something to set her belongings on, a telly to watch if she ever stayed past her training schedule—she hadn't, but one day, she might—and space heaters so she would no longer shiver in the cave's naturally chilly temperature. Now, every item mocked him with her absence, and when the extended silence confirmed that she was truly gone, he felt more alone than he had in decades.

Everything that mattered most to him had just left.

9

Bones took another few minutes to feel every bit of the blame, regret, and loneliness that his actions had wrought. Then, he resolved to fix what he'd broken between them.

Advice would help. He was hardly the first vampire to fall victim to preternaturally psychotic possessiveness. They'd found a way to function through it. He could, too.

Bones pulled out his mobile, scrolled, and hit "call" on his best mate's name. Charles answered on the second ring.

"Crispin! How goes it? Still in New Orleans?"

"I'm in Ohio now," Bones replied, used to Charles calling him by his birth name. Bones did the same despite Charles long ago renaming himself Spade—the tool he'd been assigned back when they were both prisoners at the New South Wales penal colonies in the late seventeen hundreds.

"'Fraid this isn't a social call, Charles. I'm in over my head with a particular situation."

Charles let out an indulgent laugh. "What are the lovely lasses' names? Or are there too many for you to remember?"

A grim smile stretched Bones's lips. "It's only one lass, and I'm more than a little in love with her."

A car horn blared through the line. Charles muttered something, then said, "Sorry, mate. I'm on my way to London, and traffic is murder. You were saying something about her being little in size and you loving it?"

"That's not what I said." Now Bones made sure to enunciate each word. "I said I'm more than a little in love with her."

"*What?*"

Charles's screech made Bones hold his mobile further away from his ear. Still, he heard the rest clearly.

"Who is she? And why didn't you tell me this before now? We spoke only four weeks ago!"

"I hadn't met her four weeks ago."

"Crispin." Charles's tone changed from loud shock to the softer, calm one he normally reserved for people teetering on the edge of sanity. "You're telling me you've fallen for a woman you've known less than a month?"

"What did you tell me back when I said something similar to you about Giselda?" Bones replied. "You said, 'you never have to wonder if you're in love. When you are, you'll know it.' I know it, Charles. The length of time doesn't matter."

Silence. Bones didn't know if it was more doubt on Charles' part, or because he'd mentioned Giselda. Even over a century later, Charles hadn't gotten over her death. Bones used to think that such an amount of grief was excessive. Now, he understood.

"Then I couldn't be happier for you," his best mate finally replied. "Tell me about her. I want to know everything."

Bones closed his eyes. "Her name is Cat, and she's an exceptionally strong, brave woman who's two hundred years too young for me, hates all things vampire, has already tried to murder me twice, and loathes the very ground I walk on."

He heard a screech of brakes, several horn blasts, and then finally, Charles's laughter.

"Sorry, mate, I accidentally ran the car off the road. Now that

I'm safely parked in a ditch, do repeat yourself because you *didn't* just say the object of your devotion hates you."

"You heard me," Bones said dryly. "I haven't even gotten to the best part. She's also half-vampire."

Silence stretched even longer this time. Bones broke it with a sharp laugh.

"I know. Impossible, right? If I hadn't seen the proof of it myself, I wouldn't believe it, either. But she is, and she's been taught to hate our kind—and herself–because of it."

"Oh, Crispin," Charles eventually said with a sigh. "Leave it to you to take the hardest road possible yet again."

"Someone has to walk it," Bones said, knowing Charles meant more than his new love interest. His best mate had long fretted that Bones's line of work would one day kill him, but someone had to stop the worst among their kind, and vampire law only afforded one loophole.

Kill a vampire from a powerful Master vampire's line for moral reasons, and you invited war between your people and theirs. But kill a vampire because you took a contract that someone had put on the sod's life, and that was simply the cost of doing business in a free market society.

So, when Bones could strike a blow for the better, he did. Getting paid afterward was merely the icing on the cake.

"We're not having that old argument," Bones said. "I need to know what you did to stop yourself from going barking mad whenever jealousy hit you. Just now, I berated her for not being a virgin. Can you believe I, of *all* people, did that?"

"Crickey," Charles muttered.

"Exactly," Bones said with more dryness.

Charles sighed again. "You can't learn to feel the jealousy any less. At least, I didn't. But you *can* learn not to take it out on her. When it strikes, force yourself to walk away while remembering that what you're feeling is a chemical surge turbo-charged by our supernatural natures. Or force yourself to walk away while making the phrase 'bite your tongue' a reality. Or walk away while punching yourself very hard in the face. In short, walk away while doing anything except giving voice to those out-of-control emotions."

Sound advice, indeed. "Thanks, mate. I owe you."

"No, you don't." Sadness edged Charles's tone now. Bones could almost picture him running a hand through his spiked black hair. "I'm still in your debt, and ever will be. But enough of that. When do I get to meet this wonder of biology and thief of previously-untouchable hearts?"

"When she won't kill you on sight," Bones replied, his mouth curling at Charles's instant laugh. "I'm not joking. She might look harmless, but her fighting skills are quite impressive. Soon, she'll be equal to a strong vampire."

"She wants you dead, and you're training her to be better equipped to carry out that objective?" Charles snorted. "You're going about this 'love' thing all wrong, mate."

"On the contrary," Bones replied in a light one. "I have a solid plan. But until she stops seeing all vampires as the enemy, you can't meet her, and for obvious reasons, don't tell anyone about her."

Charles grunted. "If the past is prologue, when other vampires learn what she is, half will want to claim her for their own lines, and the other half will want to kill her."

Bones's fangs shot out, and he nearly crushed his mobile from his fist instinctively clenching.

None would hurt her. He'd slaughter the lot of them first!

Time to practice the techniques Charles had just suggested. Bones bit his tongue until the taste of blood calmed him.

"Another reason why it's important that she learn to be at her fighting best," he replied in a very controlled tone.

"You, too," Charles said softly. "When Ian hears of her—"

"I'll be free from Ian's line by then," Bones said, his tone hardening. "And I'll take all who are mine with me."

Charles grunted. "And if Ian objects?"

Bones's jaw tightened until Charles should have heard the cartilage crack. "Doesn't matter. If Ian refuses to grant me my freedom, I'll challenge him and take it."

Pause.

"I hope you know what you're doing, Crispin."

Never more so.

"Thanks, mate. Until again."

He hung up before Charles could say anything else. There was no need for more warnings. Bones knew the risks. They didn't matter.

But first, he'd have to repair the hurt he'd caused her, and also resume hunting the cartel he'd been chasing. If they'd set up their new base in Ohio, as Bones suspected, he had to take them down before they endangered other innocent women.

Confirming their presence meant finding the dead, and following the money; the same formula he'd used many times. It worked, though normally, he had to find the dead by scouting out various sites according to rumors and whispers, and then start digging until he hit graves.

But Cat's lineage straddled both sides of the grave, so this time, Bones might have a short cut.

10

"We're going on a field trip," Bones announced.

Cat gave him a startled look. "Now?"

"Yes. I know you're tired from training, but this won't be taxing, promise." And it had to be done late at night, though he kept that part to himself. "Come on, moonlight's burning. The longer you delay, the longer this will take."

"Fine," she said with a sigh.

Her reluctance was an improvement compared to the first week after their fight. Then, she'd treated him only with icy anger. The second week, it had been irritation tinged with grudging respect. Now, at week four, she treated him like an over-demanding boss while also showing pride at her progress.

He couldn't decide which pleased him more; her increased comfort in the same abilities she'd previously been ashamed of, or how she was now so at ease with him, she thought nothing of brushing his arm when she bent to retrieve her bag.

Four weeks ago, she would've jumped as if scalded. Now, she hefted her bag onto her shoulder and said, "Please tell me we're not taking your Ducati."

Her dislike of his motorcycle wasn't news to him. That's why he said, "We're not. You're driving."

They walked the two miles from the cave to where she'd parked her old pickup truck. His bike could've handled the overgrown, wooded terrain, but she had to park that far away because her truck would've stalled on the first heavy bit of brush. Still, she enjoyed driving it, so he didn't point that out, or the fact that they'd arrive at their destination much faster if they took his bike.

She was mostly silent for the first hour into their drive, responding only to the directions he gave her. Then, when the city lights faded and nothing except lonely country road stretched in front of them, nervousness tinged her scent.

Bones glanced around, seeking the cause. No, nothing but bleak, barren scenery and their single-lane, unpaved road.

"Turn left here," Bones said when he spotted the sign for Peach Tree Road.

She gave him a dubious look, probably because he was steering her deeper into the woods, not out of them.

"You know, partner," she said, emphasizing the word. "You're being very secretive. What's this field trip about? I take it you didn't just get a sudden urge to go cow tipping."

Just to see the look on her face, he should tell her that he had. "No," Bones said, the truth winning out. "I need some information from a man who lives out here."

She stiffened. "I refuse to be a part of killing any humans, so if you think you're going to interrogate this guy and then bury him, you're wrong."

Any other time, he'd be offended. Right now, he laughed.

"I'm serious!" she snapped, pumping the brakes.

He didn't laugh again, but it was close. "You'll get the joke soon enough. To set your mind at ease, I promise not to touch the fellow. You're the one who'll be talking to him."

She gave him a surprised look, as if she couldn't believe he trusted her enough to do this.

He waited. When she didn't take her foot off the brake, his brow arched. "Will we be driving again anytime soon?"

"Oh," she said self-consciously, and hit the gas hard enough to lurch them forward. "Do I get any more details than that? Like, some background, and what you want to know?"

"Winston Gallagher was a railway worker back in the sixties. He also had a side business of making moonshine. One day, a fellow bought Winston's product and died the next day. Winston might've mistaken the alcohol content for the batch, or the sot drank too much. Either way, Winston was found guilty of murder and condemned to die."

"That's outrageous!" she said with all the shock of someone who'd lived a modern, privileged life. "They had no proof, no motive, and no malice aforethought."

"'Fraid the judge, John Simms, wasn't big on innocent until proven guilty. He also doubled as the executioner. Right before Simms hanged him, Winston swore he'd never let Simms have another night's peace. And since that day, he hasn't."

She stared at him, her lips parted from shock. "He hung the man you want me to speak to?"

"Pull over at that 'no trespassing' sign, Kitten," he told her. She did, still glancing at him in disbelief. "Winston won't speak to me since our kinds don't get along," Bones explained. "He'll talk to you, though, but I warn you, he's about as cheerful as you currently are."

"What part of this am I not understanding?" she asked with his aforementioned crossness. "Did that judge hang him or not?"

"Swung him right from the tree jutting over that cliff," Bones said. "You can still see rope marks in it. Many people lost their lives there, but don't bother speaking to any of them. They're residual. Winston's not."

"Are you telling me Winston's...a ghost?"

His lips twitched at her tone. Had it never occurred to her that if vampires existed, other supernatural species did, too?

"Ghost, specter, phantom, take your pick. What's most important is he's sentient, and that's rare. Most ghosts are only replays doing the same things over and over, like a record stuck on a turntable. Blimey, I'm dating myself; no one uses records anymore," he reflected. "Point is, Winston was so mad when he died, his consciousness stayed on. It's also due to location. Ohio has a thinner membrane for separating the natural from the supernatural, so it's easier for a soul to stay behind here. This particular area's like a homing beacon, too, with its five cemeteries forming a pentagram." He shook his head. "That's like a road map for spirits. Thanks to your bloodline, you should be able to see ghosts. You might also be able to feel them. Their energy's like a twinge of voltage in the air."

Her brows drew together, and then wonder flicked across her features. So, she *could* feel ghosts. Her humanity truly was the smaller half of her.

"What kind of information could a vampire possibly want from a ghost?" she asked him.

"Have Winston tell you all the names of young girls that have recently died around these parts. Don't let him tell you he doesn't know, either, and I'm only interested in deaths by unnatural causes. No car accidents or diseases."

She was giving him that look again. The one that said she couldn't tell if he was in earnest or merely pulling her leg. "You seriously want me to go into a cemetery and ask a ghost about dead girls?"

His lips curled. "Come, now, Kitten, you're half vampire. I wouldn't think ghosts would be such a stretch of your imagination."

"Guess not," she said after a pause. "And ghosts don't like vampires, so I shouldn't mention my mixed lineage. Do I get to know why ghosts don't like vampires?"

"They're jealous. We're as dead as they are, but we can do as we please while they're stuck as hazy apparitions. Makes them right cranky, which reminds me." He pulled out the bottle he'd acquired before she came over for training. "You'll need this."

She held it up and shook it. Bubbles briefly appeared in the clear liquid, indicating the high alcohol content. "What is it? Holy water?"

He laughed. "For Winston it is. That's white lightning. Pure moonshine, luv," he added when it was clear she wasn't familiar with the term. "Simms Cemetery is right past that line of trees. Make sure to bang about a bit to get Winston's attention. Ghosts tend to nap a lot, but once you've got him up, show Winston that bottle. He'll tell you whatever you want."

"You really want me to go stomping through a graveyard brandishing a bottle of booze to rouse an unrestful spirit so I can interrogate him?" she muttered under her breath. "Perfect."

"Don't forget this," Bones added, sliding a pad and pen at her. "Make sure to write down the names and ages of every girl Winston tells you about. If he can include how they died as well, so much the better."

"I should refuse because interrogating a ghost was *not* part of our agreement," she said, but an unmistakable spark of interest lit her eyes. She might deny it to him—and especially herself—but she was more than intrigued by the prospect.

"If I'm right, this information will lead to a group of vampires who need killing," Bones tempted her. "Hunting vampires *is* part of our agreement, isn't it?"

She shook her head, but held out her hand. He gave her the pen, notepad, and bottle of illegal liquor, and then pretended not to notice the spring in her step as she left the truck.

11

———

*B*ones stayed on the far edge of Simms Cemetery, watching as Cat slowly walked up to the old headstones. If you didn't know the cemetery was here, it was easy to miss, hence the human rumors that it was so haunted, it could move to change its location. When tree trunks obscured his view of her, he flew up to see over them. She didn't know he could fly, so she wouldn't think to look up to spot him, and his all-black attire made him nearly invisible against the night sky.

His new, higher vantage point let him see her again, though the trees were so close together, their bare limbs formed a spider web of branches between them. She was halfway through the cemetery when she whirled and whipped out her knife.

"All right, luv?" Bones called out.

"Yeah," she said after a second, sounding slightly embarrassed. "It was nothing."

He followed the direction of her gaze. John Simms' shade rose from his grave and crossed the length of the cemetery. Then, he flung himself off the same cliff the hanging tree protruded over. After a few moments, his shade rose from his grave and repeated the process.

Bones didn't know how Winston had managed to curse the judge who'd sentenced him, but the moonshine maker had done it. John Simms' spirit hadn't rested a single night since Winston's death. Bones wished he could say the same about the judge who'd sentenced him to the penal colonies over two hundred years ago. He'd been a nasty sod, too.

Cat paused when another ghost materialized over an age-crumbled headstone. The Weeping Woman had appeared there so often, even humans had heard of her. But she, like Simms, wasn't sentient. She was only a remnant of the energy the woman had left behind. Cat must've realized that, too, because after a sympathetic look, Cat ignored her and continued searching the cemetery.

After a moment, she stopped and knelt by another weathered headstone. "Winston Gallagher," Cat said, knocking on it as if it were a door. "Come on out!"

Winston would hear her even if that wasn't his headstone. Per Bones's instructions, she was being loud.

"Knock, knock, who's there?" Cat said next.

Bones smiled at her whimsy, and then he felt a surge of supernatural energy before a shadow formed at the nearby tree line. Cat looked in that direction, proving she felt it, too.

"Oh, Winston," she said, drawing out the last syllable of his name as if it were an incantation. "I have something for you!"

"Insolent warm baggage," the ghost muttered, materializing enough to show his stout midsection, bushy brown hair, and thick whiskers. "Let's see how fast she can run."

Winston let out an eerie wail worthy of a B-grade horror movie, and then the leaves at his feet burst outward as if kicked by a solid object. An impressive trick for a ghost.

Cat merely stood up and said, "Winston Gallagher?"

The ghost looked over his shoulder, as if expecting to find someone else behind him. That's how shocked he was that Cat could see him. Bones stifled his laugh and flew higher. Cat

71

wouldn't know to look up, but Winston might, and Bones didn't want the ghost seeing him.

"Well?" he heard Cat say impatiently.

The ghost muttered something too low for Bones to hear.

"The hell I can't," Cat replied. "If that's your headstone, then tonight's your lucky night."

"You can see me?" Winston asked, louder now.

"Yeah, I see dead people," Cat said in an amused tone. "Who knew? Now, let's talk. I'm looking for some newly deceaseds, and I heard you could help."

Bones couldn't see Winston's scowl, but it was clear in the ghost's new, belligerent tone. "Get out of here, lest the grave swallow you whole, and you never leave!"

"I'm not afraid of the grave. I was born half in it," was Cat's calm reply. "If you want me gone, fine, but that means I'll have to throw *this* in the nearest trash can."

Bones knew the moment Winston saw the bottle.

"What's that you've got there, mistress?" he crooned. Nothing like an insatiable alcohol craving to make the ghost remember his manners.

"Moonshine, my friend," Cat replied in a tempting tone.

"Please, mistress!" Winston shouted. "Please, drink it!"

"Me?" Cat said in confusion. "I don't want any."

"Let me taste it through you, please!" Winston begged.

Cat began muttering under her breath. Bones grinned. No, he hadn't mentioned this part, but now she'd learn another important lesson when it came to dealing with supernaturals: expect the unexpected. Would Cat be flexible enough to accomplish her objectives? Or would her hostility toward non-humans cause her to abandon the job?

"Fine," Cat said after a pause. "But then you're going to give me the names of young girls who've died around here. No car accidents or diseases, either. Murders only."

One month ago, she'd thought all vampires were rabid killers.

Now, she was bargaining with a ghost on behalf of her vampire partner. She had such strength. It had taken Bones years to stop hating himself for what Ian had forced him to become.

"Read the paper, mistress, you don't need me for that," Winston snapped. "Now, drink the 'shine!"

The ghost was trying to *bully* her? Bones almost pitied him.

"I've caught you on a bad night," Cat said in an icily pleasant tone. "I'll just be on my way—"

"Samantha King, seventeen years old, passed last night after being bled to death!" Winston screeched.

Bled to death.

Bones's jaw tightened. Contrary to what Cat believed, vampires rarely killed when they fed. Even if the vampire had no moral qualms, leaving bodies behind was a messy, attention-getting *waste*. Why feed and kill when a living human could provide many meals? The few humans in the know about vampires usually flocked to them, seeking the protection and care vampires gave the human members of their lines, all for the low cost of silence about their species plus a little blood.

"Mother of God," Cat said, gagging after her first swallow of moonshine. It wasn't Bones's preferred liquor, either.

"That tastes like kerosene!" she went on with a gasp.

"The *sweetness*," Winston moaned. "Give me more!"

Bones's mobile vibrated with an incoming call. One glance at the number, and he knew he'd have to take this. He flew higher, until neither Cat nor the ghost could hear him.

"Ted," Bones answered. "What did you find out?"

"Not as much as I'd like," his friend replied, a Southern accent coating each word. "I flagged every wire or transfer above ten g's, and you're right. Lots of money coming in and out of areas in Ohio that aren't experiencing an economic boom. Lots of new shell corporations here, too."

Bones had seen this before. "Let me guess; the money's being sent to shell corporations that can't be easily traced?"

"Give the fanged man a cigar," Ted drawled.

"Is Flat Creek Incorporated one of the shell companies?"

"Yes." Ted sounded surprised. "Was going to tell you that's the top receiver of all the wires, but you beat me to it."

Then Bones was right about who was running this cabal, and that wasn't good news. Hennessey was an old, powerful, well-connected Master vampire known for his expensive tastes, unbridled avarice, and absolute lack of a conscience.

"Are any of Flat Creek Inc's clients sloppy?"

There was usually at least one. Arrogance bred contempt for playing it safe.

"Sergio Ricci," Ted replied, rolling his r's. "He's been the biggest spender this past year. Probably why he's the easiest to trace. Hard to completely hide that kind of money."

Sergio. Not nearly as powerful or connected as Hennessey, but just as morally bankrupt. Killing him would be a pleasure.

"Thanks, mate. I'll need our usual arrangement soon, so don't go anywhere. In the meantime, keep your ear to the ground. Let me know if anything new comes up."

"Will do, bud," Ted replied.

Bones hung up and floated back down. He was near the tree tops when he heard Cat yell, "I hope worms shit on your corpse!"

She sounded more angry than endangered, but he hastened to the ground anyway. "What happened, Kitten?"

"You," she slurred, taking several seconds to spot him even though he was now striding right toward her. "You tricked me! I never want to see you *or* that bottle of liquid arsenic again!"

She hurled the bottle moonshine bottle at him with none of her usual skill. It missed him by several meters.

Bones retrieved it, shocked to see it was now empty.

"You drank the whole bloody thing? You were only supposed to have a few sips!"

"Did you say that?" she accused as she staggered and fell.

Bones caught her before she hit the ground.

74

"I've got those names, so that's all that matters, but you men are all alike." Cat paused to let out a loud hiccup. "Alive, dead, undead, you're all perverts. I had a drunken pervert in my pants! Do you know how *unsanitary* that is?"

"What are you saying?" Had someone else shown up in the cemetery while he was too high up to see? He'd kill them—

"Winston poltergeisted my panties, that's what!" she said with another impressive hiccup.

"Why, you scurvy, lecherous spook!" Bones thundered, swinging around to face the cemetery. "If my pipes still worked, I'd go right back there and piss on your grave!"

Ghostly laughter danced on the wind before fading away.

That was it. Bones didn't know how to kill a ghost, but finding out would become his new pastime.

Cat plucked at his jacket. She was so drunk, even that slight movement nearly felled her. Without his arm around her, she wouldn't be able to remain on her feet.

"Who were those girls?" she slurred. "You were right, most of them had been killed by vampires."

"I suspected as much." And hated for her to know it, but giving them justice was more important than him fretting about her having another reason to hate their kind.

"Do you know who did it? Winston didn't." Cat widened her eyes, as if having difficulty focusing on him despite him being right there. "He just knew who they were and how they died."

"Don't ask me more about it," Bones said, soft but stern. "I won't tell you, and before you even wonder, *no*, I had nothing to do with it."

She stared at him, her expression somber but not accusing. She believed him. It struck him with more force than he was prepared to process. He looked away so she didn't read the emotion in his gaze. Was she finally starting to trust him?

All at once, she began to laugh. "You know what? You're pretty. You're *so* pretty."

He looked back at her, fighting not to laugh himself now. "You'll hate yourself in the morning for saying that. You must be absolutely pissed."

Another cascade of giggles escaped her. "Not anymore."

"Right," he said, picking her up.

She didn't even protest. *Drunk beyond belief.*

"If you weren't half dead, what you just drank would kill you," he muttered before saying, "Come on. Let's get you home."

She snuggled deeper into his arms. At once, his body reacted despite him knowing that this was the drink, not her. Still, she felt so right in his arms, and when she brushed her mouth on his neck and inhaled his scent…it took all his willpower to keep himself from kissing her.

"Do you think I'm pretty?" she asked in a breathy tone.

"No, I don't think you're pretty." His voice was hoarse as he fought to control himself. "I think you're the most beautiful girl I've ever seen."

She smiled, and then her expression clouded. "Liar. He wouldn't have done that if I was beautiful."

"Who?" Bones asked at once.

"Maybe he knew," she said as if she hadn't heard him. "Maybe on some deep level, he sensed that I was evil. I wish I hadn't been born this way. I wish I hadn't been born at all—"

"You listen to me, Kitten," he interrupted. "I don't know who you're talking about"—aside from the world's biggest fool—"but you are not evil. Not one single cell of you. There is nothing wrong with you, and sod anyone who can't see that."

Her head fell back as if it were too heavy for her to hold up any longer. He shifted, cradling her closer.

A smile flitted over her lips. Then, with the quixotic mood fluctuation of someone drunk, she began to laugh again.

"Winston liked me. As long as I have moonshine, I've always got a date with a ghost!"

Did his feelings for her make him irrational enough to be jealous of a ghost? Yes, yes they did.

"Hate to inform you, but you and Winston do *not* have a future together."

"Says who?" she asked with another laugh.

He shouldn't. He shouldn't. He shouldn't...

He lifted her head, waiting until her gaze settled on his face. Then he leaned down so there was no chance that she could look away.

"I say."

She stared at him, her breath hitching. Her heart rate sped up, too, and not from fear. No, another emotion entirely lit his senses on fire as he caught the new, intoxicating change to her scent. His whole body tightened in response, but he didn't close the space between their mouths. He'd waited too long to kiss her to do it now, when alcohol motivated her as well as desire.

"I'm drunk, aren't I?" she asked in an unsteady tone.

He snorted. "Impressively so."

She smiled as if glad he'd confirmed that. Then her gaze flicked to his mouth. "Don't you dare try to bite me."

"Don't fret. That was the furthest thing from my mind," he replied with the absolute truth.

She smiled again. A pang hit him when he realized this was the most he'd seen her smile. He carried her to the Ford and opened it one-handed. Then, he set her down and fastened her seat belt around her hips. There was no accompanying shoulder strap. This truck was so old, that hadn't been invented when it was manufactured. Then he took the notepad from her and put it in the glove box. She barely seemed to notice.

She slumped against the truck's door as soon as he shut it, but when Bones drove off, the bumpy, unpaved road roused her. Between the lack of shock absorbs and the thin, worn seats, she had no hope of resting. She needed a new vehicle. If he thought she'd accept it, he'd buy her one tomorrow.

"Here," Bones said when he could stand her restlessness no longer, and tugged her so she could lay her head on his leg.

"Pig!" she shouted, banging her head on the steering wheel from how fast—and clumsily—she recoiled.

"Isn't *your* mind in the gutter?" he said with a chuckle. "I only had the most honorable of intentions, I assure you."

Cat gave his lap a wary look, as if assessing its potential dangerousness. Bones's lips twitched, but he didn't laugh again.

Oh, you won't have to wonder when that'll be dangerous. I promise you, you'll know at once.

Then, she looked at the cold, unforgiving metal that made up most of the interior to her truck before she flopped down and rested her head on his leg.

"Wake me when we get to my house."

12

A week later, Cat stood in front of the new, full-length mirror and stared at her reflection with horror.

"There is no way I'm going out in public like this!"

Bones leaned back in his chair, not bothering to hide his grin. "You look so smashing, I can hardly stop myself from ripping your clothes off."

If she knew how true that was, she'd do more than glare at him. Most women enjoyed a makeover plus bags of new clothes, but not his Kitten. The results were worth it, though. Her makeover didn't heighten her beauty as much as demand attention for it, as did her low-cut, short-hemmed dress. If not for the boots that reached her knees, she'd be more naked than clothed, and from her scandalized expression, she was well aware of that.

"You think this is funny, don't you?" she retorted. "This is all a big, *bloody* chuckle-fest to you!"

He jumped up and faced her. She was so used to his speed now that she didn't blink at how he went from a seated position across the room to staring down at her in less than a second.

"This isn't a joke, but it is a game, and winner takes all. If some poor undead fellow is busy looking at these"—he tugged at her bodice, earning a slap to his hand—"then he won't be looking for this," he finished, holding his latest gift against her stomach.

If she hadn't been so focused on barring another inch of her bosoms from his view, she would have paid more attention to what he was doing with his other hand. After all, her cleavage was meant to distract her *targets*, not herself.

She grabbed the gift he held out and straightened. "Is that a stake, Bones, or are you very happy with my new dress?"

She was just daring him now, wasn't she?

"In this case, it's a stake. You could always feel around for something more, though," he couldn't resist adding. "See what comes up."

She gave him one of her I'm-acting-more-angry-than-I-am looks. "That better be part of our upcoming dirty-talk training, or we're going to give this new stake a go."

Oh, he was going to enjoy this next part of her training, and for far more than its practical purposes. She might look like a seductress in her new togs, but she also needed to sound like one. Fortunately for her, he was a world-class libertine who'd spent weeks fantasizing about her. When he was done, she'd be able to handle anything her targets said.

"Now, that's hardly a romantic rejoinder," he said, as if this were only part of her lesson. "Concentrate! You look great, by the way. That bra perfectly showcases your cleavage."

"Slime," she said, but he caught her quick glance down to see if he was right. Then she quickly looked away, as if embarrassed at being caught admiring herself.

She *should* admire herself. She'd been berated into being ashamed for too long, but that was a subject for another day. For now, he had another surprise.

"Put the stake in your boot, Kitten. You'll find there's a loop for it."

She did, smiling at how her weapon was now concealed, yet still within easy reach.

"Put your other one away as well," he said, knowing she always carried her homemade silver-and-wood stake on her, too.

"That was a great idea, Bones," she said when she was done putting her weapons away. Then, her expression clouded.

Poor lass. Whenever she let her guard down enough to enjoy her time with him, she had a knee-jerk reaction of punishing herself. He hadn't been able to stop that self-destructive cycle yet, but today, he could distract her from it. Thoroughly.

"Done that myself a time or two, but something's still not right," he said while walking around her. "Something's missing." He pretended to muse a moment longer before saying, "I've got it!" with a snap of his fingers. "Take your knickers off."

She gaped at him. "What?"

"Your knickers," he repeated, using all his control to keep a straight face. "You know: panties, muff-huggers, nasty nets—"

"Are you out of your mind?" she interrupted him. "What does my *underwear* have to do with anything? I'm not flashing my...my crotch at someone, no matter what you say!"

Her color was up, but she hadn't blushed yet. He'd soon fix that.

"You don't have to flash anyone anything. Believe me, a vampire will know without you showing him that your box is unwrapped."

"How?" she snapped. "No panty lines?"

"The scent, pet." Ah, there was his blush! And such a lovely shade of red, too.

"No vamp in the world could mistake that," Bones went on, his lips twitching so much that he could barely speak. Good thing she was too incensed to notice. "Like dangling catnip in front of a bloomin' kitty. Bloke gets a good whiff of—"

"Will you stop?" she all but screeched. "I get the picture, okay? Stop drawing it! God, but you are...profane!"

He'd started this to distract her—and yes, because she was even lovelier when she blushed—but she really did need to get past her overactive sense of modesty. Her first hunt was this weekend, and she *would* be ready.

"Besides, I hardly see how that's necessary," she added, collecting herself with visible effort. "You've got me all dolled up in these screw-me clothes, and I'm going to burn their ears off with dirty talk. If that isn't enough to get our targets to take me for a ride, then it's hopeless."

"It's like this, luv," he replied. "You look right fetching, but suppose a fellow prefers blondes? Or brunettes? Or likes 'em with a little more meat on the arse? These aren't greenhorns; these are vampires with discriminating tastes. We might need something to tip the scales, as it were. Think of it as...advertising. Besides, with a vampire's sense of smell, it's not like he can't sniff you out in the first place." And if she hadn't realized that before, she would now. "For example, I can tell right off when you've got your monthlies, knickers or no knickers. Some things you just—"

"I get your point!" Now her face was fire-engine red, but to her credit, she took in a few breaths, and then met his eyes squarely. "Fine, I'll do it, when we go out on Friday for the hunt. Not before. I'm not negotiating on this one."

"Whatever you say, Kitten," he replied, ignoring her glare. "Now, to our next lesson: the nasty speak. You know the rules. For every blush and recoil you give me, you owe me ten miles running through the woods. So, which are you going to be by the end of this? A triumphant seductress? Or a tired jogger?"

"Triumphant seductress," she said with admirable confidence for someone whose cheeks were still stained from a prior blush.

He gestured to the table he'd set up. "Let's find out."

Cat sat down, giving a dismayed glance at how that made her short hemline hitch up even higher. Bones saw it and snorted.

"Going to lose our wager before I've even started?"

With a defiant arch of her brow, she yanked her hemline up another notch, and then glared at him for admiring the view.

"Are you?" she countered. "If I don't blush or pull away, *you* lose. I wonder what punishment I'll think up for you?"

"Think away," he replied with a grin. "It'll never happen." Then he sat down and held out his hands. "Game on, luv."

After a moment's pause, she slipped her hands into his. As soon as she did, Bones told her what he was *really* thinking.

"You look luscious, pet, and I'm not talking about your new dress. The only thing that could make your mouth more beautiful is if it were wrapped around my cock. I wager the sight of that could start my heart again. I can't wait to see what you look like beneath me, bent over against me, and on top of me. I want to hear how loud you can scream when you come. I bet you like it rough, too. So do I, and I'll tear into you until you're too tired to keep begging me for more—"

"My, my, someone hasn't been laid in a while," she interrupted him.

Her tone was cool, but she was already using sarcasm as a shield, and her eyes had dilated with more than embarrassment. Forbidden interest sparked there now, too, and tiny muscles twitched in her hands, as if she wanted to tighten her grip on him, but wasn't allowing herself to.

Bones rolled his thumbs over the pressure points in her palms, teasing them with light strokes. Beneath the table, her legs clenched as if she were feeling his touch somewhere else, and her eyes widened in surprise.

That's right, Kitten, Bones thought, letting her see past the mask he always wore around her. *I can make you feel things you can't even imagine. Soon, I'll do everything I'm telling you now, and that's not counting what I can do with my fangs that I won't talk about yet...*

"I'll take your breasts into my mouth, licking your nipples until they turn dark red. They'll do that," he confirmed as her brow briefly furrowed. "The more I lick and the more I nibble, the darker they'll get. You won't want me to stop even after I've completely exhausted you, and I don't tire easily. Let me inform you of a secret about vampires—we direct where the blood goes in our bodies, for as long as we want it to be there, so I can come again and again while still not stopping…"

Her breathing hitched, and when he stroked the pulse points on her wrists, he felt as well as heard her heartbeat speed up.

"I can't wait to find out how you taste," he continued, voice deepening while his tongue traced his lower lip. "I'll lick you until you think you're on fire, and after I suck all your juices out of you…I'll drink your blood."

"Huh?" she said before comprehension dawned, and she looked at his mouth with a flash of erotic expectation. Almost at once, a flush painted her cheeks from ear to ear, and she stood up so fast that her chair upended.

Triumph surged that had nothing to do with his winning their bet. She wasn't blushing from her usual prudery now. Oh, no. Her scent, pulse, and the look in her eyes showed that she was blushing because part of her wanted him to do everything he'd said…and the rest of her had just realized that.

He inhaled the heady scent of her arousal while making her a silent promise. *Soon, Kitten. Very soon.*

But not now. She wasn't ready to admit her attraction, let alone act on it. So, he'd continue on as if both of them weren't aware of the new tension between them.

He let out a low laugh. "Oh, Kitten, you were doing so well! Guess you couldn't pass up a nice stroll in the woods. Beautiful night for it, too. I smell a storm coming."

She muttered under her breath as she paced. Not her usual curses at him this time; these sounded more directed at herself.

"No wonder I had you pegged as an innocent," he went on. "I've met nuns who were more promiscuous. Knew it would be the oral stuff that did you in. I would've bet my life on it."

"You don't have a life; you're dead," she muttered.

Keep telling yourself that, luv. Even you don't believe it anymore.

84

"On the contrary, if you judge by senses and reflexes, I'm more alive than any human. Just have a few more upgrades."

"Upgrades?" She swung to face him. "You're not a computer, Bones. You're a killer."

Once again, she seemed more desperate to convince herself of that than anything else. He'd pity that inner struggle if she wasn't wrong about vampires in general, him in particular, and most importantly, about herself.

So, he only leaned back, tilting the chair until it balanced on two legs. All the while, her gaze kept flicking over him as if she couldn't help herself. He didn't want her to. That's why his shirts had gotten much more form fitting. This new gray one was tight enough to accentuate all the muscles he'd honed from working under a pitiless overseer when he was human. Back then, his lean, hard body had been a sign of his poverty. Now, ironically, it was fashionable.

"You're a killer, too, or did you forget?" he finally said in an easygoing tone. "You know, those who live in glass houses shouldn't throw stones, and all that rot. Really, Kitten, why so shy on our former topic? Don't tell me the sod who shagged you neglected foreplay."

"Foreplay?"

A new darkness in her voice made him stiffen. He tried to read her eyes but they were now shuttered, and her scent soured while her pacing became jerky with rage and remembered pain. This wasn't a normal reaction to a previous one-night stand. No, something else had happened. Something far worse.

Ice cold rage replaced his desire. Whoever the sod was that had done this to her, his days were now numbered.

"Not unless you count him taking his clothes off as *foreplay*," she went on in a brittle tone. "Can we not talk about that? It hardly puts me in the proper mood."

"Don't fret over him, pet," he told her, making sure his voice held none of the violence surging through him. "If I meet him, I'll snap him in half for you."

And I will meet him. I promise you that.

"We won't speak of him any longer," he continued. "Ready to go back to the table now?"

With that, he waggled his brows in an exaggerated way. To his relief, annoyance replaced the pain in her expression. Good. He never wanted to see that look on her face again.

"Or do you need a few more minutes to cool off?" he said in his most insinuating tone to further take her mind off the past.

She stopped pacing. "I'm ready. I just wasn't prepared before, but I am now."

She sat back down, and he stretched out his hands. This time, she took them without hesitation.

"Go on," she said in the same tone he'd heard soldiers use while preparing for battle. "Give it your best shot."

A slow smile stretched his lips. "*Love* to give it my best shot. Let me tell you just how I'd do it…"

Before the hour was through, she owed him forty miles.

13

---

ive days later, Bones met Cat by the entrance of the cave instead of in his usual spot in the makeshift living room. She gave him a surprised glance that took in his all-black attire. Unbeknownst to her, he also had a black ski mask tucked into his pocket. He wouldn't risk his dyed blond hair giving him away against the night sky if he needed to fly them away later because tonight, *they* hunted.

"Now, you're clear on all the details, right?" he said. "You won't see me, but I'll be watching you. When you leave with the target, I'll follow. Anywhere outside is fine, but do not, I repeat, do *not* let him take you inside any buildings or houses. If he tries to force you inside one, what do you do?"

Cat made an exasperated sound as she stepped around him. She was now so used to the cave's uneven terrain, she hopped over deep crevices or protruding rock formations that no human would even be able to see.

"For God's sake, Bones, we've been over this a thousand times."

"What do you do?" he insisted.

She held up her wrist. "Hit the secret pager in the watch, Mr. Bond. You'll come running. Dinner for two."

He grinned and squeezed her shoulder. "You have me pegged all wrong, Kitten. If I ever go for your neck, I have no intention of sharing."

That earned him a glare, but beneath it was a growing look of trust that tugged on his heart like a thousand tiny strings. When he'd given her the watch, she'd joked that it looked as old as the one her grandpa wore. That was the point. Her target would be wary if he saw her pressing any buttons on a Smart watch, but no one would give this aged-looking piece a second glance. It also had a special, hidden button programmed to send a signal directly to his mobile. If she found herself in danger, she need only hit the button, and he'd be there.

"Are you finally going to tell me who I'm after tonight?" she asked, ducking under the low slab of rock that hid the path to his section of the cave. "Or do I find out later if I've staked the wrong guy? You've been pretty secretive about the identity of tonight's target. Afraid I'd rat you out?"

She asked the last part with a teasing note to her voice, but from the quick look she gave him, she was serious.

"It was better for you not to know beforehand. That way, no accidental slips. Word can't get out if word isn't spoken."

After all, this was more than a simple job. It was another domino that would hopefully help Bones topple a secret undead empire.

Cat didn't answer. She just hopped over the gap in the naturally-formed stalagmite bridge, and then went up the slope that led to his current living quarters. He followed, frowning as her scent sharpened with displeasure.

He'd offended her. He hadn't meant to, but had she forgotten that only a few weeks ago, she would have cheerfully sold him out to his enemies, let alone murdered him herself?

She reached the living room area and dropped her purse onto

the sofa. Then she went inside the dressing room he'd set up for her and shut the screen. Most of her new clothes were there since Cat said her mother would throw them out if she saw the revealing garments. Once Cat was behind the screen, she spoke.

"It amuses me to think of you worrying about my Freudian slips. Maybe you didn't hear me before, but I don't have any friends. The only person I talk to aside from my grandparents is my mom, and she's being kept far out of this loop."

Bones closed his eyes. She was more than offended. She was hurt, and with her usual defense mechanism, she was covering that with sarcasm and quips.

He had to fix this.

"All right, luv. His real name is Sergio, though he might give you another one. He's about six-one, black hair, gray eyes. Italian is his first language, so his English has an accent. He may look soft to you, but don't let it fool you. Sergio's almost three hundred years old and more powerful than you can imagine. Also, he's a sadist." Bones's tone darkened. "And he likes his victims very young. Tell him you're underage, and you snuck in with a fake ID. It'll only switch him on more. You also can't kill him straightaway, because I need some information from him first. Oh, and he's worth fifty thousand dollars."

From the sudden silence, Cat had stopped changing into her evening attire. After a few moments, she opened the dressing room screen while clad in only her knickers and bra.

"Money," she said bluntly. "*That's* why you hunt vampires. You're a hit man!"

Bones took in every inch of her creamy, flawless skin, ignoring the scowl that his lengthy look earned him. If she was showing, he was admiring.

"Yeah, it's what I do, but you could also say I'm a bounty hunter. Sometimes my clients want 'em brought back alive."

"Wow," she said in a musing way. "I just thought we were going after people who had pissed you off."

A snort escaped him. "And that was enough for you to kill for? Blimey, but you're not particular. What if I were chasing some nice sweet thing that'd never hurt a fly? Still be all right with it then?"

She shut the screen with more force than necessary. "None of you are nice sweet things. You're all murderers. That's why it didn't matter. Point me at a vampire, and I'll try to kill it, because at one time they've done something to deserve it."

If she'd stabbed him, it would've been less painful. Worse, he had no defense since he'd never let anyone into his heart this way. Losing everyone he cared about when he was a lad had hardened him at a young age. Being imprisoned with no hope of release had hardened him even more. By the time Ian had turned Bones into a vampire, his heart was practically stone. Now, it felt vulnerable... and wounded.

Had he been lying to himself? Did she still see him as only a monster? Did she...did she still want to kill him?

She opened the screen enough to show her face. Whatever she saw in his expression made her close the screen almost at once.

Bones clenched his fists, trying to regain control while reminding himself that she had no favorable comparisons to draw upon. In her mind, he was the only vampire she'd met who *hadn't* tried to murder her.

"Not every vampire is like the ones who killed those girls Winston told you about," he finally said. "It's just your bad luck to be living in Ohio at this particular time. There are things going on you that don't know about."

"Winston was wrong, by the way," Cat said from behind the screen. "I looked up those girls' names the next day, and none of them were dead. They weren't even missing. One of them, Suzy Klinger, lived in the town next to mine, but her parents said she moved away to study acting. What I don't know is why Winston would make that up, but far be it for me to understand the mental workings of a ghost—"

"Bloody hell!" Bones shouted, his control evaporating. "Who did you talk to, aside from Suzy Klinger's parents? The police?"

How much danger had she put herself in?

"No one." She sounded part defiant, part unsettled. "I entered their names online at the library's computer. When nothing came up, I looked in a few local papers and then called Suzy's parent saying I was a telemarketer. That was it."

Some of his fear-fueled rage leaked away. She'd been cautious about her recklessness, if that combination were possible. He'd have Ted erase the library's security footage at once. Then, there would be no way for Hennessey or his soldiers to trace Cat's searches back to her, if they had alerts programmed on the missing girls' names.

"Don't go against what I tell you to do again," Bones said when he could speak without shouting.

She poked her head out, anger sharpening her features. "What did you expect? For me to forget about over a dozen girls being murdered because you *told* me to? See, this is what I'm talking about!" she said, as if responding to an argument she'd had with herself. "A human wouldn't act like that. Only a vampire could be that cold."

Like hell. Bones had seen more than a few of his boyhood mates swing from the gallows for the "crime" of stealing food when they were starving. Humans had also worked Bones nearly to death back at the penal colony, and he'd never forget the horrors he'd seen human slavers commit. All the above made his tone scalding.

"Vampires have existed for millennium, and though we have our villains among us, the majority of us have a sip here and there, but everybody walks away. Besides, it's not like humans haven't made their mark for ill on the world. Hitler wasn't a vampire, was he? Humans can be just as nasty as we are, and don't you forget it."

"Oh, come on, Bones!" Cat snapped the screen back, revealing that she was now clad in the slinky green and silver dress. Then she began rolling hot curlers into her hair. "Don't give me that crap. Are you telling me you've never murdered someone innocent? Never forced a woman who said no? Hell, the only reason you didn't kill me the night we met was because you saw my eyes glow, so sell that smack to someone who's buying!"

He caught a curler she'd let slip during her tirade. She saw his hand move, and flinched as if bracing for a blow. Another invisible blade ripped through him, but this time, anger salved the wound.

"Think I'd strike you?" he asked in a scathing tone. "You really don't know nearly as much as you claim. Aside from teaching you how to fight, I'd never lay a harsh hand on you. As for the night we met, you did your level best to kill me. I thought you were sent by someone, so yes, I smacked you and threatened you, but I wasn't going to kill you. No, I would have sipped from your neck and green-eyed you until you told me who your boss was. Then, I would have sent you back to the shit with both your legs broken as a warning, but I promise you this—at no point would I have forced myself on you. Sorry, Kitten. Every woman I've been with has wanted me to be there."

Blimey, in his youth, they'd *paid* him to be there!

"Have I killed any innocents in my time? Yeah, I have. When you've lived as long as I have, you make mistakes. You try to learn from them. You shouldn't be so quick to judge me on that front, either. No doubt you've killed innocents as well."

Shame, confusion, and doubt had flickered across Cat's features, but at that, they hardened. "The only people I've killed were vampires who tried to kill me first."

"Oh? Don't be so sure. Those blokes you killed, did you wait for them to try to bite you? Or did you just assume because they were vampires and they'd gotten you alone, they intended to murder you? Ignoring the very real likelihood that they were there because they thought a beautiful girl was hot to shag them."

His voice lowered. "Tell me, how many of them did you kill before they'd even shown you their fangs?"

Her mouth opened, but she didn't speak. Confusion raged across her features, followed by stubbornness, denial, and finally, that bone-deep desperation that had driven her to hunt vampires to begin with.

"Whether they showed their fangs or not doesn't change the fact that vampires are evil, and that's enough for me."

Bones knew that was her mother speaking, not her. Still, his temper snapped.

"If all vampires are the filth you claim them to be, why wouldn't I just pry your legs open now and take out some of my 'evil' on you?"

She glanced at her silver stakes and tensed, ready to lunge for them if Bones moved. Disbelief scalded him. He'd said that to point out the absurdity of her argument, and she'd *believed* it? And thought she had to protect herself against it?

He covered the fresh burst of pain with a snort. "You never have to fret about it. Told you, I don't come in unless invited. Now, hurry up. You have another evil fiend to kill."

Then, before he said something else that inadvertently terrorized her, Bones left.

14

*I*t took over an hour for his anger to abate enough to think clearly again. By that time, Bones was waiting for her at the club while wondering if she was still coming. He'd left her a note telling her to proceed with the plan, but since then, he realized he hadn't given her much reason to.

What the hell was wrong with him, using a rape taunt against a woman born of rape? It didn't matter that Bones would never do such a thing, or that Cat had been dead wrong about her part in their argument. He could've used any number of *other* ways to point out her bigoted hypocrisy. His taunt might have seemed like a ridiculously far-fetched example to him, but for far too many women, it was a brutal reality.

No wonder Cat had eyed her stakes. Right now, Bones wouldn't blame her if she'd have used them on him, too.

He hated that he'd hurt her. Again. That was the last thing he wanted. Why did he keep losing control and doing it?

The grinding sound from an old Ford's engine snapped his head around. Relief washed over him when he saw Cat park at the far end of the club's lot. She'd come. She might be angry at him, but she hadn't abandoned their partnership. Yes, she still had a long way to go when it came to overcoming her biases, but she didn't truly believe the rot she'd hurled at him. If she had, she'd never trust a vampire as her backup, and she obviously did trust him because here she was.

Cat got out of the truck, gave a final dismayed tug at her short hemline, and then strode toward the club as if she'd worn dresses like that her entire life. Heads turned, and the bouncer took one look at her before waving her to the front of the line. Cat looked startled, but then smiled with a seductiveness that had the bouncer almost tripping in his haste to let her inside.

Bones would have pitied the lad, if she didn't hold the same power over him. One day, she'd realize that, too, and God help him then.

Bones stayed on his motorcycle in the farthest, darkest corner of the parking lot. A full visor helmet hid his face from anyone who happened to notice him. Few did since most parked close to the club's entrance. Failing that, they chose the spots under the lights since this was hardly the nicest part of Cleveland. Bones let the deep shadows envelop him while he stared at the club's approaching patrons.

So far, no sign of Sergio, but according to Bones's sources, this club was the vampire's favorite weekend haunt. Bones also kept a constant eye on his mobile. The video feed from the cameras he'd hidden two days ago showed the club's emergency exits as well as the service entrances. So far, the emergency exits remained closed, and only human employees went in and out the back.

What was Cat doing? Was she still angry at him about their argument? Or was she not thinking about him at all?

His mouth twisted. No doubt she was fending off numerous admirers while downing several gin and tonics. Bones could do with a whisky himself now, but that would require doffing his helmet and revealing his face. No, nothing to do except wait.

An hour later, energy rolled over Bones like wisps from an incoming fog. Almost at once, a new Mercedes S class drove into the VIP section of the parking lot. Then a tall, dark-haired vampire got out and waved the approaching valet off.

It had been years since Bones last saw Sergio, but the vampire still wore expensive suits that flattered his softer build with hidden pads and clever tapering. He'd been a pampered aristocrat back in the early seventeen hundreds, so Sergio had none of the muscles and leanness that marked Bones's poor upbringing. Still, Sergio could destroy his Mercedes with his bare hands if he wanted to, and with his temper, it wouldn't take much to incite him. Bones had seen Sergio smash a human's skull in simply because the poor bloke had brought Sergio the wrong drink.

The thought of Sergio using those same hands to touch Cat made rage erupt through Bones. Sergio paused, turning. Bones was on the ground before the other vampire finished swinging around, cursing as he held in his telltale aura.

Fool! Alerting his target to his presence with a metaphysical rage bomb? The rankest of amateurs knew better!

After a moment, Sergio dismissed whatever he'd felt and went inside. Good. Sergio was a fool, too.

Bones stayed on the ground, locking his emotions behind the same wall that had protected them for centuries. At least, they had until he met Cat. When Bones was back in control, he rose.

Cat had chosen to be a vampire hunter long before she'd met him. She was the only one who could *un*-choose it, too. Until then, Bones would make sure she only killed vampires who deserved it, and he'd have her back so that none of them killed her. Sergio more than fulfilled the first qualification. Now, Bones needed to fulfill the second.

A mere twenty minutes later, Sergio came out of the club with Cat on his arm. She clung to him as if she needed his help to stay upright, staggering as Sergio led her to his car.

"Sorry. Think I had too many gin and tonics," Bones heard Cat say with a breathy laugh.

"Don't worry, pussy cat," Sergio replied. "I'll lick you and make you feel better."

And I'll rip off your head and spike it at her feet, Bones thought, but kept his rage tamped down. Not that Sergio would probably notice this time. The other vampire seemed oblivious to everyone except the beauteous redhead he half-helped, half-lifted into his passenger seat.

Cat giggled. "Ooh, kitty loves getting licked."

Well done, Bones thought, admiration threading through his rage. Anyone listening to Cat would never know that only a week ago, she'd have turned bright red at such banter.

"And I love cream," Sergio said, licking his lips.

Arsehole.

Sergio drove off so fast that two patrons had to jump out of his way to avoid getting hit. Bones killed his motorcycle's headlight and followed, keeping far enough back that Sergio shouldn't hear him. Good thing the stretch of highway Sergio chose didn't have much traffic since it led out of the city, not toward it. Bones throttled back, allowing more space between their vehicles, until he only saw the faint red glow from Sergio's tail lights.

Those lights stayed in a relatively straight line for a few minutes. Then, they swerved so hard to the right, they disappeared. In the next moment, a faint scream reached Bones, and the voice was too high to be Sergio's.

Bones abandoned his bike and flew. Seconds later, he saw the Mercedes in a ditch from overshooting the road's shoulder. Before Bones reached it, the back door exploded outward and Sergio rocketed through it with Cat leaping out after him. She absorbed the first blow Sergio aimed at her, and then rolled to avoid the second. Both of them were so focused on each other that they didn't notice Bones swooping up behind them.

Sergio lunged at Cat—and Bones snatched him back. Stakes protruded from Sergio's back and neck. Bones grabbed them both, and Sergio froze when he felt Bones's hands on them.

"Hallo, Sergio," Bones said with vicious satisfaction.

"About time," Cat said crossly, but relief suffused her features.

Bones felt the same emotion when he saw that she was okay. She was bleeding from her arm, plus she had a nasty bruise on her shoulder, but aside from that, she was unharmed. Sergio was in far worse shape. One more inch on the blade in his back, and Sergio would be too dead for Bones to get information out of. Not that Sergio could speak well with the other stake jammed into his throat, but he tried.

"Filthy bastard, how'd you find me?" Sergio garbled.

"I see you've met my friend," Bones said, twisting the stake in Sergio's neck. "Isn't she wonderful?"

Cat was in the process of ripping her sleeve to wrap it around her wound, but she stopped when, with almost comical shock, Sergio said, "*You* set me up?"

"That's right, *pussycat*," Cat replied coldly. "Guess you won't be giving me that tongue bath after all."

"She is something, isn't she?" Bones taunted him. "Knew you couldn't pass up a pretty girl, you worthless sod. Isn't it fitting that now you're the one who's been lured into a trap? What, did you grow short on funds so you had to go out for dinner instead of ordering in?"

The way Sergio stiffened may as well have been a confession. A stronger stench of fear wafted from him, too—another indicator that he realized Bones knew what Sergio was involved in. Still, he tried to lie.

"I don't know what you say."

"Of course you do. You're his best client, from what I hear. Now, I have one question for you, and I know you're going to answer me honestly, because if not"—Bones twisted the silver stake in Sergio's back, bringing it right against his heart—"I'm going to be really unhappy. Do you know what happens when I'm unhappy? My hand twitches."

"What?" Sergio sobbed. "I tell you; I tell you!"

Oh, you will. "Where's Hennessey?"

Cat's brows went up in question. Bones ignored that. He didn't want her to know who Hennessey was. He only wanted Sergio to tell him *where* he was.

"Hennessey will kill me," Sergio said in a bleak tone. "You don't cross him and live to brag about it! You don't know what he'll do if I talk. And you'll kill me anyway if I tell you."

Needed more persuading, did he? Bones twisted the stake in Sergio's neck while strumming the one in his back as if it were the pick to a guitar.

"See, mate, I promise I won't kill you if you tell me," Bones said over Sergio's screams. "That gives you a chance to run from Hennessey. But I swear to you, if you don't tell me where he is, you'll die right here. Your call. Make it now."

Cat's mouth dropped hearing Bones say that he wouldn't kill Sergio. Bones gave her a look that said, *for once, don't argue.*

Then he stopped twisting the blades. Sergio quit screaming, but his head slumped forward as if he were already dead.

"Chicago Heights, south side of town," Sergio mumbled.

Close enough to run the operation in Ohio, far enough away to claim ignorance if any Law Guardians came sniffing around.

"Thanks ever so, mate. Now, is this your stake, luv?"

Bones ripped the silver blade out of Sergio's back and tossed it at Cat. She caught it one-handed, understanding dawning on her features. Much as Bones would've enjoyed killing Sergio himself, he deserved to die at the hand of someone he'd tried to victimize the same way he'd victimized so many others.

"You promised! You promised!" Sergio screeched, understanding now, too.

"I did," Bones said curtly. "She didn't. Got something you want to say to him, Kitten?"

"No," she said, and shoved the blade so hard into Sergio's chest, her hand briefly disappeared. "I'm done talking to him."

15

$\mathcal{B}$ ones wrapped Sergio's body in the sheets of plastic he'd tucked inside his jacket for this very purpose. Cat shook Sergio's blood from her hand and then resumed bandaging her wound with strips from her sleeve. It would have been quicker for her to use Sergio's blood for healing, but Cat seemed more eager to get it off her than to get more of it on her.

Bones deposited Sergio's body in the boot of the car. Cat looked up in surprise when Bones then knelt next to her and reached for her arm.

"Let me see it."

"It's fine," she said in a short tone.

It was, but that didn't mean he'd be content to let her bleed. Bones brushed her fingers aside and peeled off the strips of fabric she'd wrapped around the wound.

"Nasty bite, tore the flesh around the vein. You'll need blood for that." *And better his than Sergio's.*

"I said it's fine," she repeated.

She could be stubborn all she wanted, as soon as she quit bleeding. Bones cut his palm with his knife, and then clapped his blood over the rends in her flesh.

"Don't be irrational. How much did he take?"

She glanced at her arm as if remembering. "About four good pulls, I guess. Stabbed him in the neck as fast as I could to get his mind off it. Where were you, anyway? I didn't see a car behind us."

The faintest tinge of hurt colored her tone, as if she thought he hadn't gotten there faster because he didn't care. Bones wanted to pull her against him and tell her nothing could be further from the truth, but she wasn't ready for that.

"That was the idea," he replied in as light a tone as he could manage. "I drove my bike but kept back far enough so Sergio wouldn't know he was being followed. Bike's about a mile from here down the road."

And possibly still driving itself, if it hadn't topped over yet.

"I ran that last part through the woods so there'd be less noise," he said to explain his sudden appearance without the motorcycle. One day, he'd tell her he could fly, but not today.

Her bleeding had stopped, so he could let go, except he didn't want to. She shifted as if sensing that, and then looked at the car and let out a shaky laugh.

"Wow, that's ruined. The rear door is in scraps."

Bones didn't care about the car's damage. He cared about hers. "Why did Sergio go for your wrist, if you were both in the backseat? Because he couldn't get to your neck?"

She sighed. "He got frisky in the front seat and tried to feel me up, thanks to you and the no panties idea. I wasn't about to let that happen, so I climbed in the back and put my arms around him from behind so he wouldn't get suspicious. Stupid of me, I know," she added to ward off criticism he wasn't about to give. "But I didn't even think of my wrists. Every other vampire I'd met had always gone for my neck."

"Yeah, including me, right?" Bones said while resisting the urge to pull Sergio's body out of the trunk so he could kick it. "The car swerved off the road so fast, I thought you two were sprawling inside of it. What made Sergio pull off so erratically, then?"

"I told him to come and get me."

Her words were matter-of-fact, but pain threaded her tone, and she could no longer look him in the eye. For a moment, Cat sounded as young as she was, and as vulnerable as she should have been, if life were fairer.

"Is he okay back there in the trunk?" she suddenly asked, that moment of vulnerability passing.

A laugh escaped Bones. "You want to keep him company?"

She gave him a pointed look. "No, but is he really *gone*? I'd always cut off their heads to be sure."

"Critiquing my work?" he replied, amused. "Yeah, he's really gone. Right now we need to get out of here before some nosy driver pops alongside and asks if we need help."

Bones finally let go of her wrist and rose, turning his attention to the mangled Mercedes.

"We need to move this vehicle."

Cat got up, too, giving the car a doubtful look. "How am I supposed to drive this wreck? Any cop that sees this is going to pull me over first thing!"

"Don't fret. Have it all worked out."

Bones pulled out his mobile and rang his mate, Ted.

"It's me," Bones said when Ted answered. "Looks like I'm going to need that lift after all. You'll like the ride, it's a Benz. Needs a little body work, though."

"You, not being dainty?" Ted drawled, his Southern accent thickening with his amusement. "My lawd, imagine that."

"Wasn't even me this time, mate. We're on Planter's Road, just south of the club. Step on it, right?"

"Will do," Ted replied.

Bones hung up. Cat watched him, her brows raised in silent question.

"Sit tight, Kitten, our ride will be here in a minute. Don't fret, he's nearby. Told him I might have a use for him tonight. 'Course, he was probably figuring on it being a little later in the evening.

You left with Sergio right quick, didn't you? He must have been quite pleased with you."

Bones couldn't keep the edge from his voice at that last part. His jealousy also extended to the *dead* dead, it seemed. Thankfully, Cat didn't appear to notice.

"Yeah, color me flattered. Seriously, though, Bones, even if you tow this car, there's still too much blood in it, and you didn't listen to me about bringing cleaning materials. This thing could have at least been mopped up."

She did remember that he was a professional, didn't she?

Bones took her arm again. Cat turned her wrist up, showing him that the ragged tears from Sergio's fangs were now healed. Still, Bones didn't let her go.

That's not why I'm touching you, Kitten. And you know it.

She glanced away, but she didn't move away.

Bones didn't move, either. He simply held her arm, feeling her warmth, the vibrations from her blood rushing through her veins, and her faint shivers at each stroke of his fingers. When she exhaled, he breathed it in, wishing he could draw more than those slight wisps into him. He wanted her every passionate gasp while she was beneath him. He wanted her honey drenching his mouth, her nails digging into his back, and he *needed* her cries ringing in his ears when she came.

And if he didn't redirect his thoughts, the result of his need would soon be so abundantly clear, he'd be clubbing her in the leg with it.

Bones closed his eyes. The seconds it took him to regain control felt like an eternity. She drove him to the brink without even trying. Sometimes, his feelings for her frightened him.

Cat only shifted on her feet during the extended silence. Bones opened his eyes, this time glad that she was looking away from him. Otherwise, she might glimpse his true feelings in his gaze, and she couldn't know about them yet.

"Trust me, luv," he finally said. "I know you don't, but you should. You did a smashing job tonight, by the way," he added to change the subject from the unspoken tension between them. "That stake in Sergio's back was just a thought away from his heart. It slowed him, as did the one in his neck. You would've had him even if I wasn't there."

And that's why he'd trained her so hard. If she was ever set upon by a Master vampire when she was alone, she needed to be tough enough to survive it. Tonight proved that she was.

"You're strong, Kitten," he went on. "Be glad of it."

Her gaze finally met his.

"Glad? That's not the word I'd use. I'm relieved that I'm alive and there's one less murderer prowling around for naïve girls. But glad would be if I never had this lineage. Glad would be if I had two normal parents and a bunch of friends, and the only thing I'd ever killed was time. Or if even *once* I'd been to a club just to go dancing and have fun instead of ending up staking something that tried to kill me. That's glad. This is just...existing. Until the next time."

She pulled away. Cold air splashed Bones's hand, replacing her warmth. Cat walked off a few more steps, and then stopped and half-turned as if expecting him to come after her.

No. Not this time.

"Rot," he said curtly.

Her brows snapped together with her scowl. "Excuse me?"

"Rot, I said."

He could tolerate her bitterness since some of it was well justi-fied, but this new bout of defeatism? It wasn't her, and he wouldn't pretend that it was.

"You play the hand you're dealt just like everyone else in this world. You have gifts people would kill for, no matter that you scorn them. You have a mum who loves you"—horrible person though she was—"and a nice house to go home to. So, sod your backwoods neighbors who look down their ignorant noses at you for your lack of a father. This world is a big place, and you've got an important role to play in it."

Her face darkened with anger. He ignored it. She was smart enough to know better despite this unexpected pity party.

"Think everyone goes around whistling with joy about the life they lead? Think everyone is given the power to choose the way their fate goes? Sorry, luv, it doesn't work that way. You hold the ones you love close, and fight the battles you can win, and *that*, Kitten, is how it is."

"What would you know about it?" she snapped.

He gave her all the laughter her ignorant remark deserved. Then, he hauled her close so she could see every bit of his expression.

"You haven't the slightest *inkling* of what I've been through, so don't tell *me* what I know."

Her eyes widened, and her heart rate doubled. Was he gripping her too tight? He relaxed his hands, but her pulse didn't slow. Instead, it accelerated as she kept flicking her gaze between his face and the scant distance between them.

Bones moved closer, until only the barest space separated their bodies. Her warmth breached that space, as did her scent. Both teased him, flitting over him without weight, yet still hitting him with the greatest of impacts.

Cat drew in a short, sharp breath, but she didn't move.

He stared at her, silently urging her to give into the desire he saw blooming in her eyes. Then, lust nearly felled him when her gaze dropped to his mouth, and the tip of her tongue ran along her lips as if preparing them for his kiss.

Very slowly, Bones slid his tongue along his own bottom lip, fighting his urge to yank her to him. He wouldn't ruin this moment by moving too fast.

But this is your last chance to turn away, Kitten.

She stared at his mouth, her gray eyes lighting up with pinpricks of emerald, just as a vampire's would when desire rose.

His own gaze would be blazing green if not for his control, but seeing her eyes nearly snapped it. He bent his head, about to cover her mouth with his—

A horn blared, shattering the moment. Next, Bones heard the unmistakable sound of a tractor-trailer slowing to a stop.

He turned, cursing himself for allowing a bloody *eighteen-wheeler* to sneak up on him. Then he recognized the rig, and he cursed Ted for ruining a moment he'd waited six weeks for. Why couldn't his mate have shown up ten minutes later?

"Ted, you bugger, good of you to arrive so quickly!" Bones said in a biting tone.

Ted grinned as he climbed down from the cabin. Despite having the appetite of a proverbial truck driver, Ted was still so skinny, one could be forgiven for assuming that he had an aversion to food.

"I'm missin' my shows because of you, buddy," Ted greeted him, his grin widening as he looked over Bones's shoulder to Cat. "Hope I didn't interrupt nothin' between you and that gal. Two of you looked awful cozy."

"No," Cat said in a guilt-scalded tone. "Nothing going on here!"

Ted laughed and ambled toward the wrecked and bloody Mercedes. "Sure. I can see that."

Cat glanced at Bones to see if he was buying her desperate lie. His brow arched.

Not for a moment, Kitten.

She looked away, but she couldn't hide from the truth. Not anymore. Lucky for her, now wasn't the time to confront her with it.

Bones left her to give Ted a friendly cuff on the back.

"Ted, old chap, the car is yours. Just need to get a piece out of the boot, and then we're golden. Drive us to the place, and we'll be done by then."

"Sure thing, bud. You'll like the back. It's air-conditioned.

Some boxes to sit on, too. Or you could always ride in the car," he added with a sideways grin.

Where her blood still decorated the seats? Not likely.

"The boxes in the trailer will be fine."

Ted nodded. "Then let's put this baby to bed."

Bones and Ted opened the back of the trailer. Cat wandered over and looked impressed when she saw the vehicle stabilizing clamps and reinforced steel ramp that Ted lowered. Bones hid a smile.

Told you that you didn't need to fret.

Bones drove the Mercedes onto the ramp and parked it in the back of Ted's trailer. Then he and Ted secured it with the clamps. When that was done, Bones turned to Cat.

"Be right back. Have to fetch my bike."

As expected, he found the bike toppled over about a mile down the road. Thankfully, it wasn't damaged, so he drove it back to the trailer, and then loaded it next to the car. When he was finished, he beckoned Cat up into the trailer with him.

"Come on, Kitten. Your taxi's waiting."

Her brows furrowed. "We're riding in the back?"

"Yeah. Ol' Ted doesn't want to risk being seen with me, so he keeps our friendship a secret. Smart bloke."

All true, and all unrelated to why he preferred being alone with her in the back to the two of them being in the front cab with Ted. From the look Cat gave him, she knew it, too.

"Smart, huh?" she mumbled under her breath as she climbed into the back of the trailer. "I envy that."

16

*A*t first, Cat refused to sit. Then, after lurching from side to side with the trailer's jostling movements, she chose a box on the opposite side of the cabin from where Bones sat.

That soon gave her a new concern. After her third attempt to tug her skirt down to cover more of her thighs, Bones took pity on her, and gave her his jacket.

Cat settled it over her lap with obvious relief. "Thanks."

He didn't roll his eyes, but it took a great deal of effort. Yes, he was mad with desire for her, but he wasn't about to steal peeps up her skirt like a deviant schoolboy.

Cat seemed to relax a bit after that. Bones let the silence stretch because he knew it wouldn't last. Not with the way she kept glancing at him and drawing in a breath as if to speak before discarding whatever she'd been about to say.

Of course, being her, what she finally settled on contained a thinly-veiled vampire barb.

"I know this isn't a concern for you, but is there enough oxygen in this thing?"

"Plenty of air. Just as long as there isn't any heavy breathing," he replied with a challenging arch of his brow.

She might be pretending that nothing happened between them, but he wasn't about to.

"Well, then I am safe. *Absolutely* safe," she stressed.

A smile curled his mouth. *The lady doth protest too much.*

Cat glanced at his mouth before quickly lifting her gaze back to his eyes. Then, surprisingly, she didn't look away.

Bones didn't speak. He simply stared at her, letting the silence fill with everything she wasn't able to say yet.

"Shit," she finally breathed out, as if coming to a long-denied realization.

"Something wrong?"

His tone was light, but he'd never been more serious. From the look in her eyes, she knew it, too. Her heart rate sped up, and she began to fidget while glancing around as if hoping an exit would magically appear.

"So, who's this Hennessey you were asking about?" she said in an obvious attempt to change the subject.

Ice pierced his desire at the name. "Someone dangerous."

She caught the shift in his mood, and pressed her advantage. "Yeah, I gathered that. Sergio seemed pretty scared of Hennessey, so I didn't think he was a Boy Scout. I take it he's our next target?"

Let her anywhere near that monster? Never.

"Hennessey is someone I've been tracking, yes, but I'll be going after him alone."

Cat stiffened. "Why? Don't you think I can handle it? Or do you still not trust me to keep this stuff secret? I thought we covered this already!"

Grand, now he'd offended her. "I don't think that. But I do think there are certain things you'd do well to stay out of."

From her expression, she clearly disagreed. Then, her frown smoothed, and she blinked at him in a guileless way.

"You said something about Sergio being Hennessey's best client. What did you mean by that? And what did Hennessey do to whoever hired you? Do you know, or did you just take the contract on him without asking?"

Bones stifled a laugh. She was baiting him so he'd tell her what she wanted to know in order to defend himself? Clever, but it wouldn't work.

"Questions like that are why I won't tell you more about Hennessey. Suffice it to say there's a reason why Ohio's been such a hazardous place for young girls lately. It's also why I don't want you chasing after vampires without me. Hennessey's more than just a sod who bleeds someone when he can get away with it. Beyond that, don't ask."

Cat's scowl didn't make her any less beautiful, but it did make her displeasure very clear.

"Can you at least tell me how long you've been after him? *That* can't be top secret, can it?"

Bones sighed at the acid in her voice. She still thought this was about trust. It wasn't, but if he told her why he was after Hennessey, she'd insist on being involved, and he couldn't put her in that danger. Still, he had to give her something.

"'Round eleven years."

Her jaw dropped. "Hennessey must have a *real* fancy price on his head! Come on, what did he do? Aside from pissing off someone very rich, obviously."

More baiting so she could keep dragging information out of him? Or did she really believe his motives were that shallow?

It didn't matter.

"Not everything is about money," Bones said in tone that made it clear she'd get nothing else from him.

She gave a frustrated sigh. Then, after a few minutes of irritated silence, she cocked her head at him.

"How did you become a vampire?"

Bones was both surprised and amused. "Want an interview with the vampire, luv? If memory serves, that didn't turn out too well for the reporter in the movie with that name."

Cat shrugged. "I wouldn't know. I never saw it. My mother thought it was too violent."

As soon as she said it, she laughed at the irony.

Bones smiled, too, but his smile covered his anger. What a hypocrite her mum was, more concerned with protecting her daughter from fictional violence than from the real danger of hunting vampires all by herself.

"Good thing you didn't watch the movie, then," Bones said with an exaggerated glance at the blood-spattered Mercedes. "Heaven knows how you might have turned out."

Cat chuckled, too, but when her laughter stopped, she looked at him with hopeful expectation. She really did want to know his story, then.

"All right, I'll tell you, but then you have to answer one of my questions. Got an hour to burn, anyhow."

"Quid pro quo, Dr. Lecter?" she scoffed. "Fine, but I hardly see the point. You already know everything about me."

Just for an instant, he let her see beyond his control. "Not everything," he replied with all the lust burning in him.

Her eyes widened, and her color rose—an indication of the heat flashing through her that Bones could practically feel since she was so near. He also saw it in the sudden tightening of her nipples, and he smelled it in the new lushness to her scent. Cat tried to cover her body's response by moving his jacket over her breasts, and she also concealed the new hitch in her breathing behind a cough that fooled no one.

"W-when did it happen?" she asked in a desperate attempt to diffuse the tension between them. "When were you changed over?"

Now wasn't the time to confront her with her desire, either. Not while a dead vampire rotted away only a few meters behind them, and they'd soon be interrupted by Ted again. That's why Bones shuttered his gaze and leaned back.

Her sigh of relief both annoyed and elated him. *Yes, you get another reprieve, but soon, I won't let you hide from your feelings for me, Kitten. And I won't stop with a look.*

"Let's see, it was 1790 and I was in Australia," Bones summarized. "I did this bloke a favor, and he thought he was returning it by making me a vampire."

"You're Australian?" Cat said in disbelief. "I thought you were English!"

His smile was grim. "I was born in England. That's where I spent my youth, too, but it was in Australia that I was changed into a vampire. That makes me part of it as well."

Cat leaned forward, her concern over his nearness now forgotten. "You have to go into more detail than that."

He made himself more comfortable on his box perch. "I was twenty-four, and it happened just a month after my birthday."

She goggled at him. "My God, we're almost the same age!"

"Sure," Bones said with amused snort. "Give or take over two hundred years."

"Er, you know I what I mean," she stammered. "It's just that you look much older than twenty-four."

He laughed. "Thanks ever so."

Now her color was high for a different reason. "I, ah…"

"Times were different then," he said in a gentle tone. "People aged far more rapidly. You modern folks don't know how good you have it."

"Tell me more. Please," she added almost shyly.

Bones leaned forward. Few people knew his real roots, but if she wanted to know, he'd tell her.

"It's not pretty or romantic like in the movies. You remember how you slugged those lads because they called your mum a whore? Well, my mum *was* a whore. Her name was Penelope, and she was fifteen when she bore me. I was lucky that she and the madam of the brothel were friendly, or I never would have been allowed to live there. Only girl-children were kept at the bordello, for obvious reasons."

Cat paled, but her gaze was steady. She didn't like what she was hearing, but she could handle it.

"When I was little, I didn't know there was anything unusual about where I lived. All the women doted on me, and I would do house chores and such until I got older. The madam, Lucille, later inquired as to whether I wanted to follow in the family business. Some of the male customers who were so inclined had taken notice of me, for I was a pretty lad. But, by the time Madam Lucille approached me with the offer, I knew enough to know I wouldn't want to engage in such activities. Begging was a common occupation in London back then. Thieving was as well, so, to earn my keep, I begged and I stole. Then, when I was seventeen, my mum died of syphilis. She was only thirty-two."

Cat paled more, and her hand fluttered as if she wanted to reach out for him, but she was stopping herself.

"Go on," she said in a hoarse tone.

"Lucille informed me two weeks afterward that I had to go since I wasn't bringing in enough money to justify the space. It wasn't that she was cruel," he clarified, seeing her face darken. "She was simply being practical. Another girl could take my room and bring in three times the money. Again, Madame offered me a choice—leave and face the streets, or stay and service the customers. But she added a kindness. Madame Lucille had described me to a few highborn women she was acquainted with, and they were interested. So, I could choose to sell myself to women rather than men. And that is what I did."

"You were only seventeen," Cat whispered, horrified.

Yes, and that was a good deal older than some of the other girls who'd worked at the bordello. The law hadn't caught up to morality back then, and poverty had no exceptions for youth. But Bones told her none of that. She was pale enough already.

"The women at the house trained me first," he said simply. "When it turned out that I had a knack for the work, Lucille kept me in high demand. Soon, I had quite a few regulars among the blue bloods. One of them ended up saving my life. I was still picking pockets, you see. One unlucky day, I pulled the purse off a toff right in front of a bobby. Next thing I knew, I was scheduled to appear before one of the meanest hanging judges in London. My death was all but certain, yet one of my clients heard of my predicament and took pity on me. She persuaded the judge through carnal means that sending me to the new penal colonies would be just the thing. Weeks later, they shipped me and sixty-two other unlucky buggers to New South Wales."

Bones stopped. Even after all this time, some memories still had the power to wound.

Chains bloodying his skin. The endless groans. That stench. The pleas of the dying, and worse, the guards' laughter...

Bones ran a hand through his hair. "I won't tell you about the voyage except to say it went beyond any misery people should have to endure. Once at the prison colony, they worked some of us literally to death. There were three men I became mates with— Timothy, Charles, and Ian. After a few months, Ian managed to escape. Then, almost a year later, Ian came back."

"Why would he come back?" Cat's voice was soft. "Wouldn't he have been punished for running away?"

"Indeed he would, but Ian wasn't afraid of that anymore. We were in the fields slaughtering cattle when we were set upon by indigenous people fighting against forced colonization by the British. They killed the guards and the rest of the prisoners except Timothy, Charles, and me. That's when Ian appeared, but he was different. You can guess how. Ian was a vampire, and he changed me that night. Charles and Timothy were changed as well, but only Timothy asked for it. Charles and I were changed anyway because Ian thought we would thank him later for it."

Ian was still waiting for that thank-you, and he could keep waiting until the sun burned out.

"We stayed with the Aboriginal people for a few years, and

vowed to return to England one day. Took us nearly twenty years to finally get there."

For a moment, Bones closed his eyes. It had taken him nearly that entire time to accept what he was, too. Then, and only then, had he been able to move on with his life.

She needed to move on, too, and one of those steps was by talking about the pain she'd buried inside.

"Your turn," Bones said, opening his eyes. "Tell me about the sod who hurt you."

Cat flinched as if he'd struck her. "God, Bones, I don't want to talk about that. It's humiliating."

It shouldn't be. He already knew enough to know it was someone else's sin, not hers. Time for her to realize that.

"I just told you that I used to be a thief, a beggar, and a whore," he pointed out in a gentle tone. "Is it really fair for you to cry foul over my question?"

She straightened from her hunch enough to shrug.

"It's a common story. Boy meets girl, girl is naïve and stupid, boy uses girl and then hits the road."

Bones arched his brow, waiting.

Her hands sliced the air. "Fine! You want details? I thought he really cared for me. He told me he did, and I fell for his lies completely. We went out twice, and then the third time, he said he had to stop by his apartment to get something before we'd go to this club."

Of course, he did, the manipulative sod.

"When we got there, he started kissing me, telling me all this crap about how special I was to him"—her voice cracked, and if she clenched her fists any tighter, she'd be in danger of breaking her hands—"but I told him it was too soon. That we should wait to get to know each other better, that it was my first time. He disagreed."

Bones didn't speak. She didn't need any hints of the vengeance burning through his veins like acid. She needed him to stay silent and listen because she'd *needed* to say this, even if she hadn't realized it before now.

"I-I should have hit him. Or thrown him off me. I could have, I was stronger than he was. But...I wanted to make him happy."

Cat's voice broke, her shoulders dropped, and she could no longer look at Bones. Instead, she looked at the floor.

"I really liked him," she said in a pained whisper. "So, when he didn't stop, I didn't fight him off. I didn't even move. It didn't hurt as much if I didn't move..."

Her voice cracked and she stopped, blinking hard while breathing through the memory. It took all of Bones's control not to hug her while promising her bloody vengeance.

Then, after a moment, Cat collected herself.

"That's about it," she said in a falsely brisk tone. "One miserable time, and then he didn't call me anymore. I was worried at first. I thought something bad had happened to him."

Oh, something would. Something painful, brutal, and very, very terminal.

She let out a harsh laugh. "The next weekend, I found him making out with another girl at the same club we were supposed to go to. He told me then that he'd never really liked me, and to run along because it was past my bedtime. That same night, I killed my first vampire."

Her voice turned sharp, as if made from the ragged edges of her pain.

"In a way, I owe my first vampire hunt to being used. I was so upset that I wanted to either die or murder someone. At least having some creature try to rip my throat out guaranteed me one or the other."

She met his eyes then. Hers glittered with unshed tears, and her features were a mixture of defiance, anger, and hurt.

"Did you tell anyone?" Bones asked, though he already knew the answer.

"No. My mom wouldn't have understood, and"—a jerky shrug

—"there was no one else to tell."

Once again, she'd weathered the pain, rejection and shame alone, and once again, she hadn't deserved any of it. He'd tell her that, but not with words. She'd only argue with those. Instead, he filled his gaze with all the empathy she *should* have been shown.

Cat blinked, surprised. Then, very slowly, some of the tightness eased from her shoulders. When she was no longer hunched into a defensive ball, he reached out until his hands brushed the air that was warmer from her body heat.

She looked at them, and then back at him.

Bones waited, leaving his hands within reach, an invitation she could accept or reject. Whatever she chose, he wanted her to know that he was there.

She looked at his hands again, her fingers slowly uncurling—

The truck lurched as it came to a stop. Cat grabbed the box to steady herself instead of reaching out for him. Bones jumped up with a muttered curse.

If Ted wasn't such a good mate, he'd break his legs for ruining another moment between them.

And the moment *was* gone. Her newly shuttered expression was proof of that. Bones sighed.

Ah, well. Nothing worthwhile was ever easy.

"We're nearly at the place, and there's still work to be done," he said, heading for the wrecked car. "Hold open that bag for me, Kitten."

She followed him to the boot of the Mercedes. Bones gave her a construction-style garbage bag, then unwrapped Sergio from the plastic sheets. With a single, hard twist, he removed Sergio's head, and dropped it into her bag.

"Yuck," she said, shoving the bag at him. "You take it."

"Squeamish?" After all the heads she'd lopped off herself? Bones grinned. "That lump of rotting skull is worth fifty thousand dollars. Sure you don't want to cradle it a bit?"

She wrinkled her nose. "No thanks."

Moments later, the rear door opened with a metallic screech, revealing Ted.

"We're here, bud. Hope you both had a smooth ride."

Cat caught Ted's wink and was instantly defensive. "We were only *talking*."

Ted stifled a laugh. Bones let her see his smile before he turned to Ted. "Come now, mate. We've been driving for, what? Fifty minutes? Not nearly enough time."

Ted let out a louder chuckle, but Cat only scowled.

"Are you two finished?" she asked in her prissiest tone.

Not nearly, but he did have a bit of business to take care of. "Stay with Ted and the trailer. Something I have to do."

"What?" she asked at once.

"Got a head to deliver, and I'd rather you stay out of it. The fewer people that know about you, the better."

Cat seemed glad to stay back with the trailer now. Bones gave her a last smile, and then slung the bag containing Sergio's head over his shoulder.

He was in a good mood, and for more reasons than her nearly kissing him twice tonight. Beneath all of her anti-vampire brainwashing, she trusted him as someone she could share her secrets with. She'd also accepted his past with none of the judgment she was normally so quick to dish out. Bit by bit, she was breaking out of the box that her mum, her grandparents, and her neighbors had shoved her into. Soon, she'd be free.

She'd also revealed an important detail that, unlike the other truths she'd shared with him, he could actually fix.

He couldn't undo her mum's rejection, her grandparent's ostracizing, her neighbor's ignorance, or that soon-to-be-dead sod's appalling treatment of her, but he could see to it that Cat went to a club for her coveted evening of drinking, dancing, and non-violent fun.

She'd get that tomorrow night because, unbeknownst to her, they were going on a date.

17

*B*ones landed about twenty meters from the gray sedan parked along the highway's shoulder. The car's driver didn't notice him dropping out of the sky. Humans rarely did. When you didn't know vampires existed, let alone that some of them could fly, you manufactured other explanations for how someone could suddenly appear in your line of vision.

Thus, the driver's surprised blink when Bones walked toward him. His shifting gaze indicated wariness, but he wasn't afraid. When Bones tapped on his window, the driver lowered it an inch to say, "I don't need any help. Triple A is on the way."

The line that identified him as the client, as if Bones hadn't recognized him from his gray hair, thin features, and the moles darkening his ecru-colored skin. This was George Shayne.

Bones replied with the line meant to confirm his identity, too. "Yes, but my services are guaranteed."

George's breath exploded out with relief. Just as quickly, though, his wariness returned, this time with a hint of fear wafting through the cigarette scent that clung to him.

"You're early. Does that mean it's...done?"

Bones lifted the bag containing Sergio's head. George recoiled out of instinctual disgust. Then, his features hardened, and he leaned forward to get a better look.

"It's just a skull," George said in confusion. "How do I know this is the animal that killed my daughter?"

Vampires decomposed back to their true age after death. There was now little left of Sergio's head aside from bits shriveled skin that still stubbornly clung to his cranium.

Bones held out his mobile with his free hand. When he deposited Sergio into the car's boot earlier, he'd snapped a picture. Sergio had been so newly dead then that decomposition hadn't done its full work, so his features were still recognizable as the last man that Aurora Shayne had been seen alive with.

Sergio hadn't bothered to erase the club's security footage when he kidnapped Aurora. He also hadn't bothered to hide Aurora's body after he killed her. That's how arrogant Sergio had been.

But George Shayne, a widower with no other children, wasn't content to wait for the legal system to administer justice. He wanted it in blood. George had also done a decent job getting the word out to the right places. The contract was a small one, but Bones would've taken it even if it didn't provide cover for him killing Sergio in the vampire world. Justice in the form of blood was exactly what Sergio had deserved.

"I de-fleshed the skull to make it harder to identify," Bones said. "I can provide disposal as well, if you'd like."

"No," George said in a newly savage tone. "I want to smash it to pieces myself."

Understandable.

Bones handed over the skull. George grimaced, but his hands didn't tremble as he placed it in a knapsack he'd had the foresight to bring. Then, he shoved the sack into the backseat. When he looked at Bones, tears filled his gaze.

"Tell me he suffered more than my daughter did."

Bones's jaw clenched. He'd read the coroner's report. Sergio had taken his time with Aurora. Bones would have done the same to Sergio, if circumstances had allowed.

"He died bleeding and begging," was all Bones could offer.

George made a sound between a sigh and a sob. "Good. I'm glad about that. I am. But...I don't hurt any less. I thought...I thought maybe I would—?"

Bones had George Shayne's jaw in his grip before the other man could stiffen in shock. Then, Bones unleashed the power in his gaze. When that inhuman green light bathed George's face, the man's pulse skyrocketed.

"You're safe," Bones said, and George's heart rate went from frantic back to a normal rhythm. "You feel no guilt over hiring someone to kill that sod. Doing so saved other girls' lives. Soon, you won't hurt so much when you think of your daughter. Eventually, you'll remember only the good times, and this pain will heal."

"Heal," George repeated, hope threading through his tone.

"You won't remember this moment, either," Bones went on. "Or my face. All you'll remember is the man you hired wore a mask, dropped off the head, you paid him, and that was that."

"That was that," George echoed, caught in Bones's gaze.

Bones returned his eyes to normal, and let George go.

The other man blinked for a second, and then said, "No reason to keep you. You've done your part. Here's your payment."

Bones accepted the envelope that George held out to him, tucking it into his jacket.

George frowned. "You're not going to count it?"

A smile ghosted across Bones's lips. "No need."

He'd been handed so many envelopes like these that Bones knew it was the right amount just from its weight.

George let out an uncomfortable laugh. "Guess only a fool would shortchange someone like you."

True enough, and George Shayne was no fool.

Bones gave George a wordless nod, and then walked away.

121

When he was outside the car's headlights, Bones flew, letting the rush of air clear away any residual pity he had for George. He'd done what he could for him. Now, he was returning to Cat... and to hunting people even worse than Sergio.

~

CAT WAS STILL SITTING on the back of the tractor trailer when Bones landed. As he came closer, he saw scratched-off bits of nail polish clinging to her legs like scarlet confetti. Her expression was pensive, and she was so deep in thought it took a second for her to notice that he'd returned.

"Oh," she said, and then hurried to scoot out of his way.

Still rattled from her earlier reaction to him, was she?

Bones hid a smile as he fetched his bike. When it was on the ground, he climbed on, and nodded at the space behind him.

"Hop on, Kitten, we're finished here."

She hesitated. "What about Sergio's car?"

"Ted's got a chop house. It's one of the ways he makes his living, didn't I mention that?"

"No, but what about the torso?" she said, clearly stalling.

"Ted again. Part of our deal is him planting them for me. Don't fret. Ted's a smart fellow, keeps his mouth shut."

And Ted would never betray him. Bones had taken Ted in when he was a teenager after Ted's father had thrown him out for being gay. Bones had no such bigotries, so Ted became one of Bones's people, trading the occasional blood consumption for housing, an education, and silence about the vampire race. Now, Ted was married to a wonderful man, and had not one, but two successful businesses.

"Come on, Kitten," Bones said when she still hesitated.

With more reticence than her normal aversion to riding on his motorcycle, she climbed on behind him.

Two hours later, they were back in the woods near the cave.

She'd held onto him during the long ride, but as soon as he came to a stop, she leapt off as if their prolonged contact had scalded her. Then, she hurried toward her truck.

"Off so soon?" Bones teased her. "The evening is young."

Cat did her best not to look at him as she said, "Maybe for you, but I'm tired. Go find yourself a nice neck to suck on."

Bones ignored the snark because she wished she could dismiss him that easily now. Her breath hitched as he set the bike aside and came toward her.

She did look at him then, and an almost panicked expression flashed over her features. "I-I have to go."

Yet her scent said she didn't want to. She wanted to stay, if she'd let herself admit it. That's what frightened her so.

And Bones wanted to back her against her truck and kiss her until she couldn't remember why she'd fought so hard against her desire for him. But he didn't. He'd waited this long; he could wait a little longer. It was almost dawn, so she probably was tired. Besides, they had a date tomorrow, not that she knew it.

He took a deliberate step backward, giving her more space.

"You should at least come inside and change," Bones said in a light tone. "If your mum sees you covered in blood, she might worry about you." Doubtful, but stranger things had happened. "Promise I won't peek," he added with an obvious wink.

Relief coated her smile, either at his new distance, or his feigned nonchalance. "I'll change at a gas station. When do I have to come back? This job is done, so I get a break, right?"

He bit back his snort. *No, Kitten. I might let you run from me, but I'm not letting you hide.*

"Sorry. Tomorrow night, you're on again. After that, I fly to Chicago to see my old friend Hennessey. With luck, I'll be back Thursday because on Friday, I have another job lined up—"

Her exasperated sigh cut him off.

"Fine. Just remember I start college again next week, so I'll need some slack. We might have an arrangement, but I've waited too long already to finish my degree."

"Absolutely," Bones said with feigned enthusiasm. "But since dead girls pass no exams, you won't be neglecting your training. Don't fret, though," he added when her mouth opened mutinously. "We'll work it out. Speaking of jobs, here you go."

He drew out the envelope George Shayne had given him, selected a quarter of its contents, and held it out to her.

"Your share."

Cat stared at the cash as if it were a snake about to strike. "What's this?"

He snorted. "Fellow can't even give you money without you arguing? This is twenty-five percent of the bounty Sergio had on his head. It's yours for helping him lose his head. Reckon since I don't pay the IRS, I may as well give their cut to you," he added to ward off her protest. "Death and taxes. They go hand in hand."

He'd have given her all the money if he thought she'd accept it, but she was too suspicious for that. She already looked as if she'd refuse, and it was a paltry twelve thousand.

"Um…thanks," she finally said, and took the cash.

"You earned it," Bones reminded her. This wasn't a favor. It was the literal least she'd allow him to do.

She still seemed stunned, but she was smiling now. The sight was worth more than all the money he'd ever earned.

"You just got a big chunk of change yourself, are you finally moving out of the cave?"

He laughed. "Is that why you think I stay there? Due to lack of funds?"

"Why else? You have to pirate electricity, and you shower using ice cold river water. I didn't think you did that just because you liked seeing your parts shrink!"

Now Bones's laughter held a wicked undertone. "Concerned for my dangly parts, are you? They're fine, I assure you. 'Course, if you need proof, you could always—"

"Don't even think about it," she interrupted.

"Too late for that," he assured her, voice deepening as he indulged in several explicit thoughts of that very nature.

Cat looked away, her color rising, but from the faster pulse beating in her lovely neck, she wasn't offended. At all.

Oh, how he wanted to lick that pulse from her neck all the way to where it throbbed between her legs. The thought made him hard without his intentionally sending blood to his cock.

This was the very *last* night he let her run from what she felt for him.

"Primarily, I stay at the cave because it's safer," Bones said to answer her original question. "I can hear you coming from a mile away with the surrounding woods. I also know the cave like the back of my hand. No one can ambush me there without my turning it around on them. Besides, it was given to me by a mate, so I check in on it when I'm in Ohio to make sure all's well, like I promised him."

Her brows went up. "How do you give someone a cave?"

Memories rose. It wasn't far from this spot that he'd last seen Tanacharisson, his resolute expression clear despite his face being covered in battle paint.

"Used to be an occasional winter resident of the Mingo. One of them, Tanacharisson, refused to leave after the Indian Removal Act forced his people from their lands. After seeing his people and culture destroyed, Tanacharisson went off on a suicide mission against Fort Meigs. Before he did, he asked me to look out for the cave since some of his ancestor's bones are buried in the back, and he didn't want the whites desecrating them."

Cat's eyes misted over. "How terrible."

Many things were terrible back then. They weren't perfect now. Far from it, but some of the worst injustices had ceased.

"It was his choice," Bones said softly. "He had nothing left except how he died, and the Mingo were very proud. To him, this was a death worthy of the legacy of his people."

"Maybe," she said in an equally soft voice. "But when death is all you have left, it's sad no matter what."

Yes. And infuriating, and unjust, but Bones hadn't been able to help Tanacharisson or his people. Vampires had few laws, but one of them was a strict "no interference" policy when it came to letting humans run their own societies. Sure, a vampire could take out a few terrible humans without breaking that "no interference" law, but attack a human system their society was based on, and the Law Guardians would slaughter you. The secrecy of the race came first for Law Guardians. No exceptions.

"It's late, Bones," Cat said, dragging his thoughts back to her. "I'm leaving."

He let her get into her truck before he came over and touched her arm. There was one more item he wanted to address.

"Kitten, about what you told me earlier...you need to know that it wasn't your fault. A rotten bloke like that would've done the same to any girl, and no doubt has both before and since you."

She'd stiffened when she realized what he meant. By the time he was finished, her face was set in sharp, pained lines.

"Are you speaking from experience?" As soon as the words left her, shame flitted over her features. She hadn't meant that, and she knew she'd gone too far by saying it.

Bones dropped his hand and stepped away. "I've never treated any woman that way, and most especially not a virgin. You don't have to be human to have such behavior be beneath you."

Cat stared at him, her expression changing from regret to confusion before finally, a look of longing crossed her face. She wanted to believe him, but her experiences with both vampire and human men made that difficult.

I'm not them, Bones silently promised her. *And I'll prove it.*

"Go home, Kitten," he said. "I'll see you tomorrow night."

With another look of both longing and confusion, she left.

18

*B*ones checked his phone. No, he hadn't misjudged the time. Cat was over twenty minutes late. She'd never been that late before, even when actively plotting his demise.

Worry poisoned his thoughts. Her vampire side protected her from many things, but her human half made her so...fragile. What if she'd been a victim of a random shooting? Or a car accident? With that old metal heap she drove, even a small accident could result in serious injury...

A far-off, mechanical sputtering sound brought instant relief. Her engine made that noise every time it came to a stop.

She'd just run late and hadn't bothered to ring him. Slightly inconsiderate, but nothing that merited his over-imaginative response. How did people not go mad when they were in love? These emotional highs and lows would end him faster than a silver stake.

By the time Cat made it to his spot in the cave, Bones had covered his former worry with a scowl. In contrast, she looked right chipper, and she had several shopping bags hanging from her arms, making the reason for her tardiness clear.

"Took your sweet time, I see, but I suppose everything in those bags is for me, so all's forgiven."

A sheepish expression crossed her features. Didn't she know he was joking? Apparently not because she thrust a bag into his hands while stammering out that she had gotten him something.

"This massager is great for aching muscles," she finished, and then looked as if she'd choke. His muscles hadn't ached since he was human, as she'd just remembered.

Bones pretended to examine the device. "Five speeds. Deep, penetrating action. Sure this isn't yours?"

She huffed at his inference. "Just say so if you don't want it."

He gave her the bag back. "Give this to your gramps like you intended. Blimey, but you're still a bad liar."

Yet she'd lied because she didn't want to hurt his feelings. That meant more to him than if she *had* gotten him a gift.

"Let's move onto the target tonight," she said, clearly eager to change the subject. "Tell me the details."

Bones hid his grin as he followed her deeper into the cave.

"Let's see, your target's over two hundred years old, has naturally brown hair but he colors it frequently, speaks with an accent, and is very skilled in combat. Oh, and you can keep your knickers on. Bloke will be smitten with you on sight."

All true, and she had no idea how much control he'd exercised with that *last* concession.

"What's his name?"

"He'll probably use a moniker," Bones replied with a straight face. "Most vampires do, but his real name is Crispin."

Before Cat could ask him anything else, he brushed her off with a comment about watching telly, and left.

An hour later, Cat came into the cave's version of the living room. She'd picked the most conservative of her hunting outfits, not that it mattered. Her beauty still struck him like an unexpected blow. Her skin gleamed like polished alabaster against the black halter dress, and her new curls added thick waves to her scarlet tresses. Smoky eye makeup matched her storm-cloud gray eyes, and her lips were the color of freshly spilled blood.

Bones looked away before he gave into the urge to rip her dress off so he could see her clad in only her undergarments, gloves, and those thigh-high boots. It would be worth her staking him afterward. He'd die a happy man.

"I know you like this show, but can we leave?" she asked, oblivious to her effect on him. "We have to places to be."

Oh, they'd go. Right after he dealt with his raging hard-on.

"This is the good part," he lied as he quickly sent his blood elsewhere. What was on the telly again? Right, Court TV. "They're about to deliver the verdict."

"Who cares about the verdict in that murder case when we're about to commit our own murder?" she pointed out.

Finally, his third leg vanished. Not a moment too soon. He could only feign interest in that show for so long.

"Right, let's be off," Bones said, leaping off the couch to take her arm.

She looked more surprised by his statement than his sudden appearance next to her. "Aren't we driving separately?"

"Not tonight. You'd never find the place. It's a different sort of club, very particular. Come on," he added when she still hesitated. "Let's not keep your bloke waiting."

"What is this place?" Cat demanded, staring at the front of the nightclub.

Its nondescript gray steel exterior resembled a large, industrial warehouse. It was no fewer than ten kilometers off the main road, too, with only one way in or out of the tree-surrounded parking lot. A line of people waited to get in, and in such a desolate-looking area, that would cause anyone to do a double-take.

But that wasn't why Cat stared. Soundproofing might mask

the music, but it couldn't muffle the energy emanating from the club. She should feel it even from the parking lot. No vampire could mistake it, and no half-vampire could, either.

"Let's not dawdle," Bones said in a cheery tone, and propelled her toward the door.

Some of the humans waiting in line gave him a disgruntled look as Bones bypassed them, but they said nothing. If they were here, they knew the pecking order of this club, and humans were on the bottom of it.

A tall, beautiful vampire with thick muscles, short blond hair, and cerulean blue eyes guarded the door. Trixie had been the club's bouncer for over a decade. Anyone foolish enough to doubt her capabilities soon learned the error of their ways. Her muscular build wasn't the strongest part of her power by far.

"Trixie, luv, been too long," Bones said, and kissed her cheek.

"Missed you, Bones," she replied. "Heard you left these parts."

He winked. "Don't believe everything you hear. That's how rumors get started."

Trixie laughed and waved them through while barely looking at Cat. To Trixie, Cat was just another anonymous human on Bones's arm. That's why it was safe to bring Cat here. Only vampires merited remembering in this type of place.

More tension eased from Bones once they were inside the club. Instead of a human establishment's skull-pummeling noise, the music here was set to a vampire's version of loud. The lights were also dimmer, and the three-story, spacious interior meant you'd only be crowded if you wanted to be.

On this level, a famous nineties grunge singer believed to be dead in the human world rocked the stage singing one of his most popular hits. Bloke was hardly the first celebrity to fake his own death after joining the undead ranks, but Cat didn't seem to notice him. She was too busy staring at everyone else, and her expression looked as if someone had taken shock, added a dash of anger, shaken it up, and then splashed the concoction over her features.

"What is this place?" she growled.

Bones's wave took in the dance floor, three bars, and private curtained alcoves that made up the club's first level.

"This, luv, is an undead club. The locals call it Bite. All manner of supernaturals come here to mix and mingle without having to hide their true natures. See? Right over there you have some ghosts at the bar."

Cat stared at the trio of ghosts Bones indicated. They hovered next to stools, probably waiting for a human to drink their favorite liquor so they could fly through that person's throat to "taste" it. Winston wasn't the first ghost to figure out how to enjoy liquor even after his death.

Flashes of green soon tore Cat's attention away from the ghosts. For a few moments, her head swiveled around as if she couldn't look at the club's other patrons fast enough. Even at this early hour, the lower dance floor and bars were full. Many vampires had their eyes lit up, indicating hunger or other needs. Cat glanced up, taking in the second and third levels of the club where interior balconies showed the green-lit gazes of even more vampires. Her hands clenched as if gripping invisible stakes, and she moved closer to Bones without seeming to realize it.

"My God," Cat breathed out. "There's so many of them. I hadn't realized there were this many vampires in the *world...*"

Another reason he'd brought her here.

"Kitten, nearly ten percent of the population is undead," Bones said, ignoring her gasp at the number. "We're in every state, every nation, and we have been for a very long time. Granted, certain areas attract more of our kind. Take parts of Ohio, where the line separating the normal and the paranormal is much thinner. Gives the region a faint charge. Younger vamps love that."

"You're telling me I live in a vampire hot spot?" she asked in dismay.

"Yes, but don't bother packing your bags," Bones said with a laugh. "There are scores of them around the globe."

Suddenly, she gripped his arm and yanked him toward her. He didn't mind, especially when he felt her lips brush his ear.

"What's that?" Cat whispered. "That...thing. It's not a vampire, but I can tell that it's not human."

He followed her gaze. "Oh, him. He's a ghoul. Flesh eater," he added when she still seemed confused. "Like *Night of the Living Dead*, only they don't walk funny or look hideous. The show *iZombie* had it much closer to the truth."

Cat looked revolted, which summed up how a large percentage of vampires felt about ghouls, too. The dislike was reciprocated. Ghouls and vampires had a complicated history, but their species were currently enjoying a truce. Still, ghouls tended to avoid places with high vampire populations, which was probably why Cat hadn't run into their species before.

"Sit there, have a drink," Bones said, giving her a light push toward the bar. "Your bloke will show up soon."

"Are you crazy?" Now, Cat wasn't whispering. "This place is crawling with monsters. I don't want to be their appetizer!"

That garnered a few snickers from those close enough to hear her. Cat didn't seem to notice. Or care. She was still staring at Bones as if he'd indeed gone mental.

He touched her arm. "Trust me, Kitten. Remember all the humans waiting to get in? They know about vampires and ghouls, too, and they want to mingle with the undead. They're in no danger, and neither are you. There is strict etiquette here. Absolutely no violence on the premises, and only willing blood or sex exchanges. Can human nightclubs promise the same?"

He walked away, trusting that her curiosity would win out. Or her bloodlust would. Too bad she couldn't appreciate the irony that in a club full of "monsters," she was the only person who'd come here specifically to kill.

Well, perhaps not the only one. Bones intended to kill something tonight, too: more of her ignorance about vampires. Let her see them drinking, dancing, and enjoying themselves the same way humans did. Would do more to counter her mother's bigoted teachings than a thousand of his lectures could.

After Bones had crossed the length of the club, he looked back at where he'd left Cat. She was still standing in the same spot, hesitancy written all over her. Then, she shook her head, muttered something he couldn't hear, and took a seat near the ghosts at the bar.

Bones smiled. He'd give her a few minutes to get more comfortable with her surroundings, and then he'd introduce her to her "target" for the night.

Then…let the games begin.

19

Fifteen minutes later, Bones approached Cat from behind. She should have felt him coming, but with scores of vampires here giving off inhuman vibes, her radar was off.

"Sod off," Bones said to the two human boys on either side of her. Figures she'd chosen mortals to while away the time with. When the sandy-haired boy hesitated, giving Cat another lust-filled look, Bones lit up his gaze with green.

Both lads wisely scattered. So did the vampire sitting on the stool next to Cat. Bones took that seat.

"What are you doing here?" she hissed, not looking at him. "What if *he* comes in?"

Bones laughed and held out his hand. "We haven't met. My name is Crispin."

She did look at him then. And glared. "That's not funny."

"Don't want to shake my hand, do you?" Bones said with mock reprimand. "Not nice manners."

"Will you stop?" Another furious hiss. "I have a job to do. The real Crispin's going to be here soon, and he'll be put off by your blathering!"

Bones used a single finger to turn her to face him.

"But my name is Crispin, pet. Crispin Phillip Arthur Russell the Third. 'Course, that last part was merely a bit of fancy on my mum's end. For obvious reasons, she had no idea who my da was. Still, she must've thought adding numerals after my name would give me a bit of dignity." He gave a brief smile at her memory. "Poor sweet woman, ever reluctant to face reality."

Cat's eyes were growing wider by the moment. "You're Crispin? You? But you said your name was—"

"Told you most vampires change their name after they change from human," Bones interrupted lightly. "Crispin was my human name. After Ian turned me, he laid me in the native's burial grounds until I rose. For hundreds of years, they'd buried their dead in the same place, and not too deeply, either. When my eyes opened for the first time as a vampire, all I saw around me were bones."

And blood. Every vampire rose with mindless, uncontrollable hunger. Bones didn't even remember making his first kill. All he remembered was waking up to the sightless gaze of his victim staring back at him amidst a sea of bones.

"I knew what I was then," Bones said. "For from bones I rose and Bones I became, all in that night."

Something flashed across Cat's face, and her scent changed from annoyance to something softer. Their circumstances might have been different, but she knew what it was like to have her entire existence upended in one night.

"Okay, you're Crispin," she acknowledged. "What kind of game are you playing, then? You want me to try to kill you again, is that it?"

"Blimey, no," he said with a laugh. "In fact, this is all your doing."

"My doing?" she repeated with disbelief. "How could I have anything do with *this*?"

He grinned. "When you were complaining about your life last

night, you said you'd never been to a club just to have fun. So tonight, we will drink and dance and absolutely murder no one. You will be Cat, I'll be Crispin, and you'll send me home with a dry mouth and aching balls just like you would if we'd never met before."

A scowl knit her brows, but something sparked in her gaze that she tried to conceal by taking a long sip of her drink.

"Was this all a trick to get me to go on a date with you?"

Absolutely, and I'm not finished yet.

"Let you keep your knickers on, though, didn't I?" he teased. "Don't even appreciate the willpower *that* took. Now, then, finish your drink and let's dance. Promise I'll be the perfect gentleman... until you request otherwise."

That earned him another glare as she set her glass on the counter with a loud clink.

"Sorry, Crispin, I never learned how to dance. You know, my whole lack of a social life and all that?"

"You're serious?" That other sod hadn't even taken her out for a twirl? Oh, he'd enjoy killing him for a thousand reasons.

"Yep," she said, gripping her glass a little too tightly now.

She was embarrassed. As if it were her fault that she hadn't been taken on a proper date.

Bones grasped her free hand. "You dance now."

Cat argued the entire way to the dance floor, but if she really didn't want this, she was more than strong enough to stop him. Instead, her tugs on his hand were halfhearted at best. When they were in the middle of the gyrating throng, Bones turned her back to him so she could see the other dancers.

"It's easy. Watch them, and move the way they do."

He demonstrated as he spoke, splaying his free hand across her waist to guide her movements. His other hand still held hers, and her fingers tightened as their hips brushed.

"I swear, if you try anything," she drew out.

He let his laughter hit the sensitive spot on her neck. Her shiver felt almost as good as the light brushes of her body.

"Relax. I won't bite."

That caused another shiver that he savored. Then, Cat lost her hesitancy and began to move in earnest as she copied the other dancers. Soon, her body was dipping and twisting of her own accord. Bones followed her movements, matching each bend and sway while heat slammed into him.

Feeling her this way was more erotic than every act he'd indulged in before her. He couldn't stop fantasizing about tasting the sweat that was now beading her skin. Or bending her forward until her arse cupped his cock. Or plunging so deeply inside her that her juices basted his thighs from her pleasure…

He spun her around to redirect his thoughts. A mistake. Her dreamy, sensual smile almost undid him. She'd never looked at him that way before, even when she was trying to seduce him into an early grave.

He pulled her closer, stroking her with light, sinuous touches. She raised her arms and her head fell back, baring her throat. Its long, luscious line begged him to taste it, and her arched back jutted her breasts out until the lovely globes were only a few centimeters beneath his mouth.

Taunting him, was she? Two could play at that game.

Bones bent her backward until her hair brushed the floor. Then, he pulled her up while letting her body slide along his. Pleasure knifed him at the contact, heightened by her quickening pulse and her little gasp.

Then, her brow cocked in challenge, and she flattened her hands against his chest as she twisted her hips against his.

"You were right. Dancing is easy," he heard her say above the new roar in his ears. "And I'm a fast learner."

Lust nearly felled him. He let her see a fraction of what he felt before bending his mouth to her ear.

"Playing with fire, Kitten?"

A warning and a promise. She could still walk away unscathed, if she stopped now. She could still—

Her tongue slid up his neck in a warm, wet path.

His vision went black. Only extreme bloodlust had erased his sight before, and only when he was a new vampire. Bones felt himself gripping her hair, felt her sharp intake of breath...and then all he saw was her lips.

He claimed them with all the hunger ripping through him.

20

$\mathcal{C}$at moaned, and Bones breathed it in before moving past the satiny fullness of her lips to the richness of her mouth. His tongue caressed hers, and his blood boiled when she dug her nails into his back. Her thundering pulse drowned out the music, and her heat seared him through their clothes. He ran his hands down her body until he reached her hips. She shuddered when he brought them flush against his, and then let out a sharp sound of need when he sucked on her tongue.

Two dancers collided into them, breaking their kiss and causing Cat to stumble at the unexpected contact. Bones caught her before she fell, glaring at the careless dancers.

"Watch where you're going!"

They muttered an apology. Bones turned back to Cat and—

Sweet bleedin' Christ, her eyes!

They were glowing bright green from desire. He'd never seen anything more beautiful...or more dangerous, considering where they were.

Bones tucked Cat's head into his chest in a mimic of a bear hug. Then, he half-ran, half-flew them off the dance floor.

Please, let no one have seen her eyes!

So far, no one appeared to. Or, if they did, the music had masked the fact that her now-glowing gaze came with the impossible combination of a heartbeat.

Bones picked the most deserted area of the club, a section by the emergency exit. Then, he put his back to the wall, leaving her facing him and no one else. Now, only he could see the bright glow in her eyes.

Cat didn't seem aware of the danger. She laced her fingers through his hair and pulled his mouth back down to hers.

For an instant, Bones hesitated. He shouldn't kiss her again here. He'd narrowly missed outing her as a half breed only moments ago. It would be foolish to risk that again, no matter that her lips were so soft…

Sod it. What was life without a little danger?

He let out a rough groan and covered her mouth with his. She yanked him closer as if craving him as much as he craved her, which wasn't possible. God, she tasted so good, and he couldn't get enough of her little, throaty moans, or her strong grip on his shoulders. If he were human, she'd leave bruises, but he wasn't, so he loved how tightly she held him.

He drew her tongue into his mouth, sucking on it again. She gasped before doing the same to him, until his cock throbbed as if she were sucking on that, too. Her hands left his shoulders to run down his back, stroking muscles that strained with his need. He held her tighter, letting her feel how much he wanted her. She groaned, rubbing against him with wordless demand while her heart pounded so fiercely, it felt like soft blows against his chest.

He needed her naked right now. Those private alcoves were so close…

Bones tore his mouth away.

"Kitten, you need to make a decision. Either we stay here and behave or we leave now and I promise you, if we leave I won't behave."

He kissed her after saying it. A mistake. It only made him burn more, until he might be the first vampire to die of lust-induced combustion. If he didn't love her to the point of madness, he'd already be propelling her into one of those alcoves, but she deserved better than a public quickie, especially their first time.

"Decide now," he said hoarsely, tearing his mouth away. "It's taking everything I have not to carry you off."

She stared at him, her hands clenched on the folds of his shirt. His were still at her hips, stroking them with light touches that belied his hunger. He hadn't slid them beneath her dress, but from her scent, she was wet, and it was all he could do to stop himself from dropping to his knees to taste her there.

Say yes, say yes!

"Bones." Passion made her voice a soft growl.

A familiar face suddenly caught his eye, followed by a telltale wave of power that announced a Master vampire's presence.

It couldn't be. Not here, not now!

But it was. Bones might not have seen him in years, but he knew him at a glance, and rage strafed his lust.

"Bloody frigging hell, what is *he* doing here?"

Cat tried to look around, but Bones caught her before she turned and showed anyone else her impossibly glowing eyes.

"Who?" she asked, now sounding confused. "Who's here?"

The nation's deadliest vampire, if Bones was right about him. And the sod was strolling only twenty meters from Cat while her gaze was lit up like twin streetlights.

Bones lowered his voice to a hard whisper.

"Hennessey."

Cat's eyes filled back up with gray. For once, Bones was glad for her pathological hatred of vampires. She'd recognized Hennessey's name immediately, and it doused her desire faster than a cold shower.

"Sergio said he's supposed to be in Chicago," she said in an equally low tone. "Do you think Sergio lied?"

Now that her gaze was as normal-looking as any human,

Bones spun them so his back was to the crowd and she was against the wall. He didn't want Hennessey spotting him yet.

"Black hair, mustache, thin beard, olive-toned skin, tall, wearing a white shirt," Bones said. "See him?"

Cat leaned forward casually, as if she were just resting her head on Bones's shoulder. "Got him."

"Keep your eye on him, and no, Sergio didn't lie." Of that, Bones was sure, even if he were still shaking off the effects of extreme lust. "Hennessey must've gotten word that Sergio's gone missing. He knew Sergio was in this area, so Hennessey's poking about for answers. He's no doubt rightly worried about what Sergio said to whomever made him disappear."

Cat straightened, a gleam of a different kind appearing in her eyes. "Whatever the reason, he's here. Let's go for him."

"No."

She blinked at the harshness in his tone. "Why not? He just got dropped into our lap!"

The thought of what Hennessey would do to her made his tone scalding. "You're not getting anywhere near that treacherous sod. You're going straight home as soon as he's away from the door. I'll handle him myself."

Anger drenched her scent.

"For someone who keeps telling me to trust him, you sure don't extend the same courtesy. I thought tonight was a regular job, so I'm all staked out and ready to go, and did you forget that I took on vampires before you? No one had to hold my hand through it. Now, I have training and backup, and you're still telling me to turn tail and run? Don't kiss me like a woman if you're going to treat me like a child."

How the hell did she turn this into something about *them*?

"This isn't me treating you like a child. Bugger, I clearly don't see you that way! I told you Hennessey's not just a bloke who snatches up a girl when his tummy grumbles. He's in another league, Kitten. He's a very bad sort."

"Then quit arguing, and let's go get him," she said instantly. "That's my favorite type of monster to take down."

No. Not now, not ever.

The look in her eyes stopped Bones from saying it. She wanted this, and no amount of arguing on his part would dissuade her. Quite the opposite. Now that he'd told her how heinous Hennessey was, he didn't trust that Cat would leave if he did send her away. More likely, she'd try to take on Hennessey herself. As she'd reminded him, she'd hunted vampires long before him. She would hunt them again whether he backed her up or not. He could no more stop her from that than he could stop himself from needing blood.

He let out a frustrated sigh. "I don't like this at all, but...we'll go for him, *if* you do exactly as I say."

She smiled, bright as the rising sun. "Of course."

He gave her sour a look. "I mean it, and if anything goes sideways, anything at all, you hit that panic button."

"Sure," she said in a breezy tone.

God Almighty, he hoped he didn't regret this.

"Go to the bar nearest him. He'll seek you out; your stunning skin is like a homing beacon for vampires. When he does, tell him you're on a bad first date. He'll be delighted to discover the bloke you're dissatisfied with is me."

Cat laughed. "Oh, I'll be brutal, I promise."

"I have no doubt," Bones said dryly. "But Hennessey is more dangerous than anyone you've taken on before, so do *not* underestimate him."

Her smile faded, and ice snapped into her gaze. "Got it."

This was the absolute last way he'd intended their evening to end, but...life seldom failed to surprise.

"Then I'll see you soon, Kitten."

21

ive minutes later, Hennessy glanced in Cat's general vicinity. She must have kept an eye on him because she stretched backward at once as if relieving a kink. The motion tousled her scarlet hair and made her breasts strain against her halter dress while her skin caught the club's lights as if competing with them for subtle luminescence.

Hennessey stared, and then left the leggy brunette he'd been speaking to without another word. She shook her head, offended. Chit didn't realize the favor he'd just done her.

When Hennessey reached Cat, Bones was struck with such an urge to kill, he had to stand absolutely still. If he moved, he'd slaughter Hennessey, denying vengeance to countless victims while also earning him an instant death sentence for violating the club's "no violence on the premises" rule. Bones had worried that Cat wasn't up for this fight, but now, *he* was the weak link.

He had to bury his emotions. They made him reckless, and he couldn't permit that. Until this was finished, he wouldn't allow himself to feel at all.

Bones closed his eyes, waiting for the ice to come. It had been born all the times he could do nothing after a customer beat his mum or one of the other women who'd helped raise him, grown when he saw his best mate swing from the gallows for stealing food when he was starving, and crystallized during his mum's battle against syphilis. Her love had made their brutal circumstances bearable, yet the disease hadn't only taken his mum's life. It also stole her mind. She hadn't even recognized Bones at the end. She'd thought he was merely another customer.

When that ice covered every part of him, Bones opened his eyes. The club and its inhabitants seemed to fade. Only Hennessey was sharp relief, and Bones glided toward him with the unhurried grace of a shark circling bleeding prey.

"...did you say your name was?" Cat was asking Hennessey.

Bones didn't look at her. His gaze was fixed on Hennessey. The other vampire's black hair was cropped close and his thin mustache and beard looked like an homage to the Marvel character Tony Stark. Thick black brows provided ample coverage for Hennessey's cold blue eyes, and his smile oozed with false charm as he answered Cat.

"Call me Hennessey."

"Don't mind if I do, mate," Bones said.

Hennessey's gaze flew up. For a second, he looked startled, and then his expression closed off.

Too late. He'd been caught off guard, and they both knew it. Bones gave him a slow smile as he moved behind Cat's chair.

"Been a while, hasn't it?" Bones went on as he leaned down and kissed Cat's cheek.

Mine, his gaze told Hennessey.

Cat flinched at his kiss. Hennessey caught it, and his brow flicked with an arrogance that seemed to say, *apparently not.*

"Bones." Hennessey said his name as if tasted sour. "What an unexpected surprise. Don't tell me this lovely young woman is with you. She's far too well mannered."

Bones moved closer to Cat. "She is, and you're in my seat."

"Bones," Cat said in her prissiest tone. "Don't be rude. This nice man was just keeping me company until you came back."

"Indeed," Hennessey replied while giving Cat a once-over that would've enraged Bones into violence only minutes before. "You shouldn't leave such a pretty thing alone. You never know when some monster might come along and snatch her up."

More than a veiled threat, with Hennessey's history. Hennessey must feel untouchable. Time to change that.

"Funny you should say that. I hear it's your specialty, too."

Hennessey's aura flared, hitting Bones like hundreds of invisible whips. Just as fast, Hennessey tamped it down, his mouth tightening at his obvious lapse of control.

Safe inside his ice, Bones smiled. *Temper, temper.*

"Now, where would you hear such a thing?" Hennessey asked in a falsely casual tone.

"You'd be amazed at what someone can learn, if they dig deep enough," Bones replied.

Hennessey's aura flashed out again. He knew some of his mass burial sites had been dug up. Now, he knew by whom.

The bartender came over and tapped the edge of Cat's glass. As a vampire, he'd felt Hennessey's flashes of rage, too.

"Not here, gentleman," the bartender said. "You know the rules."

Hennessey's hand sliced the air in annoyance, but when he spoke, his tone was genial. "Of course. Pesky ordinance, that, but one must abide by the rules of the house when one visits."

"Cut the fancy talk, it doesn't suit you," Bones said, allowing a hint of anger to leak through his tone. "That is my chair, and she is my date, so for the last time, rack off."

Cat stood with a huff. "That's it. I won't let you keep referring to me in the third person as if I'm not even here. You don't own me, Bones. This is our first date, and I wouldn't have even gone out with you if you hadn't kept begging me. Now, our date is *over*, so get lost!"

Hennessey let out a smug laugh while Bones manufactured some false anger. "Why, you ungrateful little chit—"

"You heard the lady," Hennessey interrupted, still chuckling. "And you know the rules. Only willing companions here and she is clearly not willing. So, as she said, get lost."

"Or we can be men about this and settle our differences outside," Bones said, his brow arching in cold invitation. If he gave in too easily, Hennessey would get suspicious. If Hennessey was thick enough to accept the invitation, all the better.

Green sparked in Hennessey's eyes. "We'll settle this, mark my words, but not tonight. Soon, though. You've been meddling where you shouldn't have for too long."

No pretense anymore. Both of them had all but admitted their roles in this, and it would end with one of them dead.

"I'm shakin' in my boots," Bones said in a sardonic tone. "Another time and place, then. Looking forward to it."

Bones left, feeling Hennessey's gaze on him the entire way.

22

*B*ones leaned against the glass half wall that marked the edge of the second-floor interior balcony. Below him, Cat was still chatting with Hennessey. She wasn't aware that Bones was watching her, but every so often, Hennessey would glance up, smirk at him, and then return his attention to Cat.

Bones's lips curled. Let Hennessey bask in his presumed victory. It would only make the look on his face when Bones killed him that much more enjoyable.

Still, he couldn't have Hennessey guessing that Bones would follow them once they left. Hennessey needed to believe that Bones was irked, but that he'd also moved on. Bones beckoned to one of the nearby human women wearing a red ribbon around her throat; the club's official mark of a potential blood donor.

She'd do as a prop. Besides, he could use the meal.

"Yes?" he asked her bluntly when she reached him. Normally, Bones would chat her up a bit, but he was pressed for time.

The woman gave Bones a hungry look of her own before pushing her honey-colored hair away from her neck. She didn't need to do anything else since her dress was strapless, and low enough to show off the tops of her breasts.

"Oh, yeah," she said.

Bones let the venom build in his fangs. The girl moved closer, running her hands over his shoulders with open desire.

"You can have more than blood, gorgeous," she crooned.

Bones brushed her hands away. "Only blood."

She pouted in disappointment, but tilted her head back.

Centuries of habit made Bones find the spot that she enjoyed the most. Just because he was rushed didn't mean he had to be a brute about this. She gasped when his fangs pierced her neck, and then moaned as his venom caused a false, yet very pleasant sensation of heat.

Her blood filled Bones with actual heat, as well as a surge of new energy. Feeding from blood bags worked in a pinch, but nothing was as invigorating as blood from the vein. Bones was on his third swallow when he caught a familiar scent, and looked up to find Cat staring at him with her mouth open in a shocked, silent O.

Would *nothing* go right tonight?

Bones didn't stop feeding, though that was his first instinct. He hadn't intended her to see this, but now that she had, she might as well see all of it.

Bones kept swallowing until he'd drained half a pint or so. Then, he nicked his thumb with a fang and pressed his blood against the girl's puncture wounds. They closed at once, leaving no trace of Bones's bite. Lastly, he snapped off her red ribbon. Now, other vampires would know not to feed from her tonight.

"Off you go," Bones said when the girl didn't move.

She gave him a last pouty smile, and then left.

Cat hadn't looked away from him once, and she still appeared shocked. Hopefully, it wasn't for the wrong reasons.

"Didn't your mum tell you it's rude to stare at someone when they eat?" Bones asked her in a neutral tone.

Cat shook her head as if to clear it. "Is she...okay?"

"Of course," Bones said. "She's used to it. That's why many of the humans are here, as I told you. They choose to be the menu."

Cat muttered something he didn't catch. When Bones took a step toward her, she backed away.

Frustration pricked him. "I promise you the girl is fine, so what's the matter? It's not as if you didn't know that I was a vampire. Did you just think I never fed?"

Something dashed across her expression that he couldn't catch because then she rubbed her face as if it ached.

"I came to tell you that Hennessey and I are hitting it off," she said in a wooden tone. "Probably leaving soon."

"You all right?" he asked when she kept rubbing her face.

Cat's laughter cut the air like a whip. "No, I'm not all right. Earlier I kissed you, and now, I watched you make a Slurpee out of a girl's neck. Add that to a headache and it makes me very far from all right."

Bones came toward her again.

She backed away as if he were poisonous. "Don't touch me."

Crack! went his ice. Blast it all, he couldn't deal with this right now! It twisted him into parts that Hennessey could easily defeat. Bones couldn't afford to let that happen.

"Fine," he said in a clipped tone. "We'll talk about this later. Go on back, before Hennessey starts getting restless."

"We won't talk about it later," Cat said as she backed away. "In fact, I never want to speak about it again."

Muleheaded woman! How long would she punish him for sins that other vampires committed?

And yet...Bones hadn't accepted what he was for the first two decades after becoming a vampire. Part of him still resented Ian for turning him. Once again, his feelings were in the way.

Bones closed his eyes, willing himself to ice over again. When he did, he welcomed that dark, inner chill.

When he opened his eyes, Hennessey was coming toward him.

"You don't learn, do you?" the other vampire hissed.

Bones glanced at the lower level of the club behind him. Through the glass wall, he saw that Cat was now back at the bar, looking flustered but fine.

"Care to elaborate?" Bones said, showing a hint of fang when he turned back toward Hennessey.

Hennessey flashed his own fangs in a sneering smile. "The redhead rejected you. Stop being pathetic and accept it."

Picturing Hennessey begging under his knife made Bones's smile genuine this time. "Unlike you, I only ever have willing companions, so I have accepted it. Besides," his gaze slid to a curvy brunette who'd been attempting to catch his eye, and he waved her over. "I won't be lonely for long."

The brunette crossed the room at once, brushing by Hennessey without a glance.

"What's your name, lovely?" Bones asked her.

"Mina," she said, giving a coy tug on the red ribbon around her throat. "What's yours?"

"Bones."

She giggled. "A name *and* a promise, I hope."

Bones laughed, brushing the tip of her nose. "Always." Then, he glanced up as if surprised. "You still here, mate?"

Anger scented the air around Hennessey like a rancid fog. Hennessey didn't like being ignored, let alone mocked.

"Soon," he told Bones. "Until then, enjoy your treat. I know I'll enjoy mine. Gingersnaps always were my favorite."

Bones waved as if rage hadn't breached his ice walls, nearly breaking them. "Unless you need instruction, we're done."

"For now," Hennessey muttered as he stalked off.

Bones glanced down at Cat again. The same two rosy-cheeked human lads who'd fawned over her before now tried to propel her onto the dance floor, judging from how one grabbed her hand while the other gave her back a light push. Cat yanked her hand free and shoved the other one until he stumbled.

Served them right. Wankers.

"Hey," Mina said, cutting off his view. "How about we—"

"Stop," Bones said, turning on the brights in his gaze. "You're a nice lass, but this isn't happening. Stay here until I leave, though. Once I do, forget all about me."

Mina stood there, her smile frozen on her face. It might be rude to use her this way, but necessity outweighed manners. With the upward angle of the balcony and Mina in front of him, Bones could now catch glimpses of Cat without being seen himself.

Hennessey returned, that oily smile stamped on his face. Cat spent the next several minutes doing an excellent impression of being inebriated. Her head bobbed as if it were too heavy for her to hold upright, and her gaze kept drifting as if she were having trouble focusing on Hennessey's face.

Hennessey had Cat out the door in ten minutes flat.

Bones followed using a secret emergency exit on the roof. He'd learned about it years ago, after being hustled out by an employee whose husband had returned from business sooner than expected. Bones was grateful for that interrupted illicit encounter now. Hennessey had glanced at the club's doors several times when they left, yet he didn't look up at the roof once.

Cat helped to keep Hennessey's focus on her by doing her usual drunken stagger to his car. Hennessey assisted Cat into it, and then the two of them drove off.

Bones flew after them. He could hardly give chase in her noisy, clunky truck, though that meant having to explain his sudden appearance to Cat later. Eh, didn't matter. She'd learn that he could fly eventually. Might as well be tonight.

The lack of streetlights on the country roads made Hennessey's black Mercedes nearly blend in with the surroundings. The club's location in a low-population, rural area made these lonely stretches of road perfect for an ambush. Cat should be making her move soon. She only needed a little more distance from the club to ensure that none of the other patrons would stumble across them.

Bones stayed high to make sure Hennessey didn't sense him. Even with his aura tamped down, Bones couldn't risk coming closer yet. Hennessey was a Master vampire like Bones was, and age didn't guarantee that status. Only unusual strength and abilities did.

Red brake lights glowed as the car abruptly stopped. Bones dropped a little lower, until the car's interior lights showed Cat falling out of the front passenger door. She stayed on the ground, flopping about like a baby bird trying to fly. Hennessey leapt out of the same door after her. Pity. Bones could've bulleted into Hennessey had he gotten out on his side and then walked around the car to Cat.

Hennessey grabbed Cat by the hair and dragged her toward the shoulder of the road. Cat let him. Smart girl. This road was deserted now, but it might not stay that way.

Cat's pale skin suddenly contrasted against the ground as Hennessey tore the top half of her dress off. Cat's bra followed suit, leaving her naked from the waist up. Hennessey cupped her breasts, and rage nearly knocked Bones out of the sky.

Why the *hell* was she letting him do that?

Then, Hennessey bent to her neck, and twin scarlet streaks rolled down Cat's cream-colored skin.

Bones's ice exploded with such force that Hennessey felt it over a hundred meters below him. Hennessey lifted his head right as Bones's mobile vibrated with the only alert it had been programmed to receive tonight: Cat's panic text.

This wasn't payback because Cat had watched Bones feed from someone else earlier, so now she was making Bones watch Hennessey feed from her. She was in trouble.

Bones aimed for Hennessey and dove.

23

*H*ennessey saw him the second before Bones hit him.
With reflexes only a Master vampire had,
Hennessey yanked Cat in front of him like a shield. Bones
swerved, smashing into the ground instead of her. Dirt flew up as
if a bomb went off.

Then, something hard and heavy landed on Bones's back
before pain rocketed between his shoulder blades. Bones flew up,
twisting at the same time. That weight fell off, but the pain
remained, bringing new, burning weakness with it.

Only one thing could do that. He'd been stabbed with silver.
Bones clawed at his back as that dangerous weakness grew.
Blasted knife must be grazing his heart. He had to get it out before
he dropped like a stone from the sky.

Two vampires were now below him: Hennessey, and a brown-
haired bloke Bones had never seen before. The car's now-open
boot explained the other vampire's sudden appearance.
Hennessey hadn't gone to the club alone. He'd had a bodyguard
hiding in his trunk the entire time.

Hennessey and the other vampire leapt up, trying to grab
Bones. Both failed. Flying was a rare ability and neither of them

had it. Bones reached for the blade in his back again, snapping tendons to hyperextend his arm. He'd managed to yank it free when Hennessey flung more silver knives at him. Bones spun and most of them missed, but one drilled him in the shoulder.

Fuck this.

Bones dove at Hennessey. This time, Hennessey wasn't close enough to Cat to use her as a shield. Bones plowed into Hennessey, driving them both into the dirt. The impact sent the knife deeper into Bones's shoulder. Pain splashed him like acid, but Bones didn't care. If he'd taken the time to pull it out, Hennessey would've had time to run.

A rush of air behind Bones made him suddenly release Hennessey and fly straight up. He wouldn't let himself get jumped twice. Hennessey's bodyguard crashed into his boss instead of Bones. From Hennessey's pained howl, the bodyguard had stabbed Hennessey, too. Perfect.

Bones leapt onto both of them. The trio ended up rolling across the ground in a punishing tangle of limbs that scissored the knife deeper into Bones's shoulder. His flesh shredded and agony exploded within him, but Bones managed to get an arm around the bodyguard's neck. One brutal yank later, and the other vampire's headless body went limp.

In the seconds it took Bones to do that, Hennessey had wrested free. Bones jumped up, finally yanking the bloody knife from his shoulder. He held the blade in front of him as he and Hennessey faced each other. Hennessey's gaze was bright green, and he smelled of rage, blood, and the even more satisfying stench of fear.

A sod like Hennessey hated a fair fight. Bones grinned as he tightened his grip on the knife—

Buh-bum...buh...bum...buh...

Cat's slowing heartbeat crashed through Bones's bloodlust.

Hennessey heard it, too, and bared his teeth in a feral smile. "You can save her or fight me, but you can't do both."

155

Filthy jackal was right. Cat's heart was skipping beats now. Bones only had seconds before it stopped altogether.

"Run, you bastard," Bones said between gritted teeth.

Hennessey turned and fled so fast that dirt and asphalt churned up behind him.

Bones waited only another second to ensure that Hennessey didn't turn back around and attack him. Then, he flew to Cat.

Blood coated the front of her in trails that slowed along with her fading pulse. Bones slashed his wrist and held the gaping wound over Cat's mouth, willing his blood into her. It overflowed her mouth and spilled down her face, but she didn't swallow, and her heartbeat skidded to a stop.

Fear drenched Bones, colder than the ice he used to deaden his emotions. He had to get his blood into her veins *right now*.

He sliced his wrist again, filling Cat's mouth with more blood. Then, he tilted her head back and massaged her neck until it drained down her throat. After that, Bones pounded on her chest, forcing her heart to pump his blood through her body.

"Come on, Kitten," he urged hoarsely. "Don't you dare leave me. Come back to me, come back, come back!"

Her heart sputtered to a start. Its sound rivaled symphonies for sheer beauty. Relief hit him with such force he felt dizzy as she coughed, and then tried to spit his blood out.

"Stop it! You know I hate that," she garbled out.

If she was complaining, then she was truly all right. Bones pulled her against him, thinking he'd never ask God for anything again.

"You scared the wits out of me, Kitten. Your heart...slowed."

He couldn't bring himself to say "stopped." Not yet. The memory was too raw.

"Where's Hennessey?" Cat murmured. Then, her head tilted toward the headless bodyguard. "And who's that?"

Bones couldn't tell her he'd let Hennessey escape to save her.

Knowing Cat, she'd either feel guilty about that or berate him for it. A modified version of the truth was in order.

"Blasted sod ran away. After I pulled Hennessey off you, we were going at it when the boot opened and this fellow popped out. Hennessey had him hiding there as his bodyguard. Bugger put up a hell of a fight, too. Hennessey took off while I fought him. When I was finished, I saw that you were barely breathing, so I opened up a vein. You really should have more," Bones added, angling to look at her. "You're still pale as death."

"No," she said, her mouth crinkling. "Ugh."

Her heartbeat *was* slower than normal, but at least it was steady now. A good night's sleep should have Cat back to normal, but first...what had caused her brush with death to begin with?

"What happened with Hennessey? Thought you were just pretending and taking it very far to goad me. Worked as well, that's why I was almost on him when your page went off. Did he catch you unawares?"

Cat's head lolled back onto his shoulder.

"I don't know. I felt sick when I got into Hennessey's car... wait, no, that's wrong. I felt sick before, at the club."

And you didn't tell me? Bones almost roared, but he caught himself. Plenty of time to hammer that point home later.

"It started when we were dancing," Cat went on. "I felt kinda... drunk, I guess. Everything was blurry and the lights seemed far off. After a while it got better, but by the time I left with Hennessey it was so much worse. My legs wouldn't work and my mind...I couldn't think. I even forgot about the panic button in the watch until it tangled in my hair. Do you think Hennessey drugged me? Maybe he knew what we were up to?"

Bones twisted so he was facing Cat. He'd been so focused on her heartbeat before that he hadn't bothered looking into her eyes. Now, he did, and fury filled him.

"Your pupils are dilated enough to belong on a corpse. You've been drugged, all right." Heavily, but her description didn't fit the timeline. "You say you felt it when we were dancing? That doesn't make sense. Hennessey wasn't there then."

Cat slowly shook her head while a soft sound of disgust left her. "It wasn't Hennessey. It was those boys."

"What boys?" Bones asked instantly.

"Ralphie and Martin, the ones you told to scram when you first sat at the bar. They handed me a drink before you got there, and they gave me another one later, when Hennessey went to find you. Those little pricks, they tried to pull me out to their car. They looked so surprised when I wouldn't come…"

Cat's voice trailed off, and she sagged against him while her eyes closed.

"Need to sleep," she mumbled. "So tired."

Bones lifted her up, the gentle movement at complete odds with the fury blasting through him.

I'll bathe in their blood before I kill them.

"You can sleep," was what Bones said. "You're safe now."

Soft snores hit his chest in reply. She was already out.

Just as well. They had to leave now. Hennessey might return with reinforcements. At least asleep, Cat wouldn't be upset when Bones flew them out of there.

Bones balanced her against him with one arm, and grabbed the dead vampire with his free hand. He wasn't leaving him behind. His body might have useful information, starting with his mobile phone.

24

*B*ones laid Cat in his bed and tucked the covers over her. She snuggled deeper into them, but her eyes didn't open. She'd only woken for a moment while he was burying Hennessey's bodyguard after he'd stripped him of anything he could use to track Hennessey. Then, she'd passed out again. Her pulse was still steady, though, so she was out of danger.

Now that she was, time to put other people *in* danger.

Bones grabbed his tactical belt, which was laden with silver throwing knives and silver daggers. After his run-in with Hennessey, he wasn't going anywhere unarmed. Then, Bones drove his Ducati back to the club. No need to waste his strength flying if he didn't have to. Once there, he parked the bike near the entrance and strode up to Trixie, who gaped at his weapons.

"What are you thinking, Bones? You know the rules—"

"And two of your guests broke them," he interrupted her.

Green flashed in Trixie's eyes. "That's a serious accusation. Do you have proof?"

"I will. Don't fret; I won't kill them on the premises."

Trixie still didn't move from his path.

Bones let his gaze turn to the hard, flat one he used when he killed. He liked Trixie, but one way or the other, he was getting in there and finding the pricks who'd drugged Cat.

"Don't make me regret this," Trixie finally said, and stepped aside.

Bones nodded, and went inside the club.

Bite was even more packed than it had been when he left. That's right, it was now midnight. Prime foraging hour both for the undead, and for humans seeking supernatural thrills.

Bones went straight to the bars. That's where the sods would be, if they were still here. Bones had only glimpsed them twice, but with his memory, that was enough.

The one who'd tugged Cat's hand had sand-colored hair, hazel eyes, and a dimpled chin. The one who'd pushed her on the shoulders had brown hair, light blue eyes, and a cowlick that tumbled onto his forehead. Both were in their early twenties; both were white—and both would die screaming.

Yet neither of them were at the lower level bars or on the dance floor. Bones went to the second floor, searching there. Nothing. The third floor was reserved exclusively for ghouls and vampires, but Bones checked there anyway. No sign of them.

They must have left. No matter, he had another way to track them. It might burn a bridge with a friend, but he didn't care.

Bones went back to the third floor, where humans weren't allowed. In the most exclusive part of the club, where a private balcony overlooked all three floors, a tall, muscled ghoul with buckeye-brown skin, a well-manicured afro, and deep brown eyes surveyed the patrons below. He was dressed in a blue velvet suit with multicolored coattails that fanned out with such peacock-like extravagance, fashion icon Billie Porter would weep with envy. He didn't have guards blocking the entrance to his sumptuous, theater-style box, either. He didn't need any. No one disturbed the owner of *Bite* without a very good reason.

"Verses," Bones greeted him.

The ghoul turned, a faint smile curling his mouth. "I've been expecting you. Trixie said you were out for blood."

"I am, and I have something to show you," Bones said.

A thick brow arched, but Verses inclined his head in the universal gesture for, *well, then, lead on.*

Bones went past the other crowded, elegant rooms that made up the third floor, turning at the service hallway. Behind him, Verses said nothing, which was unusual. Normally, Verses was hard to silence. It's how he'd gotten his chosen name: Verses, for all the poetry the burly ghoul loved to recite.

The service hallway dead-ended in a door marked "storage." Bones opened it and went inside the small, cluttered space. Cleaning supplies lined the walls in shelves from floor to ceiling. Bones turned, and beckoned Verses to join him.

A snort left the ghoul. "You might be extraordinarily handsome, but no on the closet quickie offer."

"Not what I had in mind either, mate," Bones said in a genial voice. "I'm here for this."

Bones twisted a Lysol bottle with a peeled-off label three times to the right. The shelf-lined wall behind him moved back and to the side, revealing another room. This one was state of the art, with several large tv screens mounted on the walls that revealed live video feed from all levels of the club.

The hiss Verses made would've done a seething feline proud. "You're not supposed to know about this room."

Bones snorted. "And you're not supposed to have it. Your business would take quite the hit if your patrons knew the club you advertise as a safe place for immortals featured secret surveillance video."

"Amanda," Verses muttered, shaking his head. "She showed you this, didn't she? Faithless employee, I'm glad she quit."

Bones shrugged. "Faithless wife, too, yet her husband wasn't faithful, either, so turnabout's fair play."

Verses folded his arms. The gesture made his thick muscles bulge against his velvet suit. Bones raised a brow.

"No need to be intimidating. I'm not here to blackmail you. On the contrary, I'm here to help you."

"How?" Verses asked with open suspicion.

"Two humans violated your rules right under your nose tonight. Let me access those cameras, and I'll show you."

Verses's nostrils flared and his gaze went cold. He hadn't kept *Bite* as a supernatural haven for the past seven decades because he was a weakling. The ghoul was probably mentally seasoning the humans for maximum tastiness right now.

"Show me," Verses said, and closed the storage door behind him.

They only needed to rewind the first-floor cameras two hours to find the footage. There was no audio, but none was needed. Bones caught what Cat hadn't seen when the brunet lad dropped his wallet and she helped him retrieve it—the sandy-haired boy emptying a tiny vial into her glass.

"Those little bastards," Verses growled.

"Indeed," Bones said, mouth tightening when he got to the next interaction between Cat and the boys.

Bloody hell, Kitten, you drank what two strangers gave you just because they were human? If a vampire had handed you that glass, you would've hurled it to the floor!

"That was unwise," Verses said, echoing Bones's thoughts.

Bones stiffened. He could criticize Cat. No one else could. "Or she was too trusting of your rules promising that no unwilling interactions were allowed on the premises."

Verses bristled, but his voice was even when he said, "Thank you for showing me this. It will be dealt with."

"By me," Bones said instantly.

"Are you asking me to hire you?" Verses said with a laugh.

Bones smiled even as he felt that familiar ice fill him.

"I'm not asking. You *are* hiring me, and my price is deleting all the footage with the redhead, plus you show me the parking lot footage you're pretending not to have."

"*Damn* Amanda," Verses said with a sigh. "Did she tell you that my favorite drink is a Shirley Temple, too?"

"The footage," Bones prodded in a steely tone. "I'll give you their bodies when I'm done. String them up like holiday garland to show what happens to those who break your rules."

A gleam appeared in the ghoul's gaze. Verses must be weighing the advantages of people believing he'd hired an infamous hitman to take care of this. It was common knowledge that Bones only took contracts on the undead. People would think Verses must have paid Bones a fortune to break that stance with these humans, enforcing Verses's image as a club owner not to be fucked with.

"Deal," Verses finally said. Then, a small smile touched his mouth. "The redhead must be quite important to you."

"The parking lot footage," Bones replied, his gaze warning Verses not to press him any further about that.

Verses sighed again, but five minutes later, Bones watched the two boys support a barely-conscious blonde girl between them as they left the club. Then, they loaded her into the back of a white utility van with Indiana plates, and sped off. The timestamp on the video was thirty-six minutes ago.

"Why didn't you stop this yourself?" Bones's voice was low and savage. "It's clear the girl didn't willingly go with them."

"First I've seen this," Verses replied, sounding angry himself now. "You see that this room is empty. No one monitors the video feeds as they come in since I do value my patrons' privacy. I only view them later if needed, which is rare."

Bones had to move fast, but one more thing still needed to be done. "Erase all the footage with the redhead now."

He wouldn't leave any trace for Hennessey to follow to find Cat. If Amanda had told Bones about the club's secret surveillance footage, she might have told someone else, too.

Verses's mouth quirked. "Making me do it in front of you? Don't you trust me?"

"Trust is only for circumstances I *can't* control," Bones replied with a glacial smile.

Verses grunted. "On that, we agree."

Verses erased the footage. As soon as he did, Bones left the fake storage room.

"Make their deaths painful," Verses called after him.

Bones's jaw tightened.

Oh, he would.

25

*L*ess than an hour later, Bones dropped out of the sky and landed near the club's entrance. Trixie stared at him while several of the humans still waiting to get inside screamed.

Bones didn't blame them. He had two bodies dangling beneath his arms, both in various stages of gruesomeness, and that wasn't even counting his own appearance.

"Verses is expecting these," Bones said while dropping the bodies near Trixie's feet.

She stepped back with a yelp as blood spattered her shoes. "Watch it! These heels are Renee Caovilla!"

"Tell Verses I left their van off the highway two cities over," Bones went on. "A girl's body is inside it."

Trixie's gaze hardened. She knew Bones wasn't responsible for that death. She kicked the body nearest her, no longer concerned about her expensive shoes. It bounced against the club's exterior with a bloody splat.

Many of the humans turned and ran. The few that remained muttered among themselves.

"This is what happens if you break the rules!" Trixie shouted.

Ah, Verses had filled her in on what happened. "Any of you fuckers try to roofie a drink *here*, and you'll be next!" she finished, and kicked the second body at the remaining humans.

They scattered as if running from a grenade. Still, several were hit with gore since the bodies were messy. Bones hadn't been able to save the girl, so he'd torn into her murderers. Literally.

Trixie then turned to him. "Come inside. I'll get you a drink, and we have a place where you can clean up."

Bones shook his head. "Can't. I have somewhere else to be, but do mind my bike for me. Have to leave it here tonight."

Trixie grunted. "Will do, but you should think twice about going anywhere like that. You look like you rolled around the floor of a slaughterhouse."

He did have the blood of five different people on him, but he had business to attend to that couldn't wait.

"I'm good, Trixie. Until again."

Bones flew off, not waiting for her reply.

In case Hennessey had sent spies to the club that *could* fly, Bones double-backed several times and landed on a hotel's roof before taking the stairs down and exiting another way. Only when he was sure he wasn't being followed did he go to Ted's.

Bones had already warned Ted to meet him out front so his appearance didn't upset Ted's husband. Ted was on his front porch swing when Bones landed, and he whistled when he saw him.

"Glad you said to keep Bruce inside. He'd have nightmares after seein' you. Some sumbitch must've pissed you off good."

"Two murdering rapists and the tosser who owned this," Bones replied, handing the dead bodyguard's mobile phone to Ted. "I need everything you can tell me about what and who are on it. Double the rate I normally pay you for the sleep you'll lose to do this now."

Ted smiled. "I'm a night owl anyway, but I'll take the extra money since you didn't raise a fool."

"True, that," Bones said with a laugh. "Thanks, mate."

He left, at last able to return to Cat. He needed to hear her heartbeat, feel her breathe, and soak up her warmth to reassure himself that she was still very much alive, unlike the poor lass he'd left behind in that van. His impatience made the half hour flight feel like it took hours.

When Bones reached the cave, he ran at a hunch through the low-roofed section at the beginning, able to straighten at the fork in the rock that led to his living area. But when he saw the stone pillar that covered his bedroom doorway, he paused.

Snores drifted out to him through the thick rock. Hearing them eased the knot of worry inside him. Cat was fine, but she wouldn't remain that way if she woke up and saw him like this.

Bones went to the underground river, taking off only his boots and weapons before wading into the frigid water. The mini waterfall he used as a shower wouldn't be enough this time. When he was fully submerged in the water, he stripped off all his clothes and let the current carry them away. No detergent was strong enough to get out *these* stains.

Bones washed until he couldn't scent blood on himself anymore. Then, he toweled dry as he walked toward his bedroom. Louder snores greeted him once he moved the stone aside. Cat lay almost exactly where he'd left her. Only her face peeked out from the blankets, red smears marring her flawless skin from where his blood had overflowed her mouth.

Bones dabbed the smears with his wet towel so she wouldn't see them once she awoke. When they were gone, he threw the towel aside and climbed into bed next to her. As soon as his arms settled around her, he had one clear, resounding thought:

I'm home.

Most people thought home was a place. Bones had lived long enough to know better. It was being with the people you belonged to, and Bones hadn't belonged to anyone in centuries. Now, he belonged to her, and he'd nearly lost her tonight.

A chill enveloped him that had nothing to do with his icy bath. Two more minutes, and he might have been too late to save her... unless he did something she'd never, ever forgive him for. God help him, he probably would have, too. All those centuries he'd resented Ian for siring him without his permission, and here Bones might have followed in Ian's footsteps.

Cat would hate him for it if he did. Hell, Bones would hate himself, but it wouldn't matter. He was strong enough to stand many things. Her death wasn't one of them.

And things would get even more dangerous now that Hennessey realized Bones knew about his dirty enterprise. Bones had to keep Cat away from that danger, but how? She wouldn't stop hunting vampires, and Bones couldn't stop hunting Hennessey.

Answers evaded him. Perhaps sleep would clear his head.

Bones tucked Cat tighter against him. Her warmth made up for the blankets she wasn't sharing, her heartbeat vibrated against his chest, and her snores tickled the arms he'd wrapped around her.

His passion. His love. His home.

And his downfall, if he couldn't keep her safe. He had to find a way without trying to change who she was. God knew it hadn't worked when people had tried to change him.

That was a problem for later. Now, at last, he could rest.

Bones closed his eyes and slept.

Cat's shriek sent Bones bolting out of bed. He had no idea how long he'd slept or how someone could have snuck into the cave without him knowing it, but Cat sounded so horrified that someone *must* have broken in.

"What's wrong?" he demanded, cursing himself for not bringing his weapons into the bedroom. "Someone's here?"

Cat shook her head no. Relief barely settled in when she gave him a fraught look.

"I don't remember getting into bed with you. Now, I'm wearing your shirt instead of my dress, and you're...you're...did something happen between us? Tell me the truth."

She'd shrieked him awake to accuse him of *that*?

Bones got back into bed, too disgusted to answer. Cat left the bed at once, which only increased his ire.

"Think I'd shag you while you were passed out cold? That I'm no better than those buggers who doctored your drink? Your dress was ripped off and covered in blood and vomit, so I put my shirt on you and let you sleep while I went back to the club."

"Oh," she said with such relief that his teeth ground. "But then why are *you* naked?"

"Because after I finished with your little boys and handled other business, it was dawn, I was knackered, and my clothes were a bloody mess, so I stripped them off and fell into bed. Didn't pause to think about donning jammies, sorry."

She winced at the scorn in his tone, but then concern knit her brows again.

"How did you 'finish' with the boys? What happened to Ralphie and Martin?"

"Fretting about them?" Bones asked in disbelief. "Why don't you ask if they found a new girl to ply their potions with? Ask what happened to *her*, unless you're too anxious over their welfare to bother about that."

Cat paled so much Bones braced to catch her if she fainted.

"They drugged someone else?" she whispered. "Is she okay?"

Now he regretted bringing this up, but it was too late.

"No, she is not okay. Since you didn't go down after two doses of their filthy concoction, they tripled it. About the same time Hennessey was munching on your neck, those lads were picking out a new lass. It was their own stupidity to drive her only a mile away from the club. When I went back to look for Hennessey, I came upon their van in the woods."

No need to specify how he'd known what vehicle they drove, or that he'd gone back exclusively to kill them. Hennessey was too smart to return to the club, more's the pity.

"One was on top of the girl while the other waited his turn. Neither realized she was already dead from too much drugs. I snapped the spine of the lad doing the rooting"—tore it out, actually, but Cat was pale enough already—"which scared the other lad right good. He sang, said he and his pal made sport of slipping girls drugs and then dumping them once they were finished. They preferred girls from vampire clubs because those girls tended not to report any crimes."

How could they tell the police they were at a vampire *club without being called insane?* Ralphie had said, sounding smug because Bones had compelled Ralphie to tell only the truth, and the shite was proud of his perceived cleverness. That pride had quickly turned to horror. Bones freed Ralphie from the power in his gaze before he killed him. That way, the wretch was fully aware of what was happening when Bones tore into him.

"He cried when I told him the girl was dead. Said they weren't *supposed* to die, only lie there. Those were his last words before I ripped his throat out." And his heart, and his intestines, but who was counting? "After that, I went to the club and left their bodies for the owner, who does not take to such activities. Did those snits an underserved favor by killing them quickly. The owner would have drawn it out for weeks as a warning to anyone else stupid enough to try that trick."

Much as Bones would have enjoyed that, Ralphie and Martin had to die before Verses got his hands on them. Bones couldn't have them give Verses any details about Cat that could endanger her later.

Cat sat back on the bed, her head dropping into her hands.

"What about the girl?" she asked in a pained voice. "What did you do with her?"

"Drove the van away and parked it off the highway elsewhere. Someone's probably found it by now. Police will discover who it's registered to, and assume the same sods who drugged and raped her fled after she overdosed. It won't be the first time something like this has happened."

"At least her parents will get her back." Cat's head was still bent, and now, her shoulders trembled. "They won't have to wonder what happened to her for the rest of their lives…"

Cat's voice trailed off, and then she didn't speak for several moments. Neither did Bones. A moment of silence was the least that poor dead girl and her family deserved.

"What about Hennessey?" Cat finally asked, trying to compose herself with visible effort. "What do you think he'll do? Try something, or keep running?"

Bones grunted. "Oh, Hennessey will try something. He knows I'm after him now. He only suspected that before, but now he has proof. When and where, I have no idea. He might lie low for a bit, or he might come at me straightaway."

"It's my fault that Hennessey got away," Cat said, sounding miserable again. "God, I was so stupid not to notice that something was wrong with me until it was too late."

Her voice broke. Bones came over and touched her shoulders. "It's *not* your fault, Kitten."

It was his. He should have stuck to his instincts to keep her away from Hennessey no matter what she said.

She leaned toward him, abruptly stiffened, and then jumped out of bed as if the mattress had burned her. Bones watched, perplexed, as she then faced the wall instead of him.

"Bones, I have to thank you," Cat said in a newly brisk tone. "You saved my life. I passed out right after pushing that button, and Hennessey would have bled me dry. But you know the only reason I was so…so forward with you was because of the drugs they slipped me. You know that, right? Of course, I don't blame you for taking me up on it. I'm sure it meant nothing to you. I-I just want you to know it meant nothing to me as well."

Oh. She. Did. *Not.*

"Turn 'round," Bones said in a very controlled tone.

She moved closer to the stone blocking the doorway instead. "Um, can you move this so I can get out of here and—"

"Turn *around*," he snapped.

She did with the reluctance of a condemned prisoner facing a firing squad.

Bones sprang to her side. Cat's cheeks darkened and she stared at his face as if looking any lower would cause her eyes to explode.

"I'm not comfortable with you being naked," she muttered.

"Why?" Anger turned his voice to acid. "You just said I meant nothing to you beyond mere gratitude, and you've seen a man's body before, so what could be bothering you? I know what's bothering *me*. What's bothering *me* is that you dare stand there and tell me what I do and do not feel about last night. That kissing you and touching you meant nothing to me, and to top it off, that you only responded to me because you were impaired! That's rich."

He didn't care about Charles's admonition to bite his tongue when emotions overruled his logic. Didn't bother about her being a full two centuries younger than he, and inexperienced even without that discrepancy. Right then, all that kept reverberating through Bones's mind was how she'd described what happened between them last night.

...meant nothing to me...nothing to me...nothing to me...

His temper snapped. "You know what those drugs did to you in that first dose, before the second one made you comatose? They finally killed the bug up your arse!"

Her jaw dropped with indignation. Bones turned and snatched the stone away from the doorway. "Out you go, before I lose my temper and we'll see how much you *don't* like to kiss me."

Cat gave a quick look at this mouth, and her scent flared with a new headiness. The part of her that *had* responded last night, drugs be damned, was almost daring him to do it.

He wouldn't. She'd ask him to kiss her before he did again. Hell, she'd beg him, if he were still anywhere near this angry.

"Out," he repeated.

Without another word, she left.

26

*T*ed found few leads from the dead bodyguard's mobile. It was a burner phone, so the owner's identity was still a mystery. Most of the calls the bodyguard had made were to burner phones, too. But everyone got sloppy. The bodyguard was no exception.

Bones spent the first half of his week following up on the two calls that weren't made to other burner phones. One of them led nowhere, but the other led to a trucker who'd recently been fired after taking a company rig on an unauthorized joyride. The trucker didn't remember doing it, either. All he remembered was having a beer at his favorite pub, and then waking up two states away in his company's tractor-trailer.

Under the power of Bones's gaze, the poor bloke remembered what the dead bodyguard had made him forget: he hadn't gone on a drunken joy ride. He'd been compelled to steal the eighteen-wheeler, drive it to a home supply store, and wait while the back was filled with unknown cargo. Then, he'd driven it to a dockside warehouse in Chicago, where two other vampires had unloaded the trailer's contents.

That's when the driver had glimpsed the girls. He'd only seen them for a second, and it had been very dark, so he had no useful descriptions to give Bones. But their presence was enough. So was the address of the warehouse.

Bones arrived at the warehouse that same night. It was still too late. The place was empty, and far cleaner than any warehouse should be, especially one located on the seedier side of Chicago's docks. All Bones smelled was bleach, ammonia, and other cleaning chemicals while not so much as a spare construction nail had been left on the premises.

Hennessey must have guessed that Bones would track his former bodyguard back to this place. Bones was only surprised that Hennessey hadn't arranged an ambush for him there, too. Hennessey was either being very cautious, or he'd run out of time to arrange a surgical cleaning of the warehouse *and* an ambush large enough to take Bones down.

Once again, Bones made sure no one followed him when he returned home. If he hadn't come from a line of Master vampires with flying abilities, he'd have a much more difficult time losing a possible tail. Still, inherited traits only gave a vampire the *chance* to have them. Abilities like flying had to be earned through strength and sheer will.

Bones needed both those traits to deal with a certain lovely redhead. Cat was supposed to meet him Wednesday night, but Bones decided to use their fight to put some distance between them. Right now, he had to focus on Hennessey. Cat wanted to keep denying what she felt? He'd let her by saying he was going out of town a few weeks, and their vampire hunting was on pause until he returned. She'd probably be delighted.

Wednesday night, Bones had an envelope of "vacation" cash for Cat to spend while he was supposedly away. Hopefully, she'd be too busy shopping to think about vampire hunting on her own.

Eight o'clock came and went with no sign of Cat. Then nine, and then ten. Bones rang her. It went straight to voicemail.

Bugger this.

He flew to her house. The small, barnlike structure had a gnarled oak tree close enough for Bones to hide in while he sent his senses inside. Four heartbeats, two slower from age, and two the normal rhythms of younger adults.

Then, he heard Cat's voice. "Be up later, Mom!"

"Don't watch tv all night again," Justina replied, followed by boards creaking as her mum climbed the stairs. Then, Bones saw her through the window of the room she shared with Cat.

Justina Crawfield looked nothing like her daughter. Her hair was a rich brown, her skin a tanned taupe, and she was three inches shorter and about two stone heavier. Lovely in her own right, yes, but ugly in Bones's eyes for how she'd hurt Cat.

Truth be told, he didn't fancy Cat's grandparents, either. *At night, I could hear them whispering about me,* Cat had said about her unintentional eavesdropping as a child. Her grandparents didn't seem to have warmed up much since. Why, they still made Cat and her mum share a room despite there being an office they could have converted into a third bedroom. God knew her gramps didn't use it anymore. Cat and her mum had handled all the administrative aspects of the orchard for several years.

Bones ducked behind a thicker branch when Cat came into the bedroom moments later.

"'Night, Mom," Cat said as she got into her bed.

Her heartbeat proved that Cat wasn't tired, but her mum had admonished her not to stay up late, so she'd gone to bed despite this being the beginning the evening for many humans her age, let alone one that was half vampire.

Bones's anger drained away. Once again, Cat was trying *so hard* to please people who should have loved her without such efforts. No wonder she was such shite at admitting her feelings for him. She kept getting them stomped on by everyone else.

Bones inhaled, catching Cat's scent through the open window. Her natural honey and cream fragrance was marred by the sharper aroma of darker emotions. She was upset. More family rejection? Or was she regretting not coming to him tonight?

Even if she was, her absence was for the best. When Cat eventually did come around, Bones would give her his vacation excuse. Until then, he'd give her the space she needed while he continued his hunt for Hennessey.

Goodnight, Kitten, Bones thought, ignoring a pang as he flew away. Leaving her might hurt, but not as much as seeing her bleeding out had. With luck, this would only take a few more weeks. He could stand to be away from her that long.

Probably.

Bones forced himself not to think about Cat by wrapping himself in his familiar, numbing inner chilliness. It worked until Friday night, when he answered his mobile and heard Cat's frantic voice spill over the line.

"Bones, I-I just killed someone!"

His ice shattered like it had never existed. "Where are you?"

She told him.

"Don't move," Bones said, and left at once.

27

The address Cat gave him led to an apartment complex near the university. It was six stories high, with exterior stairs instead of elevators, and lots of windows decorated with Ohio State University paraphernalia. More importantly, it had no exterior security cameras.

Ted could have the night off.

Bones went straight to room 606. The door was locked, but one hard twist of the knob opened it. He went inside—and cursed. The place stank of blood, death, and vampires. One scent in particular stunned him. Hennessey's.

What the *hell* had Cat gotten herself into?

Bones's gaze swept the living room. Upscale furnishings, state of the art computers, designer shoes near the door, and a two-thousand-dollar purse on the counter. No weapons, though, and no one here except Cat, whose heartbeat clamored like someone banging away on steel drums in the next room.

Bones went into the bedroom. Cat knelt on the floor by the wall. She only wore a tee shirt and panties. Her jeans were on the floor near the body of a pretty, petite girl with brown hair and a large bullet hole in her chest.

Bones picked up the gun Cat had discarded. It had a silencer, which explained why none of the neighbors had called the police. Saved him from mesmerizing a bunch of people. Bones unloaded it, and then put it into the bag he'd brought. Cat barely seemed to notice. She had yet to even speak. She might be able to lop off a vampire's head while whistling a merry tune, but she'd killed a human, and she was in shock.

Bones only felt anger. From the signs of struggle, angle of the girl's body, and the close-contact nature of the wound, the girl had been fighting with Cat for control of the gun when she was shot. Certainly nothing less than fear of getting shot herself would've caused Cat to kill her.

Bones knelt in front of her. "What have you touched?"

The simplicity of the question reached through her stupor.

"Umm, the phone. Maybe the dresser, her nightstand...and the closet door. That's it, I think. I'd just gotten here when Stephanie started acting nuts and saying these awful things..."

Bones took Cat's mobile phone, purse and keys. He didn't trust that she'd remember to take them with her. She might be talking, but her gaze was too wide, and if she were anywhere near herself, she would have snatched at her trousers by now.

Bones handed them to her. "Put these on. We can't linger. One of them could return any moment."

"One of whom?" she asked while woodenly complying. "Stephanie said she didn't have any roommates."

Bones filled his bag as he answered her. "This place stinks of vampires. We need to leave before they return."

"Vampires?" Cat repeated it as if she'd never heard the word before. "Stephanie wasn't a vampire—"

"What did she say about Hennessey?" Bones interrupted.

Cat's gaze grew wider. "What? Hennessey has nothing to do with this!"

"Like hell," Bones muttered, quickly checking for surveillance devices. So far, none. Good. Now, for the body.

Bones yanked the thick blanket off the bed and began rolling Stephanie's body into it. When he had her stuffed like a sausage into a crescent roll, he set her aside and continued to fill his bag with anything that might prove useful. Stephanie had a mobile phone, an iPad, and a laptop...that was open.

Bones checked it. No password required. Arrogant chit.

Bones tucked the laptop into his jacket. Ted could have the rest. Looks like Ted wouldn't get the night off after all.

"Hennessey's one of the vampires I smell here," Bones said. "Him, or someone who had recent, close contact with him."

Cat started to rub her forehead, stopped when she saw the blood on her hands, and then stared at them.

"'Out, out, damned spot,'" she whispered.

Quoting Shakespeare's *Macbeth*? She must be in shock.

Bones finished checking the other rooms for additional items before he wiped down the surfaces to erase Cat's fingerprints. When he was finished, he handed her his bag.

"Take this, luv."

She did, still moving as if she were on automatic pilot. Bones gave a critical look at the blanket-wrapped body. Good thing Stephanie was slight of build. The comforter covered her completely, and none of her blood had leaked out yet.

Bones slung Stephanie's bundled-up body over his shoulder before grabbing the nearby laundry hamper with his other hand. Anyone looking at him could surmise that he was just a bloke headed to the Laundromat for wash day.

"Nice and quick to your truck, Kitten," he instructed her. "Don't look around; don't speak. Just march right to it and get in the passenger seat. I'll be right behind you."

She obeyed without argument—more proof her shock.

Thankfully, the few residents they passed seemed focused on their own business, so Bones didn't need to stop and mesmerize anyone on their way out. When they reached the parking lot, Cat got into the passenger side of her truck, and Bones put Stephanie's body and the laundry basket in the back before laying his motorcycle over them. Now, no concern that they'd fly off if he hit a rut in the road. Then, Bones got in the front and drove them away.

∿

"Hey, bud," Ted said when he pulled up next to them thirty minutes later. Bones had parked along the side of the road to wait for Ted. Cat still didn't speak. She just kept staring at her bloody hands.

Bones got out of the truck. "Prompt as ever, mate."

"Whatcha got for me?" Ted asked, not sounding annoyed at having yet another evening interrupted. Bones made a mental note to triple Ted's usual pay.

"Electronics for a full scan, plus dinner for whichever ghoul you feel like rewarding. Make sure they clean their plate, though. I don't want a single piece of her resurfacing."

Ted's brow arched at "her." He knew Bones didn't kill human women, and ghouls only ate humans.

But all Ted said was, "Sure thing, bud. Anything I should warn them about?"

Bones deposited the body and the bag of electronics into Ted's boot. "Tell them not to chip a tooth on the bullet."

Cat's door opened, and she retched onto the ground. Understanding flashed over Ted's features as he looked at her, and then at the body in his trunk.

"Ah. Makes sense now. She going to be all right?"

Bones sighed. Cat revered human life, so no, she wouldn't recover from this anytime soon.

"She will be," Bones settled on. "Have to be off, mate. Thanks again, and let me know what you find."

Cat finished retching by the time Ted left. Bones took his flask

181

from his jacket and handed it to her. "Whisky. Not your favorite, but it's all I've got."

She snatched at the bottle, downing it with the same thoroughness as the night he'd captured her. When she was finished, she let out an extended sigh.

"Better?" Bones asked.

Cat closed her eyes. "Yeah."

Then, her eyes snapped open, and she looked more like herself than she had since he'd first arrived.

"No more cryptic shit. Who is Hennessey, and what does he have to do with a gun-toting psychotic from my physics class?"

Bones didn't care for the line of questioning, but he was glad of her new fortitude.

"Physics? You met her at college?" he asked as he drove back onto the road.

"Why don't you answer my questions *first*, since I'm the one who was nearly shot tonight?"

Fair point. "Kitten, I will answer you, but please. Tell me how you met and what happened back there."

Her chin jutted out; shades of her usual stubbornness. For a moment, Bones thought she'd refuse.

Then, she spoke. "Stephanie took psychics with me, as I said. From day one, she'd wait for me after class. First, to ask me about lecture questions she'd missed, or for notes, but then, she talked about herself. Funny, inconsequential things, like boys she liked or places she went...she seemed so friendly. Then she asked about me, and I told her I'd just transferred from a community college, didn't know anyone on campus, came from a small town—the bitch was casing me!"

Outrage colored her tone as she belatedly realized what had occurred. Anger was a useful shield, and Cat needed her shields now. So did he, because now he knew why Stephanie's place stank like vampires in general and Hennessey in particular.

"Stephanie told me she was looking for someone disposable,

and I practically slapped a big red bow on my ass," Cat went on in disgust. "Tonight, she invited me over. Said we'd hang out and then go to a bar, but when I got there, she wanted me to change clothes. I'm so used to *you* complaining about how I dress, I didn't think anything of it until I was in my underwear and she started commenting on my body like I was…meat. When I tried to put my clothes back on, Stephanie pulled a gun on me."

Rage almost made Bones swerve off the road. Mercenary bitch had stripped Cat to make sure she was defenseless as well as to asses her "marketability." If not for Cat's dual species, it would have worked, too, as it doubtless had for many others.

"Did she mention anyone's name?" he asked in a calm tone.

"No," Cat said after a pause. "She said something about paying her rent and me being what her landlord liked. Then, she said college girls were all stupid and she should tape record her kidnapping speech to save herself the effort…but no names."

Bones's hand tightened on the steering wheel until the old metal dented. Of course colleges would be a plentiful hunting ground for Hennessey, and who better to work those grounds than another student? A *human female* student, no less. Bones wouldn't have looked twice at Stephanie for that very reason, making her the perfect operative for Hennessey's business.

Cat drummed her nails against the dashboard. "How is this related to Hennessey? You said you smelled him and other vampires there. Do you think he found out who I was from the other night? That he wanted to finish what he'd started?"

"No," Bones said while ice flashed over him. "Stephanie had been coddling up to you all week, you said. If Hennessey had found out who you were, he'd have snatched you up straightaway. You and anyone unlucky enough to be around you. That's why I asked what you touched, and then wiped her place down. Though you don't have prints on file"—Ted had made sure of that—"I want no trace of you left behind for Hennessey to follow."

Cat gave him a frustrated look. "If not because of last weekend, why would Stephanie be involved with Hennessey *or* try to kidnap me? It doesn't make sense!"

It did to Bones, and the irony wasn't lost on him. He'd let Cat run from him to keep her safe, and she'd nearly run right into the meat grinder of Hennessey's operation.

Bones parked on the furthest side of the woods from the cave. No headlights had shined behind him, but he was taking no chances.

"Let's sort this out inside the cave, Kitten. Gives us a chance to go through her things while we talk."

"Fine, but you *will* tell me what I want to know," she said.

Yes, he would. All of it.

28

*T*hankfully, Cat said nothing else as they walked through the wooded terrain, allowing Bones to concentrate on every crunch of leaves that wasn't from their footsteps. So far, the forest was empty of all except them and natural wildlife. Still, he was glad when they ducked under the low roof that marked the cave's entrance before taking the fork that eventually opened up to the cathedral-like living area. In this underground labyrinth, no one could sneak up on them.

Bones went to the sofas and emptied out the few items he hadn't given to Ted. He let the papers and notebooks fall onto the floor, but caught the laptop before it toppled out.

"Have you ever heard of the Bennington Triangle?" he asked Cat as he set it up.

"I've heard of the Bermuda one," she said, her tone warning Bones that she wasn't going to let him change the subject.

He wasn't, actually, but he'd get to that.

"Bloody girl didn't password protect *any* of her files," Bones marveled. "Pure arrogance, but that's in our favor. Look, there you are, Kitten. Under 'Potentials.' Be flattered, you were first on her list."

Cat peered over his shoulder, her mouth falling open as she read "Cathy—redhead—twenty-two" topping a list of nearly two dozen other names with ages and similar brief descriptions.

"Who are these girls? 'Potentials' for *what?*"

Bones kept opening files. Most were more victim lists, but at last, he found something useable.

"Ah, Charlie at Club Flame on Forty-Second Street. Sounds like a contact. Here's hoping the twit was thick enough to write their actual names instead of placeholder ones."

"Bones!" Cat said with seething impatience.

Right. He set the laptop aside. She deserved to know what she'd almost been killed over for the second time now.

"The Bennington Triangle is an area in Maine where several people disappeared back in the fifties. To this day, no trace of them has been found. A couple decades ago, mass disappearances took place around border towns in Mexico, including a friend's daughter. I found her remains months afterward in the desert, and when I say remains, I mean I only found pieces of her. She had to be identified by dental records. An autopsy revealed that she'd been alive for months before she was murdered, and when I investigated, I found that her death fit a pattern."

Cat frowned. "What type of pattern?"

Bones sighed. "Hundreds of women went missing or were murdered in Mexican border towns around that same time. Today, there's still not any real idea who did it. Then, a few years ago, hundreds of girls started to go missing in and around the Great Lakes area. More recently, it became centered in Ohio. Most vanished with no signs of foul play, and since they were presumed runaways, prostitutes, addicts, or other high-risk types, there wasn't much of a media fuss. It's why I came here. I believe Hennessey's involved. He was near all three places when the disappearances happened."

Cat's hand crept to her mouth in disbelief.

"You think Hennessey did all that? He can't eat that much if he tried! What is he, some kind of...undead Ted Bundy?"

"I think he's the ringleader, but he's not a traditional serial killer," Bones said grimly. "Hennessey's not killing these people himself. From the bits and pieces I've gathered over the years, I think he's made an industry out of them."

For a second, Cat looked confused. Then, understanding dawned, and with it, a look of pure horror.

"You think Hennessey's running a type of Uber Eats for vampires? Turning those people into an order-in meal service? My God, Bones, how could he get away with that?"

The short version? Hennessey had gambled on the general population's apathy, and thus far, he'd won.

"Hennessey was sloppy in Maine and Mexico, but he's gotten smarter. He doesn't merely choose women that society doesn't hold in high regard; he also sends vampires to prevent their disappearances from being reported at all. Remember those girls Winston told you about? They *are* all dead. I needed confirmation that there were more girls missing than being reported, and a ghost knows who's died even if those girls' families were all bitten into believing their daughters were backpacking across Europe, or moving in with a boyfriend, or whatever else."

Cat looked as if she'd throw up again. Bones didn't blame her. He'd been sickened by it, too, and he'd seen many terrible things in his life.

"Hennessey's getting away with it because people disappear all the time. Remember all the faces on milk cartons once upon a time? Even if the police know about the disappearances, they're too busy with crimes involving the rich, powerful, privileged, or internet famous to spend too much time on society's missing outcasts. As for the undead world, Hennessey's covered his tracks well. There's suspicion, but no proof."

Cat didn't speak for several moments. She was so pale that Bones was about to get her more whisky, but then she said, "You told me you'd been chasing Hennessey eleven years, so you've known what he was doing that entire time?"

"Didn't know what I was chasing at first," Bones admitted. "Took hunting down dozens of blokes to get a whisper of what was going on, and dozens more to get a name of who might be behind it. After that, I began picking apart Hennessey's people, but only the ones who had bounties on them. That way, Hennessey only thought it was business. Now, he knows I've uncovered his operation, which means so does whoever else is involved, because he can't be doing this alone."

Cat's gaze widened. "So, even if you kill Hennessey, it might not end because his partner or partners could pick up where he left off? And you don't have *any* idea who they are?"

He snorted at the mild critique in her tone. "I've come close a few times, but then...things happened."

"Like what?" she asked at once.

"Like you," he said mildly.

"Me?" Cat repeated in disbelief.

A dry laugh escaped him. "If I didn't know better, I'd swear you were one of Hennessey's because you have an incredibly bad habit of killing people before I can get any information out of them. Remember Devon, the bloke you staked the night we met? He was Hennessey's accountant. Knew everything about him, but you staked him before I could say Bob's your uncle. Then, you went after me the very next night. Why do you think I kept asking you who you worked for? Then tonight—"

"I didn't mean to kill Stephanie!" she burst out, giving a guilty look at the blood on her hands again.

Of course she hadn't, and now that they were safe, no need for her to marinate in that bitch's blood anymore.

Bones left the sofa for the wall that bordered the living area. On the other side of it, a small, enclosed spring acted as a natural form of sink. There, he grabbed soap, cloths, and a bowl that he held under the slow trickle of water. Didn't he have an extra shirt back here, too? Yes, he did.

"Believe me, luv, I know you wouldn't kill a human unless it was by accident or they were wearing a Vampire Henchman badge. Judging by the scene, you were wrestling with Stephanie when the gun went off. She probably had a good grip on it, too. From her scent, Stephanie was hyped up on vampire blood. Would have made her much stronger, which she'd need for her job."

More silence. For the best, really. If Bones kept thinking about what Stephanie had done, he'd raise the bitch as a ghoul just so he could murder her himself. She'd died with vampire blood in her system, so all he'd need to finish the transition was a ghoul willing to switch their heart with Stephanie's. With some vampire blood to reactivate it, Stephanie would rise as a ghoul...for a few terrible hours until Bones ripped her head off.

If he didn't think she knew little beyond her job of rounding up girls, he'd do it, too. But he already had Stephanie's contact, Charlie, plus a potential meeting place. Much as he'd enjoy murdering her, it would be wasted effort.

Still, it was tempting.

"Why didn't you tell me this before?" Cat's voice was very soft. Almost wounded sounding. "You trained me to fight, but then you kept me out of the most important fight."

Did she really not understand why?

"I didn't want you involved. I'd rather not go after vampires to begin with, but that's what you need to do, so I trained you to be better at it. Not like you'd listen if I told you to stop, would you? Still, Hennessey's operation was different. Your part was supposed to end with Sergio, but your little physics chit ruined that tonight. You should be patting yourself on the back for killing her. Those other 'potentials' would, if they knew what Stephanie had in store for them."

Cat drew in a sharp breath, as if she just realized that she hadn't merely saved her own life tonight.

"Was safety your only reason for keeping this from me?" she finally said. "Or is there more that I don't know?"

"No, there's one more reason. I didn't want to give more cause to hate vampires," Bones said with raw honesty. "Not like you aren't predisposed to it. You tend to judge people for what they are, rather than what they do, if they don't have a pulse."

He heard her draw in a breath as if to argue...and then she let it out in a long sigh.

"You should know something, Bones. I lied to you when we made our deal. I was going to kill you the first chance I got."

He laughed. Her admittance was touching for the shame in her tone, but did she really think that was a secret?

"I already knew that, Kitten."

"This stuff with Hennessey...I want to help. No, I *need* to help. My God, I was almost one of those girls who never would have been heard from again! I get how dangerous it is, but if you find out where this Club Flame is, or if you get another lead, I want to be there." Cat's voice changed, hardening into the impossibly stubborn one he knew all too well. "Hennessey has to be stopped."

Bugger him dead. Truly. Would be a kinder fate than this.

"I mean it," Cat went on. "Come on, I'm the perfect wolf in sheep's clothing! How many other half-vampire girls do you know that live in an area currently being harvested by Hennessey's team? None, so you're not talking me out of this, Bones!"

Probably not. Welcome to his living hell.

"I see," he said as he returned to the living room. Then, he set his shirt, the bowl, soap, and cloths in front of her.

"Here. You can clean the blood off the front of you and change your shirt. If you go home looking like that, you'll scare your mum into thinking you've been hurt."

Cat looked at the large crimson smear on her shirt as if seeing it for the first time. Then, she whipped it off and began scouring her bare skin with the soapy cloth. Her wet bra molded to her breasts, and the cold water hardened her nipples at once.

Seeing her that way set Bones on fire. He wanted to trace every wet rivulet with his tongue and suck her nipples until she screamed with pleasure, and he *needed* her naked against him, beneath him, above him, all of it, as long as he was inside her.

"Hey." Cat finally noticed his stare, and scooted back a bit. "Dinner's *not* served. Don't get all glowy at the blood."

He would have laughed if he wasn't burning from need.

"You think blood has anything to do with the way I'm looking at you now?"

Her breath hitched, causing her voice to be unsteady as she said, "Green eyes, fangs peeking out…pretty incriminating."

Liar. She knew better, and he was done pretending that she didn't. Bones set the bowl aside and slid next to her on the sofa.

"Then I've neglected to inform you of what else draws such a reaction, but I'll give you a hint—it isn't blood."

Suddenly, Cat couldn't meet his eyes, and her hands twisted together as if she didn't trust what they'd do if she gave them free range.

Still, when she spoke, she strove for a normal tone. "Considering last weekend, I don't have anything you haven't seen before, and I doubt you're overcome with desire by seeing me in my bra."

Oh no. No deflection. Not this time.

"Kitten, look at me."

"I am," she muttered, sneaking a glance.

"You're not," he said bluntly. "You're trying to stare straight through me as if I'm not even there. You did that when we first met, when you saw me as only a vampire instead of a man, and therefore accorded me less substance. Harder to do lately, isn't it? You couldn't last weekend, when I held you and kissed you, watched *your* eyes light up with desire, and knew you were truly seeing me for all I was instead of just pretending I was only a non-beating heart with a shell around it."

Bones lifted her chin, forcing her to look directly at him. Her heart rate sped up, but she didn't look away this time.

"I dare you to look at me that way again, now, with no excuse of chemicals to fall back on, because I want you."

Her eyes widened, and a new lushness ripened her scent. His voice deepened as he breathed it in.

"I've wanted you from the moment we met, and if you think sitting next to me in your bra doesn't overwhelm me with desire, you're very wrong. I just don't force myself where I'm not invited."

She was so close each of her accelerated breaths teased his lips, yet he didn't close the distance between their mouths. Every signal from her body might be saying yes, but it wasn't enough. He wanted her fierce will the most.

Bones stayed where he was, almost touching her while achingly apart. Cat didn't back away as she had so many times before. Instead, pinpricks of green flared in her eyes and her hands unknotted.

"Kiss me," she breathed, and reached for him.

29

Only centuries of experience kept Bones from crushing her to him as he lowered his mouth to hers. Lust battled his control like a wild animal at the feel of her soft lips, and when her arms went around him, he burned as if she'd set him aflame.

Slowly, he ordered himself. *Very slowly...*

His lips caressed hers until she parted them. Whisky sharpened her taste, and he savored her little gasp as his tongue stroked hers. He only gave it teasing flicks until he'd coaxed her tongue into his mouth, where he gave it a sensual suck that made her moan.

Her hands tightened on the collar of his shirt. Then, she began undoing his buttons. Anticipation thrummed through him.

Yes. Touch me, Kitten.

When his shirt hung open, her palms bathed his chest with more heat while her nails tantalized him with light grazes. Each touch was more addictive than the last, until he needed her bare skin on his right then.

One quick yank later, he'd torn the rest of his shirt free. He only wore his trousers, and she was still in her bra and jeans. The tops of her breasts seared his chest when he pulled her closer, deepening their kiss. Each rub of her skin increased the sensuality, and she grew bolder with her tongue, exploring his mouth with shades of the same hunger he felt.

God, going slow was the best bloody torture ever!

He wanted to fill his hands with her breasts, but he only stroked their sides before caressing her back and finding the sensitive spots there. She whimpered, pressing even closer while her pulse became a song of need in his ears. He longed to bite into that flow, filling her with the heat from his venom while her blood filled him, but she wasn't ready for that yet.

He could hint to her how good it would feel. His mouth left hers to slide down her neck. When his tongue swirled around that pounding vein, and he sucked on it without breaking her skin, Cat made a sound of pure, unadulterated need.

His cock hardened until it almost ripped through his trousers. He had to hear that sound again, louder, while he was deep inside her.

"I want you so much," he breathed into her ear. "Tell me you want me. Say yes."

Another sound came from her, this time edged with fear.

"Bones, I-I didn't like sex before. I think…something's wrong with me."

He would have laughed if rage didn't knife him from the source of her insecurity. *Damn that sod who'd hurt her!*

"Nothing's wrong with you, and if you say stop, no matter when, I'll stop. You can trust me, Kitten. Say yes. Say yes…"

He kissed her without restraint this time, letting his hunger tell her what words failed to convey. Her head fell back and gasps coated his lips while her nails dug into his shoulders as if she'd die if she let him go.

"Yes," she choked out when he tore away to let her speak.

Lust almost made Bones fly them to his bedroom. He checked himself in time, carrying her there instead. When he laid her on the bed, the sight didn't just brand itself onto his memory. It seared his soul.

Her hair a scarlet storm around her, eyes half closed from desire, lips parted for his kiss while her body molded to his...

Something surged in him, too ferocious to be called need. *Before the sun is up, you will know that you are mine.*

Bones unsnapped her bra. It fell away, baring her breasts. He filled his hands with their silky weight before tasting each luscious tip. She gripped his head, her breathing coming in gasps that turned into cries when he sucked on the rose-colored peaks. Venom filled his fangs until they ached, but he didn't pierce the tips despite how much it would heighten her pleasure.

Instead, he lightly nibbled them with his flat teeth, increasing their sensitivity so much that she barely noticed when he pulled her jeans off. She jumped when he stroked her through her panties, and a harsh sound escaped him when he felt her heat and the throb of another, deeper pulse within her.

He swept her panties aside, leaving her gloriously naked. She trembled as she stared up at him, oblivious to the effect of her beauty. Her skin looked like cream made into silk, its pale expanse interrupted only by the dark red curls between her legs and the rosy peaks crowning her breasts.

"Oh, Kitten, you're so beautiful. Exquisite," he swore before claiming her mouth again. God, he loved the little moans she made, and if he allowed himself to dwell on how good her naked body felt against his, he'd spill himself here and now.

The lash. Remember the lash.

Even centuries later, its sting shored up his control, which had slipped by shocking amounts. He hadn't allowed that to happen since he was a lad. Blimey, he hadn't remembered what it felt like to be swept away, or how fast the current could get.

He'd let himself feel that later. Now was the time for *her* to feel it.

Bones left her lips to fill his mouth with her breasts again while his hand slid to her thighs. He caressed them before moving to the warm, wet depths between them. She gasped when he slid his fingers inside her, finding the spots that made her back arch like a bent bow. Then, she cried out when his thumb circled the deliciously throbbing bud of her clitoris.

He needed to taste her there. Right now.

His mouth slid down her stomach, He'd nearly reached his prize when she said, "Bones, wait!"

He froze, not moving another muscle. "Stop?"

He would, if she told him to. He'd survived worse. He couldn't remember what at the moment, but he was sure he had.

Crimson decorated Cat's cheeks in a blush, of all things, and she almost stammered out her reply.

"Er, don't stop all of it. I'm just, um, not sure that's an appropriate thing to do—"

Appropriate? As if propriety outweighed pleasure!

"I *am* sure," he said, and licked the tiny, vibrating bulb beneath him.

She shuddered as if absorbing a lethal blow. Her spine went straight up, and her eyes blazed with so much green, they looked like emeralds dipped in fire.

Another swirling lick, and her legs clenched while a cry tore from her. "Yes!"

Bones pulled her thighs over his shoulders, his tongue sliding lower and deeper. She cried out again, and he groaned deep in his throat. She tasted like flowers crushed with honey, and he could *not* get enough.

Her heartbeat thundered like an endless storm as he continued to explore her flesh. Each rake of her nails and roll of her hips urged him on, as did the cries that grew sharper and louder. Bones held her closer with one arm, and yanked his trousers down with his other hand.

The fabric split from his force, and he kicked the rest of his trousers aside. Then, the rub of her leg against his cock sent blood rushing through him as if he had a heartbeat again, leaving him feeling drunk from the sensations.

The lash. Think of the lash!

Not even its remembered sting was enough to regain control this time. Her cries and the hot honey coating his mouth tore it away. She was about to come, and unbelievably, so was he.

So be it. She'd never know.

He grabbed his cock, pumping it along with every twisting lash of his tongue. Her legs suddenly clenched, her nails tore into his arms, and she cried out so loudly it deafened the roar of her blood from the femoral artery pressed against his ear.

Bones's climax rushed through him at the same time. His nerve endings sizzled with pleasure as those spurts coated his hand. When it stopped, he grabbed the remains of his trousers, wiping away the evidence while savoring the look on her face.

Her lips were still parted from the scream that had torn past them, and her back was still half arched from the spasms he'd tasted as well as felt. But it was the sensual surprise on her features that emblazoned another permanent memory onto him.

Bones swiped his face against the sheets before sliding up the length of her body. Her eyes met his, bright green and heavy-lidded from afterglow. His fingers slid through her hair as he brought her face closer to his.

"You have never looked more beautiful."

A smile teased her lips, but when his hips settled between hers, she stiffened and a darker emotion clouded her gaze.

I didn't like it before.

An understatement, considering what she'd described to him, and she didn't yet know that this would be very different.

"Don't be afraid," he murmured.

I will never force you. You will want all of this.

Bones only let his mouth claim hers despite his loins burning at the feel of her soft, wet heat. After a few moments, she melted into his kiss, the rigidness leaving her limbs.

It returned when his cock grazed her slit with the same slow rub that his tongue gave her. He pulled both back at once, and then repeated the dual rub-and-retreat when she relaxed again. This time, her breath caught with something other than fear, and her hands tightened on his arms.

Like that, do you? he thought, deepening the kiss. *So do I.*

Bones kept grazing her, timing the teasing strokes to the flicks of his tongue, until that fear left her gaze and she arched toward him instead of away. Her juices slicked his cock and desire shortened her breaths, but he didn't press inside her despite every cell in his body screaming for him to.

She'd want this enough to say it, and if she didn't, then he'd failed to make her want it enough.

"You tell me when," he breathed against her mouth. "Or not at all. We don't have to go further yet. I'll spend the rest of the night tasting you, Kitten, I loved that." His voice deepened as he slid down her body. "Let me show you how much."

She snatched at his shoulders, stopping him. He moved back up with an undulating graze that tore a groan from her throat. Her back arched, and her eyes flared with more emerald fire.

"Tell me," he urged, his voice hoarse from need.

Her heart beat faster from nervousness, but her thighs rose to cradle his hips.

"*Now.*"

30

*B*ones kissed her, savoring her gasp almost as much as the feel of her wet depths gripping him as he slowly pushed inside her. She trembled, and each vibration heightened the incredible sensations. His head tilted back at the rush, breaking their kiss. She tucked her face into the crook of his neck, her lips a warm brand on his skin as more shivers raced through her.

He didn't stop until she gripped his entire length within her. Those delicious shivers wracked him with pleasure, but that wasn't why his eyes closed for the briefest moment. It wasn't even her beauty, and he'd seen nothing more enrapturing than the look in her eyes when he filled her.

He felt...complete. He hadn't known such a feeling was possible. If he died now, it would have been worth it.

"All right, luv?" he said, opening his eyes.

Cat nodded, her gaze wide while she gripped his shoulders. She tensed when he started to move, so he only gave the barest thrust. She sucked in a breath that ended on a surprised moan.

See, Kitten? No pain.

The last of her tenseness left her when he did it again. Then, he ceased the shallow strokes and moved with a deep, sinuous arch that sheathed him to the hilt. Her whole body flushed with new heat, and her inner walls tightened in response. He repeated the motion, faster this time, and her hands left his shoulders to clutch his back and pull him closer.

Bones pulled her hips up to meet his next thrust. It sheathed him deeper, and his groan met her rising cry. He kissed her, muffling her next cry as he did it again. Her nails raked his back, and at his next thrust, she moved against him on her own, a choked sound escaping her at the increased contact. He twisted his hips, and a single word tore from her throat.

"More!"

Lust roughed his laugh. *Oh, yes. Much more.*

He moved faster. Sensations slammed into him, shocking him with their intensity. Every thrust felt like it could bring him over the edge, each arch of her hips inflamed him, and he could not devour her mouth enough. When she tore away to breathe, Bones tasted her throat, felt her pulse hammer against his lips, and heard her blood sing through her veins.

Cat pulled his mouth back up to her, her tongue twining so greedily with his that she cut it on his fang. Hot richness flowed that he instantly sucked and swallowed.

"So sharp and sweet," he muttered when she pulled away.

"No more...of that," Cat panted, but she didn't look disgusted like she had when he'd fed from someone else. Instead, from those achingly erotic squeezes, she was secretly aroused by him drinking those illicit drops of her blood.

"It's enough." His voice was a growl. "Now you're inside me."

Her reaction inflamed him, making him move harder, faster, until he broached the threshold of too much for someone who was still half human. He slowed, and her nails dug into his arse, grinding him against her at his former pace. Her mouth went to his neck, too, sucking so strongly it was its own ecstasy, and when her flat teeth pierced his skin until she drew blood, the feel of her sucking it shattered his control.

Bones only slowed several minutes later for fear of hurting her since he'd barely checked his strength, let alone his speed. Yet nothing about her scent, body, or reaction indicated pain. Instead, all three screamed the same word she'd said before, the very one that thundered through him now.

More!

He had to be sure.

"Harder?" he said, breaking their kiss.

"God, yes," she moaned.

He gave into the wildness only she brought out in him, moving with all the passion he felt for her. Unbelievably, she matched him, gripping him with strength that made his bones creak while meeting each frenzied thrust with shouts of rapture. Her nails ripped new welts into his back faster than the old ones could heal, and she drew more of his blood from another impassioned bite. He'd known she was more vampire than human, but right now, she was barely human at all. Every training session, every fight, every moment before this one, she must have been holding back. Continuing the mirage when *this* was the real her.

Their passion moved them over the bed as if it was a battle-ground. Her sweat slicked both their bodies, and he pulled her up onto his lap, licking those drops from the valley between her breasts. The new position ground her clitoris harder against him, heightening her cries and increasing those inner clenches that drove him mad with need.

Another scalding squeeze turned his moan into a shout. She was about to come, and if it felt any better it would kill him. He gripped her tighter, staring into her eyes as he moved harder, faster. Taking her to the edge and pushing her over it.

Her spasms shook her whole body. Feeling those sweet, extended clenches rocketed him into a climax that left forceful tremors in its wake. Bloody hell, when was the last time an orgasm had left him *shaking*?

Never.

Bones finally ended their kiss. Cat gasped in lungfuls of air that were so at odds with her real nature, he hid a smile. She might breathe, but she was a vampire wearing a human suit, not the other way around. Did she even realize how many times she'd drawn his blood tonight? Probably not. At least not consciously. Her denial of her real nature went too deep.

And far be it from him to point out what she'd done. The last thing he wanted was for her to be more self-critical, especially in bed, and *especially* when he loved every uncontrolled part of her response to him. Speaking of that...

Bones brushed her hair aside to kiss her forehead. "To think you actually believed something was wrong with you."

A breathy laugh escaped her. "Something *is* wrong with me. I can't seem to move."

Grand, because you're not going anywhere, he thought, and captured her nipple in his mouth. The peak was already firm, but he teased it until it reached ruby-like hardness.

Cat made a throaty noise. Too sated for a moan, too erotic for a sigh. He smiled against her skin.

What other sounds can you make, Kitten?

He caressed her as he moved to her other nipple. When he sucked it to the same level of hardness, the noise that left her was almost a purr, and she rolled over to give him better access. Then, her eyes slit open—and widened as she looked down.

"Am I bleeding?"

Bones didn't need to follow her gaze to know what prompted the question. He'd told her that vampires cried pink due to the blood-to-water ratio in their bodies, but she must not have realized the same held true for their other fluids.

"No, luv. That's from me."

"What is…? Oh," she said, her cheeks tinting into their own shade of pink. "Um, let me up. I'll wash off."

Leave the bed after he'd waited months to get her into it? Not likely.

"It's mine," he said in a mild tone as his mouth slid lower. "I'll clean you up."

"Aren't you going to roll over and go to sleep?"

Bones paused to laugh. "Kitten, I am *far* from sleepy. You have no idea how many times I've fantasized about you like this. During our training, our fights, the nights I've seen you pawed at by other men…"

She'd never know how deeply that cut him. All vampires were territorial, and that was merely over their possessions. Make it over someone they loved, and they were damn near rabid. Bones claimed her lips to erase those memories, kissing her until he couldn't feel the burn from them anymore.

"And all the while, seeing you look at me with fear when I touched you," he murmured when he broke away. "No, I am not sleepy. Not until I've tasted every inch of your skin and made you scream over and over again."

His mouth slid back to her breasts, tongue swirling the delicious peaks before he sucked on them until green replaced all the gray in her eyes. The very notion that he'd miss a moment of this just to have a little lie-down…

That bastard had rolled over and gone to sleep.

Bones should have realized it the moment she said it. She only had the one other comparison to draw from, after all. That's why she'd assumed he would do the same.

Rage almost turned his vision red. Filthy shite had forced her and then slept like a baby. He couldn't die fast enough.

"I'm going to find that bloke and kill him," he muttered.

She'd had her eyes closed from bliss, but at that, they snapped open. "What?"

He shouldn't have said it out loud. Damn his fractured control! Now, to make her forget she'd ever heard it.

Bones sucked on her nipple again, this time using his fangs to apply pressure without breaking her skin. That plus the careful grazes heighten her sensitivity until her hands fisted the sheets and she was moaning instead of speaking. He gave her other nipple the same attention, bringing so much blood to its surface that the slightest touch would feel like an extended lick, and every lick would feel like the most sensual of bites.

He stopped to admire their new color, and because he had other places to tease into exquisite sensitivity.

"Dark red, both of them, just like I promised you. See? I am a man of my word."

"What?" she said, looking down at her breasts in confusion. Then, color filled her cheeks and her eyes widened. "You didn't actually *mean* all that stuff from your dirty talk, did you?"

A Victorian schoolmarm couldn't have sounded more scandalized. Bones laughed as he left her breasts for the decadent valley between her thighs. He had promises to keep, after all.

"Oh, Kitten, I meant every word."

31

*L*eaving the bed later was an exercise in renewed control. Only the knowledge that he had to look up "Charlie" and "Club Flame" made Bones not reach for Cat yet again when she fell back against the mattress, her gasps from her latest climax soon turning into snores.

Bones covered her with the blankets that had long been kicked to the floor. He retrieved one of the discarded pillows, too, placing it under her head. She didn't wake, but a smile briefly ghosted over her lips when he kissed her cheek.

If her eyes had opened, he would have taken her again, research be damned. But they stayed closed, and her heartbeat slowed into the even rhythm of deep slumber. He might not be knackered, but she was, and if six times wasn't enough to slake his need for her, seven wouldn't be, either.

No amount would, if he were honest. So, best let her rest.

Besides, he had no one but himself to blame. He'd taken the folders and laptop with him instead of leaving them with Ted, and the clock was ticking on their usefulness. With luck, it could be days before Hennessey sent anyone to check Stephanie's place and discover she was missing. With more luck, that person would assume the scent of blood was from one of Stephanie's victims instead of her, and with *incredible* luck, that person might reckon Stephanie left town because she'd tired of her job.

Bones would have Ted leave a trail of charges on Stephanie's credit card to further that assumption. Might buy him a week, maybe two before Hennessey realized he'd lost an operative to more than just an instance of Stephanie quitting.

Bones had to make that time count.

He returned to the sofa, picking up Cat's bloody tee shirt and throwing it away so the sight of it wouldn't upset her in the morning. He threw away the bloody cloths, too, until nothing more than Cat's purse and Stephanie's laptop, books, and papers remained. Then, Bones cleared his mind of everything except the task at hand, and got to work.

Three hours later, Bones climbed back into bed. Cat had cocooned in the blankets again, leaving only their edges for him to warm himself with. Her body was far preferable, and he pulled her against him, her heat warming the front of him while the cave's cool air chilled his back.

Bones inhaled. Her scent was now so closely mixed with his that it was something entirely new. Not hers, not his, but *their* scent, and he inhaled it again. He might continue breathing the rest of the night just to keep absorbing it.

"I love you, Kitten," he said against her skin.

She didn't hear him. She was still asleep. For the best, really. She wasn't ready to hear that, let alone believe it. As it was, she'd probably leap out of bed like a scalded version of her namesake as soon as she awoke. She hadn't intended to see him last night, let alone spend hours making love to him, and the drastic change in their relationship would likely frighten her.

It was ironic that actual monsters didn't scare her, but being confronted with the proof of her feelings for him would.

No matter. Things *had* changed between them, and she was

stronger than she realized in every way imaginable. She didn't know it, but her fear didn't stand a chance.

"Sleep well, Kitten," Bones murmured, and closed his eyes.

"BONES…"

His whispered name woke him. He felt rested, so he must have slept for at least a few hours. Cat half-rolled over, her eyes still closed.

Bones kissed her shoulder. She smiled and stretched before wiggling closer until her arse was flush against his hips.

His brows went up, as did another part of him. A *much* better reaction than he'd anticipated! Who would've guessed that she'd be a morning person?

He kissed her shoulders again before sliding his mouth to her neck. A soft moan rumbled in her throat, and her eyelashes fluttered.

"Should've stayed a prostitute. You'd make millions," she whispered in a sleep-thickened voice.

He chuckled, and her eyes fully opened. Then they widened and her whole body stiffened while her scent soured with alarm.

There's my real Kitten, Bones thought sardonically.

"Morning after regrets?" he noted as she jumped out of bed. "Thought you might wake up and flog yourself over this."

Cat didn't look at him as she grabbed a shirt from his wardrobe and threw it on. Then, she snatched up her jeans and donned them with equal speed.

"Keys, where are my keys?" she muttered.

"You can't just storm out and pretend this never happened," Bones pointed out. "It did, Kitten."

She ignored him, going into the living room. Moments later, he heard the jangle of keys.

Bones got up and stood in the doorway. She gave him a fraught look as she slung her pocketbook over her shoulder.

"Not now," she said in a desperate voice.

He sighed. "Running from this won't undo it."

As if to prove him wrong, Cat dashed toward the cave's entrance so fast that she tore up the ground beneath her. Rocks flew in her path, and a mere two minutes later, he heard the mechanical creaks of her truck's engine revving up.

Bones snorted. Ran a mile a minute, as if that wasn't proof enough of everything she was trying to deny. She wasn't merely fleeing him. She was running from her true self, again.

Eh, well. She'd be back. He had something she couldn't resist, and he didn't only mean the passion between them.

He'd found Club Flame.

BONES GAVE her five hours and four unanswered rings before he pulled up to her house.

"Wait here," he told the Lyft driver, and headed toward Cat's door. He heard her heart rate skyrocket the instant before footsteps clattered down the stairs. Ah, so she saw him.

Bones knocked. Her grandfather answered the door, his wrinkled expression fixed into a scowl. Past her gramps' shoulder, he saw Cat trip down the last few steps. She sprawled at the bottom of the staircase, her robe flying up around her legs and her expression so shocked, it was almost comical.

"What the hell?" she hissed even as her grandfather said, "Who are you?" in a decidedly unfriendly tone.

Bones lit up his gaze with green. "I am a nice young girl here to pick up your granddaughter for the weekend."

"What?" Cat gasped.

An elderly lady with long white hair and an identical scowl

appeared. Cat's grandmum had Justina's blue eyes and her husband's foul temperament, apparently.

"Who are you?" she asked in the same belligerent tone.

"A nice young girl here to pick up your granddaughter for the weekend," Bones repeated with another flash of green.

"Oh, isn't that nice?" she said with a newly glazed expression. "You *are* a nice young girl. Be a good friend, and set Catherine straight. She has love bruises on her neck and she didn't come home until this afternoon."

"Fuck my life," Cat moaned under her breath.

Bones stifled a laugh. "Don't fret, Grannie. We're going to a Bible retreat to scare the devil out of her."

Her grandfather lost his scowl. "Good. That's what she needs. Been wild her whole life."

Bones was tempted to tell them *they* were the ones who needed the Bible study, with particular emphasis on the "judge not" part, but he refrained.

"Go have a spot of tea whilst she packs, both of you," he directed them. "That's right. Off you go."

Her grandparents left. Once they did, Cat sprang toward him as if she'd been fired from a gun.

"What do you think you're doing? If only the movies were right and vampires couldn't come in unless invited!"

Bones laughed. "Sorry, luv, we can go anywhere we please."

"Why are you here?" she whispered even though her grandparents were making tea and her mum wasn't home. "And why did you mesmerize my grandparents into thinking you're a girl?"

"A *nice* girl," Bones amended with a wink. "Can't have them thinking you've taken up with a bad sort, now can we?"

She gave a fraught look at the open door behind him. "You need to leave, now. My mom will be home soon, and she'll have a heart attack that your gaze can't fix if she sees you."

"I'm here for a reason, luv. Not that I want you involved, but you were very emphatic that you wished otherwise. I found Club

Flame. It's in Charlotte, North Carolina, and I'm flying there now. I bought you a ticket, too, if you want to go. If you don't, I'll convince your grandparents that I was never here."

He wanted her to choose the latter, but he knew better.

"Why didn't you call instead of coming over?" she asked while her torn expression said she was stalling for time.

Bones answered her anyway. "I did. My calls went straight to voicemail."

"Forgot to charge my phone," Cat muttered, looking away.

Either that was a lie, or she didn't want to acknowledge what she'd been doing all night to forget about charging her mobile. In any case, Bones left it alone.

"I even called the landline here. Your gramps hung up on me when I asked for you. You might want to remind them that you're twenty-two, and it *is* appropriate for a gentleman to ring you."

"Yeah, well, they kind of lost it when they saw my neck, which was very inconsiderate, by the way," she said, her cheeks flaming now. "Leaving all those 'Been there, done that!' stamps on me for them to see."

Bones smiled at the memory. "In fairness, Kitten, if I didn't heal supernaturally, I'd be covered in similar markings, and my back would be a river of scars from your nails."

His voice deepened at that last part. She looked away, but the little throb in her neck showed the uptick in her pulse that almost begged him to continue that train of thought.

"You know I'll go tonight," she said, striving for a brisk tone. "Hennessey needs to be stopped. I'm surprised you already found the club, though. That was fast."

"Found it this morning while you were sleeping." Bones gave her pointed look. "I was going to tell you that, but you ran out like hell was chasing you and didn't give me the chance."

"I don't want to talk about that," she ground out. "I won't let my...my misgivings interfere with stopping a mass murderer, but I think it's best if we leave that alone."

"Misgivings? Oh, Kitten. You break my heart."

He said it so lightly she'd never know it was true. He'd expected this battle, but it didn't mean it was without wounds.

She gave him a sharp look. "Don't mock me. Let's focus on priorities. If you insist, we'll, ah, talk about the other stuff after the club. Now, wait here while I pack."

Bones swept his hand toward the open doorway. "No need. I already brought your game clothes plus other necessities, so just change out of your robe and we'll be off."

"Confident, aren't you?" she said under her breath.

"About certain things," he agreed, his brow arching with meaning.

She ignored that and headed back up the staircase. "Then give me five minutes to get dressed."

32

The vampire entered Club Flame almost exactly at two am. Bones didn't have a description of Charlie, so he wasn't sure if the brown-haired chap with the lightly muscled build was him. If so, Charlie was around five-nine without his tall cowboy boots, and he moved with an easy swagger that said he was very comfortable with his surroundings.

Rustling sounds crowded out the club's music for a moment. Cat didn't know it, but her pocketbook had a new accessory. A tiny listening device, courtesy of Ted. Cat had her unbreakable priorities. Bones had his, and making sure she didn't die was first on them. The panic button in her watch hadn't proved to be sufficient, so if she got in over her head again, he'd now hear it before it was too late to help her.

He'd tell her about it eventually. Not tonight.

"Haven't seen you here before, cherry pie," Bones heard a Southern voice drawl moments later. "Name's Charlie."

Bones let out a contemptuous snort that Cat couldn't hear since the bug in her purse only worked one way.

No alias? Amateur.

"Sweet to eat, and easy as," Cat replied in a teasing way. "Looking for a date, honey?"

"You bet, cherry pie," Charlie replied.

"Hey, mister, I saw her first," an annoyed male voice said.

Bones recognized that voice, and Cat had already told the bloke in no uncertain terms that she wasn't interested. Stubborn fool obviously wasn't taking no for an answer.

"Why don't you get up on outta here and go home? Best hurry, now," Charlie said. "I don't like repeatin' myself."

More rustling, louder this time. One of them must have jostled Cat's pocketbook.

"I said I saw her *first,*" insisted the belligerent drunk.

"No need to cause a ruckus," Charlie replied in a genial tone. "We'll flip for you, cherry pie. I'm feelin' lucky."

Cat muttered something that sounded like "assholes" moments later. Bones listened, but he didn't hear anything else through the bug except music and the bar's other patrons. Then, he heard the much nearer sound of the club's back door opening.

Bones froze as Charlie's aura touched him. Only the thin stretch of concrete wall that Bones hid behind separated them.

"What the...? Wait, no!" the drunk fellow gasped, followed instantly by a loud cracking sound.

"Told you not to make me repeat myself," Charlie said as the drunk's heartbeat stopped.

Bones's jaw tightened. Charlie was a ruthless killer, as if Bones needed any more proof that this was Stephanie's contact and not some random vampire with the same name.

A trunk opened and closed. Then, Bones heard the back door open and close again, too. Moments later, Charlie's voice flowed back over the receiver in Cat's purse.

"Turns out I *am* lucky tonight. Question is, are you going to make me very, very lucky?"

"Sure," Cat said in a flirty tone. "Just need a little help with my rent first."

"What's your rent, cherry pie?"

"Hundred bucks. You'll be glad you donated, promise."

"Honey child, from the looks of you, I'd say that's a bargain," Charlie replied.

"Don't worry, you're in for a real treat," Cat said in her silkiest voice.

Bones's mouth tightened. *Oh, indeed he was.*

Charlie returned to the back of the club to retrieve his car. Bones had anticipated that, and was already in his rental vehicle ready to follow at a distance. This part of town was too well lit for Bones to risk flying, what with everyone having a recording device built into their mobile phones.

Cat got into the vehicle, keeping up her sex worker charade. Charlie kept up his good ol' boy act, too, until Cat commented on how far he was taking her away from the club.

"Shut the fuck up, bitch," Charlie snapped.

Cat said absolutely nothing in reply. Charlie must have lit up his gaze when he spoke, so Cat was pretending that it had worked on her.

Charlie drove almost an hour out of the city to a semi-rural area. There, he pulled up to a small, Mom-and-Pop type complex containing less than half a dozen apartment units. Most seemed empty. Bones only heard one heartbeat aside from Cat's.

Bones drove by so Charlie wouldn't get suspicious. With how dark it was in this area, he could fly back once he was clear.

"Home sweet home, cherry pie," Bones heard Charlie say. "At least for a little while. Then, you're leaving town."

Cat didn't reply. Charlie's last order had been for her to shut up, and he hadn't rescinded it yet.

Well done, Kitten.

Bones parked a few blocks away before flying back. He arrived in time to see Charlie shove Cat inside a door marked 2D on the second floor. Then, the door slammed behind them.

"Got another one, Dean," Charlie called out.

Thanks for telling me your numbers, mate, Bones thought savagely. Since he hadn't heard Cat strike at them yet, Bones did a quick sweep of the perimeter.

"She's gorgeous," he heard a new male voice reply.

"I found her," Charlie said. "I go first."

A disgusted noise left Cat and her heart rate kicked into a new gear. She'd had enough.

So had he. Bones flew to the second floor and landed at 2D. The impact caused Dean to say "You expectin' someone—?"

The door smashing in cut off Dean's question. Cat took full advantage of the distraction, stabbing the dark-haired, naked vampire right in his baby maker.

Bones launched himself at Charlie, who lost a step staring in horror at his mate's skewered groin. Bones had a blade through Charlie's chest before the other vampire finished wincing at Dean's ear-blasting screech. Bones didn't twist it, though, which was more forethought than Cat showed. She'd flung a silver knife into Dean's back and twisted it before Bones could say "wait." Then, Cat kicked the naked vampire when she climbed off his shriveling body.

"Guess you went first after all, asshole."

Bones hauled Charlie over to the sofa. The other vampire didn't fight. Bones had a silver knife in his heart, and one twist would end him. Plus, having your heart pierced with silver nearly paralyzed a vampire with weakness and agony.

"Good thing I didn't need the other bloke, luv," Bones said, his arched brow indicating Dean's body.

Cat only shrugged. "Then you should have told me."

"Your eyes," Charlie whispered, staring at Cat.

They'd lit up right after she stabbed Dean, and their twin emerald lights now landed on Charlie's face.

"Lovely, aren't they?" Bones purred. "So at odds with her beating heart. Feel free to be shocked, mate. I know I was when I first saw them glow."

"But they're...she can't..." Charlie went on.

"Oh, don't concern yourself with her any longer. It's me you need to fret about."

Charlie's gaze shot Bones's way, and his muscles twitched as if readying himself to fight.

Bones smiled, and flicked the knife a fraction deeper. Charlie froze and his lips went white.

Good. He understood that moving meant death.

"Kitten, someone's in the other room. They're human, but don't assume that means they're harmless."

She gave a short nod and pulled out three silver throwing blades. Then, she went down the hallway, moving with careful precision. Stephanie's betrayal had taught her well.

"You're makin' a mistake, friend," Charlie began.

"Shut it," Bones said, listening for any sign of danger.

Cat's sharp cry made Bones tense. He was about to kill Charlie and fly in after her when she shouted, "We need an ambulance!"

Bones forced himself to relax and not focus on her any longer. Cat's statement meant she wasn't in danger. She'd just found what he expected her to find in a place like this.

Charlie's gaze shot his way again, a half defiant, half calculating look flashing over his features.

"That gal's fine. We don't kill 'em."

"Told you to shut it," Bones said with another knife flick.

Several ripping sounds later, Cat returned, carrying a Caucasian girl with dark brown hair. The girl was covered in bed sheets, and Cat had torn up more of the bedding to make bandages for the girl's wrists, thigh, and throat. The girl didn't speak. From the glazed look in her brown eyes, she'd been mesmerized not to, or she was in shock, or both.

"I have to take her to a hospital!" Cat said.

"Wait, Kitten," Bones replied evenly.

She gave him a horrified look. "But she's lost a lot of blood! And worse!"

216

Yes, he could smell the "and worse" part, but Cat wasn't thinking of the consequences.

"You take her to a local hospital, and you may as well kill her. Hennessey will send someone to silence her. She knows too much. I'll take care of her, but let me deal with him first."

Charlie angled his head to look more closely at Bones.

"I don't know who you are, but if you know Hennessey's name, you should know you're makin' a big mistake. If you get outta here now, you might just live long enough to regret it."

Bones gave a cold laugh. "Well done, mate! Why, some of the others groveled straightaway, and you know how tedious that is. You're correct; we haven't been introduced. I'm Bones."

Charlie's eyes widened for an instant before he suddenly smiled with false jovialness.

"No reason to be uncivilized 'bout things. Hennessey said you've been slinking after him, but you can't beat him, so why not join him? He'd love to have someone like you batting for his team. This is a big, sweet pie, my friend, and ain't nobody smart that wouldn't love a piece of it."

Bones tilted his head to better see Charlie's face. "That so? I'm not sure Hennessey would want me. Killed an awful lot of his blokes, you see. Hennessey might be cross about that."

Charlie laughed. "Hell, that's like a job interview for him! Don't worry none about that. Hennessey'd figure anybody dumb enough to get dried by you isn't worth having anyway."

"We don't have time for this." Rage sizzled Cat's voice. "This girl is bleeding to death while you're making friends!"

Bones gave her a sharp look. He wasn't pausing to have a chin wag without good reason.

"Charlie and I are talking, pet. Now," back to the vampire in his grasp, "about this pie. Afraid I'll need more incentive than 'big and sweet' to let you live. You recognize my name, so you know what I do for a living, and I'm sure I can find someone who'd pay a pretty penny for your corpse."

"Not as much as you can get playing for Hennessey's side instead of against him," Charlie said, and jerked his head toward Cat. "See the gal your wildcat is cradlin'? Each of those honeys is worth at least six figures when it's all done. We have them work the breathers first, and then we auction 'em off to one of ours for a full meal, no cleanin' the dishes afterward. And *then*, they're a perfect meal for a hungry bone muncher! I mean, these gals were never more useful in their lives—"

"You piece of shit!" Cat shouted, and came at Charlie with her knife drawn.

"Stay where you are!" Bones ordered in a tone he'd never used on her before. "And if I have to tell you to shut it *one* more time, I'm going to knock your bloody head off!"

Cat stopped, staring at Bones with something worse than disbelief. Hurt and betrayal boiled over in her gaze, and though she no longer moved, her knuckles whitened on her knife.

Frustration almost made him abandon the charade. Didn't she know *good cop, bad cop*, for pity's sake? Or was her prejudice so deep that she actually believed he meant this act?

Charlie's laugh dragged Bones's attention back to him.

"Whew, your kitty's high strung! Better watch your small 'n' wrinklies before she wears 'em on her belt."

Bones joined his laughter. "No chance of that, mate. She likes what they do to her too much to rob me of them."

Cat whitened, and he heard her stomach churn. After all they'd been through, she actually believed *this*.

Bones looked away, piling on the ice. He had a job to do. He'd do it, and then he'd deal with her low opinion of him. He eased his grip on the knife in Charlie's heart. Charlie felt it, and hope lit his gaze.

"At least six figures each, that's nice," Bones said in a mulling way, "but split up how many ways? It's not a lot if you're splashing it over a big pond."

Charlie nudged him with his head as if they were mates.

"Tally that number against hundreds of cooches, and there's only about twenty of us cashin' in on this. Plus, Hennessey's aiming to go global with his services, but he wants to keep his inner structure small. Just enough to keep those wheels movin' over that sweet track to happy land. Aren't you tired of scratchin' out a living job to job? Residual income, that's the key. We've run through our last batch of gals, so it's round up time again. A few more months of that, and then we sit back and watch the bank account grow. It's sweet, I tell ya. Very sweet."

"Indeed?" Bones drawled. "You paint a tempting picture, mate. However, there's a few chaps among Hennessey's people where there's no love lost between us, so tell me, who else is on this sweet train? Can't sign me up if I've shagged their wife or shriveled their brother, can you?"

Cat made a noise as if she'd throw up.

Charlie stiffened, and his smile faded as he finally realized what was happening.

"Fuck you," he said without a hint of a Southern accent.

Bones's lips curled and his grip tightened on the knife. "Right. Knew you'd catch on eventually. Thanks anyway, mate, you've been moderately helpful 'Round twenty of you, you say? That's fewer than I thought, and I've a decent inkling as to who the rest of them might be."

Cat sagged with such visible relief that her knees trembled and she almost dropped the girl. Seeing it, Bones wanted to shake her until her head rattled, and then hold her so close, she'd never feel alone again.

If you'd only trust me, Kitten! Blimey, what will it take?

"I don't feel anyone, but check the rest of the building anyway." Bones's brisk tone held none of the emotions raging inside him. "Break down the doors if you have to. We need to be sure no one else is here."

"What about her?" Cat said, setting the girl down.

219

He'd been monitoring her breathing and heartbeat. She should have realized that, but still he said, "She'll hold."

"If you kill me, it won't only be Hennessey that'll be after you," Charlie said with futile rage. "You'll wish your mother had never been born. Hennessey's got friends, and they go higher up on the pole than you can imagine."

"Indeed?" Bones said coldly. "Thought Hennessey wouldn't miss anyone stupid enough to get dried by me? Your words, mate. I suspect you're regretting them."

Cat left. In the ten minutes it took her to return, Bones had moved Charlie to the back bedroom. Cat stared at the metal bed frame Bones had bent and twisted until it wrapped around Charlie like a loose cage. It wouldn't hold a vampire on its own, but the silver knife piercing Charlie's heart that Bones had wedged into the metal ensured that Charlie wouldn't move.

Cat's eyes widened at the three petrol jugs near Bones's feet. "Where'd you get those?"

"Under the kitchen sink. Thought they'd have this on hand. You didn't think they'd leave this place with all its forensic evidence behind when they were finished, did you?"

She didn't answer.

Bones returned his attention to Charlie. "Now, mate, I'm going to make you an offer. It only gets extended once. Tell me who these other players are, now, and you'll go out quick and clean. Refuse, and"—Bones emptied the jugs over Charlie, who winced as the petrol soaked him—"you'll live as long as it takes for this to kill you."

Charlie stared at Bones with the kind of hatred only the condemned could muster.

"I'll tell you in hell, and that'll be soon."

Admirable loyalty. Or an admirable amount of spite. Either way, he'd burn for it.

Bones lit a match and threw it on Charlie. "Wrong answer," he said over the vampire's instant screams. "I never bluff."

33

*O*nce Charlie was dead, Bones burned the other units, too. He hated cleaning up after Hennessey, but now there'd be no fingerprints or DNA from Cat at the apartment complex. Then, Bones went over to Charlie's car, popped the boot, and pulled out the dead drunk from the bar.

Cat gasped. "Who is that?"

Bones turned so she could see the drunk's face. Shock and agony was still stamped on the bloke's features.

Cat stared. "Is he, ah...?"

"Dead as Caesar," Bones confirmed. "Charlie took him 'round back and snapped his spine. Would have felt me, too, if he'd been paying more attention. That's where I was hiding."

"You didn't try to stop him?" Anguish tinged Cat's voice.

Bones didn't have time, and even if he had, he wouldn't sacrifice many lives to save only one. She wouldn't understand that, which was why she couldn't take on someone like Hennessey by herself. Hennessey would use Cat's mercy against her, and then no lives would be saved, including hers.

"No," was all Bones said.

Cat said nothing. Just took in several breaths and looked at him with pained confusion. Bones set the drunk's body in the grass a few meters from the car. When he straightened and walked away, she finally spoke.

"What are you doing with him?"

"Leaving him here. With this fire, he'll be found soon, and get a proper burial. That's all he has left. Now, let's go."

She still didn't move. "What about Charlie? You're leaving him and Dean for the police to find, too?"

Bones went over to their car. The traumatized girl was in the backseat, still not talking although her heart rate had steadied after Bones gave her a few drops of his blood. That had also healed the deep bite marks in her wrists, thigh, and neck.

"You know that when vampires die, their bodies decompose back to their true age," Bones threw over his shoulder. "That's why some look like bloomin' mummies afterward. Let the cops try to figure out why a bloke that's been dead over seventy years ended up stuffed inside a bed frame and torched. They'll be scratching their chins for weeks over that."

Cat got into the back seat and took the girl's hand. Pain twisted Cat's features when the girl flinched at her touch. Bones's blood was breaking through the vampire compulsion on her, too. His gaze could end it, but he wasn't doing that here.

"And Hennessey?" Cat asked as Bones drove off.

"Also why I'm leaving Charlie the way he is. Hennessey will hear of Charlie's death, and he'll know who killed him because if there's a bounty on Charlie or the other plonker, I'm going to claim it. Hennessey will be nervous, wondering what they told me before I killed them, and very much wanting to stop me for good. With luck, it'll draw him out of hiding."

From Cat's expression, she wasn't a fan of this plan, but she only said, "Where are we taking the girl, if not the hospital?"

Bones was already dialing a number on his mobile.

"Tara," he said when she answered. "It's Bones. Sorry to ring you so late..."

"Never you mind," Tara interrupted, her Southern Cajun voice sleepy and pleased at the same time. "How you been, *cher?*"

"Good, but I have a favor to ask you."

"Someone needs help?" Suddenly, Tara sounded very awake.

"Yes—"

"Bring her," she interrupted. "How far away are you?"

"I'll be there in an hour. Thank you, Tara."

He hung up, seeing Cat's questioning gaze in the mirror.

"Tara lives in Blowing Rock, which isn't far, and the girl will be safe with her. No one knows Tara and I are associated, so Hennessey won't think to look for her there. Tara will also be able to give the girl the help she needs, and not just physically. She's been through something similar."

"A vampire got her?" Cat's features pinched with sympathy.

Bones looked away, his jaw tightening. "No, luv. He was just a man."

~

TARA'S CABIN was high up in the Blue Ridge Mountains, at the end of a winding gravel road bordered by thick forests. Cat looked around at the rugged terrain with awe, reminding Bones that she'd never seen any mountains before. As far as he knew, this was Cat's first trip out of Ohio.

He'd show her the world, if she'd let him. Problem was, she probably wouldn't, as her distrust tonight had proven.

Bones pushed that aside. The girl in the backseat took precedence. Tara could do many things, but she couldn't break the compulsion the girl was under. Only a vampire could.

Tara waved from her porch when they pulled up. Bones got out and kissed Tara on each cheek, noting that gray made up more than half of her raven-colored hair, and her dark teak skin now had several more lines. A pang hit him. In a mere two or three decades, Tara would likely be gone. In a mere half century, all who knew Tara would likely be gone, too. Except him.

That was the true cost of being a vampire. Seeing nearly everyone you cared about weaken, die, and then be forgotten as if they had never even existed. Tara, like many before her, had refused Bones's offer of becoming a vampire. She said she wanted to grow old, see her grandchildren grow up, and then die like nature intended. Some days, Bones envied her that. Other days, like now, he thought how poorer the world would be without her.

Tara hugged him, and then pulled away with a smile. "Gorgeous as always, aren't you, *cher?*"

Bones gently touched her face. "Not as lovely as you."

Tara laughed and swatted his hand. "Those lies are what earned you the big bucks back in the day, aren't they?" Then, Tara's expression clouded as she glanced at the car. "Are both of them in trouble?"

"Just one," Bones said, and summarized what had happened. He didn't mention who'd done it. Tara didn't need to know that.

"Kitten?" Bones finished with. "Coming?"

Cat nodded, whispering encouragement to the girl as she helped her out of the car. The girl was trying to walk, which was a good sign, but she was having difficulty.

"I'll take her up," Bones said, and picked the girl up. "Tara, this is Cat. Cat, meet Tara."

"Put her in my room," Tara said as Bones swept past her. "Cat, glad to meet you. Now, come in, child, you must be cold!"

Bones carried the girl up to the bedroom on the second floor. Tara had stoked a fire, and left different sizes of clothing on the tall-backed chair that she loved to read in.

The girl's eyes widened with alarm when she saw that she was now alone in a bedroom with him. Bones set her down at once, and pointed at the thick quilt next to the chair.

"Don't fret, I won't hurt you. Go, warm yourself."

The girl didn't move. Bones sighed, and put the blanket

around her. She flinched at his touch, her scent so thick with fear it was like inhaling sour milk.

Bones knelt so he was no longer looming over her. Then, he released the glow in his eyes. She screamed when she saw it.

"You're safe," he said, putting power into the words. If he weren't a Master vampire, he'd have to bite her to make her believe it, but since he was, his gaze would suffice.

The girl's scream ended, and the most painful sort of hope filled her gaze. Seeing it, Bones went on.

"The people who hurt you are dead. The ones responsible will soon be dead, too, and no one here will harm you. Do you understand? You're truly *safe* now."

She burst into heart-rending sobs. Bones didn't reach for her. She'd had too many people touching her without her consent. He wouldn't add to that unless necessary.

"He's done this before?" he heard Cat ask Tara. "Brought traumatized girls to you?"

"I run a domestic violence shelter," Tara replied. "Most times, I don't bring anyone here, but every once in a while someone needs extra care. When they need extra, *extra* care, I call Bones. I owe him my life, but I 'spect he told you that."

"No." Cat sounded confused. "Why would he?"

"'Cause he never brought a girl here before that didn't need my help, child," Tara replied, a smile clear in her voice.

"It's not like that," Cat said at once. "We work together, so I'm not his...er...I mean, you can have him if you want him!"

Giving him away like an extra slice of cake? Bloody hell.

Tara began telling Cat how Bones had saved her from her violent husband years ago. Bones tuned that out and focused on the girl. She was still sobbing, but it was less frenzied now.

"I know this is difficult, but I need to ask you some questions," Bones said. "You're safe, but other lasses aren't, and you could help me track down the bastards that have them."

The girl's head jerked in a nod even as she swiped at her

running nose. Bones handed her the tissue box Tara had also left close by. She'd thought of everything.

"First, what's your name?"

"Emily," she whispered. "Emily Franklin."

"Emily." Bones turned up the power in his gaze. "Those other vampires have no power over you anymore. You remember everything that they told you to forget, and you can say or do anything that you want to. Now, tell me what happened."

The story was familiar. Emily had been snatched up last week while out with friends, and Charlie and Dean had compelled her to lie to her friends so no one would report her missing. Charlie and Dean had also been the only people Emily had seen, with one notable exception.

"It seems like I blinked, and then I was in a new house. The bedroom was big, wood floors, with red and blue paisley wallpaper. The man there was wearing a mask. I never saw his face. He kept it on the whole time..."

Emily's voice broke, and rage stabbed Bones. He well remembered what it felt like to be treated as if you had no more value than a pot to be pissed in.

Emily stood. "I have to shower. I feel so dirty."

Bones rose, too, pointing at the bathroom attached to Tara's bedroom.

Before she brushed past him, Bones stopped her. "This is *their* shame," he said with all the power his gaze could muster. "Do you understand, Emily? Theirs. Not an ounce of it is yours."

Tears spilled down Emily's cheeks, but she nodded. "When you find the rest of them, kill them," she said very softly. "Please, promise me that you'll kill them."

Bones closed his fist over his heart. "I promise."

Emily nodded sharply, and shut the bathroom door.

Tara and Cat were sharing a pot of coffee when Bones came downstairs. Cat's gaze was slightly red-rimmed, either from Tara's story or from overhearing what Emily had said.

In case it was the former, Bones said, "Her name is Emily, she's estranged from her family, and she's been on her own since she was fifteen. Her mates think she's off with an ex-boyfriend, so no need to tell them otherwise and endanger them."

Tara nodded. "I'll brew another pot of coffee for her and be right up. You staying over?"

"Can't. Have a flight this afternoon, and our effects are back at the hotel. But thank you, Tara. I'm indebted to you."

Tara gave his cheek a warm kiss. "No, you ain't, *cher*. You keep safe, now, you hear?"

"And you, Tara. Kitten? Ready to go?"

"I'm ready," she said, rising. "Thank you for the coffee, Tara, and for the company."

Tara smiled. "Wasn't nothing, child. Now, you be sweet to our boy here, and remember, be good only if being bad ain't more fun!"

A breath of laughter left Cat. "I'll try to remember that."

34

*B*ones was silent on the drive back to the hotel. Cat didn't speak, either, but from her squirming, she wanted to. Too bloody bad. He wasn't breaking the silence. It was time she reached out to him instead of the other way around.

"So what's next?" Cat finally said when they pulled into their hotel's parking lot. "We find out if Charlie has a bounty on him? Or see if anyone knows who the masked asshole might be? Wonder what that was about. Kinks, you think? Or maybe he was someone Emily knew, and he didn't want her to recognize him?"

Bones put the car in park with more force than needed. She wanted to pretend they were merely work associates? Very well, that's how he'd treat her, and she'd done a poor job of things.

"Either is possible, but you're bowing out now."

Anger turned Cat's scent into something resembling burnt cherries. "Don't give me that 'unsafe' crap again! You think I can see what was done to Emily, know it's going on with countless other girls, and just hide under my bed? I was supposed to *be* one of those girls. No way am I bowing out!"

"Your bravery isn't the issue," Bones said coldly.

"Then what?" she asked, exasperated.

"The look in your eyes when I spoke to Charlie. You thought I might actually join Hennessey. Deep down, you still don't trust me, and *partners* need to trust each other, don't they?"

Anger made his hand land harder than he intended on the steering wheel. It dented and Cat winced, either from the damage he'd done or the truth in his accusation.

"You were doing a great job acting, and I got confused." Genuine regret made a ruin of her lovely features. "Can you honestly blame me? Every day for the past *six years* I've had it drummed into my head that all vampires are vicious scum, and to date, by the way, you're the only one I've met who isn't."

Bones was about to argue when he realized it was true. Yes, he'd taken her to Bite, but that had hardly ended well, and the only other vampires she'd met were targets.

Amusement suddenly pricked him. "Do you realize that's the nicest thing you've ever said to me?"

"Was Tara your girlfriend?" she asked in a sharp tone.

His brows went up. *Well. Where had that come from?*

Instantly, Cat looked away. "Never mind. Look, about last night...I think we both made a mistake. Hell, you've probably realized that yourself, so I'm sure you'll agree that it should never happen again. I didn't mean to flake out earlier with Charlie, but old habits die hard. Okay, bad metaphor, but you get my point. We'll work together to bring down Hennessey and whoever else is in his gang, and then we'll, ah, go our separate ways. No harm, no foul."

The only logical choice. She was too young, too stubborn, too narrow-minded, too temperamental...and so bloody brave it awed him, loyal to the bone to those she loved, and so secretly vulnerable that she literally used knives to protect that part of herself.

Who was he joking? Screw logic, the odds, or anything else in their way. Bones could no more leave her behind than he could shed his own skin. She was that much a part of him now.

"'Fraid I can't agree to that, Kitten."

"Why not?" she said in a frustrated tone. "I'm great as bait. All the vampires want to eat me!"

His quick smile coincided with her groan as she realized the double entendre in what she'd said. Then, Bones's smile faded, and he leaned over to caress her cheek.

"I can't let us go our separate ways afterward because I am in love with you. I love you," he repeated when her mouth dropped open and her expression went blank from shock.

Cat said nothing for several moments. Then, her jaw clicked shut, and she shook her head as if to clear it.

"No, you don't," she said firmly.

A snort escaped him. "That is one truly annoying habit you have, telling me what I do and do not feel. After nearly two and a half centuries, I think I know my own mind."

Unlike you, his tone implied.

She bristled as if she'd heard that. "Are you just saying this to have sex with me?"

He rolled his eyes. "Knew you'd think such a thing. That's one of the reasons I didn't tell you this before. I never wanted you to wonder if I were lying to cajole you into bed, but to be rudely blunt, I've already gotten you on your back, and it wasn't by declaring my devotion to you. I simply don't care to hide my feelings any longer."

Her eyes widened, and her breath became unsteady as she finally allowed herself to acknowledge that he wasn't lying.

"But you've only known me two months," she whispered.

Memory curled his lips. "I began to fall in love with you right after you challenged me to that stupid fight to the death. There you were, chained up and bleeding while almost daring me to kill you. Why do you think I struck that bargain with you? Knew

230

you'd never agree to spend time with me any other way. You had such hang-ups about vampires. Still do, unfortunately."

"Bones." She said his name as if it were a plea. "We'd never work out, so we need to stop this now, before it goes any further."

I can't bear to get hurt again! She didn't say it, but it was in her eyes, the way her hands clenched as if she were fighting not to reach for him, and in the pain tingeing her scent and voice.

Bones brushed a scarlet lock back from her face. "I know what makes you say that. Fear. You're terrified because of how that other wanker treated you, and you're even more afraid of what your dear mum would say."

"Oh, she'd have plenty to say, you can bet on that," Cat said under her breath.

"I've faced death more times than I can count. This situation with Hennessey is no different, do you really think the wrath of your mum scares me?" he asked with an amused scoff.

"It would if you were smart," she muttered.

"Then consider me the stupidest man in the world," he said, and leaned forward to capture her lips.

She melted into the kiss.

Bones pulled her closer, deepening it until her hands clenched on his back and her breath came in short, rapid pants. Then, she pushed him away when his hands found the hem of her short skirt and dipped beneath it.

"You'd better not be messing with me." Her tone was firm but her gaze pleaded with his in a way she'd never dare articulate. "I really like you, but if you're feeding me a load of shit just to get some action, I'm going to twist a big silver stake through your heart."

She'd just agreed to be his.

His joy escaped him in a laugh that he teased her neck with as his mouth slid there. "I'll consider myself warned."

She shivered with pleasure as his tongue circled the sensitive spot over her pulse. Then, she felt his fangs, extending along with another part of him, and gave him a light smack on the arm.

"And no biting."

Bones laughed again, making sure the breath from it landed on her now-thrumming pulse. Another delicious shiver ran over her.

"On my honor. Anything else?"

"Yeah." Her arms rose to encircle him. "No one else if you're with me."

Bones pulled back so she could see his smile. "That's a relief. When you told Tara that she could have me, too, I didn't know if you fancied monogamy."

"I'm serious!" she said, a wounded note threading her tone.

He framed her face in his hands. "Kitten, I said I loved you. That means I don't want anyone else."

She stared at him, her expression a mixture of hope, fear, and need. One day, Bones wanted to see love reflected there, too, but right now, this was enough.

"One more thing." The seriousness in her tone made him tense. "I *insist* on going after Hennessey with you. If I trust you enough to be your...your girlfriend, you'll have to trust me enough to let me do that."

Dating a vampire wasn't risky enough for her. She had to hunt the most treacherous of their kind, too.

"I beg you to stay out of this. Hennessey's well connected and ruthless. That's a dangerous combination."

She only smiled. "Half dead and totally dead. We're a dangerous combination, too."

He let out a wry chuckle. "Reckon you're right about that."

The smile slowly left her face. "Bones, I can't walk away from this. I'd hate myself if I didn't do everything I could to stop it. One way or the other, I'm in this fight. Your only choice is whether I'm in it with you or without you."

She'd be the death of him. The death of his sanity, at least. He'd always said "never value something more than you can afford to lose" because at one point or another, he'd lost everything and had to endure it. Now, he could *not* lose her, and Cat was insisting that Bones throw her into the lion's den or she'd hurl herself in. Worse, he knew exactly how she felt.

He couldn't walk away from hunting Hennessey, either, and Cat's courage was what he admired most about her. How could he expect her to be a coward now?

"All right," Bones finally said. "We'll get him together."

She smiled. The rising sun cast an amber glow over her features, making her so beautiful that, like the sun, it hurt to keep looking at her. Yet he couldn't bring himself to look away. Some things were worth their pain.

Then, her smile faded and she glanced at the slowly lightening sky with a sigh. "Sun's coming up."

"So it is," Bones said, and pulled her back to him.

She gasped at the intensity in his kiss. Then, she moaned when he stroked her breasts, her hips, and her thighs before reaching down between them.

"But it's dawn!" she said with disbelief.

He only laughed, deep and filled with wicked intention.

"Really, luv, how dead do you think I am?"

----

35

*H*ours later, Cat lazily traced the outline of the tattoo on his left arm. They'd finally made it to the bed in their hotel room, which was a good thing because the furniture in the living area was no longer fit for use.

"Cross bones," she murmured. "How appropriate. Where'd you get this?"

Bones drew his arms over his head and stretched. "A mate gave it to me. He was a Marine who died in World War Two."

"Sometimes I forget how old you are," she muttered.

Bones only smiled. *Yes, our age difference is truly ridiculous. No, I don't care.*

"Did you find out anything more about Charlie or Dean?" she asked, changing the subject.

"I'll check. Should have a nibble by now."

Bones got up and went over to where he'd set up his mobile. He'd sent out feelers on the dark web earlier, while she ate breakfast. She'd never had room service before, and she loved it. Now, at least he knew one guaranteed way to her heart.

"Ah, email," he said, quickly scanning it. "Nothing on Dean, but Charlie pissed off the wrong bloke. Bank wire transfer completed, one hundred thousand dollars. I'll give the location for Charlie's body, and post enough about this on the dark web for Hennessey to hear of it. That'll also be twenty-five K for you, Kitten, and you didn't even have to kiss him."

"I don't want the money," she said at once.

His brows went up and he turned around. "Whyever not? You earned it. Told you that was always part of the plan, even if I didn't let you in on it right off."

Cat sat up with a sigh. "It was one thing to take the money when we weren't sleeping together. Now, we are, and I refuse to be your employee and your girlfriend at the same time. So, really, the choice is yours. Pay me, and I stop sleeping with you, or keep the money, and we continue on in bed."

Bones burst out laughing, which clearly wasn't the response she'd been expecting. A scowl replaced her earnest expression.

"What's so funny?"

"And you wonder why I love you." He was still chuckling as he went back to the bed. "When you boil it all down, you're now *paying* me to shag you, for as soon as I stop, I owe you twenty-five percent of every contract I take. Blimey, Kitten, you've turned me back into a whore."

Embarrassment darkened her features. "That's...that's not... dammit, you know that's not what I meant!"

Bones caught her when she tried to scoot away, laughing as he flipped her onto her back. "You're not going anywhere. I have twenty-five thousand dollars to earn, and I'm going to start working on it now. Where is that pancake syrup you were so enjoying earlier? Ah, there it is."

"Don't you dare," she said when he leapt up to grab the small bottle, and then advanced toward her with purpose.

Bones yanked off her robe, baring her luscious body. Then, a flick of his wrist splashed the amber liquid from her breasts down to the tight curls between her legs. Her outraged gasp turned into a sharp exhalation when he caught a syrup-sweetened nipple in his mouth and licked it until not a drop remained.

"That's not fair," she said with a moan.

"Did you think I'd play fair?"

Whispered as he coated his fingers with more of the amber sweetness before dragging them down to her thighs. "Take every low blow, remember?" he said, and slid them inside her.

A strangled sound escaped her as he stroked her, first thrusting his fingers slowly, and then faster, until she moved against his hand as if it were another part of him.

"That's...a little depraved," she gasped out.

He chuckled as he slid down her body, following the dark amber trail to where it ended.

"Not yet, Kitten, but it's about to be."

He replaced his fingers with his mouth, licking until all the syrup was gone and he tasted only her. Then, he poured more syrup on her and started all over again. By the time he finally thrust inside her, the bottle was empty, and she'd come three times.

She came twice more before he allowed himself his own release. Then, she fell back against the pillows with a breathy comment of "Account balance zero" that made him laugh.

"Not nearly," Bones said, pulling her close again. "But a decent start."

THEY MISSED THEIR PLANE. Bones would have been fine with rescheduling until the next day, but Cat was adamant that she return home that night. She said she had class early in the morning, and she couldn't miss it.

He booked the next available flight even though he didn't want to. Truth was, he wouldn't want her to leave him whether it was

236

tomorrow or a year from now. He had everything at the moment —almost—and he was loath for it to end.

Still, Cat had agreed to be his lover, not to move in with him. He'd simply have to deal with the limitations she set while working toward expanding them. She might not yet believe that she could love him, but two months ago, she also would've sworn she'd never bed him, and look where they were now.

Cat leaned against him during the car ride from the airport to her house, but when their taxi turned onto the road bordering her family's orchard, she tensed and sat up straight. Even being in close proximity to her family made her feel ashamed again.

"Stop here," Bones told the driver, green lighting up his gaze. "All you see is the road. All you hear is music."

"If you think you're getting a quickie in this backseat, the answer's no," Cat said sternly.

A snort left him. "That's not what I had in mind, but you could convince me of it easily enough. I stopped here because I take it you don't want me to see you to the door and kiss you goodbye in front of your mum?"

Cat's eyes widened in horror. "Absolutely *not*."

Yes, because your mum would rather you risk your life killing vampires instead of being happy while dating one.

Bones didn't say that. Cat already knew it, and the fact that she wasn't angry at her mum over it spoke volumes as to her still wretched self-esteem.

"Be that as it may, I want to see you tonight."

"Bones...no. I'm barely home anymore, and next weekend I move into my new apartment. This week with my family will be all I'll have for a while. Something tells me my grandparents won't be visiting often."

Probably true. Cat had worked for free on her grandparent's orchard her entire life, postponed going to college for two years so she could care for her gramps after his heart attack left him temporarily disabled, and how did they repay her? With more judgmental coldness.

"Where's the apartment?" was all Bones said.

"About six miles from campus."

"You'll be less than twenty minutes from the cave, then." And away from those ungrateful sods. Good news all around.

"I'll call you with the address on Friday. You can come over then. Not before," she added when he opened his mouth to argue. "I mean it, Bones. Unless you get a lead on Hennessey or our masked rapist, give me a little time with my family. It's already Sunday night."

"As you wish," he reluctantly agreed, and then grinned. "If I can't see you all week, at least allow me a proper goodbye. You might not care for this back seat, but there's a nice large bush nearby where we could have some privacy—"

"No," she interrupted, looking adorably scandalized.

"Cruel," he teased, loving her blush. He'd love the day she'd be so comfortable with him that she wouldn't blush, too, and every day that came in between the two.

"Very well, driver," he said with another flash of green. "You're back to your full senses, so continue."

The driver did. Soon, a red flash caught Bones's eye. Her house, up ahead at the end of the road. Cat tensed again when she saw it, an almost palpable shadow filling her features as she looked at it, and then back at Bones.

He took her hand. "Promise me something, Kitten. Promise you're not going to start running again."

"Running?" A frown knit her brow. "I don't want to go jogging..."

His look made her stop that line of thought. Then, understanding flashed over her face and something filled her gaze that went decades beyond her young years.

"I'm too tired to run from you," she said softly. "Besides, you're too fast. You'd only catch me."

"That's right, luv," he swore, his hand tightening on hers. "If you run from me, I'll chase you. And I'll find you."

She stared at him, allowing the depth of her vulnerability to show for the briefest moment. "Promise?"

Bones raised her hand and kissed it. "Promise."

36

$\mathcal{B}$ones's mobile rang Thursday night. Disappointment filled him when he saw that it was Charles. Cat hadn't called all week. Ted also hadn't found any new leads for Bones to chase, and Hennessey had stayed in whatever hole he was hiding. Bones had nothing to kill except time, and it was killing him back.

"Hallo, mate," Bones said, answering.

"How goes the solitude?" Charles replied, sounding annoyingly amused by the question.

"I'm a mess," Bones said honestly. "Don't know if I can take it another twenty-four hours of this. I'll go barmy."

"Eh, buck up, mate. I'm sure it's not that bad."

"Oh?" Bones said acidly. "At three am, I snuck over to Cat's house just to breathe in her scent from her open window, and it's not the first time I've done that."

Charles laughed. "Very well, then, you do have it bad."

Yes, he was aware. Since he could do nothing about that, he may as well solve another issue.

"When are you next coming to the States?"

"I can be there tomorrow, if you need me," Charles said.

"Kind of you, but I rather have plans for tomorrow night," Bones said dryly.

Charles laughed again. "Of course. When did you have in mind, then?"

"If nothing changes with the job I'm doing, would Monday work for you?"

A knowing snort. "You *do* intend to make up for lost time."

"Believe me, if that's all that was on my schedule, I wouldn't want you coming 'round for months," Bones replied. "But, since I can't spend all my time in bed with Cat, and she recently reminded me that I'm the only vampire she knows who hasn't tried to kill her, I'd like for her to meet you."

"And I want to meet her," Charles said instantly. "An actual half vampire? Forgive me if I bow at her feet."

Bones grunted. "Bow all you want. Just wait for me to make the introductions, or you might not survive meeting her."

Charles chuckled. Of course, he didn't believe how deadly Cat was. No one did. It's how she'd survived this long.

"Monday, then," Charles said. "Can't wait, though I did call for another reason. Ian rang me earlier."

"Complaining that I'm ignoring him?" Bones snorted. "Ian should be used to that by now."

"His complaint was more specific," Charles replied in a newly careful tone. "Ian said that a vampire belonging to someone named Hennessey showed up at his house yesterday."

Ice speared Bones. No one aside from Cat and Hennessey knew that Bones was after him. Now, Hennessey had involved his very wily, very untrustworthy sire? Bugger him bowlegged.

"I'll ring Ian now," Bones said crisply.

"I've heard of one vampire named Hennessey," Charles went on in that unnaturally careful tone. "Hails from Greece, originally, but he's spent the past century in the Americas. Nasty sod, from all accounts. This the same bloke?"

"Likely." Bones was deliberately vague. He didn't want to lie to Charles, but he also didn't want him involved.

Charles sighed. "I know you never tell me about your jobs until they're over, but if this Hennessey *is* involved in the job you're on now, I know someone in his line who would very much like to be under someone else's protection."

Oh? That would be useful information indeed.

"Can you discreetly verify that before you come here?"

"I'll try," Charles replied.

"Thanks, mate," Bones said. "See you Monday."

Bones hung up, willing that stab of ice to grow until it was a shield, not a wound. When it had, Bones dialed the vampire he owed his life to...and yet still didn't entirely forgive.

By the fifth ring, Bones wondered if Ian was ignoring him as payback for Bones ignoring Ian's last few calls. Then, Ian finally answered, sounding irritatingly smug.

"Crispin. Spoke to Charles, I take it?"

They were all Englishmen, but Ian's accent mirrored Bones's own while Charles sounded like the aristocrat he was. Ian, like Bones, had grown up on the wrong side of London's streets, where poverty was inescapable and despair was the only guaranteed commodity. That's why Bones didn't bother to flatter Ian with lies. Ian would only see straight through them. His sire's bullshit detector was as finely tuned as a Stradivarius violin.

"Yes," Bones said. "What did Hennessey's bloke want?"

"To accuse you of trying to start a war between Hennessey and me since I'm the master of your line, and Hennessey is the master of his," Ian replied with equal bluntness. "Hennessey claims you've been killing several of his people. Is that true?"

"All business," Bones replied. "Can't help it Hennessey's line is filled with sods that have contracts on their heads."

"Hmm."

The single sound conveyed a litany of suspicion. Bones tensed. Ian was the only vampire alive who could—technically—order

Bones to stop going after Hennessey. Not that Bones would, but since he hadn't left Ian's line yet, his sire still had the ability to make things difficult for him.

"Interesting that Hennessey didn't come himself," Bones said to distract Ian from pondering what his other motives might be. If Ian discovered what Hennessey was up to, he'd know exactly what Bones was doing...and how far he'd take it.

"Yes, very disrespectful," Ian said in a sour tone. "Didn't even send his emissary with a gift for me."

"Rude," Bones agreed.

When Ian said nothing else, Bones said, "And what happened?" while nearly grinding his fangs with frustration.

"I ripped the sod's arms off." *Of course,* Ian's tone implied. "Send your lackey to my house empty-handed to threaten me, and he'll leave carrying both of those severed, empty hands."

A reluctant grin curled Bones's lips. Ian might be seven shades of a shit, but he was also ferocious and fearless. If Hennessey had thought to acquire an ally with his tactless actions, he'd thought wrong.

"Ah," was all Bones said. If he complimented Ian, his sire would know something was amiss.

"Yes, and while no one likes a tattle-tale, do be more careful about the contracts you take in future, Crispin. I'd rather not hear from this Hennessey again, unless he wants to shower me in riches as an apology for his former rudeness."

Doubtful. Hennessey would be enraged by what Ian had done, and thus more prone to make a mistake. Ian didn't know it, but he'd done Bones an enormous favor.

"I'll keep that in mind," Bones replied.

"That was almost polite," Ian noted in amusement. "You feeling all right, Crispin?"

"Have to go," Bones said, to a sardonic, "There's the insufferable sod I know" from his sire.

Bones hung up, feeling his usual mix of annoyance, grudging admiration, and frustration that Ian brought out in him.

All I had to do was not share my food with a starving, seasick bloke aboard our prison ship. Then, Ian wouldn't have felt honor-bound to repay me by turning me into a vampire whether I wanted that or not.

And Bones hadn't wanted it. That's what burned even after all these years. He'd thought he and Ian were mates, and Ian had stomped on his trust in the most permanent way possible. Yet Bones's feelings of betrayal felt further away than ever. The reason why was obvious. Without Ian's actions, Bones would never have met Cat.

Perhaps one day, he'd forgive Ian for not waiting until Bones gave him permission before he turned him into a vampire. Not that he'd tell Ian that. The sod was arrogant enough.

Once again, Bones checked the time on his mobile. Twenty-three more hours to go.

37

*T*wenty-six hours later, Bones rolled off Cat and got his first real look at her apartment. He hadn't bothered to do more than determine the location of her bedroom when he arrived hours earlier. Cat hadn't minded. From her passionate response, she'd missed him, too, even if she couldn't bring herself to say it.

She'd thoroughly cleaned her new flat, which only highlighted its broken floor tiles, the unrepaired water damage on the walls, ceilings, and baseboards, and the traces of mold that her recent bleaching hadn't been able to entirely erase. A glance through her open bathroom door showed cabinets with warped wood, a tiny tub with spiderweb cracks, and a toilet that looked almost as old as she was.

"I should slaughter your landlord for charging you money for this hovel," Bones said, only half joking.

Cat let out a breathy laugh. "You live in a *cave*, Mr. Suddenly Snooty."

"My cave is nicer than this, luv. And better furnished."

Much better. Aside from her bed and a folding table in the living room, she didn't have a stick of furniture in the place.

Her shrug turned into a lazy stretch. "I gave half the Sergio job money to my mom, so I didn't have much left after paying first, last, and security."

Bones bit back every reply that sprang to his lips. They'd only make Cat defensive and angry, but she shouldn't have done that, and her mum *definitely* shouldn't have taken it. Hadn't that woman taken enough from her daughter already?

"It's fine," Cat said, sensing his displeasure. "This place might be a dump, but it's mine, and I have everything I need."

No, she didn't, and he'd remedy that shortly. She might have refused his bounty-hunting money because of their new relationship, but Bones had every right to buy her gifts. Lovers did that all the time.

She tweaked his ear playfully. "Stop. I can almost smell the smoke coming from this thing."

"Liar," Bones said, a smile tugging at his mouth now. "Your nose only serves as decoration for your lovely face."

It was the one part of her that was completely human, and right now, Bones was glad. If she had anything close to a vampire's sense of smell, she'd know how he felt about her mum from one sniff, and it would drive a nasty wedge between them.

Cat's stomach suddenly growled. She gave Bones an embarrassed look as she tugged the sheet over it, as if covering it up could muffle the sounds it made.

"Sorry. Forgot to eat lunch."

And dinner, considering that it was nearing ten o'clock. Bones jumped out of bed and went into the tiny kitchen. One glance inside the refrigerator confirmed his suspicions. Empty.

"Yeah, I know," she said, dragging a robe on as she came into the kitchen, too. "But I didn't have time to go to the store before you came over."

No, because she was too busy cleaning this hovel and giving away nearly all her money to her mum.

"Pepperoni," Bones said.

She blinked. "Excuse me?"

"I have an insatiable craving for pepperoni pizza," Bones replied, striding over to where he'd dropped his mobile in his haste to get undressed. "A salad, too, and of course I can't forget dessert."

"You're full of it." But she was smiling, and her stomach let out what sounded like a roar of approval.

"For all you know, I invented pepperoni pizza," he teased as he entered the order into a delivery app. Ah, good. Should only take half an hour or so to arrive.

"The only things *you* probably invented were X-rated."

Bones grinned. "Would love to claim credit, but those were invented long before me. Why, when I was a young lad, the things I saw at the bordello used to turn my cheeks the same color as your hair."

"I can't imagine you blushing," she said with a shake of her head. "Like, ever."

He winked. "We were all innocent virgins once."

"Tell me about your first time."

As soon as Cat said it, she instantly backtracked. "Never mind. It's none of my business. I don't even know why I asked. Guess all that blushing and virginity stuff made me think of it, but just ignore—"

"Which one?" he asked, setting his mobile down.

She seemed very absorbed with staring at the cracks in her tile floor. "Seriously, Bones, don't worry about it."

"Which one?" he repeated. No chance that he'd let her interest go unanswered, especially since she so rarely asked him anything personal. "See, I consider my virginity lost in stages of four. Aren't you curious as to why?"

Her head snapped up. Yes, she was.

Bones came closer. "When I reached the age where such things interested me, Madam Lucille forbade me from shagging any of the bordello's residents. First, I couldn't afford to pay for it, and second, she didn't want me impregnating them. So, what's a randy lad to do, surrounded by all that forbidden fruit?"

"Bang your hand into submission," Cat said gravely.

He chuckled. "Yes, that, too. Still, one of the women had taken a fancy to me, and while she wasn't going to incur Madame's wrath by giving me a free shag, she did handle me to completion after I brought up her bath water one night." His voice deepened. "It's very different when it's someone else's touch instead of your own bringing you to pleasure, isn't it?"

"Yes," Cat breathed, her gray eyes starting to glint with the faintest hints of green. "So, that's your Stage One."

"It was," Bones said, moving even closer. "Stage Two was several nights later, when the same woman offered to let me pleasure her with my mouth. I'd never done more than kiss and cuddle a lass at that point, so the difference was…striking."

She drew in a jagged breath and her hand drifted toward her center, as if she were imagining him doing that to her. Then, she snatched her hand away as if she'd done something wrong.

Lust lit him up, and he closed the distance between them.

Don't stop touching yourself. It's so, so beautiful.

"Stage Three was her pleasuring me with her mouth the next week." Nearly whispered as he traced the V where the two sides of her robe closed over her chest. Her nipples hardened, and her breathing became shorter. "That felt better than anything I'd experienced before it, so, very notable as well."

"I-I can imagine." Her eyes were now emeralds haloed by storm clouds. "So, was Stage Four soon after?"

"No." A hint of darkness filled Bones's tone at that memory. Cat heard it and stiffened.

"Was it…bad? You don't have to tell me if it was bad."

A smile twisted his lips. "It wasn't forced, if that's what you're thinking. In fact, like most lads their first time, I enjoyed it so much that I spilled myself in about a minute. It's why I got whipped, in point of fact—"

"You were *whipped?*" Cat recoiled in horror.

This part would kill the lovely mood that the rest had elicited, but she'd asked, so he'd tell her.

"After my mum died, Madame Lucille was deciding what to do with me when one of the women remarked that I had a talent for oral pleasure. Since that wouldn't be enough, Madame had me shag one of the women in front of her to see if I had any skill at that, too, which is how I finally lost my virginity."

Cat's eyes were very wide, and all gray now. "You were ordered to have sex under observation, and then whipped when you didn't perform up to standard?"

"Yes," Bones said simply. "Not badly or it would scar, but enough to make me very invested in holding my seed until I'd done a proper job of satisfying my partner. The lasses at the bordello were not easy to please, either. Most were right sick of shagging, considering their line of work, so if I could satisfy them, I could satisfy anyone. As Madame pointed out, it's easy for women to find lovers, especially the rich women of the *ton*. For them to pay me, I had to offer what other blokes couldn't, which was guaranteed satisfaction, multiple times."

Cat still looked horrified. "That's...that's..."

"Survival," Bones supplied in a gentle tone. "Sometimes, we do ugly things for it. Believe me, I had it easier than most. After I was trained, I wasn't whipped anymore, and my clients rarely hurt me or beat me. Many of them were quite kind, and I can't say the same of the blokes who frequented the bordello."

She grasped his arms. "Even if your wound was smaller than theirs, it was still a *wound*, and it still hurt. I'm so sorry you went through that, Bones. It sounds awful."

She was so upset that her scent was spiked with pain, and she kept rubbing his arms as if trying to soothe away an invisible injury. How sweet she was. Pity life wasn't kinder to her so she had a chance to show more of that side of herself.

Bones kissed her forehead.

"It was a long time ago. I only carry what I wish to carry from those memories now. They don't hurt me anymore."

Her grip on his arms tightened. "I don't want you to do that with me. Hold back because that's how you were trained. You go ahead and blast off whenever you want—"

His laughter cut her off. "Oh, Kitten. You're priceless."

"I mean it," she insisted, so earnest it was all he could do not to laugh again.

"I can see that," he said with as much seriousness as he could muster. "However, let me assure you that I love every moment of our time in bed, and I don't want to change anything."

That familiar stubbornness filled her gaze. "I do," she said, and dropped to her knees.

His brows shot up with the same speed as his cock. She grabbed it, licked her lips, and then hesitated. She'd never done this before, and her heart rate kicked up from nerves.

"Tell me if I do something wrong."

A harsh laugh escaped him. "Believe me, nothing you could do with your mouth would be *wrong*, but there's no rush. Plenty of time for this later—"

Bones's voice ripped away when she encased him in her mouth, sucking so strongly he thought his skin would split from pleasure. The sound he made must have encouraged her because she increased the pressure.

He fisted his hands, not trusting himself to touch her. His control was already a fading memory. Bloody hell, if she kept this up, she'd get her wish for his quick "blast off." She went at his cock with the same single-minded focus she used when attacking an opponent, and it was gloriously, erotically fierce.

"…change anything?" he heard her mumble moments later.

"*No.*"

His response was so emphatic he felt her throat contract with laughter. He closed his eyes, not daring to look at her anymore. If what she was doing didn't finish him, the sight of it would. He'd been right weeks ago. The only thing that *did* make her mouth more beautiful was seeing it wrapped around his cock.

The coolness of the wall met his back. At some point, he'd leaned against it. Her free hand caressed his hip, painting it with heat that felt slight compared to her scorching mouth. Silk brushed his clenched hands. Her hair, spilling over his skin. Her heartbeat, thrumming with excitement instead of nervousness now, and her scent, perfuming the air with her growing lust as she moved faster, harder, until it was too wonderful to bear.

"Kitten." His voice was so thick, he was nearly hoarse. "I'm going to come."

She paused. His whole body screamed in protest, making him miss the first part of what she said.

"...stuff isn't poisonous, is it?"

Laughter ground from him like glass shards. "No. I was being a gentleman."

"Oh."

A pause followed the single word. Bones bent down, about to draw her up and finish inside her, when she pushed him back against the wall. Her mouth encased him again, sucking with her inhuman strength, and he let the extreme pleasure wash over him until he came with spasms that felt like they'd crack his spine.

When they stopped, he gently pulled her head away before bending down and claiming her mouth. His pleasure flavored her taste, and he savored that saltiness as he kissed her with passion that grew when he reached down and felt how roused she was. It wasn't possible that she'd enjoyed that as much as he, but enjoy it she had. Now, to return the favor, with interest.

A hard knock on the door shattered his intentions.

"Delivery!" a male voice called out, to more knocks.

Cat drew her robe closed and gave Bones a little push away.

"Food's here," she said before flashing him an uncharacteristically naughty smile. "Yes, I'm still hungry."

38

$\mathcal{T}$he next two days passed in a blur, so much that Bones forgot to get Charles a gift until Cat left for class on Monday. Then, Bones rushed to an antique dealer known for carrying items that dated back to Charles's days as a human. His mate had dropped everything to fly in from England to see him, and to verify a potential Judas in Hennessey's line. The least Bones could do was have a proper welcome gift for him.

Bones hit a traffic snag on the way back that he would have sped around if the road wasn't partially blocked by police cars. No need to waste more time dealing with the law chasing him, especially since so many cops now wore body cameras. Besides, Charles wasn't due to arrive for another hour, and Cat wouldn't be over until an hour after that.

Half an hour later, he realized he was wrong when he saw a vintage red Corvette parked along the road that bordered the woods leading to the cave. No one who could afford that sort of vehicle would leave it unattended on this deserted stretch. When Bones stopped, one sniff confirmed Charles had been driving it.

His plane must have arrived early. Eh, well, Charles was one of the few people who knew the way to the cave, and where to go once he was inside it. At least Cat wasn't here yet...oh fucking hell, was that her truck up ahead?

It was, and it, too, was empty. Bones didn't hear any crunching leaves in the woods, either. Cat wasn't on her way to the cave. She was already in it, as was Charles, and Bones hadn't told her that his mate was coming.

Please, let them not have killed each other!

Bones flew to the cave, his heart clenching as he entered it. Had he already lost one of the two people he loved most in the world? He tore around the corner that led to the living room area —and stopped short. Disbelief made him stare, unable to believe what he was seeing.

Charles was lying on the ground with Cat straddling him. Rage almost stole Bones's vision until he realized that Charles was facing the wrong way for anything sexual to occur. Charles's head was also bloody, and Cat's hands were filled with blood-covered rocks. When Cat saw him, she gave Bones such a look of relief that this couldn't be a case of illicit passion no matter what position they were in.

Still, the rabid part of Bones that roared to life at the sight of Cat atop another man allowed only one thing to come out of his mouth.

"Charles, you'd better have a splendid explanation for her being on top of you."

Cat leapt off him. Charles jumped up nearly as quickly, his long, spiky black hair wet from blood. More crimson streaks stained his ecru-colored skin, and Charles's whisky brown eyes shot Bones a baleful look as Charles slapped at the dirt covering his white shirt and expensive gray trousers.

"Believe me, I've never enjoyed a woman astride me less," Charles said with a rude glance at Cat. "I came out to say hallo, and this she-devil blinded me by flinging rocks into my eyes! Then, she attempted to split my skull before threatening to impale me with silver if I so much as twitched. It's been a few years since

I've been to America, but I daresay the method of greeting a person has drastically changed!"

Cat's guilty expression confirmed every word. Bones rolled his eyes, but he was beyond relieved. This wasn't the best introduction, but it could have been much, much worse.

"I'm glad you're alive, Charles, and the only reason you are is because she didn't *have* any silver. She'd have staked you right and proper otherwise. I warned you that she has a tendency to shrivel someone first and introduce herself afterward."

"That's uncalled for," Cat muttered.

Bones snorted. "Right. Well, Kitten, this is my best mate Charles, but you can call him by his chosen name, Spade. Charles, this is the Cat. You can see for yourself that everything I've told you about her is…an understatement."

Cat gave him a quick glower before she held out her hand to Charles. "Um, hi."

Charles gave her hand a stunned look before taking it with a bellow of laughter. "Well, hallo to you, too, darling! Pleased to meet you now that you're not flogging me unmercifully."

"I warned you to wait for me," Bones said in a low voice.

"You should have been more *emphatic*," Charles replied in the same bare whisper.

"Spade." Cat looked uncomfortable as she said Charles's vampire name. "You're white. Isn't that…politically incorrect?"

This time, Charles's laughter held an edge. "I didn't choose that name as a racial slur. It was how the overseer in the penal colonies used to address me. A spade is a shovel, and I was a digger. He never called anyone by their names, only their assigned tools. He said we weren't worthy of more."

Understanding flashed over Cat's features. She shot a quick glance at Bones, and he nodded. *Yes,* that nod confirmed. *He's one of men I knew back when I was human.*

"Sounds very demeaning," Cat replied to Charles. "Why'd you keep that name, then?"

Charles's smile turned to glass. "So I'd never forget."

Now she looked uncomfortable for a different reason. Bones redirected the topic.

"Charles has potential information on a flunky of Hennessey's who might prove useful."

Cat brightened. "Great. Should I grab my work clothes and get ready to go?"

"You should stay out of it," Charles said instantly.

Bones glanced heavenward. *If You're at all kind, don't let her erupt...*

"Is it a vampire thing to be a chauvinist?" Cat asked with all the anger Bones had anticipated. "Or just an eighteenth century one? Wake up and smell the modern age, *Spade*. Women are good for more than cringing and waiting for men to rescue them!"

"And if Crispin felt differently for you, I'd bid you good fortune and tell you to have at it," Charles replied. "Yet I know firsthand how devastating it is when someone you love is murdered. There's nothing worse, and I don't want him going through that."

Some of the anger drained from Cat's features. "I'm so sorry that vampires killed someone you loved—"

"It wasn't vampires." Pain and rage splintered Charles's tone. "A group of French deserters cut her throat."

Cat's mouth closed and shame flashed over her features. Was she finally realizing that horrible deeds were *not* exclusive to vampires, and assuming they were was both bigoted and wrong?

"I'm so sorry," Cat said again, her tone softer this time. "But I'm not like everyone else."

She glanced at Bones after she said it, her gaze silently asking, *does he know?*

Bones nodded even as Charles said, "So I've heard, and you certainly caught me off guard earlier, but whatever your extraordinary lineage, you're easy to kill. That pulse in your neck is your greatest weakness, and if I'd had a mind to before, I could have flipped over and torn it out."

Now Bones's glance heavenward was irritated. *Vengeful, aren't You?*

Instead of getting angry, Cat smiled. "You're pretty cocky. So am I, when it comes to certain things. We'll get along just fine. Wait here."

With that, Cat dashed off toward her weapons' cache, ignoring Bones calling after her.

"Where's she off to?" Charles wondered.

Bones sighed. "To hand you your arse, and for the record, if I thought I had a chance of keeping her out of this business with Hennessey, I would. Woman's stubborn beyond reason."

Charles gave him an amazed stare. "Stubbornness won't keep her alive. You almost never involve *me* in your hunts, and I'm a Master vampire. I'm astounded you'd allow her near this..."

Charles's voice trailed off when Cat returned with a wide smile and a handful of her throwing knives.

"Okay, you're a big, bad vampire who's gonna rip my throat out, right?" she taunted. "You see I'm armed—and these are steel, not silver since I don't want you to end up smelly—but you don't care since you're all that and I'm just an artery in a dress. If you get a mouth on my throat, you win, but if I plug your heart first, I do."

Charles looked at Cat as if she were barmy. Then, his gaze swung to Bones. "Is she joking?"

"Not at all." This was hardly how he'd imagined their first meeting would go, but it *would* silence Charles's arguments.

"Dinner's getting cold," Cat said with a wider smile. "Come and get me, bloodsucker."

Charles glanced at Bones again.

Bones swept out his hand. *Have at it, mate.*

Charles lunged at Cat, feinting right before aiming for her

throat. He'd almost reached it when two rapid thuds had him coming to a dead stop while staring at his chest in disbelief.

"Well, strike me pink!"

"I don't know what that means, but okay," Cat said in a cheery tone.

She had a right to be pleased. Two hilts speared Charles right in the chest. If they'd been silver, he'd be either dead from the double heart puncture or paralyzed with agony, making him an easy kill. Either way, she'd won.

Charles yanked the knives out and met Bones's knowing gaze.

"I don't believe it," Charles whispered.

Bones grunted. "Same thing I thought when I first tangled with her. She has a real talent with knives. Good thing she hadn't practiced throwing them before she met me, or I might not be here."

Charles shook his head. "Indeed. All right, Cat." He turned his attention back to her. "You've made an excellent point that you're far deadlier than you appear. I also see I can't sway you to leave this business with Hennessey alone, and Crispin clearly has confidence in you, so I bow in defeat."

Charles punctuated that with a bow worthy of his aristocratic heritage, and Cat laughed in delight.

"What were you before they sent you to prison? A duke?"

Charles straightened to his full height of six feet four inches. "Baron Charles DeMortimer, at your service."

Then, he turned to Crispin. "I have the information we talked about, if you're truly set on taking her on a hunt tonight."

"He is," Cat said before Bones could respond. Her gray gaze was almost alight from eagerness. "Who am I going after?"

39

*C*harles had done more than make a discreet inquiry. He'd also demanded proof of the Judas's intentions to betray Hennessey. That proof had blond hair and was hopping down a dark derelict alley like a vampire-sized bunny, twitching and giggling all the while. Bones watched, shaking his head.

Only one thing could cause a vampire to act that way. The wanker must be high on Red Dragon—the name for tainted blood that acted as a narcotic to vampires. Red Dragon was rare, potent, and very, very illegal.

Cat walked into the alley toward the vampire, twitching herself as if suffering withdrawals due to a human narcotic. Her bruises and dirty clothes also added to her addict charade.

"You got some horse, man?" she called out to the vampire.

The vampire let out another giggle. "Not here, chickie. But I can get you some. Come with me."

Cat hunched her shoulders. "You're not a cop, are you?"

Another stream of giggles. "Not that."

Cat backed up as if about to leave. "I don't have time for you to call someone. I'm hurtin' here."

"It's in my car," the vampire said. "Right this way."

He skip-hopped toward an even darker and more deserted alley, where shells of buildings loomed on either side of the narrow stretch of street like tattered, angry ghosts.

Cat followed, giving furtive glances around for signs of danger. Bones didn't feel any other vampires, and the few humans he did hear were probably squatting in the ruined buildings.

"Right here, chickie," the vampire called out, stopping at a faded gold Oldsmobile that looked like a literal translation of the vehicle's name. Then, he held open the passenger door.

Cat bent down to look inside. The vampire cuffed the back of Cat's head hard enough to knock out a normal human. It likely only gave Cat a headache, but Bones took no chances. He put his car in gear as the vampire dumped Cat into the front seat, closed the door, and drove off, giggling all the while.

Bones let the vampire drive until he'd exited the alleys and was on a thin stretch road away from potential witnesses. Then, Bones rammed the Oldsmobile, watching with satisfaction as the vampire's head slammed onto his steering wheel.

That should silence your giggles.

Cat's head popped up in Bones's headlights. The vampire shrieked as she shoved him back into his chair.

"Shut up, Chirpy!" Cat said in an irritated voice. "Pull over, or you'll get rear-ended again, and if that happens, guess where this knife will end up."

Bones turned off his ear piece. No need for it at this distance.

"Take your hands off me," the vampire ordered Cat, followed by a green glow lighting up the interior of the car.

"Don't waste your brights on me, buddy," Cat said, scorn in her tone. "You've got three seconds to pull over, or he's going to ram you again, and that'll be nighty-night for you."

Bones hit the brakes and gas simultaneously, causing the engine to growl in warning. The vampire pulled over and put the car into park.

Bones got out and went to the driver's side. One clear glance at the vampire's face confirmed his identity.

"Well, Tony, how goes it?" Bones asked him.

Tony recognized Bones, too, and turned whiter than his already pale skin. "I don't know where Hennessey is!"

Bones snorted. "Right, and I believe you. Kitten, if you'll drive? Tony and I are going to have a chat."

With that, Bones grabbed the knife in Tony's chest to steady it, and hauled him into the backseat. Tony whimpered between mumbles of "I don't know, I don't know."

"Where to?" Cat asked when she was behind the wheel.

"Just around, until our mate Tony tells us otherwise."

She glanced behind him. "We're leaving the car?"

"It's one of Ted's that he doesn't need," Bones replied.

"I don't know anything," Tony whined again as Cat drove off. "I'm just trying to make a buck!"

Why did they waste time lying?

"Don't tell me you don't know how to reach Hennessey. Every vampire knows how to contact their sire. Just for your miserable existence, I should kill you. Pretending to sell drugs to addicts and then mesmerizing them into thinking they've gotten what they paid for? Pathetic."

"Asshole," Cat said with an affirming nod.

Tony's green eyes slanted toward Bones. "Hennessey will kill me."

"Not if he's dead, he won't," Bones said instantly. "You're as good as that yourself now, too. Think Hennessey will allow you to live if he finds out that you let yourself get captured by me? He'll rip your bloody head off, and you know it. I'm your only hope, mate."

Tony gave a pleading look in Cat's direction. She gave him a one-fingered opinion of his predicament.

Tony huffed in offense and looked back at Bones. "Promise me you won't kill me, and I'll tell you everything."

Bones gave him a hard stare. "I'll only kill you if you don't talk, and if you lie to me, I *really* won't kill you, but you'll wish I had. Count on it."

Tony's eyes widened. "Hennessey's been secretive about his location recently, I swear, but if I need anything, I'm supposed to go to Lola. She lives in Lansing, and she and Hennessey are tight. She should know where Hennessey is."

"Address," Bones said shortly.

Tony gave it.

"Kitten, get on I-69 and head north. We're going to Michigan."

"I have a test in six hours," Cat muttered. "It took *forever* for him to show up tonight."

Bones met her gaze in the rearview mirror. "This is the job, luv. Doing it right means seeing it through."

40

*T*hree hours later, Bones had Cat pull into the grocery store parking lot across the street from Lola's building. At five am, the lot was empty, but soon, employees would show up. Hopefully, this wouldn't take long.

Bones switched the knife to Tony's back to make him easier to control as they walked toward Lola's building. Doing so also made them appear less conspicuous. Bones's arm was around Tony as if they were mates, and his denim jacket hid most of the blade protruding from Tony's back.

Lola lived in an upscale building with pretty iron balconies, excellent lighting, and security cameras at each entrance. A variety of higher-end cars dotted the parking lot. Bones nudged Tony, and he scanned the vehicles.

"Her car's not here."

"You can tell from one glance?" Bones countered.

Tony let out a half giggle, half grunt. "When you see it, you'll understand."

Once they were close enough for any vampires in the building to overhear them, Bones put a finger to his lips. Then, he mimed for Cat to stay back with Tony while he went inside.

She gave him an aggravated look, but took hold of the knife in Tony's back.

Bones crept around to the back of the building. There, he put on a ski mask and then flew at the nearest camera, smashing it. A hard yank broke the automated lock on the door, and Bones tackled the bleary-eyed man wearing a private security uniform who'd risen from his desk in alarm after seeing Bones.

"Don't scream," Bones said, his green glare compelling the man to obey. "Did you hit any alarms, silent or otherwise?"

"No," the man replied, his eyes glazed from Bones's power.

Bones pulled him to his feet. "Show me where all the security cameras feed to."

Thirty minutes and one phone call to Ted later, Bones had the building's security system disabled. Now, he wouldn't need to smash the remaining cameras, and Ted had logged in remotely and deleted the earlier feed from uploading into the cloud. Ted had also accessed older feed and transferred it so even if this morning's efforts proved fruitless, Bones could see which vampires had been coming and going from Lola's building.

"Know a tenant named Lola?" Bones asked the guard as he was finishing up.

A nod. "Hot Asian chick, great legs, *sick* ride."

"Oh?" Perhaps Tony hadn't been lying. "What kind?"

"Ferrari," the guard said with longing. "Candy-apple red."

That would indeed be easy to spot. "Thanks, mate. Now, return to your desk. You never saw me. You never left your seat. This has been a very boring morning."

The guard nodded, walking away without a backward glance.

Bones took up position in the blind spot near the front entrance, where thin walls hid exterior trash cans from view.

"I'm never making this exam," he heard Cat mutter through his ear piece.

Her own fault. If she wanted to be a student, she could be. Would be his preference in the matter. But she'd insisted on going after Hennessey, which meant she couldn't hit "pause" during a hunt simply because it had become inconvenient.

The distinctive *vroom* from an approaching Ferrari snapped Bones's attention away from Cat. He held out his mobile, using it to peer around the wall without revealing himself. True to the guard's description, a candy-apple red Ferrari pulled into the parking lot. Then, a slender, beautiful woman with high cheek-bones, dusky-colored skin, and chin-length black hair exited it. Her short green dress revealed the aforementioned great legs, but Bones only stared to determine if Lola had any weapons on her. Her shoes were strappy heeled sandals, so no hidden threats there, and her pocketbook could hold knives, but its small clutch size would allow one or two at most.

Either Lola was very arrogant, or she was a very skilled fighter. Time to find out which.

Bones waited until Lola had almost reached the front doors before he stepped into her line of sight. She took one look at him and ran, but those high heels did her no favors.

"Not so fast," he said, grabbing her.

Lola gave a brief, ineffective struggle. *Arrogant it was, then.*

When that failed, she looked down her nose at him. "How dare you touch me?"

Bones had been sneered at more effectively by much haughtier people, and he let his laugh show it.

"Dare? There's a fine word. It implies courage. Are you brave, Lola? We'll soon find out."

She glanced around as if looking for help. Finding none, she gave him another imperious glare. "You're making a big mistake."

This parking lot would fill with people leaving for work soon. Bones's grip tightened. "Wouldn't be my first. Now, then, sweet-ness, you obviously recognize me, so you know what I want."

"Hennessey and the others will kill you," Lola hissed. "It's only a matter of time—"

Bones's new grip on her jaw cut off her threat. "Normally I

don't abuse women, but you've earned the right to be an exception. So, either tell me who else is involved with Hennessey and where to find them, or you'll endure every torture and humiliation you've helped inflect on others."

A lie. Bones would kill her without pause, but he'd never do the rest. Still, the worst sort of people always expected the worst from others, so she'd believe him.

"I've met some depraved, beastly blokes in my travels who would love to give you a taste of your own poison," Bones went on, his tone deepening as if enjoying the thought. "Tell you what: I'll even sell you to them. Turnabout's fair game, isn't it? I'd say that was fair all the way 'round."

Fear turned Lola's scent sour. Tony had been right. Lola knew everything that Hennessey was doing, or the threat wouldn't terrify her so.

"I don't know where Hennessey is," Lola said. "He hasn't told me recently!"

Bones grabbed her by her hair and began dragging her away from the building. "You've just made Christmas come early for some happy deviants."

"Wait, I know where Switch is!"

Bones stopped, although he shook her. "Who's Switch?"

"Hennessey's enforcer." Scorn tinged Lola's tone. "You know how Hennessey hates to get his hands dirty. Switch handles things like silencing witnesses and body disposal. He's also recruiting now, too, since we don't have Charlie, Dean, and Stephanie anymore. With Hennessey's new protection, we no longer have to worry about any pesky human interference, either."

Very interesting. "What's Switch's real name, and who's Hennessey's new protection?"

"Head's up!" Cat shouted, coming out from her hiding place across the parking lot.

Bones looked up. Two vampires were now free-falling from

the roof. His own bloody fault for not checking that area for danger. Bones drew out his knife—

Lola lunged at him, silver flashing in her hand. Before he could shove her back, three knife hilts appeared in her chest as if by magic. Horror seized Lola's features, and she collapsed.

No time to check on her. Bones flew up between his attackers right before they landed on him. Their momentum was at maximum velocity from the ten-story drop, so Bones hooked his arm around the nearest vampire's throat and let gravity do the rest.

A satisfying rip later, Bones hurled the detached head at the second vampire's face. Brown hair haloed the two heads for an instant before the attacker hit the ground. Bones leapt on him, adding to the impact that made his attacker momentarily limp. That instant of weakness was all Bones needed. Another hard jerk-and-twist later, and Bones had two heads at his feet.

He leapt up and looked where he'd heard Cat's warning shout. She was rising from a crouch, unharmed. Thank God Lola's secret bodyguards had only focused on him. Now, to see if Lola was still alive...no. Cat's impressive toss had caused Lola to take her valuable knowledge right to hell with the rest of her.

"Lucifer's bouncing balls, Kitten, not *again*," Bones said in exasperation.

Guilt stamped onto Cat's features, and she side-stepped in front of an oddly-shaped lump of dirt near her feet. "She was going to kill you. Look at the knife in her hand!"

Wait...that wasn't dirt Cat was standing in front of. He'd been so relieved to see she was unharmed that he hadn't looked closely at the lump near her feet before. He did now, and it had once been an annoying, giggling vampire.

"Him, too?" Bones asked in a resigned tone.

"He jumped me," Cat said, part defiant and part defensive.

Every *last* bit of potential knowledge, gone, courtesy of the love of his life who couldn't stop murdering vampires even when she was only supposed to guard them.

"You're not a woman," Bones said with all the frustration boiling up in him. "You're the Grim Reaper with red hair!"

She huffed. "That's not fair—"

A horrified scream cut her off. They both turned to see a brunette woman in a Houndstooth suit staring at the headless bodies near the entrance. With another scream, she ran inside.

Bones plucked the knives from Lola's chest. Couldn't leave them behind with Cat's fingerprints on them. Then, he crossed the parking lot and took Cat's hand.

"Let's go, Kitten, before you murder someone else."

"I don't think that's funny," she muttered, but kept up with his brisk pace.

"At least I got some information out of Lola first," he commented. "Hennessey has new protection and an enforcer named Switch. We'll start by trying to find out who Switch is."

"Lola was going to *kill* you!" Fear threaded Cat's scent despite her defensive tone. She'd actually thought she was saving him, as if he hadn't had centuries to learn how to save himself.

So secretly sweet, albeit with a hefty size of murderousness.

Bones pulled her to him, kissing her until more screams warned that the law would soon be there.

"Did it ever occur to you to aim for something other than the heart?" he asked when he drew away.

No, her confused expression said.

He snorted and held open her car door.

"I love that you did it to protect me, but next time, try aiming to *wound*, hmm? Maybe throw the knives at the person's head? That way, they're momentarily incapacitated, but not reduced to a pile of rotting remains. Just food for thought, luv."

$\mathcal{C}$at had Bones rush her back to her flat so she could change clothes before attempting to make it to class in time to take her exam. Bones offered to mesmerize her professor into scheduling a make-up time for her, but Cat refused.

"That's like cheating."

He snorted. "Cheating would be mesmerizing him into giving you an A for the semester. *This* is ensuring you don't get a zero since you can hardly tell him the real reason you're late."

"Certainly can't," Cat muttered. "You coming over later?"

"Of course. Have to drop this car off at Ted's and run a few errands first, but I'll see you in a few hours."

She nodded. "Hopefully, I'll be asleep by then—"

"Hi, Cathy!"

The chipper voice made both of them look up. A tawny-haired lad with buttercream pale skin waved at Cat from the second floor. His open door was right next to Cat's flat, so this must be her neighbor. He looked about Cat's age, and his gaze was the personification of "puppy love" as he stared at Cat.

Cat gave her neighbor a smile that ripped jealousy through Bones like a skillfully-wielded knife. He'd had to work months to get a smile like that from her, and she was bestowing it on this knobhead only days after meeting him?

Bones stared back at her neighbor, and the lad's smile slipped.

"I'm sorry, I didn't know you had company," the young man said, making the wise decision to back up into his flat. Then, Cat stopped him before he closed the door.

"It's okay, Timmie. He's not really 'company' anyway."

"Oh?"

Timmie's smile was back with reinforcements, and now he reeked so much of infatuation Bones could smell it from where he stood. More jealousy tore at him, until Bones felt every inch the green-eyed monster that the emotion was named after.

"Are you Cathy's brother?" Timmie asked Bones.

Oh, that was it. "Whatever would give you the idea that I'm her damn brother?"

The words and Bones's tone caused Timmie to leap back into his doorframe. "Sorry!" he managed before slamming the door shut behind him.

Cat turned around and glared at Bones before poking him in the chest.

"What the hell was that? Either you make a sincere apology to Timmie now, or you can slither back to your cave like the festering ball sack you just acted like. Timmie's a nice guy, and you probably just made him pee his pants."

Good, was Bones's first thought. *Then he might not act on what he feels for you. Save him a world of pain.*

But the small, still-rational part of him knew that Cat was right. He *had* acted like a festering ball sack.

"I mean it," Cat said, poking Bones again. "One...two..."

She was *counting* at him? Did he look two instead of two hundred and fifty?

"Three..." she said in a warning tone.

She wanted an apology? Oh, he'd give her a memorable one.

Bones went up to Timmie's flat and knocked. The lad's heart rate increased when he opened the door and saw Bones.

Don't fret, I'm not here to eat you, Bones thought. *Yet.*

Bones gave Timmie his most charming smile. "Right, then, mate, terribly sorry for my rudeness, and I do beg your pardon. I can only explain that my curtness was caused by my natural affront to the suggestion that she was my sister. Since we'll be shagging tonight, you can imagine how I'd be distressed at the thought of rogering my own sibling—"

"You schmuck!" Cat shouted, cutting off the rest of what Bones was going to say. "The only thing you'll be shagging tonight is yourself!"

Bones turned around with feigned innocence. "You demanded sincerity. Well, luv, I was sincere."

Steam practically came from her ears. "You can get right back in that car, and I'll only see you later if you're not being such an *asshole.*"

Oh, that wasn't being an arsehole. This was.

Bones turned back to Timmie. "Nice to meet you, mate, and here's some advice: don't even think about it. You try anything with her, and I'll neuter you with my bare hands."

"Get. Out!" Cat shouted.

Bones grinned with teeth at Timmie, who blanched and scooted back into his apartment even though Bones hadn't flashed fang. Then, Bones went back down to the parking lot, where Cat was still glaring knives at him.

"Leave," she said with an emphatic swipe at his car.

"Right now," Bones agreed, swooping in to give her a quick kiss and then leaping back from her instant smack. Yes, he'd deserved it. No, he couldn't bring himself to be sorry.

"See you later, Kitten," Bones called out as he drove away.

All right, perhaps he could have handled that better, but he'd hardly challenged Timmie to pistols at dawn, had he? Back in Bones's day, that was all the rage for handling disputes over a lady's affections. At least now, the lovesick lad would remember that he'd been warned, and really, hadn't that been the gentlemanly thing to do?

Very well. It wasn't, but it was the best he could manage.

Perhaps he'd hold off on going back to Cat's until later tonight. With luck, some sleep should take the edge off her anger. Besides, Bones had a new name for Ted to run a trace on.

Switch.

Bones hadn't heard of Switch, but vampires had been known to pick more than one moniker. Perhaps Charles's potential Judas had heard of Switch? That person had certainly proved their intention to betray Hennessey by giving them Tony. If not for Cat's murder-happy ways, Bones might have learned the names of all Hennessey's partners by now.

And she thought *he'd* overreacted with Timmie. Hmmph.

Thirty minutes later, Bones returned to the cave. Charles was still there. A surprise.

"Thought you were checking into a hotel, mate?"

"Immediately," Charles said, his lip curling with disdain as he looked around at the cave's interior. "But first, I wanted to be sure that you made it back safely."

"Two mother hens," Bones said, shaking his head.

Charles's brows rose. "Beg pardon?"

Bones gave him a sardonic smile. "Cat was so concerned for me during a fight earlier that she killed the contact Tony gave us. Killed him, too, for good measure."

Charles's features froze into carved alabaster. "Crispin...are you quite certain that she—"

"Isn't a turncoat planted by Hennessey?" Bones finished with a dry laugh. "Yeah, mate, I'm certain. For starters, Cat isn't capable of such betrayal. Secondly, she could have killed me in my sleep several times by now if my death was her true aim. No, she's just very homicidal when it comes to vampires."

Charles gave him a somber look. "And reckless."

271

Bones shrugged. "She'll learn. She's already made incredible strides, but enough of that. Your contact in Hennessey's line proved their worth. Tony was a good lead, until things went sideways. Going to tell me who this Judas is?"

Charles shook his head. "Not until I have permission. I gave my word."

Bones said nothing, but Charles's chivalrousness was legendary, so it must be a woman. One that Charles had likely had a former fling with, too, for her to trust him with such a secret. That narrowed the list quite a bit, but Bones wouldn't push his mate for a name. Yet.

"Tell this person I want to meet," Bones said. "And ask if the name Switch is familiar."

"I will." Then, Charles's mouth twisted. "Every awful rumor I heard about Hennessey is true, isn't it?"

Bones met his gaze. Charles deserved the truth. "Yes."

Something hard flashed in Charles's whisky-colored eyes. "Then let me help you destroy him, Crispin."

Bones touched Charles's shoulder. "You already have. Now," his tone lightened. "I know you're anxious to check into what must be the finest suite this city has to offer, so go do that, and let me know what your Judas says."

Charles wanted to argue. It was clear in his gaze, but he only clasped the hand that Bones had laid on him.

"Not my fault I don't fancy subterranean dwellings," he said in an equally light tone.

Bones grinned. "Mock all you want, Baron DeMortimer, but this cave is the safest place for me right now. Besides, it makes me appreciate my other houses all the more."

Charles put on his coat with a jaded glance. "Poor Cat has no idea you're as wealthy as I am, does she?"

"Wealthier," Bones said, his grin widening. "I got in on the ground floor with Amazon, remember?"

Charles shuddered. "Don't remind me that I missed out on

that." Then, his gaze turned serious. "I'll let you know as soon as I hear from my contact. 'Til then, be safe, Crispin."

"I will," Bones said. "Until again, mate."

Charles left. Bones went to his computer. Ted had been giving Bones hacking tips, probably in the hopes that he'd get an uninterrupted night of sleep soon. Now, to see what he could find out about a vampire named Switch.

BONES PULLED up to Cat's building later that evening. He'd barely made it off his motorcycle when he saw Justina's car in the parking lot. Bugger. Just what he didn't need...and why was Timmie's voice coming from inside Cat's flat?

"That's right, Justina! Cathy and I are going to slay those demons with the power of Jesus. Hallelujah, can I get an amen?"

"Amen!" Justina said fervently, echoed by a less than enthused "Amen," from Cat.

What in the *literal* hell?

"I'm so glad Catherine is dating a good Christian boy like you, Timmie," Justina went on. "You don't know how worried I've been that she'd take up with the wrong kind."

Cat made a strangled sound that ended in a faked cough. "Yeah, I'm, uh, very lucky."

"So am I, praise God," Timmie said happily.

Bones's fangs shot out. *More of this, lad, and you'll be praising Him to His face within the hour.*

"But seriously, Mom, I'm tired," Cat said. "It's great to see you, but like I said, I need some sleep. We were out late last night taking care of...things."

"Doing the Lord's work," Timmie said in his gratingly cheerful tone. "Death to all demons, can I get an amen?"

Bones's scoff ended in a snarl. Her mum thought Cat had been vampire hunting with *Timmie*? The only thing that wanker could do to help on a hunt was make the vampire laugh so hard, they wouldn't see Cat sneaking up behind them with a knife!

"I understand." Justina sounded disappointed, but when she spoke next, she also sounded closer to the door. "Very nice to meet you, Timmie. Catherine, walk me out?"

"Of course, Mom," Cat replied.

"'Bye, Justina. God bless!" Timmie said.

Bones went around to the back of the unit, removing himself from sight, as Cat and Justina went out the front door.

"He's sweet, but," Justina lowered her voice to a whisper, "also a little fanatical, don't you think?"

"Not really." Cat's voice was a squeak. "He was probably just nervous to meet you."

Justina sniffed. "I can't imagine why."

Because Harpies are kinder than you, Bones thought.

"Neither can I," Cat said in her biggest lie to date. "But either way, I'm glad you two met. Love you, Mom."

"Love you, too, Catherine," her mother said.

The second biggest lie he'd heard today.

Then Cat closed her door, muttering "Thank God" a second after it was fully shut.

"Amen!" Timmie said at once.

That's it. The Almighty was about to meet his biggest fan.

Bones came around to the front of the building, slipping up to the second floor while Justina walked down to the first. If she turned around, she'd see Bones. Part of him wanted her to. But Justina went to her car without a backward glance and then drove away.

"Thanks, Timmie," Cat was saying as Bones approached her door. "I owe you one."

Bones opened it to see Cat put her arms around the tawny-haired lad. Timmie's light brown eyes widened when they met Bones's steely gaze, and then he jumped back as if scalded.

"Not interrupting, am I?" Bones asked sarcastically.

Timmie's hand clapped over his groin as he kept backing away. Cat saw it and gave Bones an aggravated look.

"Dammit, Bones, tell him you didn't mean it when you threatened to neuter him earlier."

Bones gave Timmie a single, pitiless glance. "Why?"

"Because if you don't, I'm going to get really, really celibate," Cat said through gritted teeth.

I did mean it, Bones's gaze told Timmie, but he said, "Don't fret, mate. You can leave with your stones intact. Just remember that pretending to be her boyfriend was exactly that. Pretending. Don't let the fantasy go to your head."

"You heard that?" A look of horror crossed Cat's features.

"'Death to all demons, can I get an amen?'" Bones quoted.

She came toward him, her expression pleading for understanding. "I'm sorry, but I kinda lost it when my mom came over and accused me of, of drinking!"

And? "You do drink."

She tapped her neck with meaning. "I mean of *drinking*."

Bones stared. "Bloody hell."

"In a nutshell," Cat muttered.

No wonder she'd acted so barmy. Turning into a vampire was her worst fear, and here her mum had accused her of doing that. It almost excused her desperate ruse with Timmie. Almost.

"Private time, lad," Bones told Timmie. "Say goodnight."

"Timmie, thanks again," Cat said, with a *be nice!* glance Bones's way. "I'll see you in the morning."

Timmie hurried over to the door, paused, and then said, "I don't mind foreigners. God save the queen!" before darting away.

What?

If Bones hadn't already done a thorough background check on Timmie and every other tenant in this complex, he'd think the lad was mental.

Cat caught Bones's look. "Didn't hear that part?" she asked with a sigh. "Never mind. Don't ask."

42

*T*wo full weeks passed without any word from Charles about Hennessey's betrayer or any new sightings of Hennessey himself. Worse, several of the police reports that had been filed on the missing girls suddenly vanished. According to Ted, someone had done a surgical scrub of the records, which wasn't easy.

"Another dead end?" Cat asked Bones after he leaned back from his computer with a disgusted noise.

"Hennessey's never been this cautious before. If things got messy, he'd simply pick a new area. Now, in addition to mesmerizing families into not knowing their loved ones are missing, Hennessey's also deleting the few police reports that do exist."

Cat began to pace. "Maybe he's tired of running. No police reports means no headlines, so he can get nice and comfy here."

Bones had considered that, but it still didn't fit.

"I think the new 'protection' Lola mentioned must be the wild card. Whoever they are, Hennessey's being very discreet for their sake, so they must be either vampires or humans with prominent reputations to protect."

"Corrupt cops?" Cat offered. "Say you're the chief of police, or you're running for sheriff. A bunch of disappearances would look bad, but you still want the cash that Hennessey offers, so you tell him to clean up his act a bit. Hell, you could even tip Hennessey off as to where he could find the most vulnerable girls, and you'd also have the power to make their records disappear or never get filed in the first place."

Not a bad theory, though the disappearances had taken place in different counties, so that would be out of jurisdiction for a police chief or sheriff. A cadre of them, possibly?

Bones's mobile rang. He snatched it when he saw Charles's name. "Hallo?"

Charles's voice was very low. "Crispin, can you hear me?"

"Yes, I hear you."

"She'll meet you tonight," Charles said. "At my suite."

"Who?" Bones said pointedly. "And when?"

"Francesca, eight pm," Charles replied, and hung up.

Francesca was Hennessey's Judas? That…complicated things.

"What?" Cat asked, almost hopping in place with eagerness.

"There's been a development," Bones replied in a neutral tone. "Charles is with one of Hennessey's people who wants to talk to me about switching sides."

"I'm going with you," was Cat's immediate reply.

Not a good idea. Still, if Bones were in her shoes, he'd insist on the same.

"I knew you'd say that, Kitten."

CHARLES WAS at the most luxurious hotel Columbus had to offer. It still didn't compare to his ancestral manor back in England, but Cat kept looking around at the crystal bedecked lobby until she almost tripped on their way to the elevator. Seeing it, Bones wished he could whisk her away on a trip that would stagger her from its lavishness, but until this business with Hennessey was over, he couldn't. And tonight would surely be less than a pleasant evening for her.

Charles opened the door to his suite before Bones could knock. His side-eye at Cat made his opinion clear even before he said, "I'm surprised you brought her with you, Crispin."

To Cat's credit, she didn't voice any of the emotions that flashed over her expressive face.

Bones only shrugged. "Better to have her come and know what transpired than stay back and wonder."

Charles made a sound of disagreement, but opened the door wider and stepped aside. The suite's formal living area boasted a full dining room, three elegant sofas, four chairs, and panoramic views of the city's skyline, yet Cat didn't seem to notice the finery this time. Her gaze went right to the vampire seated on the center couch, and then stopped with the suddenness of a predator spotting irresistible prey.

Francesca had hardly made herself easy to ignore. Her crimson dress was so miniscule it more resembled bathing garments from the fifties than evening attire, her long black hair was ringed with curls, her makeup was as bold as her stare, and her cinnamon-colored skin was dusted with something that mimicked the chandelier's crystals when they caught the light.

Francesca rose when she saw him, and Bones crossed the room to give her a quick peck on the cheek that politeness demanded.

"Francesca, I'm glad you've come."

"Bones..."

Francesca turned her mouth toward his. Bones's pivot caused her intended kiss to land on his cheek instead. Francesca gave him a startled glance before looking over his shoulder as if finally noticing that Bones hadn't arrived alone.

"Francesca, this is Cat," Bones said, waving her forward. "She's with me, so you need not hesitate to speak freely."

Cat approached, flashing her teeth at Francesca in much the

same way that an angry vampire flashed fang. "Hi. We're sleeping together."

Bones's brows shot up. Not her usual greeting at all!

Then the geyser of jealousy erupting from Cat's scent explained her surprising response. Charles caught it, too, and shook his head with a muttered, "Told you this wasn't wise."

Francesca was far more urbane. "Of course, *nina*." Her Spanish accent honeyed the words as her fingers flicked lightly over the front of Bones's shirt. "Who could resist him?"

Bones turned the exact moment that Cat's hand rocketed forward, fist closed. Bones caught it, and placed it in the crook of his arm in one smooth motion.

Behind him, Francesca didn't realize how close she'd come to being flattened.

"Let's sit, shall we, Kitten?"

Cat looked at her hand, now mostly hidden inside the fold of Bones's arm. Confusion replaced the rage in her features and embarrassment threaded through her scent.

"Sorry," she whispered.

Bones gave her a reassuring squeeze as he led her toward the sofa. For humans, jealousy was an unpleasant emotion. For vampires, it was a feral beast clawing through your skin, *especially* when you had no experience dealing with it.

Cat suddenly grabbed Bones's arse with her free hand while glaring at Francesca, who was licking her lips while she stared at it. Though Cat might have this coming after her charade with Timmie, Bones still pitied her when she yanked her hand away with another "sorry" that sounded even more confused and miserable than her last apology. Poor lass had no idea why she was so out of control.

"Quite all right," Bones said with a wink. "Just a bit more difficult to walk."

Cat laughed, some of the tension easing out her. When Bones

smiled at her, her scent lost most of its angry tinge and returned to its normal mixture of vanilla, cream, and cherries.

"You can let go now," she whispered, giving a rueful glance at the hand he'd still tucked under his arm.

Bones did, and they sat on the sofa. Charles sat on his other side, earning him an approving glance from Cat. Francesca took the chair across from them. Things were calm for exactly five seconds—the time it took Francesca to cross her legs, revealing that she wore nothing beneath her short dress.

Bones snatched Cat's hand and held it again. Her knuckles whitened around his while her face turned red. Rage or embarrassment, he wasn't sure. Probably both since this was the first time Cat had gotten a close-up view of another woman's shaved box, and she hadn't asked to see it.

Neither had Bones, as his cool tone indicated when he spoke. "We all know why we're here. I'm after Hennessey and you're one of his, Francesca. You and he might not be close, but it's still the highest offense to betray your sire. Make no mistake, I'm out to kill him, and any information you give me will be used for that purpose."

Cat's grip became less viselike as she realized he wasn't interested in anything Francesca offered except information.

"Why else would I be here?" Francesca replied. "If you were to do less, I wouldn't risk it. I've hated Hennessey ever since he took me from my convent and turned me."

"You were a nun?" Cat sounded shocked. "You're kidding?"

"What is her purpose, Bones?" Francesca asked sharply.

Cat might not be on her best behavior, but Francesca was also provoking her, and Bones wouldn't let that stand.

"She's here because I want her to be, and it's not up for discussion."

Francesca glared at him. Bones met her stare. He might need her, but she needed him, too, if she wanted her freedom. No one else dared to take on Hennessey, and she knew it.

Finally, Francesca's lips jutted out in a sultry pout. "*Si*, I want Hennessey dead. He's been my Master for too long."

"What does she mean, her Master?" Cat whispered to Bones.

"Each vampire line is ranked by its head, also called the Master, and every person in that line is under the Master's rule. Feudalism would be another example. There, the lord of the manor was responsible for the welfare of all on his lands, and in return, his people owed him their loyalty and part of their income. Such is the way with vampires, with a few variations."

"So," Cat drew out. "Vampire society is like Amway and a cult rolled into one."

Bones had heard less accurate summations.

"Where is my uniform? I didn't know we were attending school," Francesca barked in Spanish.

"Speak English, and without the sarcasm," Bones told her.

Green filled Francesca's brown gaze. "If I didn't know you to be the man you are, I'd leave right now."

"But you do know me," Bones countered. "And if I choose to detail our world to the woman I'm with, that doesn't mean I take your position any less seriously. You really should show Cat a bit more respect. It's because of her your fondest wish was nearly granted and Hennessey was almost dust."

Francesca looked at Cat fully this time. Since she mistook her for human, she hadn't bothered to before. Then, she laughed.

"You're the vomiter!"

Not a flattering description, but Cat said, "That's me."

"Well, *nina*, that does afford you some latitude," Francesca said with another chuckle. "Hennessey didn't say much about you except that you were a redhead. He was too incensed, and so humiliated. It was truly a pleasure to witness."

Cat stared at her. "Does he know how much you hate him? If so, how are you going to get close enough to him to help us?"

Francesca leaned forward.

Cat glanced away from the bountiful cleavage that opened up near her face.

"I've managed to hide things from Hennessey before," Francesca said with a meaningful glance at Bones.

Cat bristled at the implication. Bones gave Francesca a warning glance. No need for her to flaunt their past fling.

"But yes, Hennessey knows I hate him." Francesca's gaze hardened despite the sultry purr never leaving her voice. "He enjoys it. Vampires can only leave their sire line if they win a duel against their Master, get released as a gesture of goodwill, or get ransomed by another Master. Hennessey is too strong for me to beat, there is no goodwill in him, and he would never let another vampire ransom me. Yet not for a moment does Hennessey believe I'll betray him. He thinks I'm too fearful of what he would do to me if I were caught."

"Then you and I have something in common," Cat said. "Well, something *else*," she amended with a knowing glance at Bones. "I want Hennessey dead, too. That's all we really need to know about each other, isn't it?"

A measure of respect filled Francesca's gaze even though she shrugged as if unimpressed. "*Si*. I suppose it is."

Now that things were less tumultuous, Bones got back to business. "Aside from Hennessey's death, what do you want in return for supplying me with information, Francesca?"

"You to take me," she said.

Cat's hand landed on Bones's cock as if it were the crown jewels and Francesca a wily, circling thief. "*Not* going to happen!"

Charles dissolved into laughter.

Francesca stared at Cat's hand in shock. So did Cat before she yanked it away with another blush. Then, Cat tucked her hand into her jacket and squirmed as Charles's mirth had him wiping at the pink tears in his eyes.

"That's not what she means, luv," Bones said while fighting his own laugh. When had *anyone* grabbed him with such authority?

Never, because he wouldn't have allowed it. Now, he reveled in Cat's possessiveness because he *was* hers, as she had just declared in the most blatant way possible.

"Francesca means that with the head of her line deceased, she wants to be under my protection. I could claim her as one of mine, thereby 'taking' her," Bones continued. "Although I'm still under Ian's yoke, he hasn't exercised his authority over me in a very long time. Why I haven't bothered to challenge Ian, in fact. I've had more freedom this way, and because of my understanding with Ian, I wouldn't need his permission to take Francesca on, though normally, that would be the case."

Cat gave him a confused glance. "Why wouldn't you want to be on your own?"

Because this way, everyone Bones had sired would still be under Ian's protection if Bones were killed. With his profession, that was a distinct possibility, and Bones wouldn't leave his people defenseless if he could help it.

"Masterless vampires are open game, *nina*," Francesca said, with a sideways glance at Bones. She realized his reasons even if Cat didn't know enough of their world to figure them out. "There's no accountability for any cruelty done to them."

"That's a brutal system you people have," Cat muttered.

"A far kinder one than yours," Francesca shot back. "How many humans starve to death every year because your nations refuse to provide for them? Even Hennessey, who is a beast, would consider it a personal insult to have anyone in his line in such a condition. Think about that. The worst of our kind treats his people better than your countries treat their citizens."

"Francesca," Charles said in a censuring tone.

"I'm finished," she said with a cutting wave.

"If you bloodsuckers are such paragons or virtue, why haven't you stopped Hennessey from plowing through *my* kind?" Cat asked in an incensed tone. "Or is the kidnapping, rape, murder, and consumption of humans not that important to you?"

Bones touched her arm. "Kitten—"

Francesca shot to her feet. "What Hennessey is doing is *nothing* compared to what humans do to each other…!"

Francesca began listing several atrocities over the past two decades alone. Bones gave her thirty seconds because he agreed that vampires took better care of their people than humans did. Then, he leapt between her and Cat.

"That's enough. I remember when you had very similar views 'round ninety years ago, Francesca. Now, to answer your condition, yes, I'll take you as one of mine after I kill Hennessey. Furthermore, should your information prove directly instrumental toward that end, I'll pay you accordingly when it's over. My word on both counts. Is that sufficient for you?"

Francesca was so angry it took a moment for her to process what Bones had said. When she did, her gaze changed from bright green back to cognac brown, and she sat down.

"Agreed."

Now, finally, they could finish this up. "Do you know a vampire named Switch?"

Her lip curled in disdain. "I've heard of him, but I've never met him, and from what I gather, that's a good thing."

Disappointing, but not unexpected. "What have you heard?"

"He's Hennessey's new cleaner." Francesca's gaze flicked to Cat. "You know what that means, don't you, *nina*?"

Cat gave her a look. "I do watch action movies."

"Know Switch's real identity or aliases?" Bones asked.

Francesca shrugged. "No, but I'll try to find out."

Good. Now, to the other mystery person. "Hennessey has new protection. Someone he might be cleaning up for. Know who?"

Francesca's expression turned thoughtful. "He *has* spent more time with humans lately. I know that from the smell," she added with a not-so-subtle dig at Cat's humanity. "But answering to one of them? That I haven't heard. It would have to be a very powerful human for Hennessey to even consider it."

It would, indeed. Smart, too, to make records disappear even beyond Ted's skilled reach, and to cause Hennessey to leave behind fewer traces of his activities than he usually did.

"Try to find out who, but *don't* get caught."

Ice filled Francesca's gaze. "Oh, he'll never catch me."

Bones hoped that were true. Francesca had suffered enough under Hennessey. Cat didn't realize it, but Francesca had endured all the horrors that Hennessey's other victims had, save one. Hennessey had let her live. Not out of mercy, but because it amused him to display her like a beautiful, captive pet.

"Then we're done for now. Ring me when you have more."

Charles stood. "I'll be leaving tomorrow, too. I have some leads of my own to run down."

Bones gave him a look. "I told you not to involve yourself any further, mate."

Charles smiled. "And I'm telling you to stuff it, *mate*."

Bones snorted and clapped him on the back. Then, he turned and held out his hand to Cat. "Kitten?"

She took his hand only long enough to rise from the couch. Then, she let him go. Disappointment coursed through Bones, but he hadn't expected her to enjoy tonight, and she hadn't.

"See you later, Spade," Cat said. "Francesca…" She gave her a brief nod.

Francesca barely inclined her head in return.

Best to leave now, before one of them bloodied the other.

Bones held open the door. Cat went through it. When it closed behind them, Bones thought he heard Charles sigh with relief.

---

43

*C*at still looked keyed up, so Bones led them to the stairwell instead of the elevator. A twenty-floor descent ought to take some of her edge off.

"You never told me about vampire society before." Cat's tone was bland, but her scent was still strafed with anger. She hadn't liked Francesca insulting her entire race. Bones rather knew the feeling.

"You never asked," he said with the same faux blandness.

She shot a quick scowl his way. Then, after a moment, a thoughtful expression overtook her features.

"I guess I didn't," she said with faint wonder. "How did it happen? How did, ah, vampires begin?"

A smile ghosted across his lips. "You want the evolutionary version, or the creationist one?"

"Creationist." Cat gave him a wry smile. "I'm a believer."

Bones told her the story as he'd once been told it himself.

"We began with two brothers who had different lives and functions, and one was jealous of the other. So jealous, in fact, that it led to the world's first murder. Cain killed Abel, and God drove

Cain out, but not before putting a mark upon Cain to make him distinguishable from everyone else."

Cat's gaze widened. "Genesis Chapter Four. Mom was big on me learning the Bible."

Bones grunted. "This next part wasn't in any Bible you read. The 'mark' was Cain's transformation into becoming a vampire. As punishment for spilling his brother's blood, Cain was forced to drink blood for the rest of his days. Cain later created his own people and society that existed on the fringes of the one he'd been expelled from. Of course," he added, "if you ask ghouls, Cain was turned into a ghoul, not a vampire. Been a source of bickering ever since about which species was first, and Cain isn't around to settle the matter."

"What happened to him?" Cat's voice was soft.

"He's the undead version of the Man Upstairs. Watching over his children from the shadows. Who knows if he really is? Or if God finally considered his debt paid and took Cain back?"

Cat said nothing for so long, bitterness coursed through Bones like the sting of snake venom.

"Makes you think your mum was right, doesn't it? That we're all murderers since we're the offspring of the world's first, unless you go with the notion that vampires and ghouls are a random evolutionary mutation."

She still didn't speak. Several more floors passed by in silence, until that inner sting turned into a burn. He shouldn't have told her this. She wasn't ready to hear it—

"The first of my kind has gotten a lot of shit for what she did, too," Cat said. "That whole apple business? Kinda makes it hard for me to criticize."

Relief exploded out of Bones in a laugh, and with it, every other emotion he'd been holding back. Before he could think, he had her pressed against the wall, his mouth on hers and his hands raking over her body.

She wrapped her legs around his waist and kissed him as if

branding his lips with hers. When she grabbed his cock with the same authority as before, he ripped open the front of her jeans. Her soft, sweet flesh was already wet, and she moved against his hand in explicit demand while she stroked him.

"Now," she moaned.

Yes. Right now.

Bones pushed inside her, groaning at her heat, the sound she made, and the pleasure that sizzled through him. Her mouth went to his throat, sucking hard enough to bruise, as he moved with deep, rhythmic strokes. Her arms and legs tightened around him, and over the trip hammer of her heartbeat, he heard her cry out "yes!" while she clawed at his back as if trying to tear through his clothes.

And it was so bloody good! He couldn't think past the ecstasy slamming into him. He needed more, harder, faster...

Ah, yes, Kitten, just like that. Yes, yes, yes...!

Her climax preceded his only by moments. Their raised voices mingled in a shout as shudders overtook them. When his faded into ripples that left his whole body tingling, he gave her kiss that was interrupted by the stairwell door opening and a bespectacled man with iron-and-white hair gaping at them.

Bones glared at him, his gaze already lit up with green. "Walk away. You've seen nothing!"

The man instantly turned and left.

Cat's cheeks turned bright red and she squirmed to get away from him. "My God, what is the *matter* with me tonight?"

Bones set her down with a final kiss. "Not a single thing, if you ask me."

She gave a dismayed look at her jeans, which now resembled a pair of cowboy chaps from the missing fabric around the front.

"First, I publicly grope you, almost stab our Judas, and then, for the grand finale, I molest you in a stairwell. And I thought *you* behaved rudely with Timmie. You should demand an apology!"

Bones only laughed as he handed Cat his jacket. It was long

enough to cover most of what was ripped, so her modesty should live to die another day.

"You hardly molested me, and I will never ask you to apologize for any of tonight. I'm relieved, to be frank."

She looked at the member he casually tucked back into his trousers. "I guess that's one way to put it."

He snorted. "Not that, though it applies there as well. Do you know what you acted like tonight? A vampire."

She stiffened, but she needed to hear this because then she'd know what to expect when it happened again.

"We're territorial, every last one of us, which is why I had such a harsh reaction when I saw Timmie gaze at you with those smitten eyes. Your similar, decidedly hostile response with Francesca showed me...that you consider me to be yours. I have wondered what you felt for me, Kitten," he added with raw honesty. "Hoped you cared beyond mere rapport and physical attraction, so while I assure you that you have nothing to fear from Francesca, I was selfishly pleased to see how deep your possessiveness ran."

Emotions flitted over her features with the swiftness of stones skipping across a still pond. Surprise, vulnerability, fear, tenderness, and...hurt.

Bones stared, silently willing her to say what she was feeling instead of leaving him to glean it from her face. *Tell me, Kitten. You can share anything with me.*

As if she could hear him, she reached out...and then stopped, drawing her hand back while chewing on her lower lip. "I think we should get out of here, before you have to green-eye someone else out of reporting us to the police."

More deflection, and for a moment there, he'd thought she might actually open up to him.

Desperation suddenly leapt into her eyes as she sensed his disappointment. Then, fear followed, leaving him slightly exasperated. Did she think he'd reject her because she hadn't told him what he wanted to hear?

Of course, she did. Thus far, he was the only person in her life who *hadn't* rejected her.

"It's all right, Kitten," Bones said softly. "I'm not demanding anything. You don't have to fret."

She reached out again, and this time, she didn't pull back. Instead, her hand closed around his and tightened.

"Are you really mine?" A whisper as fragile as the hope in her gaze.

He squeezed back. "Of course."

A smile lit her face, and he felt its warmth in every cold corner of his heart.

"I'm glad."

44

*T*en days passed with nothing more on Switch's identity. Francesca did confirm that Hennessey was rounding up more girls, so Charlie hadn't been lying about that. The only other thing Francesca had gleaned was overhearing one of Hennessey's men refer to someone as "Your Honor"—a title that could be ironic, but might also be literal. A corrupt judge would indeed have the power to make records disappear.

Was a judge Hennessey's new shadow partner? Or did Hennessey have more than one judge in his pocket? His abductions had spanned the entire state, after all.

Bones had Ted working that angle while he and Charles searched for more information on the mysterious Switch. In the meantime, Francesca was keeping her ears open, and Cat was trawling the clubs as bait. One of their tactics had to pay off.

One eventually did, just not in the way Bones anticipated.

Bones waited around back of another college dive bar listening to a stream of very loud, very bad music through his earpiece. That, plus rustling sounds from Cat's purse and her repeated rebuffs of human admirers, had become so common he was almost able to tune them out. No need to pay close attention to every terrible pick-up line some sod threw her way, especially since this place was full of humans. If a vampire didn't show up soon, they'd move on to another location.

"Catherine?" a male voice said, sounding surprised.

That got Bones's attention. Her mates at college called her Cathy, not her birth name.

"My God, Catherine, is that you?" the voice said, sounding closer to her purse now.

Cat's heart rate suddenly shot up, and Bones heard a faint shattering sound, like a glass breaking.

"Wow, Catherine," the unknown man went on. "You look...*wow*."

She said absolutely nothing, which wasn't like her at all. Cat was usually very quick about sending blokes on their way. Who was this?

"Hey, you've got to remember me," the man went on. "We met after my car broke down. You helped me change my tire, *and* you can't forget that I was the first person you ever—"

"Shut up, you *imbecile*," Cat snarled.

Bones barely heard her. Rage drowned out everything else. It was *that* bloke, and he was dead.

Bones got up and moved toward the club without thinking about anything except the hot splash of the lad's arterial blood against his face. Only when someone screamed did he realize his gaze was lit up and his fangs were out *in public*, which was reckless to the point of stupidity.

Bones spun around, catching the girl who'd screamed before she could make it back inside her car.

"Sorry, luv," he murmured, backing her against her car. "You're not afraid. You didn't see anything unusual."

"See, you do remember me," the soon-to-be murdered lad prattled on. "Gee, it's been what? Six years? I almost didn't recognize you. I *know* you didn't look like this before. Not that you weren't cute and all, but you kinda looked like a baby then. You're all grown up now."

That's it. Bones wouldn't rip his throat out. He'd snap him in half, slowly, one bone at a time.

"Not afraid," the girl intoned, her body relaxing against Bones's. "Didn't see anything unusual."

"Danny, for your own good, turn around and *leave*," Cat said in her coldest voice.

Good advice. Too late.

"Now, drink responsibly, and all that rot," Bones said, releasing the girl. A quick look around showed that no one else had seen his reckless display. The gods were indeed smiling on him tonight.

Bones closed his eyes, taking a moment to rein in his rage. If he entered the bar now, he'd wind up on the evening news under the headline, "Vampires Among Us!"

"But why?" the knobhead named Danny persisted. "We should catch up. After all, it's been a long time."

Ice soothed Bones, and his eyes snapped open, no green glow spilling out to light the night anymore. The hunt was on.

"There's nothing to catch up on." Pain edged the anger in Cat's tone. "You came, you scored, you left. End of story."

Bones took his earpiece out as he entered the club. Cat sat at the bar, half turned away from a lad with light brown hair, a swimmer's build, and lightly tanned white skin. Danny's jeans were designer, as was his expensive blue blazer, and his fraternity ring had diamonds in it. Yet it was Danny's easy, smug smile that told Bones the lad was an entitled little shite, as if his actions hadn't already outed him as such.

Bones knew that smile. He'd seen it on the faces of countless noblemen after they'd abused his mum or one of the other women at the bordello. *Nothing can touch me*, that smile said. *I can hurt who I want, and I'll get away with it.*

That ended tonight.

"Oh, come on, Catherine, it wasn't all like that," Danny was saying.

"Hallo there," Bones interrupted, smiling in anticipation of ripping the sod's spine out. "What have we here?"

Cat paled, but said, "This person was just leaving," as if Danny were no more than another stranger trying his luck.

"Not yet, Kitten, we haven't been introduced," Bones replied, holding out his hand. "I'm Bones, and you are?"

"Danny Milton," he said, taking Bones's hand. "I'm an old friend of Catherine's."

Fucker actually winked when he said, "old friend."

Cat was too busy staring at Bones to see it, but it demolished Bones's control. He'd intended to maim Danny outside, away from Cat's view, but after that, Danny didn't deserve to live another moment without pain.

Bones's hand tightened, slowly at first, causing Danny to frown as he attempted to tug away.

"Hey, man, I don't want any trouble..."

Bones hauled him closer, green flashing in his gaze. "Don't say a word," he ordered, and then crushed Danny's hand.

An agonized moan tore past Danny's lips. Not even a Master vampire's power could stop that. Hands were so sensitive with their abundance of nerve endings. It's why torturers usually started with them first.

"Stop it," Cat said in a horrified tone.

Her sweet side really was to her credit, but it didn't serve her here. Danny deserved none of her mercy.

Bones's hand kept tightening.

Danny's face became soaked with tears and sweat while harsh grunts forced past his closed lips. Bones's grip tightened even more, until Danny's hand collapsed like a deflated balloon.

"Bones." Cat's voice was urgent as she touched his arm. "He isn't worth it, and you're not changing anything that happened."

"He hurt you, Kitten," he said without looking at her. "I'll kill him for it."

"*Don't.*" Her tone became more urgent. "It's over, and if it wasn't for him using me, I'd have never gone for that first vampire. That means I wouldn't have eventually met you. Things happen for a reason. Don't you believe that?"

In fact…he did.

Bones finally looked at her. Cat's gaze was beseeching, and when she touched his face, her slight tremor broke him. She was *very* upset, and no matter his rage—or how the sod deserved it—he couldn't stand to see her this way.

"Please," she breathed. "Let him go."

Bones dropped Danny's hand. The filth fell over, vomiting and crouching over his bleeding, malformed hand. No one except the bartender seemed aware that anything had happened, and from the disgusted glance the bartender gave Danny, he assumed his retching and falling over was caused by a different reason.

Bones threw several bills on the counter for Cat's tab. "Bartender, he needs a cab. Poor bugger can't hold his drink."

Then, Bones knelt next to Danny. "Say one word about this, and the next thing I'll be crushing is your stones. You'd better thank your bleedin' stars she stopped me, or you and I would be having a party you wouldn't live long enough to regret."

Danny sobbed out something that might have been an affirmative. Bones didn't care. He knew Danny's full name, so he'd be easy to track down later. Maybe he'd even make Danny's death look like an accident in case Cat heard of it.

"Best be leaving, pet," Bones said, taking her arm. "This has attracted a bit too much attention."

"I told you to leave it alone," she hissed as she followed him to the parking lot. Then, she slammed her door as she got into her truck. "Dammit, Bones, that could have been avoided!"

"I saw your face," was all he said. Tonight wouldn't be the night he told her about the receiver in her purse. She was upset enough already. "You went white as a ghost. Knew who it had to be, and I know how hurt you were by it."

"But what did smashing his hand accomplish?" she shot back. "Now, we won't know if one of Hennessey's guys comes to the bar. What if they do, and they nab someone? Danny isn't worth some woman's life because he slept with me and dumped me!"

He'd done more than that. From Danny's perspective, she'd said no, and he'd overpowered her. Not only did he lack remorse for his actions, Danny had been proud, as his wink had proved. None of that was forgivable, even if Cat downplayed it now.

"I love you," Bones said simply. "You have no idea what you're worth to me."

She stared at him for a few seconds longer than was safe to do while driving. She must have realized that because she pulled off the road a few moments later.

"Bones, I-I can't say the same, but you mean more to me than anyone else has. Ever. I hope…I hope that's worth something?"

Her gaze pleaded with his again, for a different reason this time. *Give me time*, it said. *I'm still so afraid…*

Bones touched Cat's cheek, her jaw, and then finally, her lips. "It's worth something, but I'm still holding out to hear the other."

For a split second, he thought he saw what he wanted to see in her eyes. But he couldn't be sure. He longed for it so much that it might be his mind playing tricks on him, like a dying man chasing mirages in the desert.

"You realize tonight is the first time I've heard someone call you by your real name?" Bones said to change the subject.

She shook her head. "That's not my real name anymore."

How well he understood. Only Ian, and Charles, and the first vampire Bones had sired still called him Crispin. To everyone else, he was Bones because that was the real him.

"What's your full name?" he said, adding, "I already know it, of course, but I want to hear you say it."

She smiled. "Catherine Kathleen Crawfield, but you can call me Cat."

"I think I'll stay with Kitten," he said with an answering smile. "It's what you reminded me of when we met. An angry, defiant, brave little kitten, and every once in a while, you're cuddly like one, too."

Her smile widened, and then fell as her expression grew serious. "I know you didn't want to walk away at the bar before, and I also know you're numbering Danny's days. But I don't want his death on my conscience. Promise me you'll never kill him."

He could sooner promise to stop drinking blood!

"Why? You can't still have feelings for that wanker."

"Oh, I have feelings for him, all right." Anger flooded Cat's tone. "I'd like to put him in the ground myself. Still, it would be wrong, so promise me, Bones."

Very well. He knew plenty of blokes he could outsource this task to. "Fine. I promise I won't kill him."

Something sharp filled her gaze. "Promise me that you will also never cripple, maim, dismember, blind, torture, bleed, or otherwise inflict any injury on Danny. *Or stand by watching while someone else does it,*" she added as if reading his mind.

"That's not fair!" Bones nearly sputtered.

"Promise me," she insisted.

His own fault. He should have waited until she wasn't there to deal with Danny. He hadn't, and she knew him too well to assume that he wouldn't finish the job later.

"I promise," he said at last. "Bloody hell. Didn't I teach you too well to cover all of your bases?"

"You did," she said without a hint of pity. "Now, since we can't go back to the bar, what do you want to do?"

Mesmerize you into forgetting the promise you just coerced from me, but since I can't do that... "You decide."

Cat thought for a moment. Then, with a secretive smile, she pulled back onto the road. Bones didn't realize where she was going until an hour later, when she turned off onto a small gravel road leading away from the highway. Then, he smirked.

"Taking a trip down memory lane, are we?"

"So you *do* remember this place," she said with a grin.

"Hard to forget. This is where you first tried to kill me. You were so nervous, and you kept blushing. Never had someone who tried to stake me blush as much as you did."

She put the car in park about twenty yards from the lake and took off her seat belt.

"And you knocked the living daylights out of me. Want to try it again?"

Bones laughed. "Fight? Blimey, but you do like it rough."

"Not that." Mischief and something even more enticing danced in her eyes. "Let's try the other. Maybe you'll have better luck. Want to shag?"

Oh, hell, yes.

"Still wearing your stakes?" he teased as he took off his jacket. "Going to make me rest in pieces?"

Her brows wagged suggestively. "Kiss me, and find out."

Bones did, enjoying her tiny gasp at how fast he moved, and then *really* enjoying her taste, how her arms wrapped around him, and how green her eyes were when he finally pulled away.

"Not much room in here, luv. Want to go outside so you can stretch out?"

"Oh no," Cat said, lust and laughter thickening her voice. "Right here. *Love* to do it in a truck."

He laughed as he pulled her onto his lap, pushing aside her knickers until her bare flesh pressed against his already unzipped trousers.

"Let's find out."

45

A fortnight later, Hennessey still hadn't surfaced. They also hadn't come across his people at any of the pubs and clubs Cat had spent her evenings at. Francesca was still trying to find out about Hennessey's new protection, and Bones was casting a net online to see if Hennessey had switched locations and was now rounding up girls in another area. Until then, they waited, which he was used to and Cat was...not.

"Maybe we should try again tonight," she said when she came out of the bathroom. She was still wearing the lingerie he'd bought her, although it was wrinkled from their recent activity.

Bones cast a meaningful glance at the school books she'd stacked on her new dining room table.

"You said you needed to study. Besides, it's Sunday. Not a big night for carousers, undead or otherwise."

"I am tired," Cat admitted.

No doubt. Attending college during the day and hunting nearly every night would tax anyone's stamina. That wasn't even counting their other exertions, the most recent of which had taken place on her new couch with her new television turned up so she didn't fret about her neighbors overhearing.

She'd objected to Bones furnishing her apartment, of course. He'd ignored that with the same obstinance she used when ignoring his urgings to take her cut of their jobs.

"You refuse to be my employee, and I refuse to be a cheapskate lover," he'd said when her new bedroom set arrived. "Now, if you're quite finished, we have a mattress to christen."

She'd stopped protesting after that. At least her flat no longer made him wince every time he entered it, even if the new furniture and rugs didn't completely conceal the hideous flooring and the new pictures couldn't hide all the wall stains.

Three sharp raps sounded at her door. Her pizza was early. Bones got up, but Cat stopped him with a smile.

"Stay there. You're not eating it anyway."

She put on a robe over her silk and lace nightie before opening the door. Then, she slammed it shut with a cry.

"Sweet *Jesus!*"

Bones already was on his feet, a knife in his hand. Seeing that, Cat screamed with even more terror.

What in the blazes—?

"Catherine, what is the matter with you?" her mum yelled through the door. "Open this at once!"

Bloody hell. No wonder Cat had screamed. Her mum's presence elicited the same inner reaction from Bones.

"Holy shit, it's my mother!" Cat said in a panic. "Hurry, you have to hide!"

She began shoving him toward her bedroom while calling out, "I'll be right there, Mom. I'm…I'm not dressed!"

"Still haven't told her about us?" Not like a few more months would make a dent in her mum's prejudice. Or a few more years. "Really, Kitten, what are you waiting for?"

"The Second Coming of Christ, and not a moment sooner!" With that, she opened her closet and pushed him inside.

Bones let her, but his look told her how little he appreciated it. This was hardly the first time a woman had hidden him away from an unexpected guest, but it was the first time he was brassed off at being treated like a dirty secret.

"I'll be right there," Cat shouted to her mum before saying, "We'll talk about this later," in a frantic whisper to him. "Just stay here. I'll get rid of her as fast as I can."

The closet doors shut, although Bones could still see Cat through the slats. She ran around her room as if possessed, kicking Bones's clothes and shoes under her bed.

"Catherine!" her mum shouted, with a kick instead of a knock this time.

"Coming!" she shouted back, running out of the room. "Mom," he heard moments later. "What a surprise."

The front door shut none too gently.

"I drop by to say hello, and you slam the door in my face? What is the matter with you?" her mum demanded.

How much time do you have? Bones thought cynically. *I have a list, and it doesn't even include everything that's* your *fault.*

"Migraine," Cat said before adding a note of pain to her voice. "Oh, Mom, I'm glad to see you, but it's a bad one…"

"*Look* at this place," Justina interrupted with shock. "Catherine, where did you get the money to pay for all of this?"

It's the least she deserves, Bones seethed as he pulled on the spare set of clothes he kept here. *And she could have bought most of it herself had she not given all her money to you.*

"Credit cards," Cat replied. "They'll give 'em to anyone."

"Hmmph," her mother said. "Those will get you in trouble."

Can't say a single nice thing to your daughter, can you? he thought in disbelief. *Why she cares so much about your approval, I'll never know.*

"Mom, it's great to see you, really, but…"

Cat's voice trailed off, and fear suddenly strafed her scent. What had the woman done to her now?

"Is that a new *bed* as well?" Justina asked waspishly.

If Bones made it through tonight without bleeding her mum, he deserved an award.

"It was on sale," Cat said, sounding ill for real now.

A pause, and then Justina said, "You don't feel warm."

"Believe me," Cat said with feeling. "At any second, I could throw up."

With another disapproving "hmmph," Justina said, "Fine, I'll call before I come over next time. I thought we could go out to dinner, but...I could bring you back something?"

"No!" Cat said at once. Then, she quickly added, "Thanks, Mom, but I don't have an appetite. I'll call you tomorrow."

"That headache is making you act very weird, Catherine," her mum said.

"Yeah, sorry, love you, 'bye!" Cat replied, to the sound of the door shutting.

Love you.

Words he'd kill to hear, and her mum didn't even bother to say them back. Yet Bones was the one Cat was ashamed of. Him, and herself. Glass hurled from a great height couldn't shatter as thoroughly as his heart.

Bones finished dressing and left the closet. He'd reached Cat's bedroom door when she turned around, relief and guilt stamped on her features.

"Whew," she said with strained laugh. "That was close."

He stared at her for a long moment before saying, "I can't stand to see you do this to yourself any longer, Kitten."

Confusion knit her brows. "Do what?"

"Continue to punish yourself for your father's sins," he replied bluntly. "How long are you supposed to pay for them? How many vampires do you have to kill until you and your mum are square? You're one of the bravest people I've ever met, yet you're scared to death of your own mum. Don't you realize? It's not me you're hiding in a closet, Kitten. It's yourself."

She puffed up in anger, yet she sat on the sofa as if her legs could no longer hold her.

"That's easy for you to say, your mom's dead," she replied with uncharacteristic cruelty. "You don't have to worry if she'll hate you for who you're sleeping with, or if you'll ever *see* her again if you tell her the truth! Am I supposed to ruin my relationship with the only person who's been there for me? My mom will take one look at you, and all she'll see is fangs." Cat's gaze suddenly turned pleading while her voice cracked. "Don't you understand? *She'll never forgive me.*"

As soon as she said it, her eyes brightened with tears. To hide that, her head dropped into hands which now shook.

Yes, it was brutal to realize the person you loved didn't love you. Bones knew that all too well. But he couldn't fix her relationship with her mum. He couldn't fix her shattered sense of self-worth, either, no matter how hard he'd tried.

Only she could.

"You're right, my mum's dead," he replied softly. "I'll never know what she would have thought of the man I've become. If she'd be proud…or despise me for the choices I've made. I will tell you this, though. If she were alive, I'd show her what I was. All of it. She would deserve no less, and quite frankly, neither would I. But this isn't about me."

He went over to the counter where he'd left his keys. The scrape of metal on fiberglass snapped Cat's head up.

"I'm not insisting on meeting your mum," he said, in case she misunderstood. "But I am saying that sooner or later, you'll have to come to terms with yourself because you can't wish away the vampire in you, and you shouldn't keep trying to atone for it. So, take some time to figure out who you are and what you need, Kitten. When you do, don't apologize for it. Not to me, your mum, or to anyone."

Pain filled her gaze and knifed her tone. "You're leaving? Are you…are you breaking up with me?"

Bones wanted to snatch her up and tell her he loved her and would never leave her. But he'd done that several times, and it hadn't so much as dented the shell around her. Only she could penetrate that shell, let alone tear it down.

"No, Kitten." His voice was thick with everything he wasn't allowing himself to say. "I'm just giving you a chance to think about things without me around to distract you."

She rose, reaching for him before she clenched her hands at her sides. "But what...what about Hennessey?"

Even now, she couldn't bring herself to say she wanted him to stay. If she had, he probably would despite knowing better. But no. She was pretending her only real concern was the job.

"Francesca still doesn't have anything, and we've struck out searching for him on our own. Won't hurt to give it a small rest. If anything comes up, I'll ring you, promise."

He opened the door. Cat's gaze brimmed with tears, but she said nothing to stop him.

Bones didn't speak, either, save for one word.

"Goodbye."

46

$\mathcal{O}$ ne thing a vampire was very familiar with was the relativity of time. It could blink by, making decades feel like days, or it could stretch until each second felt like a knife sliding into a festering wound.

The past four days made torture seem preferable. Cat didn't ring him, and Bones didn't ring her, nor did he allow himself to catch glimpses of her from afar. He didn't listen to her through the microphone in her purse, either. He'd gotten that to keep her safe on vampire hunts, not to be his personal spying device.

Instead, Bones threw himself into the hunt. His nights were spent scouring clubs for any trace of Hennessey's people, and his days were spent scouring the internet for Hennessey's cyber footprints. So far, Bones hadn't uncovered any spike in disappearances outside of Ohio, so either Hennessey hadn't left the state, or he'd hidden every bit of evidence.

On one positive note, Francesca had insinuated herself deeper inside Hennessey's circle. She still didn't know who Switch was, but she had a lead on Hennessey's new protection, and she was updating Bones with more on that tonight.

Bones was leaving the cave for another night of bar trawling when his mobile rang. He felt a familiar pang when the number wasn't Cat's. He didn't know who this was, in fact.

"Hallo?"

"Yes." Francesca's voice, sounding strained. "I need to make a reservation."

Bugger. That was her predetermined code for "Things are too dangerous, pull me out."

"We have several slots," Bones replied, going along with the "reservation" act. "What time tonight is good for you?"

"As soon as possible," Francesca said, with a laugh that sounded like ground glass. "The recipe I attempted was a disaster. The ingredients went higher up than I anticipated."

Not predetermined code. Francesca was trying to tell him something.

"We offer car service," Bones said. "All I need is an address."

Francesca's voice lowered to a whisper. "Someone's coming. I'm at—"

The line abruptly disconnected.

Bones called it back at once. It only rang before a mechanical voice announced that this number didn't have voicemail. He rang it again, to no avail. Then, he called Ted.

"Need a number tracked back to its location," he said without preamble. "It's urgent. Call me on my other line when you have it. I need to keep this one free."

"Number?" Ted said briskly.

Bones gave it.

"On it," Ted replied.

Bones hung up. He wanted to try Francesca's line again, but whatever had happened was bad. If she were running from someone, Bones couldn't risk his call giving away her location. He'd have to wait for Francesca to ring him back, or for Ted to find her.

Minutes ticked by, flaying his nerves like a skilled whipmaster. Had he heard anything in the background that hinted at her location? Not that he could remember, and aside from the "reservation" charade, she'd only said the recipe she attempted was a disaster because the ingredients went "higher up" than she'd anticipated. Had to be a hint about Hennessey's new protection... and Francesca telling him that in the few seconds before the line went dead meant she knew she might not get a chance to say it to Bones's face later.

Blast it, why hadn't Ted called back yet?

Bones paced, which did nothing to lessen the tension that raged within like an animal flinging itself against the bars of its cage. To distract from that, and from his ominously silent mobile phone, Bones focused on her last message.

"The ingredients went higher up." So, Hennessey's partner wasn't a mere judge or sheriff, then. A mayor? Possibly, but that still limited their reach to a single city, and that didn't fit with the statewide disappearances. Unless Hennessey had multiple mayors in his pocket? *That* broadened the scope, and Francesca would rightly be afraid if she'd discovered that. Such a feat would be real feather in Hennessey's cap, making it worth Hennessey's while to leave no traces of his trafficking behind.

And mayors had the resources to have their own Teds scrubbing the internet of any disappearance reports. Or looking for anyone who might expose them, such as Bones or his lovely, redheaded accomplice...

He had to get to Cat. Now.

Bones strode out of the cave and fired up his Ducati. Then, he tore through the rough terrain without care for the hundred-thousand-dollar bike. He'd just left the woods when his mobile finally rang.

"Francesca?" he answered without looking at the number.

A sharp intake of breath. Even that brief sound was enough for Bones to realize who this was.

"Kitten, it's you," he said in relief. "I'm already on my way to you. Something's wrong."

"What is it?" she asked at once.

He didn't have time to explain. "Get dressed if you need to. I'm hanging up; I have to keep this line clear. I'll be there shortly."

Bones hung up, gunning the motorcycle again. Sod any cops who tried to stop him. They'd have to catch him first.

He made it to her flat in ten minutes. She opened the door before he knocked. Must have been watching the parking lot. A sniff revealed her neighbor's scent heavy in the air, but Bones was too concerned about Francesca to bother about that.

"I think Francesca's been caught," he said.

Cat winced and shut the door. "What happened?"

Pacing didn't help, but Bones couldn't stop. "She rang me two days ago, said she was getting closer to finding out who was pulling the legal strings for Hennessey. Then, 'round an hour ago, she called and said she needed out. We were arranging a place to meet when she said, 'Someone's coming,' and the phone cut off. I haven't heard from her since."

Cat's wince deepened. "Do you know where she was?"

"Of course not," Bones snapped. "If I did, I'd be there, not here!"

His tone and the words made her take a step backward.

"Sorry, Kitten," he said, catching her to him. "This has twisted me into nastiness. If Hennessey caught Francesca spying on him, there's nothing he won't do to her as punishment."

The hurt left her expression, and her hands made soothing circles on his back.

"I understand. Look, let's assume for a moment that it's not as bad as it looks, and go from there. If Francesca had to get out in a hurry and she couldn't contact you yet, where would she go? Is there any place she'd feel safe?"

He had zero hope that things weren't as bad as they appeared, but on the off chance that he was wrong...

"She might go to *Bite*. It's the only place in the area where violence isn't allowed on the premises, so that rule would protect her. Worth a shot, anyhow. Will you come with me?"

308

"You think you can stop me?" Cat asked dryly.

Bones didn't want to. If she was at his side, she was safe. "Right now, luv, I'm glad that I can't."

～

TRIXIE HADN'T SEEN FRANCESCA. Bones did a sweep of the club in case Francesca had managed to sneak past the blonde bouncer, but she wasn't there. Bones left his number with Trixie, who promised to ring him if she saw Francesca. Then, he and Cat tried the next place where Francesca might seek refuge.

Bones used the power in his gaze to get past the human couple renting the hotel suite where he and Cat had met Francesca weeks ago. Then, he thoroughly checked the suite in case Francesca had mesmerized the couple the same way Bones just had. No sign of Francesca, though.

Bones rang Charles. He hadn't heard from her, either, and Ted hadn't been able to trace Francesca's location because she'd called from a burner phone. All Ted had determined was that Francesca's call had been routed from a cell tower in Columbus.

Out of options, Bones tried *Bite* again, searching it even more carefully this time. No sign or scent of Francesca. He even went back to the bloody hotel suite even though he knew it was useless. Still, it was doing *something*, and a useless something felt better than a helpless nothing right now.

Dawn was breaking when Bones felt Cat stifle a yawn against his back. If she hadn't been clinging to him to keep from falling off the motorcycle, he wouldn't have caught the slight movement. Of course, Cat would be tired, but she hadn't uttered a word of complaint during their fruitless, nightlong chase. She'd only offered support, encouragement, and hope even though her gaze reflected the same grimness he felt.

No need for Cat to keep searching. There was nothing she could do, and infuriatingly, little that Bones could, either. It had now been over nine hours since Francesca had called him. Far too long for him to believe she'd managed to get away. Now, Bones could only hope that Hennessey was stupid enough to ring him and brag about what he was doing to Francesca. Ted was ready with a trace on Bones's mobile, if Hennessey did that.

He was about to turn around and go to Cat's flat when police lights caught his eye. About a mile ahead, two of the three lanes were closed off, causing traffic to back up even at this early morning hour.

"There must be an accident," Cat said, raising her voice to be heard. "We should take another route. Wait...does this road look familiar?"

It did indeed, and rage turned Bones's blood to ice.

"This is where Hennessey dragged you away to bleed you. Well, not right here. Up where the police cars are."

Cat stared at the lights with growing horror. "Oh, Bones..."

"I can hear them." No emotion colored his tone. Ice was already spreading to every part of him. "They found a body."

Cat shuddered. Then, she gently touched his back.

"It might not be her. Keep going."

Oh, he would, and if Hennessey attempted to ambush him, he'd see what Bones was *really* capable of.

"Keep your helmet on," he told Cat. "Don't take it off no matter what."

Traffic crawled along as three lanes were reduced to one, making what should have been a five-minute ride take over half an hour. Bones could have swerved around the other cars, but he didn't want to attract any attention. His helmet had a full-face visor like Cat's, so they were two anonymous people to anyone watching.

And Hennessey probably *was* watching. This was his creation, as surely as if the road had been his canvass and he an artist.

Accidents always attracted rubberneckers. This was no different, even if it hadn't involved another vehicle. Still, the crime scene tape, road flares, police officers, and medical examiner van gave onlookers plenty to stare at as the cars rolled slowly past.

Bones stared, too, expecting what he saw, but still feeling its punch when he glimpsed Francesca's long, lustrous hair spread out like a black silk scarf near her skeletal remains. Francesca's body lay exactly where Hennessey had nearly bled Cat to death, and the message couldn't be clearer.

Bones's jaw clenched until it snapped. Cat made a soft, pained sound that the wind snatched away as the bottlenecked traffic cleared and Bones gunned his motorcycle.

47

*B*ones backtracked for over an hour before he drove to the woods bordering the cave. Then, he carried the bike to eliminate everything except the soft sounds their feet made as they walked through the woods. If anyone had managed to follow them, Bones would hear them. And then he'd tear them to pieces.

Cat didn't speak until they were deep enough inside the cave to see the light from the telly he'd forgotten to turn off. Even then, her voice was soft.

"I'm sorry, Bones. It's not adequate, I know, but I am so, so sorry Hennessey killed her."

"He didn't," Bones said with all the bitterness in him.

Surprise mixed with the pity on Cat's face. She didn't understand. He did, all too well.

"Hennessey would've done many things to Francesca, but killing her straightaway isn't one of them. From the police scanners, her body was dumped only two hours after I last spoke to her. Hennessey would've kept her alive for days, until he'd found out every detail of what she'd relayed to me. None of Hennessey's people would've gone behind his back and killed Francesca, either."

"What are you saying?" Cat asked in the careful voice of someone trying not to startle a rabid animal. "Who killed her?"

Bones smiled with no humor. "Francesca killed herself."

Cat's mouth dropped. "No…"

"It's the only explanation," Bones said with more bitterness. "Francesca must've been trapped, saw there was no escape, so she killed herself. It would only take a second to twist a silver blade through her heart, and then there's nothing Hennessey could do except rage at her corpse. His leaving her where he nearly killed you was just his way of saying he knew who Francesca betrayed him to."

And an explicit warning: Cat was next.

"Your part is done in this, Kitten," he said with icy finality. "Finished."

Anger sparked in her gaze before sympathy drowned it out. "Bones, I know you're upset—"

"Bollocks," he cut her off. "I don't care how pissed you are or what you threaten me with. End our relationship, never speak to me again, whatever you fancy, but I will *not* continue to dangle you out as bait to the same people Francesca killed herself over rather than be at the mercy of."

He was now gripping her too tightly, and he couldn't make himself stop. Francesca's skeletal body kept flashing in his mind. How easily that could be Cat, reduced to nothing more than bones and hair along the side of a road.

"I couldn't bear it if it was you I was waiting for a call from that never came." His voice shook with something far worse than rage. "Or if it was your body I found on the ground…"

Bones released her, spinning around before she saw the new wetness in his gaze. He'd rather leap into his own grave than be the cause of Cat's death. It would be far preferable to living with the knowledge that he'd gotten her killed.

Her warmth touched his back before her hands did. Then, they curled around his shirt, tugging gently.

"You're not going to lose me," she said, pulling him against her. "Francesca was on her own. She didn't have you shadowing her. Her death isn't your fault, but you owe it to her to keep after Hennessey. She gave it all she had, for her own reasons, maybe, but that doesn't change what she did. You're not giving up now and neither am I. We've got to have faith."

Faith? He'd run out of that centuries ago. Oh, he believed there was a God, but if the Almighty bothered to stop bad things from happening to good people, Bones would be out of a job.

"Hennessey's got to be scared," Cat went on. "Wondering what Francesca told you. Scared enough to make mistakes, I'd bet. You've hunted him for eleven years; you've never been this close before. There's no turning back now, and I'm not running away even if I'm afraid. We're going to get him." Her voice strengthened. "We're going to stand over *his* dead body on the ground, and every greedy bastard on his team, too. Then they'll know they were taken down by you...and your little Grim Reaper, who hasn't met a vampire she didn't try to kill first."

Laughter tore from his clenched throat. He'd called her that in anger, and here she'd turned it into a nickname.

Bones turned around to brush the scarlet locks from her face. "You're my Red Reaper, and I've missed you terribly."

He folded her into his arms, feeling the reassuring thuds of her heartbeat, the warm puffs of her breath, and the silkiness of her cheek against his throat. This past week had left him feeling as if half of him had been ripped away, leaving the rest raw and bleeding.

"Bones." Her voice was very soft. "When I called you before... before I found out about Francesca, it was to tell you that I'd finally figured out who I was and what I needed."

What...? Oh, right, he'd told her she should do that. It felt like a thousand years ago.

"You told me when I did," a new tremor filled her voice, "I shouldn't apologize to anyone for it. So, I'm not going to."

Bones stiffened. If she'd picked *now* to tell him she was finished with him, he'd have to commend her for her cruelty.

He drew away. "What are you saying?"

A lopsided smile curled her lips. "I'm saying I'm a moody, insecure, narrow-minded, jealous, borderline-homicidal bitch, and I want you to promise me you're okay with that, because it's who I am, and *you're* what I need. I missed you every minute when you were gone, and I don't want to spend another day without you—"

He must be high. Had to be, and he'd give every cent to stay on this drug.

"—and if my mother disowns me for being with a vampire, then that's her decision," Cat went on, her jaw jutting out in that familiar, stubborn way. "I've made mine, and I refuse to apologize or back down from it."

Had he really heard that? Or had stress finally broken him?

She kept staring at him. Only when her brows drew together in a decidedly annoyed manner did Bones allow himself to believe that he hadn't hallucinated what she'd said. Still...

"Would you mind repeating that? Think I've lost my wits and just imagined what I've longed to hear."

She threw her arms around him, kissing him as if she'd die if she stopped. Elation covered his grief and rage. They'd be there later, but right now...there was only this.

Bones deepened the kiss while he stroked her arms, back, and hips. He couldn't get enough of touching her. She rubbed against him, her breath coming in gasps that turned into moans when his head dipped to her throat. Her pulse thundered as he teased it with slow licks, slight grazes of teeth, and then suction that brought dozens of blood-dot roses to the surface.

She shuddered with pleasure, tugging her collar down to bare more of her neck. He chuckled as he pulled her shirt off, leaving her in only her bra and jeans. Then, he trailed his mouth to her breasts, surprised when she stopped him and drew him back up before he could give her nipples the same treatment.

"What's wrong?" he asked in a husky voice.

Her gaze was green, but more than desire filled it as she brought him back to her neck.

"Don't stop," she said in a slightly unsteady tone.

If the words weren't enough, the new way her pulse jumped confirmed what she meant. Hunger instantly rose, until his fangs throbbed with almost as much need as his cock.

Still, he was wary. "What are you doing?"

"Overcoming my former prejudice," Cat said with the faintest laugh. "You're a vampire. You drink blood. I've drunk yours, and now, I want you to have mine."

Bones pulled away before that hunger erased his willpower.

"No," he said after a pause. "You don't really want that."

She touched his face, trailing her fingers down until they rested against his mouth. "Your fangs don't scare me and neither do you. I want my blood inside you, Bones. I want to know that it's running through your veins—"

He spun around, clenching his fists before he snatched her to him and drank her until she begged him *not* to stop.

"You can't tempt me like this," he ground out.

Cat filled his vision, moving in front of him and holding his arms so he couldn't turn away from her.

"I'm not tempting you. I'm *insisting* you drink from me. Come on, Bones. Tear down this last wall between us."

Oh, he *had* to be hallucinating.

"You have nothing to prove to me," he tried again, but his gaze kept returning to her throat, both in hunger and in assessment. Her pulse was steadier than it had been when she first made her invitation. She might be a little nervous, but her heartbeat, scent, and the look in her eyes all indicated that she meant what she said.

For now. That could change tomorrow.

Her arms slid around him, bringing him closer to her neck while her lips teased his throat.

"I'm not afraid," she breathed against his skin.

God. Help. Him.

With the last of his willpower, Bones said, "I am. I'm very afraid you'll regret this afterward."

Yet he couldn't stop his arms from encircling her. She rubbed her body along the length of his, taunting him with its lushness, and when she bit his earlobe with her flat little teeth, a bolt of lust made him shudder.

"I want this," she whispered into his ear. "Show me I shouldn't have waited so long."

Hunger scorched away the last of his hesitancy. Oh, he'd show her, and she would absolutely love it.

48

---

*B*ones moved her hair aside, baring that tempting vein in her neck. Then, his mouth covered it. Excitement and nervousness made it beat like a bird's wings against his lips, and she gasped as his tongue teased it. Then, her breath caught when he sucked it without breaking her skin, bringing that vein closer to the surface, until the lightest puncture would pierce it.

Venom built in his fangs, until the pressure from it throbbed with nearly as much intensity as her thundering pulse. Vampire bites only hurt if a vampire held back their venom. Bones was doing the opposite. These drops he readied would numb the sting from his bite. More would fill her with heat, and more still would make her dizzy from pleasure. But first...

"You're sure, Kitten?" he asked roughly.

"Yes," she breathed out. "Yes—"

His fangs slid in, venom shooting out of them. Cat didn't even have time to stiffen before it hit her bloodstream. Then the tension suddenly left her, and she made a soft, throaty sound, almost like a purr.

Her blood seared his throat before filling him with addictive fire as he swallowed. The effect exploded along his nerve endings like thousands of popping champagne bubbles. Her blood was as dual-natured as she, and drinking her was like swallowing honey while getting stung by a bee; so sweet you barely noticed the sting.

A primal moan escaped her when he sent more venom into her. Then, he sucked on the over-sensitized spot. She cried out and clutched his head closer.

"God, yes!"

He slid his fangs deeper, that flow of blood increasing when he pulled them out to swallow more of that crimson nectar. Cat swayed a little, and he tightened his grip, supporting her. Her pulse accelerated, and she pulled him harder against her neck even when her legs buckled and his grip was the only thing holding her upright.

"Don't stop," she gasped.

He wouldn't. Not until she felt every incredible sensation he did. He sank his fangs in again, giving her a few more drops of venom. Her moan grew louder, and she gripped him so tightly, her nails dug into his skin.

"Yes," she moaned.

Her pulse sped up with her pleasure, increasing the delectable flow. Each swallow was better than the last, but he had to slow the amount he took or she'd lose too much.

Bones closed one of the holes with a few drops of his blood. Then, he licked the remaining puncture before giving her another drop of venom. She ground her hips against his and held him to her neck as if she'd never let him stop drinking her. Lust and heat sang through him, fueled by her blood, her touch, and those infinitely erotic rubs that tempted him to take this to a new level of sensuality.

He didn't. She'd only said yes to this. Time enough for the rest later.

Bones gave a last, deep suction that lolled her head back even while a rapturous cry escaped her. Then, her eyes closed and she finally released her grip on his head. Bones held her as he closed that final hole, feeling her warmth within and without. Her blood now filled his body with the same thoroughness that she filled his heart.

"Kitten?"

No response. She was asleep. Blood loss combined with his venom would likely have her out for hours. More, if she'd slept as poorly as he had this past week.

Bones carried her to the bedroom, taking off only her shoes before he wrapped her in the covers. Then, he paused, thought about it, and stripped her to her skin before hiding her clothes outside the bedroom. Then, he climbed into bed next to her.

If she regretted this tomorrow, she'd do many things, but fleeing naked wasn't one of them.

Then, with her safe in his arms, he finally slept.

Bones awoke before she did. A glance at his mobile showed he'd slept five hours. Longest rest he'd had in weeks.

He checked his email and text messages. Nothing useful. No taunting messages from Hennessey for Ted to track, no hits on his online feelers to track Hennessey. Still, he should resume hunting, both online and in person. There was much to do.

Bones set his mobile down. He wasn't ready to leave Cat. She was curled next to him, taking all the covers as usual, and holding her while she slept was a balm to his battered psyche.

Francesca's face flashed in his mind. She'd hardly been perfect, but she was brave, strong, determined, and she'd deserved far better than this. Despite Hennessey kidnapping her, forcibly changing her into a vampire, forcing her to become his mistress, and then forcing her to remain in his line for nearly a century, Francesca hadn't let him break her. Instead, her final act had been a "fuck you" drenched in her own blood.

Hennessey must have been enraged at Francesca for escaping his wrath. So enraged that he'd scalped her.

Bones had been too upset to put it together last night, but if Francesca's hair had stayed on her head, it would have turned white from aging to her full years along with the rest of her. Yet it had been as black and lustrous as the day Hennessey had turned her into a vampire. That was only possible if Hennessey had cut if off before Francesca's body deteriorated fully into true death. Even dead, Hennessey couldn't stop tormenting her.

"I'll get him, Francesca."

Cat stirred, and Bones tensed. He hadn't meant to say that out loud. His emotions must've gotten the better of him. Hard for them not to. He'd promised Francesca that he'd protect her, and he'd failed.

Cat stirred again, her breathing changing. She was waking up. Selfishly, Bones wished she'd sleep a bit more. He wanted to hold her a little while longer.

"Is it dark out?" she murmured, opening her eyes.

Too late. She was awake, and already reaching for her neck to feel where he'd bitten her. Nothing was there now, though. The marks had healed with his blood, but their memory remained, and partaking in such a purely vampiric act went against every prejudiced teaching her mum had instilled in her.

"Yes, it's dark now," Bones said, bracing for the fight to come.

Cat rolled over, and then snatched her feet back when they brushed his. "You're freezing!"

"You took all the covers again."

His voice was bland, but at any moment, her sleep fog would fade and she'd get upset about sharing her blood with him. Any moment now...

She wiggled, unwinding from the blanket cocoon she'd wrapped herself in. Then, she scooted closer after throwing part of the blanket over him.

"You're like ice," she muttered. "And why did you undress me while I was asleep? You didn't take advantage, did you?"

Bones rose on his elbow so he could see every nuance of her expression.

"I took precautions. I stripped you and hid your clothes so if you woke up angry about what happened, you wouldn't be able to run out without talking to me first."

Instead of getting angry, the briefest smile curled her lips.

"You sure learn from experience." Then, her expression became serious. "I'm not angry. I told you I wanted you to do that, and I meant it. It was…incredible." Wonder filled her voice. "I didn't know it would be that way."

Relief crashed into him. He wanted to hold her to him, kiss her breathless, give her the world, anything, as long as she kept looking at him that way.

"I'm so glad to hear you say that. I love you, Kitten. You can't imagine how much."

Her gaze welled up and then spilled over while the faintest tremor ran over her body. Bones stroked her cheek, catching the first shiny drops as they fell.

"What's wrong, Kitten?"

She drew in a shuddering breath. "You won't stop until you have all of me, will you? I've given you my trust, my body, my blood…and still you want more."

"Yes, I want your heart the most." His voice vibrated with intensity. "Above all else. You're exactly right; I won't stop until I have it."

Her tears splashed the blanket while a myriad of emotions splashed over her features. Then, she tensed as though readying herself to absorb a blow.

"Bones…you have it already, so now you can stop—"

If she said anything else, he didn't hear it. Blood roared through him, its sound drowning out her voice. Only battle had made him unconsciously blitz his blood throughout his body this way, and no battle ever had stakes this high.

"You mean that?"

His quiet voice belied the armageddon going on inside him. Cat nodded, her gray gaze wide and shiny with tears.

"Say it." Need made his tone harsh. "I need to hear the words. Tell me."

Her voice cracked at first, but then she squared her shoulders and cleared her throat.

"I love you, Bones."

Light exploded through him. He'd never known joy could detonate like a bomb, but it did, and it filled his whole soul.

"Again," he said, a grin breaking over him.

She smiled back even as her tears fell faster.

"I love you, Bones."

He yanked her close, kissing every part of her beautiful face before resting his lips over hers.

"Once more."

She wrapped her arms around him, and happiness burned so brightly inside him, he half expected to see beams shooting from his limbs.

"Bones, I love you—"

His kiss cut her off.

"It was well worth the wait," he murmured, and then didn't stop kissing her for hours.

49

The mayor of Columbus was so. Bloody. Boring.

That's all Bones had determined after nine days of spying on him. Ted had the mayor's home, office, and mobile devices tapped, but they'd gleaned nothing incriminating from those, so Bones had tailed the mayor in person to see if he'd been Hennessey's "higher up" partner.

So far, nothing but the usual corruption, adultery, and partisan bickering, none of which led them any closer to Hennessey. Bones would give it one more night before turning his attention to Cleveland's mayor. If she didn't pan out, he'd tail the next mayor of a populous city. One of them had to be Hennessey's secret partner. It couldn't be anyone of lower authority.

The sound of multiple snapped twigs jerked Bones's attention away from tonight's stakeout. Someone was in the woods bordering the cave. When the sounds came closer, he grabbed his weapons' belt. Cat wasn't due for four more hours, and this wasn't a random deer. Not with how it came directly toward the cave's entrance.

Bones kept low as he ran toward the opening of the cave, a silver knife already in his hand. He lowered it when he heard accelerated breathing combined with a human heartbeat, and sheathed it when Cat's familiar scent preceded her.

He rose to his full height, walking toward the entrance instead of running now. Cat was coming into the cave at a run herself, dressed as if she'd planned for a winter jog in a thick black spandex top, black spandex trousers, and sneakers.

"Kitten, didn't expect you so early," he began, and then stopped. She looked frightened. He'd never seen her look frightened before, even when she should have.

"What's wrong?"

Cat barreled into him, breaking into tears. Bones caught her, carrying her back into the living area while wondering what the hell had happened. Had she told her mum about them? That would explain her tears and her fear. Nothing scared Cat more than the thought of losing her relationship with that woman.

"Danny," she choked out, stunning Bones. What did that sod have to do with anything?

He set her on the sofa. "You're not making sense, Kitten."

Cat's tears cleared up, fury replacing them.

"Danny Milton. He fucked me again, only this time, he kept his clothes on! Guess who's the new prime suspect in an unsolved crime involving a young mother and a strange, mummified corpse? Danny gave the cops my name when he tattled on you for crushing his hand, *and* he told them that six years ago, he saw me leaving a club with the same guy wanted for questioning in Felicity Summer's disappearance. Two detectives came to my apartment this morning. They found Felicity's car and the corpse of the vampire I beheaded, but of course they don't know about vampires, so they think I reburied some long-dead guy in a freaky occult ritual or something. You need to drink them and change their minds, or I'll never graduate college—"

Bones rose so fast, she stopped speaking.

"Ring your mum." Ice and fear splintered his tone. "Tell her to get your grandparents and bring them here, right now."

Cat jumped up in disbelief. "Are you *insane?* Your presence aside, my mom would run out of here shrieking since she's afraid of the dark. The police aren't worth—"

"I don't give a rot about the police."

His tone finally made her realize something far worse was going on. She quit speaking and stared at him.

"Hennessey's looking for anything he can find on me, or, failing that, on you." Bones tore open the Velcro version of a purse that she had belted around her waist. "If the police have your name in connection with a strange, shriveled corpse, then Hennessey will, too. You're not anonymous anymore. You've been linked to a dead vampire, and all Hennessey needs to do is look at your photo to know you're the same girl who almost got him killed, so"—Bones pressed her mobile into her now-shaking hand —"ring your family and get them *out of that house.*"

Cat turned pale as death, but instantly hit "Mom" on her contacts. Bones began snatching up more weapons, each unanswered ring increasing his urgency. When the call went to voicemail, Cat tried again. Still no answer.

"I spoke to her this morning, before the detectives came." Cat sounded like she was moments away from screaming. "She said there was someone at the door…"

Bones strapped on more weapons before handing Cat a pair of arm sheaths, thigh holsters, and her combat boots. All were filled with silver knives.

"Put these on, Kitten."

She did, moving with speed born of practice and desperation. Bones grabbed his motorcycle keys, and they both ran toward the cave's entrance.

BONES PUSHED his Ducati to the limit, covering the eighty-mile distance in only twenty-five minutes. Cat kept ringing her mum along on the way, never getting an answer. When Bones drove up to her porch, Cat leapt off the bike, evading Bones's attempt to grab her. She was almost a blur as she ran through the open front door, and then immediately slipped in the wide red puddle that coated the floor near the entrance.

Bones snatched her up with one hand, the other ready to fling knives at anything inhuman. Cat wasn't looking for danger. She was too busy staring in horror at her grandfather's body. He was crumpled on the floor of the kitchen, his hands still clutched around the torn mess that used to be his throat.

Her pain pierced him, but Bones buried that as he gave her a hard shake. He didn't hear anyone else in the house, yet he was taking no chances.

"Hennessey and his men could still be nearby. You're no use to anyone left alive if you break now!"

Anger pierced Cat's shock and grief. Good. It made her finally pull out two of her knives and look at her surroundings with menace instead of horror and desperation.

More blood trails and crimson handprints painted the worn wooden steps leading to the second floor. Bones inhaled, smelling death coming from Cat's former room at the top of the stairs. He grabbed her before she ran up there, this time anticipating her new burst of speed.

"Stop," he said firmly. "I think Hennessey and whoever was with him is gone, but you keep those knives ready, and you unleash them at anyone you don't know. I'll check upstairs."

"No," she snarled. "I'm going up there."

"Kitten, don't. Let me. You keep watch."

She shoved him hard enough to dent the wall behind him. "Get out of my way."

Her gaze glittered a bright, dangerous green, and she'd put him into the wall using only one hand. She shouldn't have been able to do that. She also shouldn't have been faster than him earlier when she'd run into the house before he could stop her. Hairs rose on the back of Bones's neck as he stared at her.

At this moment, she was something even more impossible than a blending of human and vampire. She was a Master vampire.

He moved to the side.

Cat ran up the stairs, not tripping in any blood this time. Bones followed, sending his senses throughout the house and outside it. He didn't hear, smell, or feel any vampires, but that didn't mean they weren't lurking nearby.

The sound Cat made turned his attention back to her. She stood in front of her old room, the door in pieces at her feet, and her grandmother dead on the other side of the threshold.

Bones was glad Cat could only see what had happened instead of smell it, too. From the thick scent of terror, her grandmother had been alive when Hennessey's men had kicked in the door. She must have locked herself in the room after being injured. For some reason, they'd let her run up here, probably because it amused them. Then, they'd kicked in the door, thrown her around the room a bit, and finally torn out her throat.

But where was her mum?

Bones didn't smell death anywhere else in the house, and the only heartbeat he heard was Cat's. Justina's scent was heavy in this room, but it was her room, so that was expected. Had Justina run up here with Cat's grandmother? And if so, was any of the blood spattering the room her mum's?

Bones crouched near Cat's grandmother, sniffing the deep tears in her neck. A familiar scent scorched up his nose along with the smell of her grandmother's blood. Hennessey had been the one to deliver the killing bite.

Rage speared him. Bones forced it back. He had to see whose blood painted the carpet and walls. Time enough for rage later.

Now that he had her scent, Bones sniffed the crimson streaks. Most of it was her grandmother's blood, but one of the smaller spatters wasn't. Must be her mum's. So, Justina *was* here during the attack. So were two…no, three more vampires aside from Hennessey, judging from the scents in the air. One of those scents was familiar, but Bones didn't remember who it belonged to. In this case, it was like seeing someone's face and recognizing it while completely forgetting that person's name.

Bones went over to the bed, where additional streaks marred one of the pillows. He sniffed it. Yes, this was more of Justina's blood, but only steady drips. Not an arterial flow. He checked the last set of bloody streaks, and then turned to Cat.

"I can smell them. There were four vampires including Hennessey. Your mum was here, too. They took her, and there's not enough of her blood here for her to be dead."

Cat's eyelids fluttered, and her knees trembled as if she were fighting to stay upright. Then, she stood ramrod straight and gave him a short nod, but that brief glimpse razed him. Such desperate hope in her gaze, mingled with such terrible pain.

I'll get her back, Kitten, whatever it takes.

"Stay here," Bones said, and went over the staircase more closely, realizing that, from the scents, Justina had dragged her injured mother up the stairs. Brave of her. Even in the face of her worst nightmare—vampires—Justina had risked her life trying to save her mum instead of fleeing as fast as she could.

Bones examined the blood near the front door next. All of it was Grandpa Joe's. From the splatter pattern, her grandfather had opened the door to his unexpected visitors, and immediately gotten his throat torn out. Then, they'd let him crawl away, his blood soaking the floor, until he died in the kitchen.

Bones went to his body, inhaling again. More blood and death. Hennessey's scent wasn't on the kill wound, though, so he hadn't been the vampire to murder him, but it was stronger near her gramps' torso. The bastard didn't do anything by accident, so Bones turned her grandfather over, checking his body—

A folded note was tucked inside her gramps' shirt, carefully away from his blood. Bones took it, his fist clenching when he heard the sound of a car approaching.

"Get down here, Kitten, someone's coming!"

She ran down the stairs, her gaze still lit up with green. Bones concentrated, but he felt no telltale vampire power, and moments later, he heard the double thud of heartbeats.

"Is it them?" Cat asked in a savage tone.

"No, they're human."

Green bled out of her gaze until only thundercloud gray remained. "Oh."

She sounded disappointed. Bones understood her need for vengeance, but now wasn't the time.

"Let's go," he said, taking her arm.

She didn't move. "How will we know where they've taken my mom? We're not leaving until we do. I don't care who's coming!"

The car was almost here, and worse, he heard sirens in the distance now, too. Bones got on his bike, revved it up, and spun it until the back end faced her.

"They left a note in your grandfather's shirt. Come on, Kitten, they're here."

With that, a black Chevy Tahoe roared into the driveway, a red siren flashing on its dashboard. Two men were inside, one with white skin only a few shades darker than his silvery hair, and one with slicked-back black hair and tawny brown skin.

"Police!" the older man shouted, coming out with his gun drawn. "Hold it right there, Crawfield. Don't you fuckin' move!"

Bones flew to Cat, standing between her and the pointed guns. The cop knew her name, so he must be one of the detectives she'd mentioned.

"Don't fucking move!" the cop shouted at Bones, clearly alarmed at how he'd suddenly appeared in front of Cat.

"Get on the bike, Kitten," Bones said low. "I'll get on behind you. They have backup on the way."

"Drop your weapons! Hands in the air!" the younger man shouted, to the sound of both guns cocking.

Bullets wouldn't hurt him, but they could kill her. Bones dropped his knives and held up his hands.

Come closer, he silently urged them as both cops approached him. The younger one already had his cuffs out, too. A few more steps, and Bones would knock them on their arses—

Silver flashed by Bones, followed instantly by screams. Both guns dropped and the cops' clutched wrists now pronged through with silver knives. The younger one tried to grab his gun with his other hand, and a new silver knife pinned it to the ground. Another one followed, slamming into the older cop's wrist before he could try the same thing.

Cat sheathed her remaining knives and got onto the bike.

Bones said nothing. She'd wounded two humans; something she'd normally never do. She wasn't in the mood for a chat.

He got on behind her, his arms long enough to reach the handles while his back was a shield in case more officers arrived and fired at them. These two couldn't. All they were good for now was a trip to the nearest Emergency Room.

"I'll get you, bitch!" the white-haired one screamed.

Be glad you won't, Bones thought as he sped off.

Even he didn't know what she was capable of right now.

331

50

*B*ones avoided the roads and only drove through wooded areas. Every so often, he heard police helicopters and sirens, but even in early December, the tree canopy was still thick enough to hide them from sight.

When darkness fell and he hadn't heard a chopper for almost an hour, he risked approaching a nearby highway. Good, no cops or roadblocks, and there was enough traffic for this to work.

Bones killed the bike's engine. "Hop off, Kitten."

She did, giving him a questioning look.

"Wait here, won't be a moment," he said, and tore off branches from the nearest tree. Then, he laid the bike in a small ditch and covered it with those branches.

Now, to get a new ride.

Bones stepped out onto the shoulder of the road. Headlights appeared, getting closer. Bones moved into the center of the road, fixing his gaze on the driver while his eyes lit up.

"Stop," he mouthed, staring at the driver.

Fool didn't see him. The driver was glancing down, probably at his mobile. Bones should wreck him out of sheer principle.

"Stop!" he shouted, his gaze turning a brighter green.

Finally, the driver looked up. Then, he slammed on the brakes. Still, the car's bumper nearly kissed Bones's belt.

Idiot. But the car would do. Not too flashy, not too old.

"Park," Bones mouthed, indicating the side of the road.

Caught in the power of Bones's gaze, the driver did.

Bones opened the driver's door, giving a disgusted look at the phone in his lap. It was open to Twitter, of all things. As if that couldn't wait until the bloke was home.

Bones led the driver to where Cat was half-concealed by the tree line. Then, he hauled the driver close, biting him and drinking nearly a pint. Aside from the energy boost, that was the least the man deserved for Tweeting while driving.

"You're tired," Bones told him when he was done. "You're going to have a little lie-down now. When you wake up, you won't remember me or fret about your car. You went for a walk, and you'll walk home after you've rested."

The driver immediately curled up on the ground and fell asleep. Wasn't too cold out, so he'd be fine.

Cat's stare grew pointed.

"We needed a vehicle no one was looking for," Bones said.

"Oh."

That was all she said until they were in the car and driving away. Then, she said, "Show me the note" in a hard tone.

Bones gave it to her. "You won't understand it, but they knew I would."

She opened the wadded-up paper and stared the five words. RECOMPENSE. TWICE PAST DAY'S DEATH.

"Does it mean she's still alive?" she asked hoarsely.

Bones grunted. "That's what it's supposed to mean."

Hope flared in her gaze. "Do you trust Hennessey in this? Is there some kind of...vampire code not to lie about hostages?"

Even if there was, Hennessey probably wouldn't follow it.

"No, there's no code for hostages, and I don't trust Hennessey in anything. But he might reckon that he has a use for your mum beyond being a hostage. She's a lovely woman, and you know what Hennessey does with lovely women."

Rage made Cat's cheeks red while the rest of her face went dead white. "When are we supposed to meet them? What time? And what do they want from us?"

Our horrible deaths.

Cat already knew that, past her grief, anger, and fear. That's what they had to thwart while still getting her mum back.

"Let me find a place to stop off, and then we'll talk. Don't want a police roadblock making a bad situation worse."

Frustration seethed from her scent, but she nodded.

Bones drove until he reached a derelict part of town. Then, he looked for a hotel that would suit his needs. When he found one, he pulled around to the back.

"Wait here," Bones said, putting on a coat the driver had left in the backseat. Now, his weapons were covered, at least.

Bones went into the lobby. The single tv had a crack in the screen and no sound, but one glance confirmed he'd been right to leave Cat in the car. *Grisly Double Murder Rocks Small Town*, the headline said, followed by Cat's driver's license photo. Under that were the words *Armed and Dangerous*.

No picture of Bones, curiously. Perhaps the cop's unmarked vehicle hadn't come with a dashboard camera.

"Help you?" the desk clerk asked, sounding bored.

Bones turned to him. "Yes. I need a room, and I'd prefer to pay cash. Don't want my wife seeing the credit card charge."

The clerk's gaze turned shrewd. "We're not supposed to take cash."

Supposed to. Not "can't."

Bones dropped several bills onto the counter. When the clerk's eyes fastened on them, Bones knew he wouldn't need to bother mesmerizing the clerk into accepting the offer.

"I *really* don't want to use my card," Bones said.

The clerk snatched the money, pocketed it, and began typing on his keyboard. "Let me guess—your name's John Smith?"

"That's it," Bones replied in a pleasant voice.

Moments later, he had his room card. A glance at the tv still showed Cat's face, now with the headline "Officers Injured In Attack. Reward For Information Leading To Arrest."

"Some shit, huh?" the clerk said, following Bones's gaze.

Some shit, indeed, and all his fault. If he'd refused to let Cat go after Hennessey that night at the club, none of this would have happened.

Bones tried not to think about that as he returned to the car and drove them to the farthest corner of the hotel. Regret led to doubt, and doubt led to hesitancy, which he could not afford when dealing with Hennessey. He needed to be clear, cold, and merciless. That was the only thing that would help Cat now.

She said nothing until he led her into the hotel room. It smelled worse than it looked, and with the worn carpet, dented furniture, and frayed bedspread, that was saying something.

"Why a hotel room?" Cat asked in a wooden voice.

Your face is on the news, so we have few options left.

She had enough to fret about, so Bones only said, "We're off the road, so less chance to attract attention, and we can talk without interruption here. No one in this area will notice much beyond a drive-by shooting. Also, you can wash up."

Not even Cat's all-black clothing could hide the fact that she was covered in blood. Her hands were also stained scarlet, as was her cheek, and more blood darkened her hair.

"Do we have time for that?" she asked.

"We have hours. They want to meet at two a.m. That's what 'twice past day's death' means. Midnight is the death of every day, and they chose two hours past it, giving you plenty of time to hear about your grandparents and mum, and contact me."

Or time for them to take Cat themselves. Pure luck that Hennessey must have gotten her old address. If Cat hadn't moved into that apartment a few months ago, she could have been the one to open the door to Hennessey this morning.

Bones couldn't afford to feel everything that thought elicited, so he focused on Cat when she said, "How considerate," with open loathing. "Now, tell me what they're offering. Me for her? Does Hennessey want the bait that almost got him killed?"

She still wasn't thinking clearly. Residual shock, no doubt. It also protected her from the worst of her grief, which was why he hated what he had to do next.

Bones sat her on the edge of the bed. She let him; further proof of her shock. Then, he knelt in front of her and took her hands.

"Hennessey wants me, Kitten. He's given no thought to you beyond how he could use you toward that end. You realize he'll be making your mother talk. With luck, they won't be asking the right questions. I didn't believe you when you told me what you were, so even if your mum is coerced into telling them about you, chances are they'll think she's raving and pay her little heed."

Cat's hands had been limp and cold when he started speaking. Now, they were tightening, and some of that abnormal chill left them. Anger was strengthening her.

"Those detectives probably saved your life by coming to your flat this morning and scaring you into leaving," Bones went on. "Hennessey and his men have no doubt discovered where you live by now and searched the place. They'll find your weapons, but they'll probably surmise they were mine, and that I kept them there for convenience."

"So, me and my family are nothing to them," she bit out.

"It's to our advantage," Bones said, his hands tightening. "They want me, and I'll go, but they won't be expecting you."

After all he'd done to protect her, it had come to this.

If Bones had another option, he'd take it, but there wasn't time to summon his allies. Even if he could, the sudden arrival of Charles or other members of Bones's line would enrage Hennessey into slaughtering her mum. No, he and Cat had to face

Hennessey and his men alone. Bones could no sooner expect Cat to leave her mum to die than he could expect himself to fall out of love with her.

Some things were inevitable, it seemed.

"You don't have to do this," Cat abruptly said. "You can tell me where my mom is, and I'll go on my own. As you said, they won't be expecting me."

She wasn't in shock. She was *mental*.

"How can you even suggest that?" His voice was heavy with disbelief. "First of all, this is my fault. I should have never allowed you to hunt Hennessey with me. Then, I should have killed Danny that night like I intended. At the very least, if I'd stolen Danny's memory of how his hand got maimed, he wouldn't have given your name to the police. But I was angry, and I wanted him to know why it had happened. *Of course I'm going*, Kitten. Even Hennessey, who hasn't the slightest idea that I love you, knows I will go. Doesn't matter if your mum's already dead and there's nothing to gain from it except vengeance, I'll still go, and I'll rip off every hand that touched her or your grandparents."

Cat's gaze filled up with tears. "Aren't you afraid?"

His head briefly bowed under the weight of everything that question elicited before Bones raised it and met her gaze.

"Yes, I'm afraid. I'm terrified that you'll see me as a monster again because it was vampires who did this. That's what I'm afraid of, Kitten."

She knelt and enfolded him in her arms. He didn't realize how much he'd needed it until that moment. Guilt wasn't the only emotion he'd been suppressing. That fear was, too.

"I will never stop loving you," she said, her lips a soft brand against his skin. "No one can change that. No matter what happens, I will *always* love you."

He closed his eyes, breathing her in while letting her warmth soak into him. What came later would be terrible even if they did save her mum, but right now, this moment...it was theirs.

"I love you, too, Kitten. Today, tomorrow, forever."

She made a choked sound. He held her closer, brushing her hair aside to stroke her cheek. Dried blood clung to his fingers like scarlet grains of sand as she turned to kiss his hand.

"Bones." His name whispered past her lips. "Make love to me. I need to feel you inside me."

He drew away to look at her. Desperation filled her gaze, not desire. She might need this, but she didn't truly want it.

Not yet.

Bones stilled her hands and took off his weapons before removing his shirt, letting the fabric slowly slide over him. Enough moonlight filled the room to highlight his skin when he threw the shirt aside and unbuckled his trousers. Green flecked her gaze when they, too, were tossed aside, leaving him naked.

An ember. Time to turn it into a flame.

Bones removed Cat's waist, arm, and thigh holsters before taking off her boots. Then, he peeled off her spandex, seeing her wince as the dried blood crunched from his actions. It had soaked through to stain her entire right side. Her jaw tightened as she glanced at the red smears coating her.

Bones tilted her chin up until she looked only at him.

"I know what you're thinking and you're wrong. This isn't goodbye for us, Kitten."

Guilt flashed over her features, followed by grief. She did believe that.

He didn't. His voice strengthened as he stroked her face. "I didn't survive over two hundred and fifty years to find you only to lose you within six months. I want you, but this isn't goodbye because we *will* get through this."

She clutched him to her, her hands running over him as if she could force every other thought away through tactile overload alone. Bones kissed her, deliberately slower than her frantic movements, and touched her as though any suddenness on his part would startle her away.

After a few minutes, her breathing changed from fraught intakes of breath to something slower. Deeper. Edged with sensuality instead of desperation, and when he stopped kissing her to see her eyes, they now glowed with a soft emerald light.

A flame. Now, for fire.

Bones replaced his hands with his mouth, kissing every part of her with the same slow thoroughness. This time, she clutched him to her with desire, not a need to forget. When he tasted her, she twisted around to take him into her mouth, and when she came, she drew upon him so strongly that he lost himself, too.

Afterward, he slid inside her, more pleasure mixing with the aftershocks from his climax. She wrapped her legs around him, drawing him in deeper while her nails scored his back. He moved slowly until she demanded otherwise, and then he let passion carry them both away.

51

*C*at lay next to him, silent but not sleeping. The bedspread was on the floor, half covering their discarded clothes. A faint blue light from the nightstand clock was now the only illumination in the room. The moon had been hidden by clouds.

She stroked his shoulder, pain darkening her features when her touch left behind a reddish smear. Sweat had moistened the dried blood on her, making the stains easier to transfer.

"There's a shower in the bathroom," Bones said quietly.

She drew her hand away. "You go. If I wash it off, it's like I'm erasing what happened, and I can't do that." Her tone hardened. "I want to wear my family's blood when I kill those bastards. I want it to be the last thing they fucking see."

She'd need every bit of that fierceness. She also needed to be *what she was*, without limitation or regret.

Bones steeled himself against everything he felt for her as he asked, "What are you willing to do to ensure that?"

She gave him a startled look. "Anything."

"You sure?" he asked bluntly. "If so, you'll need more than your family's blood. You'll also need mine."

Cat stared at him, ice cold determination filling her gaze.

"How much?"

"A lot," he said with more bluntness. "Not enough to turn you, but enough to make you more vampire than you've ever been."

Any other time, those words would have sent her running in the opposite direction. Now, her brow only cocked.

"Will I be as fast as you? As strong?"

"Nearly. You'll also heal almost as fast as vampires do, and your other senses will be heightened."

Cat left the bed, rooted under her discarded clothes for a moment, and came up with a silver knife.

"Let's do it," she said, grabbing for his wrist.

He stopped her before she cut his wrist. "Not yet. There's something I need to do first."

"What?" she asked with an impatient glance at the clock. Only ninety minutes left until they had to meet Hennessey.

"Feed," Bones said.

She pulled her hair aside, baring her neck.

He let out a short laugh. "I'd love nothing more, but I can't drain you and then fill you with my blood. That *would* turn you."

"Oh."

She let her hair fall back and began pulling on her blood-stiffened clothes.

"You don't have come with me. I know that's not your favorite thing to see," Bones said as he got dressed, too.

She gave him a look. "We're in this together. All of it."

God, how he loved her.

Blood was easy to find here. They only needed to wander to the darkest part of the alley between the hotel and the nearby convenience store before Bones heard footsteps behind him. He turned, seeing four men eying him with predatory expectation.

"Evening, gents," Bones greeted them.

"Evenin', guv'nor," the tall, muscular one mocked with a fake English accent while the other three started to circle them. "'ow's

341

about you hand over your wallet, then you and your hottie won't get hurt?"

"Terrible imitation of Brit-speak," Cat muttered.

Bones agreed. That's why he didn't take the time to mesmerize them. That, and their threat to Cat, of course.

Bones spun in a circle and felled them with a single punch. Then, he drank from each of them, until he was more than full.

"You're so washing out your mouth before you kiss me again," Cat said. "I don't want a face full of hepatitis."

Bones only snorted as he followed her back to the hotel. Cat pointed at the bathroom as soon as they were in their room, and he went in and rinsed out his mouth.

"You couldn't catch hepatitis if you tried," he said when he was finished. "No germs or viruses can survive in vampire blood. You haven't been sick a day in your life, have you?"

She thought about it for a second. "Actually...no."

Bones sat on the bed, anticipation thrumming through him despite the terrible circumstances that necessitated this.

"Come here, Kitten."

She did, her gaze searching his as she reached for his wrist.

"No," Bones said, tilting his head to the side. "Here."

"Why not your wrist?" Her voice was higher from nerves, but the same amount of determination filled her eyes.

"Because then I couldn't hold you," Bones said, encircling her in his arms.

Some of the tension left her. She scooted closer, embracing him now, too.

"You'll tell me when to stop?"

"Promise," he said, fighting to keep the new huskiness from his voice. She couldn't know how much he'd enjoy this. It would distract her at best and disturb her at worst.

Cat's breath tickled him with warm puffs before her mouth closed over his neck. Then, she pulled back.

"Why my teeth and not a knife?"

"Silver would drain my strength. This won't. Now, quit stalling and do it, Kitten."

"Right," she muttered against his skin. "Guess 'life sucks' is an instruction manual as well as a saying."

His laughter turned into a hiss as her teeth clamped down. Their flatness required force to break his skin rather than the easy puncturing that fangs provided, yet her biting him was so purely *vampire* that pleasure and pain entwined. When she drew his blood, she sucked it with more strength than she had at her most passionate. Bones stifled his moan as he directed his blood to his neck, allowing her to swallow in greater quantities.

"Again," he said when the punctures healed, closing off that flow.

She complied. The pain only heightened the intensity of the pleasure when she sucked until his blood filled her mouth.

"More," he growled when she pulled away. Her vampire side hadn't taken over yet, which was the whole point.

Cat grimaced but bit him again, swallowing the next mouthful, and the next one, and the next.

Her grip on him slowly tightened while faint swirls of energy rose from her skin. She began biting him without encouragement, swallowing without hesitation, and drawing out greater quantities of his blood than before.

That's it, Kitten.

Bones slid his hand into her hair when she bit him so hard that she split his skin on the first try. Then, she sucked so strongly he didn't need to will his blood out. She was drawing it with her own strength, spiking pain and pleasure through him.

She bit an even larger puncture into his neck when the last ones closed. Then, she widened the tear, sucking harder and yanking his head back to bare more of his throat. When that still wasn't enough, she wrapped her legs around him, holding him in a grip that was becoming viselike.

"So good," she muttered in a new, animalistic tone. "So, so good."

Bones pushed her head back. "Enough, Kitten.

She lunged at him, her teeth snapping while her gaze was now so wild, nothing human remained in it. Bones held her head away, twisting to free himself from her legs, all while she clawed at him and a single word spilled from her mouth.

"Moremoremoremoremoremore—!"

"I said *enough*."

Bones yanked her arms behind her back, grimly pleased at how much strength it took him to do that. Then, he flung himself on top of her, leveraging both of their weight to keep her arms pinned behind her. He needed his hands free to hold her away from his neck, which she was snapping at like a deranged shark.

"Stop fighting!" Bones said while tangling his legs in hers to keep her from using them to flip him over. "Just breathe. Ride it out, Kitten, it will pass."

He kept repeating that while countering her attempts to knock him over and rip his throat out. Eventually, the madness left her gaze, her breathing evened into pants instead of frenzied snarls, and she stopped thrashing beneath him.

"How do you stand it?" she finally asked in a rasp.

Bones loosened his grip, although he didn't get off her. She might not be entirely free of the blood lust yet.

"You don't, not for the first several days. New vampires kill anyone near them when the hunger hits. After a week or so, you learn to control yourself."

And if any new vampire *didn't* learn control, it was their sire's job to kill them or that sire forfeited their own life. That became law after some careless sires let their newly-turned offspring rampage to the point that enough humans heard of it and vampires become enshrined in myth and legend.

"This is what it feels like to be a new vampire?" she asked in a soft voice.

344

No, or you'd still be trying to tear my neck open, and the only thing that would stop you is a great deal more blood.

"No. This was only a taste, and it's temporary. By next week, most of the affects will be out of your system. You'll be back to yourself."

Cat didn't say anything for a moment. Then, she inhaled, and awe filled her features.

"I can smell you. I smell myself on your skin. I smell everything. My God, there are so many scents in this room..."

She inhaled again, her nose wrinkling as she took in some of the room's less pleasant aromas. Still, that wonder remained.

"I didn't realize how different things were for you. I could be blind and still know most of what was around me by scent alone! Although, how do you walk by a public bathroom without passing out?"

Bones chuckled as he kissed her forehead. "Willpower, pet. And choosing not to take a breath in at that moment."

She smiled, and then her features clouded.

"Is this what you feel like every day? Stronger, more alert...superior?"

She almost whispered the last word, apprehension competing with the lingering wonder in her expression.

Bones chose his words with care. "You had about two pints of vampire blood aged for nearly a quarter of a millennium. That means you're a hitchhiker on my power now, so in a way, yes, you feel the way I do. Are you telling me you like it?"

So much guilt smashed into her expression, he knew the answer was yes. And she couldn't handle the thought. Even now, she still believed her vampire nature was evil.

It wasn't. It was just her, more amplified. People were the evil ones. Not enhanced abilities.

To distract her from that guilt, Bones kissed her, enjoying her surprised groan as she kissed him back. Heightened senses had many advantages. Feeling pleasure more intensely was also one of them.

But that wasn't why Cat had drunk his blood, so he ended the kiss. Then, he stared at her, forcing his emotions back and replacing them with battle ice.

"When it is time, no matter what we find, you need to unleash everything within you. Hold nothing back. Use all your strength, all your abilities, all your rage. Give them free rein and let them carry you. Kill anything, vampire or human, that stands in your way from retrieving your mum, because if they're there and they're not in chains, they're your enemy."

Her features seemed to turn to stone, matching the new steel in her gaze. "I'm ready."

If she truly was, then nothing could stop her. She didn't know how powerful she was, but he did. All she had to do was let it out.

Bones jumped off the bed, cracking his knuckles and rolling his head around his shoulders in his pre-battle ritual. Cat did the same, her movement nearly as fast as his. Then she met his gaze, hints of green burning in the stormy depths.

"What's the plan?"

Bones gave her a brief, savage smile. "Let them take me in supposed exchange for your mum. When they renege on the deal, we kill them all."

52

*R*ecompense.

For Hennessey, that meant meeting at the same spot where Bones had ambushed him, and where Hennessey had left Francesca's body. For Bones, it meant what would come later.

"What if they just kill you on sight?" Cat whispered as they approached that stretch of highway, speaking for the first time since they'd gone over their lines for tonight.

Her nerves were understandable. The most stressful time in battle was typically right before it. When the fighting started, there wouldn't be time for nervousness. Only action.

"Not Hennessey," Bones said. "He'll want to drag it out for weeks. He doesn't do quick, merciful kills, especially to a chap who's caused him this much trouble. No, he'll want to break me and hear me beg. There will be time."

Cat looked like she'd throw up, and she gripped his hand.

"Bones..." *I can't lose you!* her gaze screamed while fear soured her scent.

He covered her hand with his. "It'll be all right, luv."

Four SUVs were on either side of road up ahead. Bones drove up and came to a stop between them. At once, several vampires surrounded their car, coming not from the SUVs, but from the trees on either side of the highway.

Clever, Bones thought coolly. *But I didn't come here to run, so your ambush is wasted.*

Bones leaned over the armrest toward Cat. "Let them smell your fear," he whispered. "It'll lull them. Don't be strong until you have to be."

Fools wouldn't know she wasn't afraid for herself. They wouldn't even care that she was wearing all her weapons. They'd only see a human, and thus utterly dismiss her.

A vampire approached Bones's window. He had reddish brown hair, freckles, and the typical milky skin of a ginger. His gangly form still held hints of unfinished adolescent growth, but Bones had met him a decade or two ago, so he only looked like a teenager. He was around sixty, judging from his aura.

"Hallo, Vincent," Bones said, rolling down his window. As soon as he did, he caught Vincent's scent. *He* was one of the other vampires at Cat's grandparent's house. Bones knew he'd recognized that scent even if its owner was forgettable.

"You came after all," Vincent drawled before grinning. "And call me Switch."

Bones schooled his reaction, but Cat's mouth dropped.

"*You're* Switch? You? You look like a Boy Scout!"

"Don't I?" Switch agreed in genial tone. "Works great for my job. No one suspects me of anything." Then, Switch returned his attention to Bones. "I'm surprised you brought her."

"She insisted," Bones said, as if frustrated by it. "Wanted to see for herself that her mum's still alive. Couldn't sway her from it."

Switch's smile turned nasty. "Nice family you have, Catherine. Sorry about your grandfather. I know it's rude to eat and run, but I was short on time."

Anger drenched Cat's scent, but not a hint of green filled her gaze. "Where's my mother?" was all Cat said.

Switch gave a vague wave. "We have her."

A dark-haired vampire with walnut-brown skin came up to Switch. Unlike Switch, he had several weapons on him, and from the wary look he gave Bones, he was ready to use them.

"Drones aren't picking up anyone else, and neither are our sentries. They appear to have come alone."

"Well, let's be on our way, then," Switch said in a cheery voice. "I trust you won't lag behind?"

Bones flashed fang in his smile. "Don't fret about me."

Switch flicked his fingers in a dismissive manner and then walked away, getting into one of the SUVs.

"I'm afraid," Cat said, as rehearsed.

Switch and the others would be listening to every word. She even manufactured a quaver in her voice, but her gaze was laser steady as it focused on the other vehicles, and the scent of her anger filled their car like billowing smoke.

Bones replied with his predetermined lines. "Once we get there, stay in the car and don't come out. When your mum gets in, you leave straightaway."

"Okay."

Cat began to cry. The little hiccup sounds she added were a masterful touch. Bones heard Switch snort in derision.

They drove for nearly an hour, away from town, of course. No shock that Hennessey chose a deserted area. Bones only saw winter—deadened cornfields for the past several miles. Then, he glimpsed a home at the end of a gravel road that was surrounded on one side by withered cornfields, and on the other by tall, thin trees whose branches reached up like skeletal hands. If they passed by an open work shed filled with bloody chainsaws, it would be macabre perfection.

The four SUVs hung back, leaving the long driveway open. Bones drove up and parked on it, facing the house. At once, the other vehicles pulled in behind him and on either side of him. Cat met his gaze, her eyes wide, but her stare steady.

Bones had barely stopped when Switch yanked open his door, which had automatically unlocked when he put the car in park.

"End of the road," Switch said with a smirk. "Hennessey said we'll send her mom out after you come in."

"Don't think so, mate," Bones replied. "Bring her to where I can see her, and then I'll come. Refuse," his tone hardened, "and you and I dance here and now."

Switch's smile faltered. "You can hear her heartbeat in there. That's proof enough that she's alive."

Bones gave a derisive snort. "I hear seven heartbeats in there, and who's to say any of them are hers? What's the point of hiding her from me? Is this a bargain or not?"

Switch muttered "bastard" under his breath, but waved at one of the vampires, who went into the house. Moments later, the front window curtains jerked open and a heavily tattooed vampire held Justina against the glass.

Cat gasped, and it wasn't rehearsed. Bones was more clinical as his gaze swept over Justina. Blood trailed from her head, but her cuts appeared minor, she was fully clothed, and she looked terrorized but not broken. Hennessey must have been too occupied plotting Bones's torture and death to focus on her.

"Your proof," Switch said. "Satisfied?"

Bones got out of the car. Half a dozen vampires instantly surrounded him. All were armed, all had notable power levels, and all had a "try me" expression on their faces.

Bones only grinned. *Hold that thought, mates.*

Cat scooted into the driver's seat, locking the doors.

"Wait here, we'll bring your mom out," Switch said to Cat as the other vampires hustled Bones inside the house.

"Look who joined the party," Hennessey drawled once the door closed behind Bones and his guards.

Bones's gaze swept the interior room. Wood floors, plain plaster walls, and hardly any furniture, which was necessary since over two dozen vampires were now in here. That was twice the number he'd expected, and all for him since Hennessey had no idea that Cat was a threat. Bones would be flattered if this didn't make it harder to get Cat's mum out alive.

Instead of taking Justina to Cat, the tattooed vampire dragged her mum further inside the room. For a moment, Justina's eyes met Bones's as she passed him. Anger, hatred, and grief were clear in her gaze, no surprise. Bones was a vampire, and Hennessey had just given her a thousand more reasons to hate vampires. But Justina also looked confused as she glanced at Bones, and then at the window where Cat's headlights pierced through the curtains.

"Yes, I came because of her," Bones said quietly.

Shock suffused Justina's expression, and then she lunged at Bones, trying to hit him with her bound hands. "Lying monster!"

Hennessey and the others laughed. Bones only shook his head. Insulting him and trying to assault him despite being bound and helpless. Wasn't that déjà vu all over again? Perhaps Cat had gotten some of her incredible bravery from her mum.

The tattooed vampire shoved Justina into the room's far corner. She tripped and fell since her feet were also bound, but now Justina was low to the ground and out of the way. Perfect.

"Be careful what you wish for, Bones," Hennessey said, delightedly smug. "You tried for years to find out who was in my operation, so look around. Except for one, we're all here."

Bones recognized several faces among the vampires, although the three humans were unfamiliar. Bones heard three more heartbeats in the back of the house, but the soft sobs that came along with them indicated captives, not more conspirators.

No Ohio mayors, prominent judges, sheriffs, or even Congressman among the humans in this room. Where was Hennessy's "higher up" partner? Was he the missing "except for one"?

As for the vampires, they were all armed with silver knives except for three who held thick lengths of chain with even thicker cuffs at the ends of them. Hennessey jerked his head at Bones, and the three vampires surrounded him.

Titanium with silver spikes, Bones noted as the first of those chains bit into him. Hennessey had spared no expense.

Hennessey visibly relaxed when Bones didn't struggle as the first set of cuffs were slapped around his wrist. Hennessey had also dressed for the occasion, wearing a charcoal gray suit that had a subtle sheen only very expensive fabrics boasted. His black hair was perfectly combed, and his thin moustache and beard looked freshly trimmed. Brown eyes bristled with green highlights as he stared at Bones.

"I would've let your girl go and only killed you, but I believe in an eye for an eye, and you have to pay for turning Francesca against me. She was the only woman I ever loved."

Ice filled Bones until he half expected to see his breath when he spoke. "You didn't love Francesca. You only loved controlling her. There's quite a difference."

Hennessey charged toward Bones, only stopping when Switch ran up and tugged at his arm.

"Boss, the girl!"

"...just a few miles from Bethel Road," Cat was saying in a calm voice. "Earlier today, I speared Detectives Mansfield and Black through the wrists with silver knives. Come and get me."

"Bitch called the police?" Hennessey said in disbelief.

"Didn't see that coming, did you?" Bones taunted him.

Rage darkened Hennessey's face. "Get her!"

Switch ran out the door. Cat was already revving her engine. Hennessey's eyes widened.

"She can't mean to—"

The car smashing through the front windows cut him off.

$\mathcal{G}$ lass exploded like shrapnel. Switch hung onto the car's hood with one fist shoved through the windshield in a failed attempt to stop Cat. Bones took advantage of his captors' shock to rip the remaining chains from their hands. Then, he ducked.

Not a moment too soon. Cat dove through the ruined windshield, rolling past Switch, and came up flinging silver knives. Screams merged with the sounds of twisting metal and falling plaster as those knives found their marks. With how tightly Hennessey had packed this room, Hennessey's guards had nowhere to run.

Justina wisely stayed on the floor, and the still-moving car rolled to a stop only a few feet from her. A rage-filled scream roared out of Cat, and her eyes lit up with emerald fire.

"What the *fuck?*" someone shouted when they saw it.

One of the heavy cuffs was still locked around Bones's wrist. The other cuff was free, and it was at the end of a long chain. Bones swung the chain at the nearest vampire, looping it around their throat. The cuff caught, preventing the chain from slipping free. With a brutal yank, Bones tore the vampire's head off.

Bones repeated the lethal combination until he was jumped. Fire replaced his ice as battle rage took over. Bones didn't even feel the knife someone slammed into his back. Since it missed his heart, it didn't matter. Bones smashed his fist through the vampire facing him, whirled, and head-butted the vampire who'd stabbed him. The blow was so hard that the vampire's eyes exploded. Before they could heal, Bones ripped his head off, and whirled to face his next attacker—

Cat flew through the air, landing on a vampire reaching for her mum. She ripped his back open with a silver knife before another vampire jumped at her. Faster than he could react, Cat rolled under her attacker's leap. The vampire sailed over her, and Cat had him knifed to the wall moments later.

A rush of incoming air made Bones spin, causing the stab meant for his heart to land in his side. His attacker was too close for Bones to swing his chain, so he pulled a length over his knuckles before slamming his fist into the vampire's face. Blood spurted as the vampire's face dented, but another vampire was right behind him. Bones shoved the now-faceless vampire at his new attacker before sliding on the blood-slicked floor to come up behind the new threat. One vicious twist later, and that threat was permanently negated.

Cat's snarl whipped Bones's head around. Lucifer's flying fuck! Both her arms were speared through the chests of rapidly shriveling vampires and she was using their bodies as shields while fighting off two more vampires. He hadn't taught her that, and it was so gruesomely magnificent Bones would have applauded if another vampire wasn't sneaking up behind her.

Bones yanked the knife from his back and flung it at the vampire. It landed in his heart, and he went down like a stone. Cat never saw him. She was too busy stabbing the vampire in front of her so deeply that her arm briefly disappeared. Then, Cat threw one of her "shield" bodies at the remaining vampire stupid enough to try her. It staggered him before her knife rammed straight into his open mouth.

Four more vampires charged Bones, claiming his attention. Bones killed one, but the second grabbed Bones's chains and held on while the third yanked Bones's knife from his hand. The fourth vampire was nearly upon him, and now Bones was unarmed and fighting one-handed.

Bones kicked at the glass littering the floor, sending shards up toward the charging vampire. One shot into his eye, giving Bones the second he needed to rip his cuffed arm free. Bones swung those chains at the vampire he'd half-blinded, knocking away the silver knife aimed at his heart. Then, Bones looped the chains around the vampire's neck and yanked until there was nothing left on his shoulders except a bloody hole.

"Head's up!" Cat shouted.

Bones turned, seeing a literal head fly across the room. It drilled into the vampire who'd been lunging at Bones from his blind side. Bones swung his chains, smashing them into that vampire's skull. Then, Bones grabbed the knife meant to kill him and twisted it through the other vampire's heart.

The next few minutes were a blur of blood and screams. Every chance he got, Bones checked on Cat. Each time, his concern was wasted. Blood coated Cat, most of it not hers, as she smashed two vampires' heads together so viciously pieces of bone flew. Then, she staked them before their skulls healed. Her movements were so fast and deadly, the few remaining vampires started to run away from Cat instead of toward her.

"Where you going?" she snarled as she stabbed another one. "I thought this was a party!"

Yes, it was Hennessey's party, and now Bones didn't see him. Had Hennessey escaped during the melee?

Sirens cut through the night, followed by a caravan of blue and red lights. Cat's phone call had finally netted results.

"Police!" shouted an electronically amplified voice. "Drop your...the fuck?"

Bones ripped the arm off the vampire he was fighting, not caring that spotlights from the police cars now blazed onto him. Then, Bones's brutal twist-and-tug removed that vampire's head—

Gunfire ripped through the air. Two bullets stung Bones before he dropped down, keeping out of their range. The few remaining vampires were less gracious in their response to being shot at. The ones closest to the hole that Cat's car had made in the house charged at the police. Soon, screams mixed with sharp retorts of even more gunfire, and Bones saw two of the vampires escape into the woods.

"Hennessey!" Cat's shout sliced the air, and she popped up from her crouch near the front of the smashed car. Bones followed her gaze, seeing Hennessey, with Switch right behind him, also trying to make it to freedom.

"I'm coming for you!" Cat snarled, leaping at Hennessey.

Switch crawled faster, but Hennessey paused. Cat landed on him, her momentum slamming them into the side of the house. The impact shook it as if another vehicle had rammed into it. But Hennessey twisted around faster than Cat, landing on top of her. One of Cat's arms was stuck behind her, and the wall penned her in on one side while the car blocked her on the other.

She was trapped.

Bones flew toward her. He was halfway there when agony rocketed into his back and he dropped like a stone. All at once, Bones's strength abandoned him and he could hardly move. He knew what that meant, and ice of a different kind filled him.

He'd been stabbed in the heart with silver.

Every instinct told Bones to flip onto his side and try to pull the blade from his back, but he didn't move. He had one chance to survive this. A slim one, but a chance nonetheless.

Bones lay absolutely still, eyes closed, tuning out every other sound except the footsteps of the vampire approaching him. The knife had been thrown, not stabbed, which was why Bones was still alive. Whoever had thrown it still had to twist it. Granted, sometimes a deep-enough toss lethally shredded the heart, so that's what Bones pretended to be as the vampire came near. Already dead. It helped that Bones was so covered in blood, the vampire wouldn't see that he hadn't started to shrivel yet.

"Got you," an unfamiliar voice muttered in satisfaction.

Perhaps, Bones thought coolly. *But not without a fight.*

Bones's chains, which had seemed so light when he was whipping them around before, now felt like felled trees across his right arm. He couldn't move them without giving away his "dead" ruse, so did he have anything to use as a weapon near his left hand?

Only glass shards from the shattered windows, he realized, in pieces barely bigger than Cat's fingernails.

Cat. His Kitten. God, had Hennessey already torn her throat out? Hennessey had been so close to her neck...

Stop, Bones's glacial logic argued. *You're no use to her dead, so get through this first, and help her afterward.*

The glass pieces were too small to use as a knife. They were barely big enough to position into the cracks between Bones's fingers, but he did. Women had been using their keys as makeshift weapons that way for decades. The vampire was on Bones's left side, too. He had one shot. Only one.

Bones felt the vampire lean over him. Over the ominous ringing in his ears that was unconsciousness or death coming for him, Bones heard Cat shout. Frustration boiled inside him, matching his pain. Cat might need him, and right now, he could do nothing to help her.

Please, let that shout be in victory, not in pain...

The blade in Bones's heart vibrated as the vampire's hand landed on it. Agony struck like lightning, but Bones forced himself not to move while he summoned the last of his strength.

Almost...now!

Bones rammed his glass-spiked hand into the vampire's groin, scent guiding him since the sod wasn't diligent when washing his balls. The vampire screamed and dropped the knife to protect his shredded groin. Bones immediately rolled to the side and yanked the knife out of his back. Pain flash-fried him and everything went black even though his eyes were now open. Bones only knew he wasn't dead because he still hurt too bloody much.

He couldn't see and his strength hadn't returned, and now, he had one very brassed off vampire pouncing on him.

The vampire pummeled Bones while trying to wrest the knife away. Bones didn't defend himself, sending all his lagging energy into holding onto the knife. They both rolled, and Bones managed to tangle his legs in the vampire's limbs. Now, the sod couldn't dash away to get *another* knife.

Bones's heart still felt like grenades had gone off inside it, and each punishing blow made it worse. But with every passing moment, Bones felt a little less weak. His vision returned, and he no longer needed the weight of his body to help hold onto the knife. His hands were now strong enough, and Bones tightened his grip as he flipped over, catching his first glimpse of the vampire who'd nearly killed him.

The swarthy, dark-haired bloke who'd told Switch that he and Cat had come alone earlier.

"You're dead!" the vampire snarled at him.

"Would've been, but you valued your balls more than your life," Bones said, and rammed the knife up between them.

It tore beneath the vampire's ribcage and went up into his heart. Immediately, Bones wrenched the blade from side to side. The vampire went limp, but just in case, Bones scissored the knife one more time.

"And never hesitate to twist," Bones muttered.

His chest still felt on fire, and he hadn't felt this weak since he was a human. He needed blood, yet he ignored that and the continued hail of bullets to leap up and look for Cat.

Relief almost leveled Bones when he saw her, still alive, and ramming a blade into Hennessy's back. She twisted it as if trying to dig a path through to the other side, and Hennessey's whole body jerked before becoming absolutely still.

Yes!

Bones only allowed himself a moment of relieved exultation before he dropped down and found a body that was still warm. Whoever this human was, he'd been stabbed through the forehead with a silver knife. Good. Such a quick death meant he'd still be filled with blood.

Bones sank his fangs into the man's neck while squeezing his chest in rhythmic pumps. Blood began flowing into Bones's mouth, foul tasting from death, but still useful. That fire in Bones's heart ebbed and more of his strength returned.

Not an instant too soon. Two vampires crashed into Bones, one from the front, and one from the back. The crunch of multiple fractures from their impact briefly deafened Bones to Cat's shout. A silver knife flashed in front of him. Bones blocked the attempted stab to his heart, but the knife sliced through Bones's arm so deeply it severed it above the wrist. His right hand, still cuffed, fell to the floor along with the chains.

Bones bashed his forehead into the stabbing vampire's face. Blood spurted, and the vampire's grip on the knife loosened. Bones grabbed it with his remaining hand. One brutal stab-and-twist later, and the vampire landed on the floor next to Bones's severed hand.

Bones whirled, about to stab the vampire behind him when Cat's shout reached him again.

"Switch is getting away. He's going for the trees!" Cat yelled.

The other vampire grabbed Bones's remaining hand. Bones let him, and shoved his ragged stump all the way through the vampire's neck. The vampire froze, his head half-severed, and Bones yanked his remaining hand free. Then, Bones ripped that silver knife through the vampire's heart.

For that good deed, Bones got shot by the police again. He glared at the officers before looking where Cat's wild wave had indicated. Switch had broken through the blockade of police cars and made it to the tree line. Even now, Switch was disappearing into the forest.

More gunfire stung Bones. Cat was crouched by the car, too low for the bullets to hit her, but there were too many trigger-happy police for her to escape. She needed Bones to get her out of here without getting shot, but if he did, Switch would be long gone.

As if reading his mind, Cat shouted, "Get Switch now, come back for me later. *Don't* let him get away, Bones! Get him!"

If he didn't, she would. It was clear from the rage in Cat's voice, not to mention her gaze. And only one of them could survive getting shot to chase after Switch.

She'd get arrested, but that was all right. These police weren't on Hennessey's payroll or they wouldn't have shot at Hennessey's men. No, they were regular cops, which meant Bones only needed to give them a few flashes of his gaze for them to release Cat to him later.

I'll come back for you, Bones thought, and ran after Switch.

54

*M*ost of the bullets didn't hit Bones as he ran. Having a vampire charge right at the officers clearly rattled several of them into missing as Bones cleared the blockade they'd set up. Switch was now nowhere in sight, but Bones could smell him, and he flew into the forest after him—

—and immediately fell to the ground. Fucking hell! The effects of his near handshake with the Grim Reaper weren't out of his system yet. Probably wouldn't be until tomorrow, but Bones didn't have all night to recover if he was going to catch Switch.

I'll rip off every hand that touched her or your grandparents.

That vow held new meaning since his own hand had just grown back, but he wasn't running at his usual speed. The energy reserves that had seen Bones through that near-lethal fight and the ones after it felt like they were depleting with every step. A silver-punctured heart didn't immediately heal like every other wound, and Bones hadn't drunk enough blood to make up for his new weakness. Plus, he'd only had corpse blood, which barely sufficed in any amount. Only living blood would help replenish Bones's strength. Lots of it.

Soon, each lift of Bones's legs felt heavier, until he could've sworn the ground had turned into quicksand. He had to rest, and after he rested, to feed. Even if Switch got away now, Bones could always hunt him down later...

Nice family you have, Catherine. Sorry about your grandfather. I know it's rude to eat and run, but I was short on time.

Anger lit a fuse under Bones's flagging resolve. Switch had taunted Cat to her face with how he'd murdered her grandfather, yet she hadn't let her eyes glow from the rage that must have been boiling over in her. If Cat had that much strength, Bones could find the strength to run down Switch and make him pay *now*.

Weakness was fleeting. Vengeance was forever.

Bones forced himself to keep going. Switch's scent was still heavy enough to follow, but in a few hours, it wouldn't be. This was Bones's best chance. He couldn't lose it.

An hour passed. Then two. Then three. By that time, Bones was so exhausted, he was breathing in regular intervals to keep going, but Switch's scent was also thicker, so Bones wasn't the only one tiring. Switch was slowing down.

A mile ahead, Bones heard traffic and other sounds that indicated a city. From his trajectory, Switch was running right toward it. If Switch made it there before Bones caught him, he had a good chance of disappearing. Cities were notoriously smelly, making it hard to catch anyone one person's scent. Plus, it was now dawn, when many people were heading to work, making it easy for Switch to blend in with a crowd.

Bones couldn't let Switch reach that city. From his scent and the sounds Bones could now hear, Switch was only about fifty meters ahead. Problem was, Bones wasn't sure he could take Switch in a fight. He had almost nothing left.

Cat's tear-stained face flashed in Bones's mind, and his hand tightened on the single knife he'd grabbed before chasing after Switch. He might not have much left, but he had enough.

Bones ran faster. Soon, he saw Switch up ahead, and past him, a body of water that Bones recognized as Cedar Lake. Switch had run all the way to Indiana. Bloody gashes and multiple bullet holes left Switch's clothes barely hanging on him, and more blood streaked his hair and arms.

"Who's chasing me?" Switch called out before risking a glance behind him. Then, he swore. "You fucking kidding me? *Come on!* Hennessey's dead, his operation's ruined, and your girl's fine. Stop chasing me and have a victory drink!"

"Later," Bones growled as he closed the distance between them.

Switch spun around, one hand extended in a "wait" gesture. "How about we make a deal? I'll tell you which human was pulling Hennessey's strings, and believe me, you'll want to know."

Bones slowed to a walk. "In exchange for what? Your life?"

"Bingo," Switch said, winking.

Bones pretended to think about it.

Switch gave him an exasperated look. "Come on, this will save you months more of digging. Plus, you can always try to kill me later. Just let me go now. Besides, you don't look so good, if you don't mind my saying."

"I look a damn sight better than your former boss," Bones replied curtly.

Switch waved that off. "His own fault. I wanted to keep the operation small, but then Mr. Big Shot entered the picture and told Hennessey he'd help make the records disappear as long as Hennessey made up the majority of his inventory from street girls, addicts, the homeless, and other types that drive up crime numbers. Ohio was only supposed to be the start of it, too. They were going to take this show on the road nationwide." Switch gave Bones a crafty smile. "Sure you don't want to know who Hennessey's partner is? Because he could find another vampire to replace Hennessey, and then you'll just end up hunting someone else—"

Bones flung the knife Switch hadn't seen. It landed in Switch's heart. Switch dropped to the ground with a pained, disbelieving gasp. Bones came over, stepping on Switch's arms when he tried to pull the blade out.

"Thanks for rambling on. Gave me a moment to catch my breath, so to speak. You were right; I'm not at my best right now."

"Don't," Switch gasped out when Bones grabbed the knife. "Wait—"

Bones twisted the blade four times; once for Cat's grandfather, once for her grandmother, once for her mum, and once for her. Then, even though Switch was dead, Bones ripped his hands off.

He'd promised, after all.

Finally, Bones walked toward the city that Switch had almost made it to. Once there, Bones would mesmerize a driver into taking him back to Ohio to get Cat out of jail, and help himself to a drink from that driver, too.

෴

CAT WASN'T at the jail nearest to the house where she'd been arrested. Bones didn't need to mesmerize one of the police officers to find that out. A "Breaking News" alert interrupted the station that Bones's driver was listening to.

"We have shocking news. Ohio governor Ethan Oliver was assassinated at his residence this morning. Details are still coming in, but as of now, we know the suspect is in custody and has sustained serious injuries…"

"Pull over and give me your mobile," Bones ordered with a flash of green in his gaze.

This couldn't be coincidence. Switch had called Hennessey's partner Mr. Big Shot, and Francesca had been frightened when she learned of his identity. A governor *would* be frightening, and a governor would also have more than enough power to make records disappear all across the state.

The driver complied. It only took a second of scrolling to find GOVERNOR MURDERED leading every headline, followed by pictures of the rising political star and a multitude of platitudes. Finally, Bones found a blurry image of the suspect.

A redheaded woman. Her face wasn't visible since police officers surrounded her, but who else could it be? And she was being loaded into an ambulance.

...suspect sustained serious injuries...

"Bloody hell, Kitten!" Bones swore before ringing Ted, who answered at once.

"Ted," Bones began.

"I saw," Ted interrupted. "I already hacked into the hospital they took her to. Paramedics show she was shot three times, but her vitals were steady, and there's nothing posted under her name as far as surgeries, so she's not critical."

Shot three times. Anger and fear boiled through his veins.

Why, Kitten? If you found out that the governor of Ohio was Hennessey's partner, you should have waited for me, not gotten yourself nearly killed going after him alone!

Bones forced himself to calm down. The picture had shown Cat walking to the ambulance, so she hadn't been mortally wounded, and with the amount of blood he'd given her, her bullet wounds should heal very quickly.

"Where is she?" Bones asked when he could speak calmly.

Ted told him, adding, "Don't go there now. It's a media circus, plus the FBI and ATF just arrived. Let everyone realize this is a 'lone wolf' attack and not something coordinated, and then things'll settle down."

"Might be difficult for them to realize that," Bones bit out. "Cat should have been arrested at an abandoned farmhouse this morning, where we left a slew of vampire and human bodies."

Ted blew out a sigh. "I saw somethin' about that, and hoped it had nothing to do with you. Whelp, I'm here if you need me."

"Thanks, mate. Speak to you soon."

Bones hung up. His driver, a young bloke who'd had the

misfortune to turn onto the street bordering the forest right as Bones staggered onto it, gave him a questioning look.

"Still want me to stay parked?"

"Yes."

He had to think, coldly and clearly. Not easy since he was exhausted, weak, and now worried. Mesmerizing a few police officers into freeing Cat was one thing. Mesmerizing the police, the FBI, ATF, and every other law enforcement initialism the Americans would throw at a political assassin was quite another.

At least Bones could do something about the vampire uproar that would follow Hennessey's death. Bones taking out another Master vampire would normally drag his sire, Ian, into a war with Hennessey's allies since Bones couldn't claim that it was only business. Not this time. No one had dared to put a price on Hennessey's head.

Still, Bones had a way around that. All it would cost him was a bit of pride. Easily disposable commodity right now.

Bones rang Ian, who answered with, "I don't recognize this number, so if you're a telemarketer, you're dead."

"It's Crispin," Bones said. "I killed Hennessey and several of his associates early this morning."

Silence, then Ian's waspish, "What part of 'be more careful' did you take as 'whee, murder spree!' Crispin?"

"Hennessey was collaborating with the newly-deceased governor of Ohio running a trafficking ring selling humans to vampires and ghouls. They harvested hundreds, at least."

"Terrible, but I wouldn't have chosen to go to war with Hennessey's allies over it," Ian said in an icy tone.

"I'm not finished," Bones responded as pleasantly as he could. "Hennessey did the same thing in Mexico. I have proof, and such blatant harvesting didn't go unnoticed. Furthermore, Hennessey intended to widen his operation, going national and possibly going global."

"Imbecile," Ian spat. "If the Law Guardians found out about

that, they'd slaughter Hennessey for drawing so much unwanted attention to our species..."

Ian's voice trailed off. A sardonic smile twisted Bones's lips. Ian might be an arse, but he was no fool.

"Crispin," Ian said in a newly bright tone. "I'm so pleased you followed my instructions to take out this threat to our species' secrecy. I'll be sure to inform the Law Guardians at once. They'll be delighted with my loyalty to the vampire cause, and they can deal with any of Hennessey's allies that might be foolish enough to openly mourn for him."

"Glad to be of service," Bones said dryly. "I'll forward the proof I mentioned later."

"Yes, do that." Ian was almost crowing with delight. "Now, if that's all, I have a call to make."

Bones hung up. Yes, that was all. Let Ian take the glory. Bones needed the anonymity for when he fled with Cat...and her mum. Hardly the happily ever after Bones had imagined, but every rose had its thorn.

"Now you can drive," Bones told the lad, who'd been staring aimlessly out the window. "Take me to your house."

Bones needed to feed from several people in order to get back his strength, and he couldn't do that until he showered and changed. He was still covered in blood, bullet holes, and various slashes; not a trusting image when you were trying to get people alone long enough to bite them into a quick meal.

Hold on, Kitten, Bones thought grimly. *I'm coming.*

55

Six hours later, Bones waited outside the hospital where Cat had been taken. Media still swarmed it, but curiously, many of the law enforcement agencies had now left. Only a regimen of unknown government agents remained, their vehicles stationed at every exit and more of them screening each person who entered the hospital.

Bones didn't need Ted to tell him they had Cat on the eleventh floor. They'd cleared it of all other patients shortly after noon. That had caused quite a stir, adding to the noisy, controlled chaos that every hospital had. With all the loud upheaval, it was impossible for Bones to hear Cat, if she were even speaking at all.

She might be asleep. She might be unconscious. He had no idea, but Cat was alive. Of that, he was certain. There was too much security still here for her to be dead.

A little after four p.m., a flurry of activity ensued. All the media were cleared from the premises and the back of the hospital was completely cordoned off. The government vehicles, all unmarked, formed a gauntlet from that back area to the hospital service road, which was also cleared of any traffic.

Bones left his perch on the roof of the building across the

street. Then, he glanced at the sky. Not night yet, but rain threatened, so the clouds were low and dark. Bones flew up, his denim jacket and trousers blending in with the clouds.

Twenty minutes later, a convoy of four vehicles left the hospital, three in flanking positions around a black SUV. They'd cleared the service road, but they hadn't bothered to clear the highway that the convoy pulled onto.

Thanks for that, mates.

Bones flew ahead of the vehicles, looking for a good spot. Not there. That was too near to an exit. Not there. That was too close to bridge. Ah, there. Close to a tree line. That would do.

Bones dropped down to the side of the road and waited. Several cars drove by. Even better. Rush hour traffic meant more cars, and more cars meant more confusion.

The SUV leading the convoy got closer. Its windows were darkly tinted on the sides, but the windshield wasn't, showing a male driver and male front passenger. Past them, Bones glimpsed two women in the backseat. He couldn't see their faces, but one had brown hair and one had...red.

When the vehicle was almost upon him, Bones stepped out into the middle of the road. Screw not displaying vampiric powers in public. The Law Guardians owed him after Hennessey. Besides, Bones would have Ted delete any videos that popped up online if anyone caught this on their mobiles.

The black-haired driver gaped at Bones, but the brown-haired bloke did something surprising: he pulled his gun and shot Bones right in the chest.

Definitely the right vehicle!

The gun's loud retort covered Justina's scream. "That's him!" Bones heard the instant before the vehicle hit him. "That's—!"

The crash cut her off. Bones gritted his teeth as three tons of metal slammed into him. It hurt like the very devil, but he ignored the pain and forced the SUV to a stop. Glass and air bags exploded, metal screeched, the engine smoked, and brakes squealed as the government convoy careened around them to avoid ramming into them. Then, the convoy tried to spin back around, only for two of their vehicles to get hit by oncoming traffic.

Bones ripped the front passenger door open. Couldn't have that bloke shoot Cat next, if he had "deliver or kill" orders. But he and the other sod were now bloody and unconscious.

Cat and her mum weren't. Abrasions from the side airbags scraped both of them, but Cat looked fine, to his great relief.

Bullets suddenly tore into the back of the SUV, narrowly missing Cat. Bones gave the agents firing them a nasty look as he tore the passenger door free. The agents behind them were using their car as cover while they fired. That wouldn't last.

Bones hurled the car door at them. It tore through their vehicle and the car immediately exploded. The agents ran, but other agents from the cars in front of them started firing at them, too. Bones gave their second vehicle the same treatment with the driver's side door. Soon, thick, dark smoke filled either end of the highway, concealing parts of the road.

Time to make the most of that cover.

"Hallo, Kitten!" Bones said as he ripped her seatbelt free. Then, he caught Justina by the arm as she tried to run away.

"No, you don't, mum. We're in a bit of a hurry."

The bloke who'd shot Bones woke up and flailed as if trying to pull his gun again. Bones cuffed the back of his head, but Cat grabbed Bones's arm when he was about to hit him again.

"Don't kill him. They weren't going to hurt me!"

Did she miss all the bullets being fired at them?

"Oh, right," Bones said sarcastically. "I'll just send them on their way nicely, then."

Bones bit the trigger-happy sod, getting in a few quick swallows before tossing him by the shoulder of the road. Justina gasped in horror, but technically, Bones had done him a favor. It was safer there since the heavy smoke caused more collisions by the minute. Pure luck that they hadn't been hit yet themselves.

"Get out of the car, Kitten," Bones directed her.

She did, going to her mother, who was now trying to bite her way through Bones's grip on her arm.

"I can't wait for them to kill you, you animal!" Justina raged. "They know what you—!"

Cat clipped her mum in the jaw, knocking her out.

Bones's brows rose. Yes, that was the quickest way of ensuring Justina's cooperation, and he certainly understood the urge. He just couldn't believe that Cat had done it.

More bullets ripped past them. Cat dropped low, taking her mum down with her. Bones didn't. He'd had enough of people shooting at her.

He grabbed the SUV's frame and hefted it up. Cat's eyes bulged. Guess she hadn't believed him when he told her what a Master vampire could do. She'd believe it now.

"Take your mum and back up."

Cat leapt back, carrying her mum with her. A breeze briefly cleared some of the smoke, showing the remaining government agents crouched behind their last vehicle. No other cars were near it. Good. He only wanted to hurt these arseholes.

Bones tightened his grip on the car's frame and spun. Then, he hurled the SUV at the agent's final vehicle.

The double explosion shook the ground and shot a tornado-sized plume of black smoke into the air. At once, more crashing sounds came from the other side of the highway as cars going in the opposite direction rear-ended each other after staring at the massive fireball.

"Time to go, luv," Bones said, hefting Justina's unconscious form over his shoulder. Then, with Cat's hand in his, they ran into the nearby tree line.

56

Several miles later, Bones deposited Justina into the back of the black Volvo he'd left along a side street. He'd had other vehicles similarly parked around the city, not knowing which route the agents would take Cat when they moved her. Nice coincidence that the Volvo was the vehicle they ended up using.

"You don't get your meanness from your father," Bones remarked. "You get it from your mother. She bit me."

Cat grabbed the roll of duct tape Bones had brought just in case. Then, she wrapped a long piece over Justina's mouth and bound her mother's hands with more tape.

"So she won't bite either of us," Cat muttered.

When she was finished and they drove off, Cat stared at Bones as if she hadn't seen him before.

"How did you do that? *Any* of it? You stopped a car going sixty with only your body! If vampires can do that, why didn't Switch stop me from driving into the house last night?"

"Switch couldn't stop a toddler on a tricycle," Bones said dismissively. "He was only 'round sixty in undead years, and not very strong at that. You have to be an old, powerful Master like me to pull such a trick without regretting it dearly afterward. Believe me, it hurt like blazes. That's why I took a nip from your two captors before chucking them off. What government agency were they with, anyhow? And where were they taking you?"

Cat's expression shuttered. Clearly, this wasn't a pleasant subject for her. "Um, they didn't say. Weren't real chatty, you know? Maybe they were taking me to a special holding cell or something because of what I did to Ethan Oliver."

Speaking of that... "You should have waited for me, Kitten. You could have gotten killed."

Anger suffused her features. "I couldn't wait! One of the governor's dirty cops got me into his car and tried to shoot me, *and* he was supposed to plant a bomb at the hospital where they took my mother. Oliver was Hennessey's human partner, Bones," she added, as if he hadn't figured that out yet. "He practically bragged to me about how Hennessey was 'cleaning up' his state for him, as if all those innocent people were garbage. He was going to run for president and do the same thing nationally! God, if I killed him ten times, it still wouldn't be enough."

The same thing Switch had said, minus Oliver's name and a few other particulars, like the hospital bomb. Of course, Cat had rushed after Oliver if her mum's life was threatened. She'd do anything for those she loved, danger be damned.

"Why do you think the agents carting you off weren't more of Oliver's men?"

"They weren't," Cat said, adding, "Besides, you hardly treated them like you were giving them the benefit of the doubt. You chucked two car doors and an SUV onto them."

"They kept shooting at us," Bones reminded her. "They also jumped free before the explosions, and if they were too thick not to, then they deserved to die for their stupidity."

Cat said nothing to that. They drove in silence for a few minutes before she fingered the leather seats in an absent way.

"This is nice. Whose vehicle is this?"

Bones hid a smile as he looked at her. "Yours. Like it?"

"Not whose is it *now*, whose was it?" she asked pointedly. "As in, will it be reported stolen? Or is it one of Ted's?"

"It's yours," Bones repeated. "This is your Christmas present. It's registered under the name on your false license, so there's no way the law can trace it to you. Sorry to have you miss out on the holiday surprise, but under the circumstances, I thought you wouldn't mind getting your present two weeks early."

Cat's expression wasn't just shocked. She looked incredulous. "I can't accept this. It's too expensive!"

Laughter rumbled from his throat. "Kitten, for once, can you just say thank you? Because really, aren't we past this?"

For the briefest second, she looked stricken. Then, it was gone, and she wobbled a smile at him. "Thank you. It's…this is incredible. All I got you was a new jacket, I'm ashamed to say."

Bones smiled. "What kind of jacket?"

She drew in a deep breath that caught in her throat, as if she were fighting not to cry. He doubted this had anything to do with either of their Christmas gifts. Now that they were safe and their enemies were dead, every emotion Cat had been suppressing was doubtless coming to the surface.

"Well, it was long, like a trench coat," she rasped out. "Black leather, of course, because vampires are supposed to wear that instead of blue denim," she added with a mock-censuring glance at his jacket. "The police probably ransacked whatever was in my apartment that the vampires didn't destroy, but I doubt anyone found this. I hid it under the loose floorboard by the kitchen cabinet so you wouldn't find it."

Her voice quavered at that last part, and she blinked away tears. She must be realizing she'd never go back to her apartment. It might have been a hovel, but it had been *her* hovel. Now it, her grandparents, and most of the other staples in her life were gone for good.

Bones reached over, taking her hand. Cat blew out a halting sigh before meeting his gaze.

"Switch?" she asked quietly.

"Shriveled in Indiana," Bones replied, glad he could give her good news on this, at least. "Bugger ran at full speed for hours. Sorry I didn't take my time with him, Kitten, but I wanted to head straight back to you. So, when I caught him, I left him to rot in the woods by Cedar Lake. With all the other bodies the police have found, one more isn't going make a difference. In fact, Indiana's where we're headed now."

"I'm glad Switch is dead."

She was still speaking softly, and Bones didn't think it had to do with fretting that she'd wake her mum. Delayed shock, probably. She'd been through so much the past twenty-four hours.

"Why Indiana?" Cat finally asked.

"Got a mate there who will get you and your mum set up with new identification. We'll bunk at his place tonight and leave tomorrow. Just have to run a few errands in the morning, and then we're off to Ontario. We'll stay there a few months, but don't worry. We *will* track down those sods that escaped. Just have to wait until this business with Oliver cools down. Once your government lads can't find a trace of you, they'll look for other fish to fry."

Cat's expression said she doubted that, but she only said, "How did you know when they were moving me?"

"By watching," Bones replied with jaded amusement. "When they cleared the entire back exit road and had armed agents waiting with several vehicles, I just stayed ahead of the convoy until the time was right."

Furious grunts suddenly came from the back of the SUV, followed by repeated kicking sounds. Bones gave Cat a wry smile.

"Your mum woke up."

57

A few hours later, Bones drove up to Rodney's house. The two-story, ocher-colored brick home with the wrap-around porch and summer and winter garden looked warm and unpretentious, much like the man himself.

Bones parked, and Cat got out of the back seat. She'd been there since Justina awoke. Cat had to hold onto Justina to keep her mum from trying to kick her way out of the vehicle. Cat also kept the duct tape around Justina's mouth. She must not be anxious to hear more of her mum's tirade about Bones. Soon enough, they'd both have to listen to all the different ways that Justina thought he was a monster, but until then, a few hours of silence had been welcome.

"Get out of the car, Mom," Cat said.

Justina glared at Cat and didn't move.

Bones opened the door and reached for Justina. That's all it took for Justina to bolt out of her seat into Cat's arms. Then the front door opened, revealing a bearded, brown-haired man with warm beige skin, hazel eyes, and a ready smile.

Rodney's shirt stretched over his barrel-thick chest when he spread his arms out. "Bones, it's been too long!"

"It has indeed, Rodney," Bones said, getting out of the car and hugging Rodney.

Bones had chosen to stay at Rodney's for two reasons. One, Rodney was a ghoul, and after what Justina had been through, Bones reckoned any creature was better than a vampire to her. Two, Rodney was so nice that everybody liked him. Oh, Bones was sure that Justina would hate him regardless, but Rodney would make her work for it. Ted Lasso had nothing on Rodney.

"Rodney, this is Cat," Bones said.

Cat kept a tight grip on Justina's arm while shaking Rodney's hand. "Nice to meet you, Rodney, and I hate to impose right off, but can we use your bathroom?"

"No imposition at all," Rodney said. "Follow me."

Once they were inside, Rodney pointed toward the hallway. "Second door on your left."

"Thanks," Cat said before turning to Bones. "Be back in a minute. I want to get her cleaned up and have a word with her."

"Take your time, luv."

Cat propelled her mum into the bathroom. Moments later, she had the tub running. Bones didn't know why Cat would want to try giving her mum a bath, but he wasn't about to ask.

"Here," Rodney said, handing Bones a whisky. "You look like you could use this."

Bones hefted it in appreciation before taking a seat at the nearby table. Rodney had redecorated since Bones was last here, still keeping with earth tones, but now the furniture was deep navy, the carpet was sand colored, and the walls were light sienna brown. Rodney's true passion, however, was cooking. The kitchen took up half the downstairs, with several chairs around the large center island and a number of brass, cast iron, and other specialty cookware hanging from the ceiling.

"I hope they like mushrooms. I made *coq au vin* with truffle risotto," Rodney said. "Figured they probably hadn't had much of a chance to eat."

377

Bones sighed. "That's very kind, Rodney, and you're right. But even with your culinary skills, I doubt they'll be very hungry. Things are...quite tense between Cat and her mum."

"Bones killed the vampires who murdered Grandpa Joe and Grandma," Cat was saying to her mother. Rodney's brows rose. No, Bones hadn't had a chance to tell him that part yet.

"He won't hurt me, and he won't hurt you," Cat went on. "I know you hate vampires and this will be hard, but you've gotta trust me for now. Just give me a little time. Our lives *depend* on you trusting me. We're staying here tonight, and then tomorrow we're leaving the country. Do you understand, Mom? *Tomorrow.* It's the only way."

Justina must still be gagged because Bones didn't hear her argue, and even with the water running, he doubted Justina's anger would allow her to keep her voice low.

As if to confirm that, Cat said "Well? Are you going to be reasonable? Can I take the gag off you now?"

"Apologies in advance," Bones said to Rodney. "Her mum's had truly terrible experiences with vampires, and she's very loud about expressing her hatred of them."

"You can trust me, Mom," Cat said, sounding almost desperate. "I promise you."

Bones was shocked when, moments later, a silent yet un-gagged Justina entered the room with Cat. What had Cat done, said all the above with the brights on in her gaze?

"Be nice," Cat hissed at her mother as she gave Justina a little push toward them.

"I'm sure you'll want to settle in," Rodney said, coming over to them. "Take your pick of the guest rooms. There's one upstairs and one in the basement."

"Show me the basement one," Cat said, her smile strained to the breaking point.

"Of course. Follow me."

Bones stayed where he was. His presence would only agitate

Justina, and she was being shockingly compliant right now. Let Rodney show them around. Justina might even confuse Rodney with a human, easing her tension a bit more.

"This will be perfect for you, Mom," he heard Cat say a few moments later.

"Where do you think you're going?" Justina demanded.

"Upstairs with Bones," Cat said, to an instant protest from Justina. "Good night."

More protests and pounding sounds started at once. Cat must have locked her mum into the guest room. Bones was surprised by both actions. After everything that had happened, he'd assumed that Cat would stay with her mum tonight.

"We'll talk about this tomorrow, Mom, when we're alone." Now Cat sounded curt. "Stop causing such a fuss. Rodney's a ghoul, and all your screeching is making him hungry.

Bones's brows shot into his hairline. Cat had apparently lost *all* her fucks when it came to her mother's prejudice. Bones had been willing to give Justina some latitude because of what had happened, but Cat obviously disagreed.

Justina quit yelling and banging on the door. Bones almost felt sorry for her, but she was in no danger. Even if Justina weren't his guest, Rodney only ate "cruelty free" humans. Rodney got his parts from the local mortuary the few times a year he needed to eat something other than grocery-store food. Justina couldn't be safer no matter how much of a fuss she kicked up.

But Cat must be at the end of her rope, to be so unusually harsh with her mum. Bones doubted Cat would be up for small talk with Rodney, so Bones waited for her in the other guest room. Women's and men's clothing were laid out on one dresser while the other held a fruit and cheese assortment, a bottle of wine, a bottle of whisky, and several bottles of waters.

Rodney truly was the kindest bloke.

Cat went straight to the bedroom, not bothering to ask

Rodney where it was. That's right, she could scent him now. Bones wondered if she'd miss that ability when it was gone.

Perhaps she will, he thought when he enfolded her in his arms and Cat inhaled deeply, as if trying to absorb his scent.

"I told you we'd make it through this," Bones murmured long moments later. "You didn't believe me."

She started to tremble. "I didn't, but you were right. Now, both you and my mom are alive. That means more to me than everything else, Bones."

He drew back. "*You* mean more to me than everything else."

She kissed him, her mouth moving against his as if she'd never get another chance. He held her closer, and it still wasn't enough for her. She tightened her grip until she could barely breathe while tears leaked from her eyes.

Bones kissed them, trying to gently loosen her grip before she hurt herself. "What's the matter?"

Cat looked away, her hand dashing beneath her eyes. "I just…I couldn't bear it if anything happened to you. I can stand a lot, but I can't stand that."

Her tears came faster, and she was trembling so much now that she was almost swaying from it. Was this a delayed shock response? Understandable grief? Both?

"Nothing's going to happen to me, Kitten. I promise."

"I promise, too," she whispered before raising her chin and staring at him. Now, her gaze was steady even though tears still streaked down her cheeks.

"I want you to know that despite everything, I'm so glad I met you. That was the luckiest day of my life. If I hadn't, I never would have known what it was like for someone to love all of me, even the parts I hated. Without you, I would've gone through life empty and guilt-ridden. You showed me a whole new world, Bones. I'll never be able to thank you for all you've done, but I'll love you every day until I die."

She'd never been more honest or vulnerable with him, and the trust that took pierced his still-healing heart.

"Kitten, I only thought I was living before I met you," he said hoarsely. "I didn't know I was only half alive. You'll love me until the day you die? I'll love you *forever*."

Then, he showed her how much she meant to him, until her shudders were from passion instead of whatever had caused her tears, and they both finally fell asleep.

ones awoke to a pair of deep gray eyes staring at him. That was different. Usually, he woke up well before her. Then again, quite understandably, Cat had a lot on her mind.

"Can't sleep?" he murmured, reaching for her.

"Guess not," she said, looking away even though she slid into his arms. The scent of anguish wafted from her like heavy cologne, and her eyes were red-rimmed from recent tears.

Bones held her, stroking her with soothing motions, until the worst of the stiffness left her. She still smelled of anguish, though, and now another emotion doused her scent.

Guilt.

"You're upset about more than your grandparents, aren't you?" he said quietly. "It's your mum, isn't it?"

Cat tensed with the suddenness of someone who'd been stabbed. "What makes you say that?"

"You kept her bound and gagged the whole way to Rodney's despite how traumatic that would have been to her after Hennessey kidnapped her." No judgment colored his tone. Only matter-of-factness. "Then, you dragged her off to the loo as soon as you arrived and ran the tub despite neither of you bathing.

From both, I reckon you're trying to keep me from hearing something your mum has to say."

If he thought Cat was tense before, now, she felt like a living statue. "You're being paranoid."

"I'm right," Bones said, soft but insistent. "So, tell me, Kitten. I'll find out what it is eventually."

She pushed him away and sat up, covering herself with the sheet. That action only solidified his suspicions. She didn't just smell guilty; she was also subconsciously putting more barriers between them. What was she hiding?

Cat said nothing for several minutes. Just breathed as though trying to control something uncontrollable within her. Then, she squared her shoulders and glanced over at him.

"My mother hates me." The words were straightforward, but her tone was an open, bleeding wound. "Guess I can't blame her. I did get grandma and Grandpa Joe killed, and don't bother telling me I didn't. You warned me, Bones. Over and over again, you warned me to stay out of it with Hennessey. I refused, and my grandparents paid with their lives. I don't blame my mom for hating me for that. I don't even blame her for hating me over you." A brief, bitter smile. "This was the worst possible way she could have found out that I was dating a vampire, after all, but I gotta say, I didn't like her calling me a 'whore for the undead.' I mean, that sounds so *indiscriminate*, as if I was out there banging anyone without a pulse…"

Now, Bones tensed. *No one spoke to her that way. No one.*

"So, I kept her gagged," Cat went on, donning sarcasm as a shield. "Hard for her to call me names through that duct tape, right? As for the bathroom, I don't know why I bothered to run the tub. Not like you can't hear past it, so maybe I was just fantasizing about water-boarding her if she started calling me a whore again. Or saying she wished Hennessey had killed her because that was better than her finding out that her daughter was fucking a corpse—"

Bones grabbed her, holding her against him while rage scorched his veins. If anyone else had hurt her this way, he'd eviscerate them, yet he couldn't so much as give her mum a piece of his mind. Cat would only be angry at him if he did.

Besides, the rational part of Bones knew that Justina was speaking out of her own great pain. Justina had never experienced anything except grievous harm at the hand of vampires. Little wonder she didn't take the news that her daughter was dating one with a smile.

No, he had to bite his tongue and show Justina that she was wrong by giving Cat all the love that Justina had failed to lavish on her. Eventually, her mum would realize that not all vampires were the same. Or Bones would mesmerize Justina into being less of a hateful bitch toward her daughter.

Whichever came first.

Cat remained stiff for several moments. Then, she turned around and buried her face against his neck. Wetness slicked him from her tears, and her breaths fell in ragged puffs against his skin.

"I know you probably hate her for this, but don't. She can't help herself, the same way I couldn't help myself when you and I first met."

So forgiving. Justina didn't deserve her. Then again, neither did Bones.

"Do me a favor?" Cat went on. "Mom's ribs got bashed up during the brawl at Hennessey's, and the car crash didn't help. She'd never willingly drink your blood and she's in pain, so can you sneak a couple drops into her coffee this morning?"

"Of course." He'd do whatever she asked. Didn't she know that?

Her arms slid around his neck. "How long until you have to leave? You said you had errands to run this morning with Rodney to...to get us all set to go to Canada."

Bones's hands slipped beneath the sheet she'd wrapped around herself. "I don't have to leave for another hour or so—"

She crushed her mouth against him, kissing him with the same frantic hunger as last night. Then, she shoved him back against the mattress and straddled him. Lust roared through him as she grabbed his cock, bringing it against her center, but beneath that, a colder realization prevailed. Her extreme need wasn't just enhanced desire due to her consuming so much of his blood. It was too visceral, as if Cat were using his body to run away from a pain too crushing for her to feel.

Well, if this was what she needed, she could have him. All of him.

Bones let her ride him until she spent herself. Then, he flipped her over and drove her to the limits of passion, until she shouted herself hoarse and he owed Rodney a new bed.

They were very, very late to breakfast.

Justina moved the food around her plate with the grimness of the damned. Rodney's cooking wasn't at fault, of course. His crepe pancakes and sautéed spinach omelets were delicious. Cat asked for seconds, which relieved Bones since she hadn't eaten for almost two days before this.

"More coffee, Justina?" Rodney asked.

"No," Justina said. Then, after a glare from Cat, Justina added, "Thank you."

Rodney received short, chilly responses from Justina, but she hadn't spoken a single word to Bones since Cat let her out of the guest room. Justina also refused to look at him. Both suited Bones. If Justina decided to "punish" him with the silent treatment all the way to Canada, he'd consider it a win.

Rodney glanced at his mobile. "We need to leave soon if we're going to pick up your passports and the other things."

Other things. A polite way of saying weapons and blood. Bones wasn't traveling any distance without either, and Rodney lacked both since he had almost no enemies, and he had very different dietary requirements than Bones.

"Right you are, mate," Bones said, rising.

Justina actually smiled when Bones got up. Cat shot her a look that withered the smile from her mum's face. Then, Cat ran to Bones and held him as if he was dangling from a cliff and her grip was the only thing preventing his fall.

"What's this?" Bones said with gentle teasing. "Miss me before I've even left?"

"Yes." Her voice was a rasp. "I'll *always* miss you when you're gone."

Bones kissed her, and she tightened her grip on him even more. When he finally pulled away, he caught a glimpse of Justina over Cat's shoulder. Loathing suffused Justina's features as she watched her daughter embracing a vampire. Then, Justina's eyes met Bones's, and something odd flared in her gaze before she quickly looked away.

Why would Justina look *satisfied*? Was the bitch planning to verbally roast her daughter again as soon as Bones left? If she did, Bones might bite her into a state of niceness after all.

Cat stopped Bones when he turned to go. "Before you leave, give me your jacket."

His brows rose, but he took it off and handed it to her.

"In case we have to leave and meet you," Cat said, answering his silent question. "It's, ah, cold outside."

An obvious lie, not to mention that Rodney had coats here that they could borrow. Still, perhaps Cat just wanted something with his scent on it, and she would hardly say that with her mum glaring holes into her back for simply touching him.

Bones leaned down, kissing Cat's forehead. She looked up at him with more of that pained longing.

"Be careful, Bones. Just please…be careful."

386

He smiled to ally her fears even though she had no need for them. He wasn't in any danger. Yes, two of Hennessey's men had escaped, but they'd be running away from Bones. Not hunting him, and soon enough, they'd also be dead. Bones now knew their faces, if not their names. He'd find and kill them after he had the three of them settled in Ontario.

Still, if anyone was entitled to a little paranoia after the past few brutal days, it was Cat.

"Don't fret, luv," he said, caressing her face. "I'll be back before you know it."

Then, with Rodney at his side, Bones left.

59

The forger Rodney knew was thorough and quick. Cat and her mum now had new driver's licenses, passports, insurance cards, and bank accounts, all under aliases. From there, he and Rodney went to an undead weapon's dealer and left with enough silver to fight a small army. Bones had been planning to fill up on fresh blood before making a bagged withdrawal from a local blood bank, but he decided to skip that. Cat was obviously having a hard time, so he wanted to get back to her as fast as possible. He could forgo eating for a few days without it harming him.

The only extra stop Bones made was at a florist. The shop was on the way back to Rodney's, and the scarlet roses in the window looked springtime fresh even though it was winter. The first time he'd given Cat flowers, she told him she'd never gotten any before. Bones had given her a bouquet a week since.

Rodney bought a bouquet for Justina, too, despite Bones telling him she'd only hurl them to the floor. Rodney just smiled and said that was up to her. Even now, Rodney held the lilacs and tulips bundle gently, as if they wouldn't be scattered all over his living room floor soon.

When Bones pulled onto Rodney's street, ice pierced his spine. Why wasn't Cat's Volvo in the driveway? Bones had left her the vehicle in case plans changed and she needed to meet him, but Cat hadn't said anything about leaving for another reason. Bones checked his new mobile. No missed calls or texts from Cat, and he'd given her the number. Why would she leave without telling him where she was going?

Unless someone had *made* her leave?

Bones gunned it to the house, tearing up a section of lawn with how fast he spun into the driveway. Then, he leapt out of Rodney's car, the ghoul following close behind him.

No damage to the front door, which was unlocked, and it hadn't been when he and Rodney left. Bones had heard Cat turn the lock behind him. No damage or signs of struggle inside the house, either. Everything looked as exactly as it had when they left, except for the folded note on the countertop...

Bones snatched it up, disbelief ripping through him as he read.

Don't come after me because I'm already gone. Those agents knew about vampires, and they were going to kill you. I'm dressing Switch in your jacket and telling them his body is yours, so they'll think you're dead now. You'll be safe this way, and so will my mother. We could never be safe if we stayed together, and I won't kill you or her trying. I already have enough blood from people I love on my hands...

The ink blurred into dark blotches where her tears had hit the page, making the next part almost too blurry to read.

...and everything I said about how much I loved you was the truth. You are my life, Bones, and now consider me dead because with the job I'm taking, I will be soon. But I will love you forever, right down to my final breath, where your name will be my last word, I promise.

"Bloody fucking hell!" Bones shouted, flying out the door. He didn't care that it was still daylight. Didn't care that someone's mobile phone might be pointed at the sky. He had one chance to stop this.

I'm dressing Switch in your jacket and telling them his body is yours...

The words haunted Bones as he flew toward Cedar Lake. He'd come home an hour early. Cat hadn't expected that. If he could make it to Switch before she did, he could stop this madness.

Bones kept himself high because cell towers and electric lines were obstacles that would slow him down. Even if someone did see him, he was so fast he should only be a blur. Still, Bones wasn't as fast as he would've been before that near-lethal stab. His strength still hadn't fully returned, but that didn't mean he wouldn't murder every bastard who'd threatened her if they were at that lake with her.

...they were going to kill you...

No, they weren't. He was going to kill them. He should've done so on the highway, but he hadn't wanted to slaughter some poor sods whose only crime was being picked for Cat's security detail, as Bones had thought at the time. Now, he knew better.

...consider me dead because with the job I'm taking, I will be soon...

Oh, he could imagine the kind of jobs the government would delight in sending someone as strong and fierce as Cat on. She'd be the best weapon they'd had since the hydrogen bomb, and he bloody well should've *known* they weren't average G-men! That one bloke had fired at Bones as soon as he saw him. Not the standard response at all when one sees a man in the road.

Those agents knew about vampires...

Clearly, but they didn't know enough since they'd used regular rounds instead of silver, and *no wonder* Justina had looked at him with such satisfaction earlier! The bitch knew that Cat had been frightened by those sods into leaving him.

That's the real reason Cat had gagged her mum and kept her locked away. Also must be why Cat had knocked her mum out on the highway. Bones hadn't bothered about what Justina was saying at the time, expecting only insults, but in retrospect, Justina had said "I can't wait for them to kill you, you animal!

They know what you—!" right before Cat clocked her into unconsciousness.

They know what you are. That's what Justina had been about to say before Cat had stopped her.

Cat. His Kitten. Stinking of anguish and guilt while holding onto him as if death itself couldn't break her grip. She'd been silently saying goodbye to him because she thought leaving was the only way she could save him, and here Bones had thought she was only gutted because of her grandparents' murder and her mum's incessant bigotry.

...I will love you forever, right down to my final breath...

Didn't *this* personify "be careful what you wished for?"

Bones had wanted Cat to love him with all the passion, stubbornness, and fierce bravery that made her who she was. Now she did, and that's why she'd left. She would do anything for those she loved, damn the danger or the consequences. She'd drive a car through a house filled with vampires while fully expecting to die...or she'd leave with a band of unknown government agents even if it meant ripping her heart out in the process.

Ahead, a smudge of dark blue broke up the green and brown landscape below him. Cedar Lake. He'd made it.

Bones flew faster while sending his senses out. The only sounds he heard were from the nearby city. No one else was near the lake or in the forest below. Was he early? Or too late?

He aimed for the spot where he'd left Switch's body. From this height, he couldn't see if it was there or not. The branches were too thick. Bones torpedoed through the canopy, snapping those branches and then tearing up dirt with the force of his landing. He whirled, looking for Switch's body—

"*No!*"

Bones's shout scattered every bird that hadn't already fled after his violent landing. Their cries as they flew away echoed through the new roaring in his ears as a breeze brought him faint hints of Cat's scent.

She'd been here. She and several other people, one of whom had been in a wheelchair, judging from the twin tracks in the dirt. Bones smelled fuel and ran ahead, closer to the lake. In the clearing not far from the water's edge, far deeper parallel impressions indicated a helicopter had landed there recently.

Fucking hell! That meant no tire tracks for him to follow, and he hadn't seen a helicopter on his way over. Bones flew up again, scouring the sky around the area. Nothing. Whatever chopper had been there was now gone, and with them, Cat.

Rage made Bones smash down onto the ground again. Then, he started pummeling trees until his blood stained the earth and it looked like a logging crew had cleared the area around him. But the violence carved a path through the part of his mind that had gone rabid at Cat serving herself up as a sacrificial offering because she thought it was her life or his.

Very well. She'd done it, and that's all there was to it. Now, Bones had to *undo* it.

Cat hadn't realized it, but she'd left him a few clues to follow. The first was saying "they" knew about vampires, and "the job" she'd be doing. That, combined with the official convoy guarding her yesterday, meant that the government had snatched her up. Not some private organization. Good. The government would leave more footprints to follow, starting with the chopper they'd used to whisk her away. It would have radioed into an air control tower at some point, so there would be records that Ted could hack.

There were also agents that Bones could interrogate. At least one of them should be hospitalized after the highway crash yesterday. Bones only needed to find out which hospital had received car crash victims, and go there to have a little chat. Since Cat had so helpfully told them he was dead by masquerading Switch's body as his, they wouldn't be expecting Bones.

Now, to start the hunt.

Bones reached for his mobile...and realized he'd left it back at

Rodney's. At least Rodney's house wasn't that far away, but that was why Bones had been too late. Cat hadn't had far to go, and she must have left immediately after he had this morning. That meant she and the people who'd taken her had at least a three-hour head start. Not ideal, especially since they'd flown her out instead of driven, but not insurmountable, either.

Bones crackled his knuckles and rolled his head around to loosen the constrictor-tight muscles in his neck. Then, he gave a final look toward Cedar Lake, where Cat had pulled off her greatest ruse yet, though she and Bones were the only ones who knew it.

Don't come after me because I'm already gone...

"Oh, I'm coming, Kitten," Bones said out loud as he launched himself into the sky. He'd told her before: if she ran from him, he'd chase her.

EPILOGUE

Four and a half years later.

ones stood next to two other groomsmen beside a tall, flower-covered nuptial arch. Flower petals also lined the aisle that split the two sections of chairs on either side of the ballroom. Randy, the groom, waited in the center of the arch, and he grinned as the band began playing Pachelbel's *Canon in D*, signaling the start of the wedding ceremony.

The first bridesmaid began walking down the flower-strewn aisle. The guests murmured with appreciation as she passed them. The bridesmaid smiled with the confidence of someone used to being admired, and her bold stare stayed on Bones as she added a little sway to her hips.

Bones didn't smile back. He was here for one person alone, his friendship with the groom notwithstanding. And she was soon to walk down the aisle, too.

Of course, if Bones looked at the guest list, Catherine Crawfield's name wouldn't be anywhere on it. She'd supposedly died over four years ago after trying to escape a prisoner transfer. That's how the government had covered up the multi-vehicle crash on the highway when Bones had rescued her. The government had even deleted all incriminating mobile phone footage of the incident, too, saving Ted some time.

But a Ms. Cristine Russell *was* here, as the maid of honor to Randy's fiancé, Denise. Over four years of looking for her, and Bones had found Cat not because of his exhaustive efforts, or even the information her worthless ex had unwillingly provided him. No, Bones had found her because of striking up a friendship with a human named Randy six months ago.

Randy had a rare, natural immunity to vampire mind control. Bones discovered that when Randy couldn't be mesmerizing into forgetting that Bones hadn't breathed the entire hour Randy had sat next to him at a bar. Randy also hadn't been afraid to find out that vampires existed. Instead, Randy had been curious, and Bones had been…lonely. That was the real reason Bones had allowed his friendship with Randy to grow. Who knew that fate had other plans for it?

The second bridesmaid, a petite woman with black hair, walked down the aisle. Bones barely looked at her. As maid of honor, Cat would come after her.

In moments, he'd finally look into her eyes again. They'd always been so expressive, as if telegraphing what was in her heart. The last time he'd done so, he'd seen love and anguish in Cat's gaze. What would he see now? Her using his last name as her alias' surname made him hopeful that she still cared for him, but… she could have chosen that surname years ago and ceased caring since. After all, she'd never reached out to Bones, and he'd kept the same mobile number this entire time, plus given her a new way to contact him only a few months ago in Chicago.

Had Cat continued hiding from him because she still cared too much? Or did she do it because she no longer cared at all?

He was about to find out, and he'd more than earned the answer whether she was ready to give it to him or not. That's why Cat had no idea that he was here, let alone that he was one of

Randy's groomsmen. Bones had deliberately shown up late to avoid Cat spotting him until she walked down the aisle. Then, *she* would have nowhere to run. Not without wrecking her best friend's wedding, and if Cat was still any part of the person Bones had known, she'd never do that to Denise.

The music increased in volume as Cat appeared at the back of the ballroom. Not a muscle on him moved, but inwardly, Bones braced. It still wasn't enough. His shields cracked, letting some of his supernatural aura escape.

God, *her face.* So beautiful in a way that had nothing to do with her expertly applied makeup. Her upswept hair was now the same platinum blond shade his had been when they first met, and her body was curvier, filling out the lavender lace bridesmaid dress in all the right ways. Then, her scent hit him, and he breathed in its mixture of warm vanilla swirled with cream and cherries. He wanted to keep breathing it until he was dizzy from inhaling too much oxygen, and her eyes—

—swept either side of the room with sharp, measured glances while her muscles tightened and wariness edged her scent. Cat had felt the power from his aura when it leaked out, and government-sanctioned vampire hunter that she was, she was now looking for its source.

Bones let his battle ice come, covering everything beneath a thick, glacial wall. She'd made him wonder for over *four years* if she still loved him, let alone if she was even still alive. He'd be damned if he let her see how deeply he still loved her when he had no idea if she felt the same.

Even if she did, he still wouldn't show her what he felt. Not yet. First, she'd have to admit that she never should have left him in the first place. He wasn't some victim she'd had to sacrifice herself for. He was a powerful Master vampire, and if Cat didn't know that before, she bloody would now.

At last, she looked at the wedding party in the front. Bullets were softer than that unyielding gray metal of her gaze as it raked over the other groomsmen before landing on Bones. Then, she swept him from his shoes to his shoulders, no doubt seeking out any telltale bulges of weapons beneath his black tuxedo, before finally meeting his eyes—

Bones knew the instant she recognized him. That predatory look vanished, replaced by so much shock that her heart skipped a beat and Cat tripped and nearly fell. She caught herself with those inhuman reflexes, her movements so fluid none of the wedding guests even noticed, all the while staring at Bones as if one blink would make him disappear.

Bones stared back, his mouth curling ever so slightly.

Hallo, Kitten. Yes, I found you.

The End

ACKNOWLEDGMENTS

This November marks the fifteen-year anniversary of my debut novel. I'd wanted to be a writer since I was a child, but while I started dozens of stories, I never finished them...until I dreamed about a half vampire woman arguing with her full vampire ex about why she'd left him years before. From that premise, the Night Huntress series was born.

Flash forward to today, when I finally get to tell Bones's side of their story. To say I feel grateful is a vast understatement. That's why, with this and every other book, my first thanks go to God because all this time later, it still feels like a miracle that I can write for a living.

After that, a heartfelt thanks go out to my wonderful agent, Nancy Yost; to Melissa Marr, for your editing skills and your friendship; to Ilona Andrews, for your friendship and support; to Natanya Wheeler, for cover design plus all the formatting/technical intricacies; to Cheryl Pientka, for assistance with the audio edition; to Will Watt, for audio narration; to my family, for always being there for me; to my husband, for literally everything, and last but definitely not least, to readers, for giving this and every other book of mine a chance.

ALSO BY JEANIENE FROST

Author's Note: The Night Rebel, Night Huntress, Night Prince and Night Huntress World series all contain stories set in the same paranormal universe. The Broken Destiny series is set in a different paranormal universe that's unrelated to those series. Thanks and happy reading!

– *Jeaniene Frost*

Night Huntress series (Cat and Bones):

Halfway to the Grave

One Foot in the Grave

At Grave's End

Destined for an Early Grave

One for The Money (ebook novelette)

This Side of the Grave

One Grave at a Time

Home for the Holidays (Ebook Novella)

Up From the Grave

Outtakes from the Grave (Deleted Scenes and Alternate Versions Anthology)

A Grave Girls' Getaway

The Other Half of the Grave

Night Huntress World novels:

First Drop of Crimson (Spade and Denise)

Eternal Kiss of Darkness (Mencheres and Kira)

Night Prince series: (Vlad and Leila):

Once Burned

Twice Tempted

Bound by Flames

Into the Fire

Night Rebel series (Ian and Veritas):

Shades of Wicked

Wicked Bite

Wicked All Night

Broken Destiny series (Ivy and Adrian)

The Beautiful Ashes

The Sweetest Burn

The Brightest Embers

Other Works:

Pack (A Werewolf Novelette)

Night's Darkest Embrace (Paranormal Romance Novella)

ABOUT THE AUTHOR

Jeaniene Frost is a *New York Times* and *USA Today* bestselling author of paranormal romance and urban fantasy. Her works include the Night Huntress series, the Night Prince series, the Broken Destiny series, and the new Night Rebel series. Jeaniene's novels have also appeared on the Publishers Weekly, Wall Street Journal, ABA Indiebound, and international bestseller lists. Foreign rights for Jeaniene's novels have sold to twenty different countries.

Jeaniene lives in Florida with her husband Matthew, who long ago accepted that she rarely cooks and always sleeps in on the weekends. In addition to being a writer, Jeaniene also enjoys reading, writing, poetry, watching movies, exploring old cemeteries, spelunking and traveling – by car. Airplanes, children, and cook books frighten her.

Jeaniene loves hearing from readers and you can find her on her website www.jeanienefrost.com or socials:

         facebook.com/JeanieneFrost
         twitter.com/Jeaniene_Frost
         instagram.com/jfrostauthor
         youtube.com/JeanieneFrost
         goodreads.com/Jeaniene_Frost

CPSIA information can be obtained
at www.ICGtesting.com
Printed in the USA
LVHW082308200522
719225LV00013B/264